Praise for *The First Se* ~~D1167911~~
also by A.B. L~~_____~~

Amazon's *Hot New Releases in Spy*
Stories and Tales of Intrigue - #4

Amazon's *Top Rated Spy Stories and Tales of Intrigue - #5*

Goodreads *Best Spy Novels of the Twentieth*
and Twenty-first Centuries

"That's only the beginning of the globe-trotting adventure that transports readers from the Caribbean to Cambridge, Massachusetts, to Cairo and other international locales. Bourne deftly juggles the action with informed yet accessible writing about the dot-com boom and subsequent bust while advancing the story through the perspectives of a gallery of vividly drawn supporting characters." – Kirkus Reviews

"Thumbs up…a knock-down, drag-out action adventure thriller."
– Wilderness House Literary Reviews

Quotes from Amazon Reviewers

"This is a heart-stopping, spaghetti bowl of a thriller. Smart, complex, graceful and filled with the type of insider information (the tech world, government intelligence, Jihadist hierarchy) that drives me, as a reader, to distraction…. Edwin Hoff is a leader - the kind we ache for…and a spy of the highest caliber."

"A.B. Bourne takes us not only through the evolution of the characters she's written, but the reinvention of the world as we know it, and with a skill that's uncommon for a first time novelist. She's like Daniel Silva in a dress..."

"This thriller was impossible to put down- even with my toddler climbing all over me while I read it at times! The suspense of Edwin's next move kept me on the edge of my seat. Characters who initially seemed inconsequential to the plot came back with a bang. The references to Boston brought me back to a fascinating time in the historic Internet boom. I look forward to seeing what's in store for Edwin in the Second Secret.
LONG LIVE EDWIN!"
"This fun, exciting read reminded me of early, fresh Nelson DeMille. Not predictable, edge of my seat reading."

"An intense thriller revolving around the events of 9/11 and the Dot Com Boom/Bust. Known history doesn't change, but A.B. Bourne creates a fast-paced drama with vividly-drawn characters. Secret agents, uber-villains, Boston cops, and tech entrepreneurs all dodge and weave in unpredictable ways in a race-the-clock chase to stop a bio-terror disaster and keep a company afloat. Completely enjoyable – a *non-trivial* and *obstreperous* ride!"

"I agree with the other reviews. I thought the depth of plot and character development was phenomenal and the way the book was structured built up the suspense. It always left me wondering to the point I couldn't put it down and then didn't want it to end. The book is at the same time an uplifting book if you remember that Edwin is based on the co-founder of Akamai Technologies, Danny Lewin. It's given me pause for thought."

"This book is so enjoyable that I couldn't put it down. I didn't know what to expect and was intrigued by the concept. I knew Danny and love the references that make him come alive throughout the book. I kept wondering if maybe, just maybe, this could be true. It's definitely one of those books that keeps you thinking long after the last page has been read. I can't wait for the next secret to be revealed."

"A.B. Bourne does a masterful job developing characters and weaving together several stories that orbit the main character's journey. This book is a feat that provides a window into the inspiration one person can provide to those around him. I can't wait to read about Edwin's next adventure!"

"Don't even think of buying this book unless you have some available time for the next few days! For if you find you need to sleep, have impending deadlines, and so on, you will find them totally overridden by the compulsion to continue with this amazing novel. I stayed up far too late, missed far too much work, neglected far too many things–when two days later the book ended and released me from its jaws."

"The First Secret of Edwin Hoff is a terrific thriller, with a strong theme of redemptive and hope."

"A friend recommended this to me on Friday; I was finished by Sunday."

"I.Could.Not.Put.It.Down."

Also by A.B. Bourne

The First Secret of Edwin Hoff

Rising Aces

An Edwin Hoff Thriller

A.B. Bourne

Watch Hill Books

Weston, Massachusetts

Printed in the United States of America

ISBN (print): 978-0-9839807-3-5

ISBN (e-book): 978-0-9839807-4-2

For Julian, S, and J

AUTHOR'S NOTE

The fictional character Edwin Hoff is inspired by a real person, Danny Lewin, the genius mathematician and legendary entrepreneur who started Akamai Technologies. He was a remarkable leader who died much too young.

Danny deeply affected most people who had the chance to work with him. As with others, Danny spun me out with more strength, more strategy and more courage.

If this is your first introduction to "Edwin", I hope you enjoy meeting him. If you met him in <u>The First Secret of Edwin Hoff</u>, thank you for asking to see him again. This book is for you.

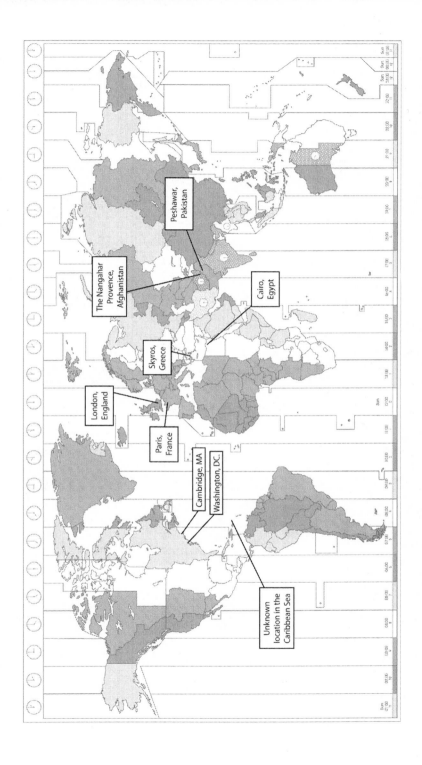

Names

al Khaleef   Translation: "the Successor," in this case to the terrorist organization al Ra'duzma.

al Ra'duzma   The global terrorist organization bent on destroying the West. It operates in Pakistan, North Africa, Europe, and Saudi Arabia. Translation: "greatest thunder."

Ali Hamini   Orphaned at six in Saudi Arabia, educated under the pseudonym Yassir Metah at the Rugby School in England and at Yale College in Connecticut. Software developer at D6 in Massachusetts. Long considered the Successor to lead al Ra'duzma.

Ascher Silver   FBI Agent, Assistant to the Chairman of the Joint Chiefs of Staff.

The ASP   The Association for the Society to Protect. A covert organization dedicated to fighting biological weapons regardless of national borders.

Badi Badi   Ambitious terrorist from Yemen.

Bunny617	Online poker player.
Dr. Bart	Geneticist at Oxford DNA Laboratories in Oxford, England.
Charles Lincoln	Chairman of Finley's Auction House in England.
Camille Henderson	CIA analyst turned operative. Graduate of Yale College.
D6	The technology company started by Edwin Hoff. Based in Cambridge, Massachusetts.
Edwin Hoff	Mathematician and MIT student-turned-legendary entrepreneur, billionaire founder of D6. Believed killed in plane explosion.
Finley's	Renowned auction house headquartered in London.
Fiona Tate	Up-and-coming English auctioneer.
The Helper	Provides shelter, food, local jobs and other life support for young men sent by al Ra'duzma to live briefly in France.

Hudson Davenport	Head of sales at D6.
Imad Iqbul	Tribal leader of all North African terrorist factions in al Ra'duzma.
Khalid al Hamzami (KAH)	Uncle of Ali Hamini, serving a life sentence in Supermax prison for terrorism.
Lars Grundek	ASP operator assigned to recover the remains of the Raptor, who is considered Rogue Until Proven Dead.
The Leader	The Leader of al Ra'duzma for twenty years. America's most wanted criminal.
Matilda Mace	The founder and head of the ASP.
Oliver Kestrel	Reclusive billionaire.
Rais Abdullah	The Influencer in al Ra'duzma. The European commander of foot soldiers needed to carry out terrorist plots.
The Raptor	Deep-cover commando, gone rogue from the ASP.

Sheikh Malikh Mukhtar	Saudi Sheikh, chief financier of al Ra'duzma attacks.
Usman	Houseboy to Ali Hamini and message runner.
Vernon Keely	Director of Central Intelligence Agency Egypt Field Office.
Whaleed Zubani	al Ra'duzma terrorist in U.S captivity.
Yassir Metah	Yale College classmate and boyfriend of Camille Henderson. Ali Hamini's cover for status.
Zed	ASP technician and partner to the Raptor.

EVIDENCE

Some humans carry a variant of the Monoamine Oxidase A (MAOA) gene. Known as the "Warrior Gene," those with this variant are more likely not only to use weapons and join gangs, but also to be among the most violent gang members.

Beaver, Kevin M., Matt DeLisi, Michael G. Vaughan, and J.C. Barnes. 2009. "MAOA Genotype is Associated with Gang Membership and Weapon Use." *Comprehensive Psychiatry*.

PROLOGUE

2:00 p.m., July 4
Thirteen years ago
The Nangahar Province, Afghanistan

The convoy of four small, tan trucks kicked up dust driving through the open desert. They slowed some when they reached the mountains, the road turning often as it rose through rocky cliffs.

Inside the third car sat a man with black hair, trimmed short, parted on the side. He had straight white teeth, and he licked the grit collecting in his teeth. Every breath in the desert brought in dirt.

In his lap, the man flexed his left hand so the edge of his palm made a blunt, hard blade. With the other, he braced his thumb against his taut fingertips, and tucked his wrist down. The beak of the "crane's neck" karate form could, in one strike, blind a man or break the bones in his hand.

Ali Hamini was thirty-two. He wore a striped tie with his dark navy summer wool suit and custom-fitted white shirt. The thick blue, red, and yellow diagonal lines woven into the silk proved to some that the wearer belonged at a long table in a hallowed hall of an elite western school. But to Ali's colleagues, any tie was a scorned symbol of the west.

This often compelled Middle Eastern leaders to leave their collared shirts open at the neck.

Ali knew the tribal leaders of al Ra'duzma expected to see the tie. For many years, they had invested in his western trappings, his perfect orthodonture. This was how they had prepared him. But Ali regretted the dark color of his suit, the way it trapped the heat and showed the dust accumulating in moist creases.

As the truck lurched over the rough path, Ali relaxed his left hand and slipped it into his pocket, where his thumb grazed the small, slick stone. Polished by hand with honey, the agate was black and white. This one was called *djaz*, which meant "fear." Long ago, his uncle had told him some believed the mere presence of this stone could arouse terror in the hearts of men.

Ali imagined the face of his uncle, Khalid al Hamzami. The Americans had put it on a playing card and called him "KAH." His was a face card, one of the highest value.

Ali wondered what his uncle was doing, at that moment. Probably sleeping. He imagined the narrow bed, a thin mattress on a cement slab bolted to the wall facing a small television. There would be no window, not where he was. Not locked in a cell in a federal prison under a mountain somewhere in Nevada.

The convoy suddenly stopped. Doors opened and twenty men left the cars and formed two flanks in the road. Each shouldered a Kalashnikov rifle.

One soldier opened the door next to Ali.

"We walk from here," he said. He turned to take his place at the front of the line.

Ali twisted, looking behind him, beside him and through each window. He saw the tan, rough mountains where little vegetation grew. Steep cliffs surrounded the cars. Behind the caravan, the dusty road retreated toward the valley, passing through a small village.

He squinted in the bright sun. He searched for a silhouette edging behind a rock. A shrub moving along the ground. A glint of sun on a steel barrel, pivoting its point to him.

Heat warped the desert air.

When Ali was content that nothing seemed out of place, he put his feet on the gravel and stood up. At six feet tall, he towered over the soldiers. He shook his legs to straighten the trouser crease.

"Do you see the caves?" the soldier asked.

Ali scanned the cliffs. He saw no caves.

"There," said the soldier. He shifted the rifle and pointed over his shoulder.

Ali glanced up. He still saw no caves. He looked at the two lines of armed men surrounding him.

Suddenly Ali saw the opposite of every image. These men with guns were not guiding him, the honored guest. They were guarding a prisoner. This was no escort. It was an ambush.

How could he have been so stupid, at this moment of all, to ignore the risk that followed him everywhere? Pride was a sin for so many good reasons.

The muscles in Ali's neck spasmed. It was a protective reflex, but it disabled him. The fibers tightened into hard armor to protect against a perceived assault on his spinal cord. The pain made him want to sit, drain the excruciating force of gravity. He stood absolutely still. He put the pain where he always did, buried in the vault in his brain, behind a thick, slick iron bolt.

With the two lines of armed men on either side, Ali picked his way up a steep, narrow goat path.

After nearly an hour of strenuous climbing, the soldier at the head of the line stopped. They were at the edge of a promontory, where the narrow path seemed to end.

Ali was sweating. His tie trapped the heat in his suit.

The soldier pressed his back against the cliff and motioned to Ali.

"Here," he said. "The Leader asked for you to walk alone from here. The opening is just around the corner."

Ali peered over the edge and saw the trucks far below, on the road. They looked like stones strung at the end of a string.

"The path beyond this turn is quite narrow," said the soldier, who braced against the cliff wall. "Step with care."

Ali nodded. He stepped past the soldier. His elbow brushed the man's gun. The soldier inhaled.

Ali moved forward on to the promontory. Rocks slipped under his leather wingtips. With his right hand, he felt around the point. He pressed his back into the wall. Inch by inch he turned his toe, then his heel, then his toe, until he had edged around the sharp corner.

There the ledge curved like a sheltered cove. It widened comfortably to a fifteen-feet-wide plaza.

Then Ali saw them. The honeycomb of small, black caves had been invisible until Ali stood right in front of them.

Two soldiers guarded one small opening. One pointed his finger, and Ali ducked through the dark opening.

Ali saw blackness, and the flicker of kerosene lamps bouncing off the walls. It took a moment for his eyes to adjust to the darkness. The stone floor was even, swept free of the loose rocks from the path that had gouged his hand-stitched Italian shoes on the path.

In the darkness, Ali moved forward slowly, drawn to the lamp light. It came from a small cavern off the hallway. Two more armed guards squatted on either side of the entrance. When Ali approached, they did not move. Ali passed them, and entered the small room that held the kerosene lamp.

In the middle of the floor sat a man with a long beard and white robes. His legs were crossed. His feet were bare. He looked up at Ali with the stony gaze of the Western world's Most Wanted. The Leader of al Ra'duzma, the global terror network of tribes intent on destroying the Western world.

Loosely translated, al Ra'duzma meant "the greatest thunder."

They will be heard, thought Ali. *But in between, living in a cave, is their Dust King. And all this could be mine.*

Ali dropped to his knees before the Leader, repeating his pledge of obedience. His *bay'a*.

The prospect of playing this part was a far cry from another one that al Ra'duzma once had made Ali play: the College Boy. He thought of the down comforter over his bed at Yale College, on the east coast of the United States. How the blanket trapped warm pockets of air as he napped there with Camille Henderson, who was then only nineteen, her red hair splayed across his pillow. He remembered the clanging radiators summoning the heat on dark afternoons in the small suite of rooms across the courtyard from the dining hall, which just opened to offer steak "with au jus" and daily Jell-O.

He pushed the thought aside. That was many years and several identities ago.

From his seat on the stone, the Leader gazed intently at Ali. His cold stare shone light to a very small part of the world and pitched blackness to the rest.

Ali kneeled on a dark red carpet stitched with blue, tan and white geometric patterns. He pressed his torso forward, nearly as low as he bent in prayer five times a day.

"You are ready, then?" asked the Leader.

Ali stayed low and lifted his gaze. "Yes, if it is Allah's will."

The Leader nodded.

"I must go now. They are after me," said the Leader. "It is time for my successor to be named. It must be someone who is westernized, with better access to a world of assets to fund the business of al Ra'duzma. Someone above suspicion. Someone well prepared."

"I am ready," said Ali. "My life has been but a vessel for this day."

"Has it?" The Leader cocked his head to one side. "You have left no...liabilities? From your time in the West?"

Ali bowed. He hoped the move would seem like a gesture of humility.

But he was thinking of something else. A regrettable decision. That day when he had committed the act of such betrayal that if the Leader, or anyone else, knew of it, Ali would never receive the honor he had pursued throughout his entire life. And not just that: the tribal leaders who formed al Ra'duzma would make his punishment a public service message. He would be decapitated. Or boiled. Fried. Disemboweled. Dragged. Burned.

Or, Ali thought, *all of the above.*

Liabilities. Ali pictured the freckled face of Camille Henderson, and the glare of Edwin Hoff.

Camille. When they were together at Yale, she claimed she saw his soul. But she never knew that his life at Yale was a long-planned cover. That everything about him was a costume, tailored to fit a profile sketched by others, many years before they met in the college quad. That what she saw, peering into his depths, was simply what Ali put there, so she would see something.

Camille knew exactly how Ali had betrayed al Ra'duzma because he had done it with her. In fact, she knew something else. He had done it for her.

In the dark cave, prone before the Leader, Ali thought next of Edwin Hoff. In his cover some years after "College Boy," Ali had worked for Edwin's company, D6. There, Ali became "Software Engineer."

That turned out to be a colossal mistake. Edwin Hoff, the founder of D6, MIT genius mathematician turned billionaire overnight, had seen starkly who Ali was, and who he was not. And when Edwin, too, had discovered what Ali had done, he made this promise:

"Never assume I am gone. I will always be watching for you. And I will come get you."

These were the last words Ali had heard Edwin speak, years earlier. From his brief time working for him at D6, Ali knew two things about Edwin Hoff.

First, Edwin always did what he said he would do.

And second, Edwin Hoff, the legendary entrepreneur, genius billionaire, had his own secrets.

In the cave, on his knees, before the leader of al Ra'duzma, Ali sat back on his haunches and looked up at the Leader.

"Liabilities?" Ali answered. "Only that I am but a man."

"Then it is done," said the Leader. He waved to a guard hanging back in the shadows of the cave. "Notify the media and strategy groups. My successor has been named. Bow to him, after I am gone."

PART ONE

CHAPTER ONE

11:18 p.m., May 22
Present Day
Kandahar, Afghanistan

The translator buckled a harness around his Belgian shepherd. He checked the pack. The parachute was in position if needed. He held the dog's leash and crouched shoulder to shoulder with ten other elite soldiers on the MH-60 Black Hawk helicopter.

The rotors spun and the helicopter lifted into the air. It flew through the dark night behind its twin, without lights, without sound, without leaving a heat signature.

The flight would take eighty-seven minutes.

The two aircraft carried twenty-one Navy SEALS and one dog across the border between Afghanistan, where they were permitted to fly, and Pakistan, where they were not.

CHAPTER TWO

12:00 a.m., May 23
Peshawar, Pakistan

The van crawled along the cracked pavement. Inside, six bleating goats slipped on loose straw and streaked piles of their own feces. Crouching in the corner, his fingertips pressed against the cool metal walls, Ali Hamini tucked his nose under his shirt and took short gulps of the rank air.

Though Ali was now well into middle age, his beard was black, as black as the straight locks that dropped over his dark eyes. Beneath the loose kurta, his body was tight from the rigorous routines he performed each morning in the dark on the mat stretched over the cool cement floor of his small room. In these years, Ali Hamini had gone from a dot com millionaire to a servant, one the Leader would summon in the middle of the night to his private residence.

"He calls, I come," Ali muttered. "I wade through goat shit to find out if this is the day I rise. As promised to me, and as I have earned. But not yet been paid."

Years had passed since the Leader had tapped Ali in the mountain cave, and announced to all of al Ra'duzma that he would be the successor. But the Leader had not yet

4

relinquished his throne. He kept Ali close. Ali made sure no one else came between them.

Ali's thoughts drifted into the future - one that could not be so far off - when he would be like a king. When at last he would have the power to swing the world on its hinges. Until then, Ali would continue to manage and organize and funnel to the Leader well-shaped plans of attack that came from the diaspora of inflamed men bent on claiming their own piece of power.

Until Ali had that control, and the pledged loyalties of all tribal factions, he would wield the power of access to the one who did.

Sliding in the goat truck, Ali pulled a prepaid cell phone out of a deep pocket and pressed one digit. He heard a series of chimes, a pulse, and the voice of a man.

"What's the traffic report?" asked Ali. "How long will it take you?"

"I'm close," said the urgent voice of a young man. "I have reports of traffic patterns from ten cities, collected over six months. Their gas and oil trucks get stuck in traffic and become giant, sluggish bombs. They line up twice every day, in the same places, in every city, like clockwork."

It was a good plan. Ali imagined hundreds of gas tanks blowing like a long, lingering, firecracker. The clouds of smoke and fire, the drivers trapped in traffic jams.

"Pick the five best cities," Ali said. "You're done planning. I will tell you when there is a green light. Keep this phone. Be ready. You are next."

Ali checked his watch. He had several more minutes before the goat truck would reach the headquarters.

Ali punched a different digit. When a man's voice answered he spoke again.

"I'm thirsty," Ali said.

The man on the other end chuckled.

"You are not alone," he said.

"What drink are you making?" asked Ali.

"Every city has drinking water treatment facilities," the man reported. "I have the chemical in hand to treat every major U.S. city, all at once. It may not poison them, but it will contaminate the water and the lack of water itself will be the weapon."

"And if I say go, today?" Ali said.

There was a silence.

"Well, it's just a matter of getting the chemical across the border."

"Where is it now?"

"Germany. It's quite a lot to move."

Ali curled his upper lip.

"You do what I say," Ali barked. "Rent a shipping container. Pack it in barrels with sausages. Dogs can't sniff through them. Send it to Canada. Put the container on a truck and drive it through North Dakota. Cross the border at exactly 11:30a.m., when the guards will be getting hungry for their own lunch. The suggestion of sausage will make it worse for them and they'll push you through."

"Okay," said the man.

"I want to hear from you in two weeks that you have the shipping container, the barrels, and the sausages," said Ali. "If you need my help then, I will help you. If you need it again, I won't."

Ali clicked the phone off. These attack leaders were zealots but usually highly impractical. This made Ali essential.

To Ali, this war was not a question of what prayer book one held. Ali had learned very early on that only one thing mattered, and it mattered absolutely. It was this: did you wield power and pain, or did you feel it?

As the goat truck bounced along the rough road, Ali noticed the flies hovering over the excrement pushed against the truck wall.

Bees, he thought. Parasites could destroy their bees. Then nothing would pollinate. Nothing would grow - except the bugs. This would cause massive food shortage, starvation.

So much was possible. Yet as Ali saw things, the Leader had done nothing in many years. Nothing at all. He had wasted his power. He just clung to it, hidden away like a prisoner. Many times Ali had presented him with well-formed plans, ready to pull the trigger, but the Leader would shake his head. It was as if the Leader's only plan was to remind Ali who was in charge.

It had been thirteen years since that searing summer day when Ali had met with the Leader in his mountain cave. But despite the promises, Ali had not risen. He had paid his dues, and far more, yet he had gone nowhere.

Ali grew fierce as the pointless delay continued. He had always been promised this role. If he knew nothing else about himself, Ali knew this: he was to be the successor. He was to be *al Khaleef*.

So no matter how long it took for the Leader to go, Ali made sure he was first in line to be the successor. Every serious plan had to pass through him. He helped shape them into viable plans.

And he had worked up a stunner of his own.

Ali smiled, thinking of his masterpiece, and how cleverly he had used the hours of these stultifying dull years while the Leader of al Ra'duzma held on to control instead of getting out of the way.

Greatest thunder indeed, Ali scoffed. *When I am al Khaleef, I will make it rain like their first flood.*

In the rank darkness, alone with the goats, Ali imagined the tribal leaders bending to his own knee with their pledge of *bay-a,* total obedience.

From urchin to overlord, penniless to millionaire. I am nothing at all, then all that ever mattered, Ali thought.

The idea brought on a surge like heat in a teenager.

Ali recalled very little of his early childhood, and what he did often surfaced when he felt certain temperatures and textures. The musky warmth when he wriggled under his mother's arm as she slept. The steam rising from the hot tea as his father poured a thick, even arc of just-boiled water, slowly, evenly, before he left for the hospital to take care of his patients. Cool bed sheets that the maids would fold crisply every day. The papery hard filaments of his quartz collection, bits of glistening rock that his mother would give him for each birthday, each special holiday. He would line them up, then organize them by shape and color and value. Then he would mix them up gently in their velvet purse, pick new categories, and reorganize them like they were a king's ransom. Sometimes he would wrap one in a scrap of paper and leave it on his mother's pillow.

But then the American bombs fell, and took this all away from him.

When he was just six, after his parents both had died so abruptly, Ali was left orphaned and lost in the chaos. He thought someone would come get him.

No one came. That night, and many nights after, Ali slept against a frozen cement wall. He remembered the cold dirt he would draw in circles around his eyes, hoping street people looking for prey would think he was awake, or just crazy, and leave him. Sometimes it worked, but not always. Sometimes nothing worked but to shut his eyes and sever his senses. After particularly hard nights, the gravel pillow left bleeding scrapes on the underside of his jaw, his cheek, his forehead.

Ali stole food. He learned to fight. Once he left a small child lying still on the ground while Ali snatched his crust of bread. It tasted of yeast and tar and blood.

Then one night came when someone else changed everything, again.

Ali was sitting against a building, fighting to stay alert through exhaustion, thirst and hunger. He trailed his fingers in the ground filth, separating large pebbles from small, sharp glass from smooth paper bits.

A man in his thirties squatted in front of him. He watched the young boy at the edge of consciousness, and still his hand made orderly piles of the rubbish.

Ali looked at the man. Then his eyes went black and his pupils lost focus. Ali began to turn onto his hands and knees.

"No, no," the man said. "That's not...Take this."

The man opened his palm, showing Ali three plump figs, and slick slices of orange. The sweet juice of the orange was warm, the temperature of Ali's swollen tongue.

That day, the man Ali would come to know as "Uncle" told Ali who had killed his parents. He told Ali who he had been, and who he would become, and who he would become next. And that was who Ali became.

Many years later, Ali would pay for those sticky figs, and that juicy orange. They would cost him Camille. They would cost him nearly every dime of his thirteen-million-dollar fortune earned in a stock windfall working under the cover of Software Engineer for a company called D6. But

Ali accepted these costs because he owed Uncle everything. And because this was the price of paving his path to power.

Some pressures bubbled right at the surface, and released quickly. But Ali's fury built from so deep a source that it fueled a tolerance for a path taken in small steps over a long period of time, while his surface appeared unsettlingly calm.

Uncle sent him to school in the madrassa. It was clean; rules were clear. There was order. Ali showed his unusual intelligence and natural ability to inspire his classmates and organize their earliest efforts at innovation. He thrived, and he gained stature. He was rewarded with fine clothes, praise, and position. His good looks, his cunning, and the praise of his classmates lifted Ali above them all.

And then one day, Uncle said he was ready. He sent him to boarding school in England, to begin his march to leadership through curious roles and places. This time, Ali understood why someone else had flipped his life again.

But he did not know that in one of these roles, in one of these places, he would make a grave mistake that would risk his only chance to live with the bat in his own hand.

As the truck banged over the rough ground, and the rank goats bleated their objections, Ali readied the report on the existing attack plans for the Leader. Ali permitted a brief fantasy, wondering if this day would at last be the day the Leader would step down and finally let him up.

The truck lurched. Ali's foot slipped. His shoulder bashed the side of the truck.

And, as it always did, his dream began to leak. He felt cold, and his wet palms slid against the steel.

But maybe, maybe he finally found out what I did, Ali thought. *So this van...this ride...stinking goats...this could be the last of it.*

The truck rocked over a curb, sending Ali onto his knees. He cursed.

Metal gates whined. The van pulled forward. It paused for a second set of gates, the rough idle rocking the van roughly. The goats pressed together in one corner. Ali coughed. Then the wheels crackled over the dirt and stones for a few more seconds. The van stopped. An emergency brake strained. Then both doors opened and the goats trundled down a wide wooden tailboard.

Or, Ali thought, muttering a quiet prayer, *he just called me because his crap computer is on the brink again.*

Ali landed on the dirt, his legs wobbled from the rough ride. He bent over and retched. The smoky smell of charred garbage from the pile in the corner usually helped cleanse his airways of the fecal stink. His hands on his knees, Ali gathered himself.

The walled yard in the inner courtyard of the compound made a moat around the white main building, which stood three stories tall. In one corner of the compound, goats, a cow, and chickens roamed inside a pen surrounded by twelve-feet-tall cement walls. In a corner there was a pile of ash where the residents burned their trash.

And there's his pen, Ali thought. He looked up at the top of the main building, which he could just see edging over the seven-feet-tall wall that bordered the balcony on the third floor.

Dirty old tennis balls littered the yard, errant shots, lost forever, of neighborhood batsmen playing in the suburban streets.

Ali noticed a real prize: a cricket ball, wrapped in leather. He shook his head, imagining the chagrin of the boy who had lost that over The Wall. He picked up the pricey ball and heaved it into the black sky with enough force to clear the high wall.

Ali peered at the open black sky. It was midnight. Just then, the glow of the streetlights beyond the wall flickered, and failed.

Strange, Ali thought. *The power has gone out.*

The stars looked like lasers, thousands of well-lit lenses fixed on him. Was the single eye of a high drone passing overhead?

Or worse.

Ali ducked under the eave. He rapped softly on the door. As usual, just two quick knocks. The door opened a crack. He went in.

A man stood behind the door, pointing an assault rifle at Ali.

"Better go up quickly. He's mad," said the man. He swung the AK-47 back over his shoulder. Ali nodded, glancing at the two men sitting at a table in the front room. He had not expected to see any of the women, except perhaps a glimpse, entirely covered. But now it was nearly midnight. They would be asleep in their quarters with their children.

Ali opened the gate made of iron lattice. It blocked the foot of the internal staircase from floor to ceiling. He took a step.

It's a bug fix. It's just another call about a broken computer.

He forced deeper breaths in through his nostrils, out through his throat. At the top of the stairs he turned down a short hallway to the open door. He knocked, again, two short raps. His abdomen flexed.

"Yes, come in," called a deep voice, strung tight with irritation.

Ali entered the small room. He saw the Leader was sitting at his desk. It was small and made of wood, pushed up to the wall. He sat in a small chair, his long legs sticking out akimbo. Candles flickered from a shelf. In the corner hung a dark curtain that often framed the background of his video communiqués. This was the bedroom - and the media studio. On the desk Ali saw the old computer monitor and large hard drives stacked below on the floor. There were two wooden file cabinets.

When Ali entered, a woman, her face uncovered, lowered her gaze and left the room.

The king-size bed was unmade. The house was ready to sleep but the Leader apparently could not.

The Leader smacked the top of the old monitor. It made Ali cringe. He had patched this rickety network together from pieces. It would not tolerate a tyrant's tantrum.

Ali bowed.

"Allahu ak bar," he said.

The Leader looked at Ali, his long features wrinkled in disgust.

"The only think that stinks worse than goat shit..." he paused, "is failure."

He stood up. The Leader was taller than Ali, nearly six and a half feet tall. He pointed at the screen. "I hope you can fix it this time. It's broken again."

"The power is out all over the city," Ali said, eyeing the plug. "Maybe the battery is old."

Ali moved quickly to the chair, passing the unmade bed. It was only a foot off the ground, an ornate carpet spread wide across the floor below the king-size bed frame.

Ali's eyes darted to the pillow.

And then, he saw it. Right there in front of him. Exactly what he sought, what he needed, just to seal every crack that seeped cold doubt.

Ali was entirely prepared to assume the mantle of leadership. He had sown carrots, and sharpened sticks, for certain tribal leaders. When necessary, he would use them to affirm their loyalty. This would not happen one single moment before the Leader was gone, of course, since no one would tolerate premature ambition. No matter what promises they had made.

To assure his ascension, Ali had invented, tested and all but deployed an attack on the West that would shift the world's power on its axis, in a moment. He had based it on logic, on human weakness, and on acute knowledge of where the West put its attention. All those precious souls to save. This priority gave him power. This priority, Ali noticed, left other flanks exposed.

But somewhere deep inside Ali, perhaps logged in the memory of a swirl of steam rising from a cup poured long ago, or of the glint of a pebble of lapis lazuli, a heaviness bore down on him.

Hesitance showed weakness, and this infuriated Ali. So he would obliterate this flaw. As with every challenge worth completing, he had planned for it. Through planning he would overcome it.

What Ali needed to complete this part of his plan was lying right there on the Leader's pillow. All he needed to do was reach over, cover it with his palm and find the special pocket in his kurta, the flowing tunic that covered his loose trousers.

He must turn away. He cannot see me do it.

"The battery is fine," said the Leader. "It's new. Come quickly. I have been waiting too long for you."

The Leader pushed back his chair, and stood up. He reached the bed in two strides, and sat down on the end of it.

Ali nodded meekly. "Okay. I will take a look."

14

But Ali swore under his breath, as he turned back to the keyboard. His fingers flickered across the buttons. It went blank; green symbols appeared on left hand side as he unlocked the computer's brain and took control of it. In moments the screen flickered and held the image of a blue sky, rolling green hills and the logo of a warped windowpane.

"Aha!" The Leader clapped Ali on the shoulder. "You did it again! Now, move. I'll drive."

Ali relinquished the throne and stood as the Leader scanned reports of Al Ra'duzma that had been assembled all around the world and brought to him on a small memory chip that he could hold between his thumb and forefinger.

Ali stepped back from the computer. He eyed the Leader, who was absorbed with the computer.

There would not be a better moment.

Ali eased back toward the side of the bed. He stretched out his arm, casually.

"Stop," the Leader said without taking his eyes off the screen.

Ali froze.

"Don't go yet."

"Yes?" said Ali. He coughed.

The Leader turned in his chair. His dark eyes settled on Ali.

"Your time in the West was well spent, in the end. Your computer skills will do well when it is time. It is all about communications. Getting the messages out. And in. You have done very well with the plans, as my right hand. Do you think you can be even more ... al Khaleef?" he asked. The Successor.

"Insha Allah," said Ali. God willing. His breath eased with the familiar chant.

Ali glanced at the Leader's pillow again. It was so close. He swallowed. "You know you are still my choice," continued the Leader. "You have been for many, many years. But, of course, there are others now who may…disagree. You will have to win the allegiance of each tribal leader, when it is time. I trust you have my instructions well protected."

"Yes, I do," said Ali quietly. "But that will be a very long time away."

The Leader shrugged. As his realm shrunk, he had obsessed about the power he could never lose: to declare who would succeed him. Al Khaleef. His primary topic of conversation involved how he would deliver his kingdom, and to whom.

"Who, do you think, are other potential candidates?" Ali asked.

He spoke with a convincing air of objectivity. But his gut clenched. In all the different covers and cloaks they had made him wear since he was six years old, this was the one consistent thread. He would become al Khaleef. This drove every decision of his life.

Except for one catastrophic mistake.

"Many of them now like Badi Badi, of Yemen," offered the Leader. "He has been very resourceful. The shoe bomb. Packing bombs into computer printers, and such things. He is smart. And he acts. He visits the tribal fathers often and treats them with respect. Perhaps there is another person who has shown an interest, too," the Leader trailed off. "You, of course, made your contributions to The Awakening years ago. But of course, the tribal heads do have to remember that."

Ali forced himself to look down and loosen his throat to speak factually, without aggression.

"The mission received every dollar Allah gave me from my company's stock offering. It was thirteen million dollars," Ali said. Roughly, he thought. Ali also had prudently invested some in a special resource, and kept it secure throughout this purgatory while he waited for the call. It was his insurance policy. Part of his plan.

"Yes," said the Leader. "And your uncle could not have attempted his plan without your financing."

The Leader gazed at Ali.

"Even though that plan failed. Completely. Even though he is living out his days in an American prison."

Ali kept his head bowed.

"But that is why we always plan for contingencies," said the Leader. "The other parts that day worked very well indeed. The planes. The buildings. Just not the 'big bang' we were planning. You are still my choice of course, but some... have questioned... your contributions are a bit stale now. Except for fixing this." The leader patted his keyboard. "Which is nice."

"But I have brought you plan after plan," Ali protested. "I have worked with the men to hone them. The military barracks in Afghanistan. The football game in Dusseldorf."

"Yes," said the Leader. "You have planned. But you have not acted. There is a difference. The tribal leaders know it."

Ali wiped the fury from his face. All he could do now was listen or lose the chance forever. Patience was power also, he reminded himself. The Leader was testing him. Provoking him. Could he still wait? Or would he become a threat before there was a need for a successor?

The Leader waited. He studied Ali's subdued face. He nodded.

"There are three people you need on your side. You need Imad Iqbul, who has stitched together all of the tribes in North Africa. Not an easy accomplishment. Without him, they fracture. He makes them come to him in London, where they cannot bring their guns."

"Thank you," said Ali.

"You'll also need Malikh Mukhtar," said the Leader.

"The Sheikh?"

"Yes, the Saudi with rubies dripping from his pockets. He decides which plans get our money and our backing," said the Leader. "He likes shiny things. He enjoys fine cuisine, and the theater."

"He's in London too," Ali said. This he already knew.

"It is safer for them there," the Leader said. "It is harder for a rival to shoot them down in a market and ride off on a motorcycle unmolested."

Ali could tell the Leader was enjoying the day's plotting when he began drumming the tips of his fingers on the bed sheet.

Ali glanced beyond him to the pillowcase. The object he needed was still there.

"And there is one more person you need to persuade that you are al Khaleef," said the Leader.

This startled Ali. He knew of the Sheikh, and he knew of the North African. As far as Ali had known, these two men were the levers of influence in al Ra'duzma.

"Who is that?" Ali asked.

The Leader tightened his lips.

"Above all you need the support of Rais Abdullah, who they call 'the Influencer.'"

"Who is he?" Ali said. "What does he influence?"

The Leader's lips twisted in a curious smile. Then it disappeared.

"Only the largest army of deployed foot soldiers," he said. "All of our smaller tribes do what Abdullah wants, to gain the power of these feet on the street. Without them the plans come to nothing. The Influencer has the ear of every tribal head. They must listen, no matter how much they resent it."

Ali was not surprised to hear the names of Imad Iqbul, the strategist, or Sheikh Malikh Mukhtar, the financier. He had well-developed plans in place to ensure their support.

But Rais Abdullah was someone new.

Ali had made a serious oversight. He would have to fix it before the time came that he needed that support.

"Where is Rais Abdullah?" Ali asked.

The Leader brought his lips together. He was about to answer, when they heard rocks and pebbles clattering into their third story windows. Something suddenly whipped furiously at the air over the roof.

There was a loud explosion. Then another, closer.

They heard gunshots.

Machine gun fire rattled on the first floor, spraying the bullets one way, then back.

"They are here," the Leader said. Slowly, he stood up.

Ali would remember the faint smile that spread across the Leader's face, as he stood in the middle of the bedroom. How he turned to meet one of his wives, who had raced in from the hallway. Ali watched the pair back into the bedroom, the Leader holding his wife by her shoulders, in front of him, as they faced the doorway.

"Where is Rais Abdullah?" Ali shouted at the Leader's back. There was no answer. Ali felt fury mix with shock. But he would get his answer.

Ali reached down to his calf.

Gunfire exploded on the floor below.

"Paris," the Leader said softly. "Rais Abdullah is in Paris."

Ali took his hand away from his leg. He shrank toward the bathroom, and locked the door. He saw a thick window on the wall next to the toilet. There was a towel on the rack.

Another explosion shook the building. Ali heard the metal gate door on the top of the stairway crash open. Automatic weapons fired rapidly, blunted by silencers.

Ali kicked off his shoes and tied the laces to each other with a double square knot. He slung them around his neck as he climbed up on the toilet. He yanked the towel off the rack with such force that the screws came out of the plaster.

The metal pole clattered on porcelain.

He heard sets of footsteps charging up the stairs.

Ali wound the towel around his fist. Then he punched the glass window as hard as he could.

Ali scraped the shards of glass out of the frame, and shoved his head and shoulders through it. He rolled forward like a gymnast. Both feet hit flat on the floor of the balcony.

The cement wall at the edge of the balcony was ten feet away, and seven feet high. Ali ran at the wall, using his momentum to scrabble up an extra three feet. He got his fingers around the top ledge.

He hung there.

Ali could see the silhouettes of soldiers wearing helmets and four-eyed night vision goggles moving quickly around the Leader's bedroom.

With all the strength he could muster, Ali hauled his body up flat on the top of the cement block wall and dropped over the other side.

CHAPTER THREE

1:18 a.m. May 23
Peshawar, Pakistan

Ali hung from the edge of the balcony, three stories above the goat pen. He gripped the small grooves in the mortar along the top ledge. He pressed his bare toes into the cracks. There was less than half an inch of purchase.

The small joints in his digits soon ached.

Ali looked down the wall. Fifteen feet away, a group of wires were bolted to the corner. The cords stretched out over the animal yard to another post.

Shoes still slung around his neck, Ali edged along the building until he reached the corner where the wires connected. No power ran through them. But that could change at any moment.

Ali swung one shoe over the wire. Then he gripped each rubber sole and pulled. The knot would have to hold for a few seconds.

Ali reached to his calf and drew a five-inch serrated hunting knife from a narrow scabbard strapped to his leg with soft leather. He bit the blade. Then, a shoe in each hand, he jumped.

The nylon laces slid along the wire, Ali dangling from the pair of old sneakers, until he reached the wire's lowest point. Ten feet in the air, he hung still.

Then Ali wrapped one arm around his shoes and, with the other, took the knife from his mouth.

Just the touch of the sharp edge on the taut wire split the line. He needed the laces. He would have to move quickly.

Ali dropped hard on the dusty ground. He bent his knees and rolled to absorb the impact. In the dark night, against the edge of the building, Ali stuck the tip of the knife into the tight knot of his shoelaces until it released. His hands shook as he pulled them on to his feet and tied them tight.

Ali scanned the area. He had landed in the courtyard. The Americans would be monitoring the perimeter of the compound and would catch anyone escaping.

But Ali was not looking for an exit.

He had to find a way back in.

There will be a moment. One split second after the Americans go and before the Pakistani police get here.

He could hear one helicopter approaching, then the sound of another inbound from a different direction.

Someone has sold out the Leader, Ali thought, as he clung to the shadows. *But this time, it wasn't me.*

Two Chinook helicopters beat the skies. Flames rose over the rooftop.

Four soldiers ran out of the building, a heavy white sling suspended over six feet between two pairs of them. They pushed the heavy oblong object into the rear of one helicopter and jumped in with it. The helicopter rose immediately, its blades beating the air, but it made little sound, just above a slight hum.

Ali crouched low. He crept quickly around the edge of the building. He watched other soldiers rush out with computer files, hard drives, and papers. They boarded the second helicopter, which lifted off while the soldiers' legs dangled.

For the moment, they were gone.

Ali slipped through the broken front door.

Inside a woman wailed. Children whimpered from a room where they had been gathered, then left. The guard, who had opened the door for him moments earlier, lay motionless on the cement floor, blood pooling around his head.

Ali climbed the same stairs he had just used. When he reached the top, Ali saw a woman lying dead on the floor at the foot of the bed. The mattress was bare and soaked in red blood, still slick and bright. The Leader's body was gone, ferried off to an American DNA test in his own bed sheets.

"The sheets," groaned Ali. "No!"

Ali looked at the closet; the clothes were gone.

Ali's heart raced. "It's gone. It is all gone."

Moments ago, he had nearly had the missing piece in his hands.

Ali scanned the floor. Nothing. Then he noticed the small bathroom attached to the bedroom.

Only the leader would have used that, Ali thought. He sprang toward the room, pulled back the dingy shower curtain.

He crouched, examining the drain.

And there, Ali finally saw what he sought: it was about six inches long, a spiraling grey hair released from the tangle of a fist-long beard.

Ali pulled a piece of white paper from his back pocket. He folded it around the piece of the Leader's hair. Then he tucked the small package into a pocket sewn in the folds of his kurta.

He shuffled down the stairs, nearly tripping as he hurried.

When Ali edged the front door open, the sky was dark and quiet. The Americans were gone. He could hear sirens approaching.

But it was not the police he watched for. It was not the Americans. It was not a rival to lead al Ra'duzma.

Ali broke into a full run along the perimeter of the house to the back gate, risking for just a moment the sharp eyes he knew were peering at him, through lenses he would never expect to see.

Never assume I am gone.

The last words Ali had heard from Edwin Hoff echoed in his mind as he ran down the street.

The Leader is dead, thought Ali as he ducked down narrow alleys. *Succession begins now. And I - only I - am al Khaleef!*

By the time Ali reached his apartment, he was glistening with sweat.

It was happening almost exactly as he had planned. Ali would have to move very quickly – this he had always known, and the plan accounted for the pace. But now, there was one new component. Ali had to find the Influencer, and win him over.

But every plan encountered problems and Ali had practiced to adapt.

Ali would win votes with a juicy carrot and a punishing stick. He would eliminate any risk that his one terrible, unforgivable error could rise up now.

Once the key leaders had pledged their support to him - by will or by force - Ali would show all of the tribal heads what he had built. His technology would earn the fear worthy of the role. That alone should convince them all that he was, as they had always told him, the successor. al Khaleef.

And while Ali worked to convince the tribal leaders that he was the rightful successor, Ali also had a plan to convince himself. He spat on the ground, still soured by remembering his revolting, inexplicable behavior.

Chapter Four

11:30 a.m., May 22
Somewhere in the Caribbean Ocean

On the eastern edge of the Caribbean Sea, where the currents began their northwesterly swirl, a small, abandoned oil rig clung to four cement columns that plunged through the water to the seabed and were anchored firmly into the Caribbean plate. To the aircraft that occasionally passed tens of thousands of feet over it, the structure was ocean litter. To the oil company that had built it, the barren well was sunk costs, sold to a law firm representing a client, which was in fact another law firm, representing a reclusive client.

Once the lawyers had purchased the old rig, they filed papers to declare the rig a sovereign nation, and named Oliver Kestrel its monarch. No one could recall ever having met Oliver: not the lawyers, not his only known associates - the people with whom Oliver played hours of poker, night after night, and only online.

All they knew was that the name Oliver Kestrel also belonged to the sole beneficiary of the estate of Edwin Hoff, multi-billionaire entrepreneur and founder of the technology company D6, who years earlier had perished when a plane exploded several hours after he had boarded.

The rig had a steel platform that hung over the sea, suspended between the cement stanchions. The platform supported a small cabin. Above the cabin tall girders reached forty feet high, once used to steady the deep sea drill.

The living platform contained a stateroom, a 'head' - naval terminology for a tiny but functional bathroom, a small kitchen, a utility room, a windowless central room and modified crew quarters.

One former bedroom had been stripped to the studs. It was lined with shelves and stored with supplies – coffee, sugar, canned food, desalination tablets, duct tape, antibiotics, multi-colored whiteboard markers – enough to sustain one man for several months. The shared wall between two other crew quarters had been demolished. Bunks and built in cabinets had been removed and replaced with wide metal shelving. These racks lined the room from floor to ceiling. Another rack ran down the middle of the eight-by-thirteen room.

These shelves held stacks of blinking computer servers. The computers pulled in data feeds from all around the world, all different sources, and ran them through a special software program that crunched the data into logical conclusions. The data feeds and results then appeared on monitors bolted to the walls of the windowless central room on the rig.

A narrow hallway led through the modified crew quarters, past the captain's quarters to the central command room. Opposite the command room, a door opened to a small, steep staircase that reached up to the roof and the base of the tall girders.

A small brown Gore-Tex knapsack hung on a hook four inches to the right of the door.

For the previous occupants, the central room had been a kitchen and gathering place where roughnecks, after their shifts, drank beer and played cards around a grey metal kitchen table.

Now flat screen monitors covered the windowless walls. Eighteen-inch monitors covered one wall from floor to ceiling. Another held a whiteboard covered with scribbles and arrows, next to a counter, cabinets, coffee machine and refrigerator. The markings were algorithms worked out by hand, each argument color-coded in a different dry erase marker.

Whiteboard paint covered a third wall from floor to ceiling. Bright blue capital letters posted this schedule in military time.

SCHEDULE:
00:00-02:00	POKER
02:00-06:00	SLEEP
06:00-6:20	EAT 1 (Coffee. Dried fruit. Granola w powdered milk)
06:20-6:30	BIO BREAK
06:30-7:10	CLIMB
07:10-7:30	SWIM
07:30-8:00	SHOWER & DRESS
08:00-10:00	CODE
10:00-12:00	WATCH
12:00-13:00	EAT 2 (PBJ, V8)
13:00-15:00	BUILD
15:00-16:00	STUDY
16:00-18:00	PRACTICE
18:00-19:00	CLEAN (RIG, SELF)

| 19:00-21:00 | EAT 3 (fish if caught, rice/pasta, beans/peas) |
| 21:00-24:00 | WATCH |

REMINDER: DO WASH ON TUESDAY.
DRY SHIRTS, SHORTS FLAT ON DECK.

The fourth wall was the focus of the room. It held a seventy-two-inch flat screen that was split down the middle. On the left side, a photo never changed. It was the face of a man, unmarked by time, taken years earlier. It was an employee ID photograph from the company called D6, based in Cambridge, MA. Disdain lifted the corner of the man's lip. His flat black eyes looked down his nose at the camera. His black hair, parted on one side, fell forward over his eyebrows.

There was a name beneath the ID photo.

Ali Hamini, Software Engineer

On the other side of the split seventy-two-inch screen flashed a scroll of photographs of faces that never had matched the ID photo. Not in all the years the software program had been looking for one.

The grey metal table still stood in the center of the room, but now the desk had six eighteen-inch flat screen computer monitors, one row stacked above the other. There was one chair. It was made of tight black mesh with short arms and it swiveled on rolling wheels.

In this throne sat Edwin Hoff.

Edwin rolled his chair close to the desk, and rested his chin on both fists. His eyes flashed from one monitor to the next.

Edwin was studying the photos and feeds, like he did each day. His clear green eyes bore into the pixels on the screens for hours at a time. For most people the constant image would have become wallpaper. But not to Edwin. Each day he focused on a different feature and its relationship to another. Each day he knew it better. Each day he watched the scrolling images pause on a potential match, but always discarded it.

Edwin's stomach was tight, a feeling that had become very familiar over the past two weeks. And his head hurt. Food was luxury.

But he needed coffee.

Edwin spun in his chair. Then he pushed his hands on his thighs and stood up. He was nine inches over five feet tall and lean. His perpetually tanned skin stretched tightly over his thick muscles; the veins bulged. He was losing weight, as he always did at this time in the calendar, when it had been months since the last supply drop. But his thighs were still thick cables, his arms and shoulders strong sinew. The daily regimen of climbing the steel rigging up and down kept him lean. The softness around his waist was long gone.

Edwin never had needed much sleep: three hours a night was plenty, though he allocated four in the schedule.

His black hair was neat, and he had let it grow to mid-length, a more adaptable length should he suddenly need it. He shaved every morning. A few years back he noticed grey shards in the stubble. The jeans he wore were loose. He had used his awl to poke new holes in his leather belt. Edwin was wearing cut-off shorts and a grey cotton t-shirt. He rotated three pairs of cut-off shorts and five t-shirts. When he let them dry on Tuesday afternoons, he made sure they did not flap in the wind. He could not risk the chance, however slight, that someone would notice life on the abandoned rig.

Edwin also wore contacts. They had a slight yellowish tinge that made a light ring around his green irises.

Whether or not Edwin was looking at the photo dominating the wall or not, he knew the highest point in the natural arch of the eyebrows of Ali Hamini. He could measure the distance between Ali's pupils. He could calculate the rise of his cheekbones and the angle of his jawbone. He knew that each strand of hair that grew from the crown of his head was exactly $1/140^{th}$ of an inch in diameter at its base.

Edwin saw this face as a collection of numbers, numbers that would remain the same regardless of age or disguise. These numbers defined the measure of each feature and its relationship to one another.

Even surgery could not change the distance between the center points of these black pupils. Not by a nanometer.

This was the face of the man who had helped to cause the deaths of thousands of Americans several years earlier in the worst terrorist attack ever on U.S. soil. Edwin would find Ali Hamini, wherever he was hiding in the world. To do this, he had built a software program he called Crosspathz. The program collected information about purchases of anything that could fashion copper wire, nitrogen, or C4. It clocked the registration and removal of chemicals and nuclear substances. It monitored violations of compliance, silent warnings that drawers of dangerous materials were mysteriously emptied. It captured facial prints, framed full-on by small cameras behind screens at ATM machines, or by closed circuit cameras at airports and train stations, or from security systems lurking beneath the eaves of storefronts.

In the Network Operations Control Center, each flat screen monitor flashed with a different display. There were news feeds in multiple languages with English subtitles flashed on the bottom script. There were maps showing yellow and green spots across a globe, none red. One patch of

screens scrolled images of automobile license plates enter-
ing and exiting Manhattan, London, Paris, Munich, San
Francisco, Chicago, Miami, and Washington D.C.. Another
processed traffic incidents and recorded operator licenses
involved. ATM feeds across America and Europe fed fish-
eye photographs of faces withdrawing money into a facial
recognition program. Interpol warrants and arrests also fed
the system.

Millions of faces, images collected from cameras
throughout the world every second of the day, shifted in a
blur beside the unchanging photo of Ali Hamini.

Crosspathz linked the information about purchases
and location of faces to the location of mobile phones, and
the owners carrying them. It recalled and recorded every
number dialed, to whom someone spoke, and the digital
signature that encoded exactly what they said, in one hundred and thirty-two languages and dialects. With the command "chain out", the program could draw a visual graph,
mapping everyone a person spoke with, and everything he
bought.

By knowing what one bought, where one went and with
whom one spoke, the program could – near enough – pre-
dict what one would do next, when and where, and with
whom.

But Edwin had been looking for Ali for years. Crosspathz
crawled the earth and vacuumed what it found, sending the
data back into the program. But Ali Hamini had not surfaced. So Edwin would wait. And he would watch. He would
do nothing else.

Waiting was not Edwin's natural state. He itched to feel
the speed of motorcycle wheels leaning into curved, paved
hills. He missed the battle in the boardrooms. He missed

making new things happen. But until Ali Hamini raised his head and Crosspathz caught it, Edwin would wait.

It still grated to know that, years ago, Ali had been right under Edwin's nose.

"Once I made the mistake of letting a soft woman convince me to let you go," Edwin told the image, while the screen beside it cycled through irrelevant mug shots. "I never should have taken that knife off your neck."

His lips folded into a tight, angry line.

"Never assume I am gone," Edwin said aloud, as he thought of the last time he had seen Ali. It was in Cambridge, Massachusetts, and many years before.

In the dark hallway, Edwin watched silently. He breathed evenly, feeding oxygen to his coiled muscles.

Camille Henderson sat on a wooden chair in a two-bedroom house in East Cambridge. Her hands were locked to her ankles in steel cuffs. Ali and his uncle, Khalid al Hamzami – KAH - had taken her shoes.

"Don't," Camille had whispered to Ali. "Put the gun down."

Tears wet Ali's eyes. The gun barrel waved in his shaky hand. Uncle started to laugh. It was a giddy, bitter crow. He tossed his head back, taking in the pleasure of smashing people into each other. Then he screamed in pain. His hands dug frantically at his eyes. He crashed around the room.

Because as KAH had gorged on Ali's weakness and Camille's fear, he did not notice her small fingers. How they pressed gently against her heel. He did not hear the handcuff gears release.

But Edwin did. From behind the hallway door, he smiled. She was a titan.

In that split second when al Hamzami took his focus off Camille, she got on her feet. In her tight fist Edwin saw the rubber duck toy he had given her earlier in the day.

Camille squeezed it with all her might, sending a sharp spray into KAH's eyes. The bleach blinded him. He could not see Camille heave her whole body at his knees. She cut him down. The duct tape held firmly as she wound it around him.

"Wow," said Ali. "Camille!" He wiped his eyes with the back of his left hand. His right held the gun, still pointed at her.

"What are you doing?" she asked.

"It's time for all of us to move on," said Ali.

"So go," pleaded Camille. "You haven't done anything wrong, not yet. You can still be free."

"I can't. Uncle has much bigger plans for me. I have much bigger plans for me. So my weaknesses here in America can never be told. It's over for me here anyway, now."

"I'm not going to tell anyone," Camille said.

"Oh, you will. You are an American first. You all are. I am an outsider. I look like the worst of them. I'm related to one of them. Maybe I am one! They are my people. Not you. Not that... arrogant... Edwin Hoff!" Ali flared. "I will never suffer him again. No. Uncle is right. It is time to become who I really am."

"And who is that?" Camille asked.

To this Ali said nothing. His eyes were dry as he switched off the safety catch. His forefinger curled around the trigger.

"I hold the gun," he whispered.

Only Camille saw the shape in the hallway.

Suddenly, Ali felt sharp, cold steel press against his jugular vein. Edwin's bicep flexed around Ali's neck.

"Stop," Edwin said. The word shot like a bullet.

"I don't care if I die," Ali said.

"You do," said Edwin, his bicep bulging around Ali's neck. "You're no blind moron tricked into doing the dirty work to die for

someone else's glory, money, ego. You want to give up the chance to be king? Right when the moment you have waited for your entire life has come? The old leader is on the run now. They will need you – the westernized man with a pure soul. And millions in valuable stock options. Who else would be better? You know you want the power. You are no suicide."

"Let me go, she lives," Ali growled through his clenched teeth. He still pointed the gun at Camille. Ali was pinned down, on his neck, like a boy with a gravel pillow. Rage boiled.

It made him seethe to bargain with Edwin. There would be no more dealing.

Bound on the floor, KAH unleashed a torrent of Arabic.

"Go back! Find the Leader. He wants to see you! You will make me proud again. To think this is where it has all been leading for twenty-five years!"

But Arabic was as clear as English to both Edwin and Camille, who had studied it in college, had learned that dialect from Ali and several others in her job as an analyst for the CIA's middle eastern desk.

"Who wants to see you?" asked Camille.

Edwin flipped Ali onto his back.

"I know what you are about," Edwin hissed. "I know what you did, and what you are going to do next. I will always be watching you. Never assume I am gone."

Ali made a quick move. He broke Edwin's grip and twisted to his feet. He whipped a chair at Edwin's legs, then grabbed the shade off a bedside lamp and smashed the bulb. He jabbed the jagged glass at Edwin, but missed. Then Ali flipped backwards onto the double bed. He landed on his feet and ducked through the open window.

Edwin and Camille heard the sound of rusty metal screeching until Ali reached the ground. He was gone.

And then, so was Edwin.

CHAPTER FIVE

12:15 p.m., May 22
5,000 feet above sea level in the Caribbean Ocean

The pilot of the small craft watched the white streaks appear and fade on the dark blue expanse far below. He monitored the coordinates on the dashboard of the small plane. They were close now. He marveled at the physics of it. The speed of the plane. The lift beneath the wings. The distance of the drop. The pull of the current. Zed loved being in the cockpit of a relatively simple but miraculous machine.

Behind his aviator glasses, his eyes were still good. Since his sixtieth birthday, Zed had a twenty-five-dollar pair of readers from CVS but rarely used them. His short hair was black with streaks of grey, which fell over his left eyebrow.

"I hope he finds this. Somehow he must."

Zed scanned the ocean below. He was over the Caribbean, somewhere, but he could not see anything below signifying human life - not even a white triangle of a sailboat shuddering over the afternoon swells.

Zed put the controls on autopilot and buckled on the harness strap slung from a bar bolted to the spine of the cabin. He inspected the straps folded around the large mass of black rubber, six feet long, four feet high, and five feet wide. He checked the large backpack that lay on the top, in the center. He pushed the load into position; it rolled easily on the casters he had placed beneath it.

By now, this drop procedure was routine for Zed. Though he never repeated the exact time, day or distance between his excursions.

Satisfied with the pre-drop check, Zed buckled back into the cockpit seat. He was on course. Just a few minutes more. He could not overshoot. It had to be precise or the entire load would be lost; and he would never know. He still never knew if, each of these ten years, the drop ever reached its intended recipient. Yet still he made the drop. Every three, four or five months, without fail. Without doubt.

It was only in the most desperate circumstance that Zed would contact his beneficiary directly. This had not happened yet.

The warning peal sounded. The coordinates veered toward one another on the dashboard display. He was very close to the drop site now. There.

Zed pressed "release." Two doors folded open behind the wheel well. The large package slid down the track until it fell through the opening and was gone.

Zed continued along his course for another mile, then looped back. He peered down through the cockpit window. Far below, Zed thought he could still make out a khaki circle: the dome of the parachute. By now, it would have sprung the lifeboat into its proper landing position, packages intact.

"He's probably out of sugar by now," Zed said and smiled.

In the past lonely decade, Zed had discovered that recalling the smallest habits of his old friend would bring him back the fullest.

Nearly three hours after making the drop at the designated location over the Caribbean, Zed lowered the landing gear of the small plane and taxied down the private airstrip cut into the thick woods of central Maryland.

What he saw at the end of the runway made his eyes widen. Zed was glad the aircraft required several hundred yards to slow to a stop. He needed the time to breathe down, to mask his accelerating heart rate.

A man with shaggy blonde hair, thickly built and solid at five feet ten inches, stood in the middle of the runway. He wore wire-framed glasses, and often pushed them up the bridge of his nose with the back of his thumb. Zed knew Lars Grundek well. Over the years, Zed had built many tools for Lars to use on operations for the Association for the Society to Protect.

"So now the Head sends the pit bull for me?" Zed's lips tightened as he shut down the engines of the airplane. Lars stood close to the door Zed would have to exit through. Lars extended a hand and smiled. Zed watched the other man's lower eyelids stay flat, so he ignored the grin and the hand. There was no pleasure in this summons.

Zed jumped down square on his feet. He was agile and fit as the ASP required, even of its technical staff.

"She wants to see me," Zed said.

Lars nodded. "In a manner of speaking."

The ride into Northwest Washington D.C. took thirty-six minutes. They passed the National Zoo, and pulled up behind a yellow brick apartment building. Zed's escort unlocked the passenger door only after he himself had exited the car and could open it for Zed by hand. They took the elevator to the penthouse where the Head of the Association for the Society to Protect held forth.

It had been years since Zed had had a private audience with the Head.

The elevator opened on to a long hallway where paintings hung in gilded frames, lit by tilted golden rectangles that pointed soft light down on them.

Lars pushed through the double doors, and then nodded to Zed.

Zed walked over the ornate geometric patterns on the flat carpet that covered the large floor.

A woman sat in a wing chair. She wore a dark brown velvet coat with a zipper that ran from the center of the collar to the trim. A thin clear plastic tube bit gently into her nostrils. Her skin was papery and bluish; her hair white wisps that barely followed the course an old, thick wave once shaped.

"Zed," she said.

"Ma'am," he responded. His hands clasped behind his waist. He stood with his shoulders straight and square. His eyes met hers.

"You've been flying." "Yes. I need my hours, ma'am."

"Picking up a new skill? Or perhaps, not so new, now?"

How long has she been watching me? He thought. *Hide in plain sight.*

"Yes. I began flying several years ago," Zed said.. "I find it relaxing to be in the air. It's like being the first to ski on fresh powder."

"Especially over the sea, I would imagine," she said. "Where there's nothing at all below you."

"Yes," he said. "Exactly. It's wonderful. Very freeing."

She beckoned with a finger.

Zed approached her.

She crooked it again. Closer.

He stood by the side of her chair. She gripped his wrist.

Zed felt her bony finger land on his pulse point, the spot where she could feel any skip in his heart rate.

Without letting go, she spoke.

"Do you think often about your old partner? While you are flying like a Raptor yourself?"

"I do," he said. Her fingers pressed into his wrist. "I think about him every day."

"As do I," she said. "In all these years, we have not found a trace of him. Not a trace anywhere. Perhaps he has washed out with the sea."

"I have not seen him, ma'am. I have not heard from him. I have not spoken to him."

The Head kept her fingers on his wrist for a few beats more. When the pattern did not quicken, she let go, and patted the top of his arm.

"It must be quite a loss to lose your partner and friend. After all these years, you should find a new one."

"I find I'm better at serving all of the operators, ma'am. Edwin – the Raptor - was quite demanding of my time and skills."

"Of all of ours," said the Head.

Zed dipped his head. She waved him off. Lars, who was standing by the double doors, opened them for Zed. They walked to the elevator in silence.

Lars pressed the button, and then watched the doors close in front of Zed's face. He returned to the living room.

The Head covered her mouth with the mask and drew in her oxygen.

"Let him go," said the Head. "Tell me what you know."

"He did not file a flight plan," Lars said. "He was in the air for seven hours. He fueled up with enough for ten hours but used only seven, and came back nearly empty."

"So he went out loaded and came back light," the thin voice came coated with mucous she tried twice to clear. "The aircraft must have made a drop somewhere in a three and a half hour circumference."

"I agree," Lars said.

"Sweep it," said the ancient woman. "I know he's there somewhere. A boat? A small island? Look for something capable of sheltering a Raptor, but not feeding it."

Lars Grundek worked for the Association for the Society to Protect and was put in charge of the mission to find a former colleague - the elite commando known as "the Raptor.".

Once the best operator among the most elite in the ASP, the Raptor had disappeared thirteen years earlier, unexpectedly, after completing a difficult mission. As was its practice in such rare circumstances, the ASP designated the Raptor as "Rogue Until Proven Dead." Lars Grundek had the duty to establish proof of both.

CHAPTER SIX

12:15 p.m., May 22
Somewhere in the Caribbean

E dwin had a lunch date, but no lunch. He sat in front of the six monitors on his desk. Each one showed different arrays of playing cards: hearts, diamonds, spades and clubs. Edwin moved the mouse, clicked, entered a few keystrokes, and the cards flipped over on one screen. He moved rapidly; the screens shifted constantly. He counted and played. Edwin was playing a different hand of poker on each screen - six different but simultaneous matches.

"You're toast," he muttered, dropping a full house and watching images of gold coins rattle into a velvet sack with a golden string. The dollar signs scrolled on the border and delivered $22,004.00 into the account of one Oliver Kestrel.

"Well played, Oliver," typed the opponent, screen name BUNNY617, the one who had contributed most of the coin to the pot. "Bye for now. Have to catch a plane."

OLIVER KESTREL: Same time tomorrow? You'll be back?

BUNNY617: We'll see.

There was a long pause. Edwin stared at the blinking cursor on the chat screen. His knee bounced under the desk.

BUNNY617: Yes, of course, Oliver. You have $132,055 of mine, all tallied, these years. I want it back.

Edwin typed: Glutton. I will crush you. Same time.

The games were mental calisthenics. Edwin played daily. BUNNY617 usually showed up, too.

Edwin marched rather than walked, even when he went to get a cup of coffee. His Nikes squeaked on the painted cement floor as he strode across the small room to the counter, which stood next to a refrigerator. He pushed the button on the espresso machine and heard it hum. He peered into a carton of coffee pods. A single pod rattled when he shook the box.

"So," said Edwin, holding the dark gold pod up to his eye. "It's just you and me now."

Edwin often spoke aloud. It was important to use his vocal chords regularly.

He put the pod into the machine and folded the box in a pile of flat cardboard. He squeezed a clamp on a rubber tube and a finger-width stream of clean water flowed from an upside bottle through a desalination distillery, through the tube and into the reservoir of the coffee machine. The mug filled with a dark, intense brew, settling a light brown crema on the surface. Edwin reached for a crinkled bag of sugar, turned it upside down and shook it over the cup. Granules fell from the creases. He opened a drawer. Empty except for a few torn white shreds of sugar packets.

He took a sip and winced. "Today really better be the twenty-second day of the month," he muttered.

This was another of his little measures to fend off the unceasing loneliness of his circumstances: quite often he spoke to himself. And he listened, too. Thankfully, thus far, nothing he heard came as news.

Edwin hopped up on the counter and drank the last cup of coffee in his stores.   It was the last of anything he had to eat. And it was bitter.

"About four sugars short," he said.

Just then, a jingle from a small device strapped on his wrist disrupted him.

"Mmmm good. Mmmm good." The mechanized voice on the curved clear polymer transmitted the message he waited for. It was a poor mimic for an old soup commercial, but it made drops collect at the tip of Edwin's tongue.

Edwin glanced at the wearable computer, a treasure from one of the last deposits. Only one person could communicate with this device.

"Zed, you soup-loving titan!"

He put down the mug and trotted to the door.   He opened it to the warm, light, afternoon breeze of the Caribbean Sea.   On the holograph that his lenses created, adding a layer of information to Edwin's field of vision, he could see the feed that also played on a monitor in the control center: the breeze was from the south; the current running north and west at eight knots.

"I have eight minutes, thirty-two seconds," Edwin calculated. He would have to move quickly to intercept the drop before the currents swept it past the rig.

Edwin pulled on the thin black frog suit. He tied the Nikes back onto his feet. He stretched the elastic strap of black rubber goggles behind his head. He trotted out of the room and down a hallway to a reinforced steel door. He slid back the bolts and hauled the door sideways into the pocket in the wall that held it. Immediately the wind buffeted him and thudded against the walls as it raced into the hallway. Edwin held the edge of the door and looked down. The waves were high against the stanchions, even seventy-five feet below him.

This was the fun part.

Edwin stood on the rounded steel girder that framed the outside of the door. He dropped his arms to either side. Then he simply bent forward.

But he did not fall. He spun, his feet staying fast to the metal. The magnets in his Nikes clung to the steel and he skated, upside down, to the vertical stanchion that supported the platform. When he grabbed it, he kicked his feet loose, and climbed arm over arm down to a lift that held a power-boat well over the choppy surf. Once inside, he pressed a lever. The platform tipped up, and shoved the boat into the ocean. Just as the engines submerged, Edwin throttled up. The bow reared up and he shot through the cement towers that balanced the living quarters of the rig above the seas.

Edwin scanned the horizon. He saw the sonar display before the background of the waves.

A dark dot closed in on a light green spot that was easing northwest at about eight knots.

He should intercept it within a minute.

But just then, Edwin saw another dot moving across the field. It was bearing down on the target. On him. He could not flee.

They'll hear the outboard.

So he cut the engine. The waves slapped at the sides of the small boat; he could feel the dizzying roll of the ocean swell now that one hundred and fifty horsepower was not leveling off and cutting through them. He crouched low over his black boat, glad the frog suit covered his skin, and would let him blend into the dark waves.

The dot neared. This craft, too, was approaching slowly.

"Mmm good! Mmm good!"

Edwin slapped his wrist. The device went silent.

I should be right on top of the target now.

Edwin peered over the rail, scanning the dark blue ocean.

Then he saw his quarry. A hundred yards off his port bow, a black twelve-feet-long inflatable dinghy, tented with a plastic sealed tarp and trailing a parachute. His food for the next several months. He exhaled.

But then, Edwin heard the heavy low rumble of diesel engines, and the scrape of chains as large wheels spun. The wind carried the sound away from him.

The other dot was nearly as bad as it could be.

A commercial fishing boat. Trawling.

The ship was letting out hundreds of yards of netting right where Edwin's groceries were drifting. And the fishing boat was moving very slowly.

That's not going anywhere soon.

He processed the facts quickly.

1) The dinghy was floating into the nets.
2) If it reached the nets, the parachute would get entangled.
3) The fishing boat would notice and stop. And investigate.
4) He could not start the engines on his boat.
5) His boat was drifting into the nets too. It had to change course without an engine very quickly.

Edwin considered his options. The afternoon wind was beginning to pick up.

Wind...good. Bad day for the boat.

He pulled his mask and breathing gear on and slipped soundlessly over the side of the boat. In his hand he held a large plug. Because the only way to keep his boat from drifting into the nets was to send it straight down. Even if Zed would not be pleased.

"Powerboats are for slackers," Edwin said.

Edwin dove fifteen feet where the water was calmer and the chop of the surf did not shift him. He swam toward the dinghy as fast as he could.

The parachute extended the craft's footprint by 50 feet, languishing like a bloated anchor.

He could see the floats of the fishing netting bobbing twenty-five feet away.

Edwin pushed the parachute to the surface, spilling the heavy water like a leaking bag. As it emptied, he rolled it, until he could reach a strap around and pushed the bundle over the edge.

The silver grid of fishing netting eased beneath them.

Edwin unsnapped one side of the tarp and grabbed each corner. He opened the lid of a black plastic box tucked near the transom of the dingy and extracted a roll of duct tape.

By now, the dingy had drifted entirely over the netting, which was settling a yard or so beneath the surface.

Edwin spun the tape around one end of the oar and a corner of the tarp. In an instant, he did the same to the other side. Then he lifted the oar and the expanse of plastic tarp over his head. The bottom edges stayed anchored on the side of the dingy.

He heard large metal spools grinding. The fishing boat, a hundred yards east, was preparing for another cast.

They're reeling in the netting. They're reeling in their catch, which very nearly includes me, Edwin thought. He swore.

Edwin pulled the diving knife from its sheath on his calf. He put the pointed tip into the inflated bellow of the supply raft.

But after a second, he pulled it away.

I can't sink this load. It's been five months since food arrived. I'm out of sugar, and I'm starving.

Edwin always created options. The powerboat was useful but superfluous. He had other ways of moving fast on the water.

I can't lose this dinghy or its contents. And I can't risk anyone finding it.

Now the netting stretched beneath him, and around him, as far as he could see. He could not turn on a motor; it would tangle in the net and stall.

Wind fluttered at the edges of the tarpaulin. Edwin braced himself. But as the wind caught in the tarp and slid past its edge, it began to push the dingy forward. The tarp made a sail, Edwin the mast and mainstay.

The nylon web ghosted beneath them.

Edwin tilted the oar so the handle nearly touched the inflated gunnel; the boat pointed toward the direction of the breeze, gathering speed. The netting slipped beneath them, and soon he was sailing over dark blue water, the prince returning to his sovereign nation, a principality on cement stilts forgotten somewhere in the warm Caribbean sea.

When the loaded dinghy cleared the netting and drifted out of sight of the fishing boat. Edwin rolled down the tarp. He unbuckled a locker beneath a center seat and extracted a ten-horsepower outboard motor. In moments Edwin was buzzing back to the rig like a mosquito in the dusk.

It took two hours to unload the supplies into the elevator. There were twelve boxes, two feet wide by one foot, eight inches high. Some of the boxes were heavy. He stacked them in piles on the floor, and put one on the counter. He stuck his fingers next to the tape and ripped the cardboard open. He pulled out cans and stacked them quickly on the shelf. Cans of baked beans, peaches, pineapples, and pears. Four large cans of coffee. Two five-pound bags of sugar. Ten pounds of rice. An entire box of microwavable pasta. Four boxes of MREs – meals ready to eat. Five jumbo bags of chocolates.

"Fun size!" Edwin said, his green eyes bright with delight. He ripped the plastic and crammed two small snickers into his mouth.

Food filled his shelves.

There was one more box. It felt light.

Edwin placed this one gently on the counter. He pulled his ballpoint pen out of his back pocket. He pressed the button with his thumb. A thin blade, sharp on both edges, slid out. This he tucked under the taped flaps. With a quick swipe the top sprang open.

"Whatcha got for me, Zed?"

He lifted the top of a large box of white Styrofoam. Inside was a piece of paper and a pile of what appeared to be black and yellow marbles. He picked up the paper. It was a map of the world. Someone had drawn crude stars in gold permanent ink on each country.

"Deployments," Edwin said. Zed had been pre-populating his fleet in strategic locations around the world.

Then Edwin picked up one of the black and yellow marbles. He held it gently between his thumb and forefinger.

"Buzz buzz," said Edwin.

In his fingers, Edwin held a plastic bee, one inch long. Its wings folded back from the thorax over its back. He studied the patterns on the wings, where solar circuits ran currents through what looked like veins in the nearly transparent wingspans.

Edwin held the small insect to the light. Then he pressed his thumb on the abdomen, where a small scan ran a tiny blue beam across the whorls of his fingerprint.

The eyes opened. The wings lifted. The bee flew around the room and went out the door and down the hallway.

Edwin's focus adjusted to a holograph his contact lenses set in the field of vision. There he could watch high definition footage appear. It showed the hallway in the oil rig, his unmade bed. It hovered near the framed picture on the wall.

It was a WIRED magazine cover. The title read "Meet Edwin Hoff, MITs next billionaire." The picture showed Edwin's face and his hairline from years ago. The footage paused at the bookshelf, where a single, small volume lay, warped with humidity. "Howl," by Alan Ginsburg. It had been a parting gift from Lula.

The footage streamed in as the bee left his private quarters, and moved to the dark stairwell, eventually opening on to the bright platform below. The screen showed the ocean waves, growing stronger in the afternoon as the wind picked up.

The bee rose. It filmed down on the rig from above the tallest stanchions, inspecting the small platform Edwin had installed there, with a few critical pieces of gear.

Edwin was relieved. "So Zed is still well. And he's still ahead of the ASP."

Edwin checked the time.

"15:15. Time to study," he said. He pulled up a website that showed fourteen common facial emotional patterns. Without human company, all these years, Edwin had found studying human facial expressions to be fascinating. He liked knowing what faces and bodies were saying whether or not anything came out of the mouths.

Then suddenly, Edwin looked up. His chin dropped and his hands braced square against the desk.

Three monitors on the wall flashed red.

CHAPTER SEVEN

3:15 p.m., May 22
Somewhere in the Caribbean

Edwin dropped to his feet. He pushed the coffee cup behind him on the counter. His body tightened as he studied the alarm monitors.

There's a blackout in Pakistan. Pretty wide-ranging coverage.

The monitors told him that telephones, Internet and electricity had all gone out at 12:15 a.m. in Peshawar.

To most people, the blackout would appear to be a temporary inconvenience. But to Edwin it meant something quite else. He knew the likelihood of "a broken line" or "workers needed a temporary shut-down" across so broad a territory was improbable.

Someone's going in. They shut off the lights so no one can see. And they shut off the phone so no one can tell.

Edwin perched on the edge of his chair, eyes darting from one monitor to the next.

Someone jammed power and communications in Peshawar. So what don't they want anyone else to see? Or tell?

The screen shifted and zoomed in on a green and black image, night vision cameras showing a patch of a suburb in Pakistan, its grid now black.

"Where are we exactly, fleet?" he muttered.

He thought for a moment. Then he typed in a string of code. It was an old authentication, a trap door he had built into a network he once created so he could take a peek whenever he wanted to see what his creation, the D6 network, could see.

"Come on, slackers," Edwin said. "Did you find my little Hobbit hole yet?"

The screen pinged. Edwin had successfully tapped in to the same video feed that streamed into a single, secure computer address in Washington D.C. The feed now blindly reflected to Edwin's monitor. It appeared to come from a powerful set of cameras with both a wide scope and powerful zooming telescope.

Edwin knew exactly who else would be watching this same show. But they would have no idea that Edwin was in the room, too.

The video was coming off one of their drones flying at fifteen thousand feet. He watched the soundless video stream as Seal Team 6 commandos flew two oddly shaped helicopters low over suburban streets.

They are invading an ally. No wonder they want the lights out.

The helicopters flew in darkness over the suburban streets. No lights went on in the nearby houses.

One helicopter hovered fifty feet above the roof of a three-story building.

Tighten those gloves. That rope can burn.

He watched the black lines drop straight down from the Blackhawk helicopter. The night vision video feed picked up light green bulges sliding down the ropes. These, Edwin knew, were the commandos with guns in their packs and black heat-resistant gloves on their hands, sliding down the ropes. They let go at the roof, where they ran for cover to a predetermined location.

The soldiers wore night vision goggles with four conical lenses instead of two. Black gloves shielded their hands.

A second helicopter landed in the yard. Edwin watched more light green shapes run toward the building, as the soldiers approached.

Next to the dotted line of heat sources the soldiers' warm bodies made, Edwin saw small white dots also racing around chaotically on the video.

Chickens. A cow. Some goats.

He watched nine commandos blast through another gate and reach the wall of the building, where they edged toward the front door. They went in, rifles high and blasting.

Outside the walls of the compound, Edwin saw another soldier standing with a dog. A few people approached, and then retreated.

They do not want to pet that dog.

When Edwin had trained, their team had several shepherds. Fierce looking, fiercely loyal. By discouraging onlookers, they bought extra time for missions. By sniffing out explosives, they saved limbs and lives.

They were not lap dogs.

Nineteen minutes after they went in, Edwin saw four soldiers emerge carrying the ends of a long, white bag, over six feet long, slung between them something wrapped in white sheets.

During the next nineteen minutes, Edwin watched other SEALs emerge with files, discs, hard drives, and an old square computer monitor. They carried the keyboard gingerly.

A large Chinook landed. A soldier knelt by the corpse in the white bag. He stuck something into the arm, and then, after a few seconds, withdrew it. Then he repeated the sequence. The soldier then stuck two long swabs into the mouth. He snipped two clumps of hair. Each went into a small clear plastic bag; then into a clear jar with screw on top.

Two matching DNA sets. They're splitting them up in case one helicopter doesn't make it back.

One person ran with the samples in a cooler to the Chinook helicopter. The other went to the Black Hawks. The soldiers loaded the body into the Chinook.

The two invading Blackhawks and the rescue Chinook lifted off.

Edwin watched the video stream carried through the small eye of the drone, filmed fifteen thousand feet above Peshawar. The helicopters left the view.

What Edwin saw next changed everything.

Through the video feed, the drone showed a man creeping around the wall of the compound.

They left someone? No. No chance.

The man edged along the building, moving slowly but surely toward the front door. The small hairs stiffened on the back of Edwin's neck.

So - who did they just get? Why'd the U.S. just risk an act of war? Breaching the national sovereignty of Pakistan - to go in and take him out in a white sheet in the space of thirty-eight minutes?

He swung in his chair to the left, to the right.

"You got him," he said. "I bet to hell you got him."

Edwin flicked a few keys on the keyboard. He reset the program, directing his own drone network.

"Go hive," he said.

Across the seas, over the mountains, thousands of bees moved into place, each capturing a certain view and feeding each small bit into the hive mind that fed Edwin's network and Crosspathz software program.

The software crunched this massive amount of data with the stacks of computers blinking on top of one another in what once were crew bedrooms for the oil rig. Crosspathz zoned in on this figure that was inching along the edge of the Leader's lair, moments after the U.S. Special Forces had removed him.

The program measured the man's height, gait and stride. And when he glanced upward at the sky for several long moments, perhaps watching the departing helicopters, cameras captured the distance between his pupils, two points that could not be disguised. It catalogued the bridge of his nose, the rise of his cheekbone, the angle of his jaw - and the small mole below his left ear.

Then the man slipped back into the house.

Edwin looked at the giant monitor on the wall of the cabin. After years of waiting, he watched the image that had never found a match from any feed in the world, not from the camera beside any ATM, at any crosswalk, on the platform of any train, beside any subway queue, or at any airport or tollbooth. Finally, it shined in green. Finally, it had paired with an exact match. The frenetic scrolling ceased. It froze on one single face, years older than the image in the ID photo on the left. It was the same man.

The hair was longer but still deep black. He wore a kurta open at the neck, instead of a button-down blue chambray shirt. And Crosspathz had just caught him, slipping back into the Leader's lair, the moment after the Leader had been killed.

This was the man who tipped the plot that, had it succeeded, would have added millions to the death toll on the day of the worst attack on U.S. soil.

This was the terrorist who had lived his own deep-cover life – right under Edwin's distracted nose - as an engineer at D6, in Cambridge, Massachusetts.

"It's Ali," Edwin said.

The deduction was simple.

Who lived in that house? Who was the U.S. military after so badly that they were willing to risk breaching Pakistani sovereignty to raid at midnight, kill and capture?

"They got him," Edwin said. "They finally got the Leader of al Ra'duzma."

He clapped his hand on the desk.

"Success! And now, there will be a successor."

Edwin moved quickly to the next phase.

Ali is the first person back inside. So Ali must be the successor, or he wants to be. But I've got him now. Which means he's toast.

Edwin tucked the box of bees under one arm. He climbed the stairs two at a time until he was out on the roof of the living quarters. The rigging extended another fifty feet. With a length of doubled-up duct tape for a strap, Edwin slung the box over his neck and shoulder and climbed the metal girders, arm over arm, until he reached the small platform sixty feet higher at the top.

The wind was howling. He braced his feet against the corners and crouched low over the box. He popped his ballpoint pen, and with its narrow blade, sliced through the box top. He opened it.

Gingerly, he took a bee model in his hand. He passed his left hand over the small lenses that looked like eyes and waved it again beneath its abdomen.

The cameras imbedded there read the swirls of Edwin's fingertip prints, authenticated him, and turned the tiny drone on. The bee made a small hum. It was now a flying camera, a robot no more than one inch wide, its destination determined by Edwin's computer program running off the servers below, and which would feed back whatever it saw to the Crosspathz software. Its filaments of wings spread out, capturing light and feeding the tiny drone with enough energy to sustain flight at a certain height. By falling rapidly, the bee would generate friction. The heat exchange would be stored to recharge the battery when it needed a burst.

Edwin tossed the bee into the air. He saw it catch, hover, then dart with an astonishing burst of speed through the twilight, to the north and east. It was soon joined by nineteen more bee drones, the latest installment in a fleet of tiny drones that Zed would send in his packages each year, and which Edwin would then program and deploy. These would join the squadrons that Zed had dispersed regularly over the years. There were thousands of them now deployed around the world, their sensors creating a wide, responsive grid. Each captured a small view, but together, they snapped into a cohesive, detailed and broad picture.

The bees were much more subtle than a satellite, with more detailed coverage. Hidden away on his oil rig, Edwin watched the world change through the multifaceted eyes of his increasingly large hive.

One monitor in the control center looked like air traffic control. It was filled with clusters of small green dots moving and shifting location with each refresh of the screen. Twenty new red dots fanned out from a spot in the Caribbean, heading east.

Edwin stared into the small round metal mirror in the tiny washroom. His green eyes blazed back at him. After years of isolation, he would engage again, at least for a brief time. He would be among other people.

"Focus," Edwin scolded his image. "Be better now. Get Ali. And don't let the ASP catch you. You are behind."

Edwin knew the Association for the Society to Protect thought he was dead, which meant they would have assigned their considerable resources to find him and make it so. Even if it took years.

Edwin Hoff once had been a deep cover operator for the Association for the Society to Protect, the ASP. He was assigned to a technological logistics support person named Zed.

The ASP accepted only the most elite commandos, and without regard to flag. World leaders did not acknowledge the ASP, and the ASP answered to no government. The ASP had only ever had one Head – the person who had created the organization with considerable personal wealth, and for only one purpose. The single mission of the ASP was this: to defend humanity against its smallest threats. As disease vectors could pass unseen through borders, the ASP would do so as well to pursue and eliminate these invisible killers. ASP operators were trained and willing to stop bio-attacks without approval, process or authority. They came from U.S. Delta Force, Israel's Sayeret Maktal, Pakistan's ISI, Britain's SAS. They were trained in every skill a deep-cover operator needed to stop an act of bioterror: hand-to-hand combat, munitions, breaching buildings, rooms, vehicles, and planes. They were expert at Survival, Evasion, Resistance and Escape. Spy tradecraft was built into their muscle memory. ASP Operators touched down in communities for a time – for years even – remaining unnoticeable, unexceptional and unattached.

This last was so important that the ASP put in the Operator's contract.

Sec 1.2.10 No Attachments:
The operator shall not form or maintain any signifi-
cant personal relationship(s) during the Term of this
Agreement other than with the assigned technical support.
Any such attachment will lead to immediate termination.

Isolation simplified the inevitable extraction. Worse, attachments could compromise an operator's loyalty and discretion, and expose the existence of the ASP. So the ASP was mortally jealous of any it discovered, and turned the termination clause into a deadly serious matter.

People were supposed to think Edwin was a boring graduate student in Cambridge, Massachusetts, studying an obscure field in MIT's mathematics program. In the buzz of the dotcom boom, when everyone else was doing it, Edwin had started a small technology company, called D6. This was supposed to extend and add authenticity to his cover.

But the company boomed. D6 brought Edwin unexpected fame, fortune and popularity, an unexpected formula for kryptonite. The buzz of his cover life distracted Edwin, and so did the chocolate eyes of a dark-haired barista named Lula Crosse, who smelled of coffee and cinnamon and roses.

It was during this time that Edwin's company D6 had employed Ali Hamini, a brilliant software engineer with a bad attitude.

There was no way around this truth. Edwin had broken the cardinal rule of the Association for the Society to Protect by forming an attachment – a delicious, intoxicating, compelling attachment – with Lula Crosse.

Ali was right under Edwin's nose, while Edwin was preoccupied with the rich pleasures of playing a tech billionaire.

Ali used the stock windfall from D6's initial public offering to finance the purchase of weaponized pneumonic plague, which his associates in the terror world had planned to release over New York and Boston. They very nearly did. Edwin caught on just in time to stop the attack, but Ali escaped. He had his own grand plans to fulfill.

When the ASP made Lula pay for Edwin's breach, he left the ASP, his cover, D6, and that world where he had found himself so suddenly engaged, so alive, and so enthralled at his responsibility to a thousand individuals who depended on him for a weekly paycheck. Even though he was supposed to be faking.

When it all went so terribly wrong, Edwin knew exactly who to blame. So he made two promises. First, with the exception of Zed, Edwin would have no attachments. Never again. He would not put anyone else at risk ever again. He would not be lured. On this he would never weaken.

Whenever he began to tire of the view from the rig, of every shade of blue reaching in every direction as far as he could see, he singed himself with the memory that he had cost Lula her life.

Second, Edwin would get Ali and put an end to his murderous ambitions.

So for as many years as it had taken, and as many as it would take, Edwin focused on finding Ali Hamini, the westernized link to the leadership of the global terrorist organization al Ra'duzma. Edwin studied the feeds and adjusted the algorithms of the net he created to sense and trap his prey. Every day, every hour, Edwin would focus on finding Ali.

And when Ali eventually raised his head above the slime he had sunk beneath, Crosspathz would spot him. And then Edwin would go get him, and stop the next head of al

Ra'duzma before Ali could take over and demonstrate he was even more fearsome than the predecessor.

"I will watch until you make a mistake," Edwin had promised. "Just one. When you surface - and you will - I will come get you. And I will destroy you."

Edwin found a place to hunt for Ali that was remote. So remote that it would prevent any encounter, much less any attachment. So remote that Edwin could find Ali before the ASP found Edwin.

The ASP always made sure that an operator who went rogue never could return.

CHAPTER EIGHT

1:32 a.m., May 23
Peshawar, Pakistan

Ali was soaked in sweat by the time he reached his apartment building. This time, he took care to sprint beneath awnings; through narrow alleys with covered rooftops, so no eye above could follow him. Outside the high walls of the compound, neighbors would be waking and peering through their windows.

Ali took the stairs three at a time. But he was not winded. He was strong, nimble, fast and fit. The day had come when he needed to be. Because from the moment the Leader fell, the clock had begun to tick. It was time to fulfill his own legacy. The orders were in his apartment.

He pressed his fingers against the back of his neck. It was all that ever bothered him. Sometimes, without warning, the nerves along his spinal cord heard a silent warning and – crunch. They spasmed, flexing instantly against a perceived assault. To move, even a flinch, was torture.

But this evening the muscles were smooth and relaxed.

Ali locked the door behind him. He scanned the room as his eyes adjusted to the light. A younger man slept soundly on his mat, one arm bent over his head. Near the wall lay the rest of his possessions, a few kurtas and leggings and underclothes, folded politely in an old carpeted suitcase that he had retrieved from Ali's refuse.

"Sleep while you can," Ali muttered to his assistant. "There will be plenty to do when you wake."

Usman was a runner, and had delivered the message that night that the goat truck would be coming for Ali. He was in his mid-twenties. He ran fast. He ate as much as he could fit on his plate. He slept hard.

Ali crept across the floor and pulled back a corner of the curtain on the single front window. The street was pitch black. He dropped the curtain.

In the kitchen, Ali tugged at a drawer. The utensils inside clattered and slid. He cringed at the noise.

Usman slept.

Ali felt for a small, sharp paring knife. A toaster was on the counter, crumbs scattered around it. Ali unplugged the cord and put the toaster on the small kitchen table. Then he felt along the wall. His fingers soon found the faint indentation where the plaster split behind the paint.

The blade slipped easily into the groove. Ali wiggled the knife. A panel fell from the wall into his other hand. He placed it carefully on the counter, and then stuck his hand inside the dark space.

His fingers quickly felt the slick surface of the plastic bag. Ali held up the small thumb drive.

The Leader had given this drive to him two years earlier.

"You are not to look at this until such time as I give the order," the Leader had said. Ali remembered how his gaze had drifted. "Or when that time comes that I can never give that order. Then you must open it immediately. Then this is all that will matter."

Ali heard a door creak. He froze. Listened.

Silence.

Ali put the bag down on the counter. He reached back into the hole in the wall, his arm crooked as far as he could reach. He felt the rough plaster against his shoulder.

This time he retrieved a thin, leather-bound case. A zipper ran around three sides. Ali pulled the zipper around one corner, then the next.

The leather case held several plastic sleeves, each with a zipper. Three were empty. One held an old, dried, toothbrush.

Ali reached into his kurta, and from a small pocket stitched near his hip he felt the pointed edge of a folded piece of paper. He opened it gently. In the crease he saw one long, coarse, grey hair.

Carefully, Ali tucked the delicate package into one of the empty sleeves within the leather case and zipped it closed.

Ali started to push the plaster square back into its place in the wall. But then he laid it on the counter again. He reached back in. This time he pulled out a photograph. It was a strange picture, an angled shot of the surface of an old wooden table. It caught, out of focus, the edge of a round, flat, tin platter. A few black crumbs scattered on it near a few thin strings of white cheese, curling in globs at the end.

The camera had focused on some letters carved amid generations of others in the brown tabletop.

YM & CH

TLF

'Yassir Metah and Camille Henderson...: True Love Forever' Ha. We're a long way from Nicko's Pizzeria, Camille.

Ali tucked the photograph into a sleeve of the leather case and zipped it closed again.

When his computer hummed, Ali inserted the drive. He closed his eyes and breathed deeply. His clothes clung to his skin, the heat and moisture reviving the stench of the goat truck.

"I'm ready," he said. "I must be ready."

"Ready for what?" Usman asked. He stood in the doorway, stretching.

A mile away, they heard sirens squealing. Jet engines ripped the sky, waking Peshawar.

"What has happened?" Usman asked, suddenly alert.

Ali looked up. He held Usman's eyes as he slipped the thumb drive into its socket on the computer.

"They found him."

Usman's eyes flared. "Who?"

Ali nodded.

"No..."

Ali nodded again.

Usman rushed to Ali's side. He knelt on the ground and took both of Ali's hands in his. He bent over Ali's outstretched palms and kissed them.

"Then, Ali, it is you now. Al Khaleef," breathed Usman. "It is Allah's wish."

Ali blinked. It was a heady moment. He had been told for so long what he would be given. Now the promised reward was so close. Succession.

"*Insh' Allah*," Ali managed to remember to say. If Allah wills it. "The Leader has left instructions."

"How will he say it, do you think?" Usman said, as the computer clicked and hummed, registering the discovered drive, asking what to do with it. "How will he anoint you?"

"I don't know," said Ali.

There was a single file on the drive. Ali's finger hovered.

"Push it," Usman said.

Ali did not move. Finally Usman pushed the button. The file opened.

Ali read the short message. But what the Leader had written was not what Ali expected. Not the phrasing, not the content, not the result. It was even worse than the Leader had hinted at earlier that evening.

Ali was not the named successor. He was not even mentioned.

Usman stared at the text. "What does it say?"

Ali cleared his throat. "It says: 'Upon my death, select my successor in this way. All tribal leaders shall meet forty-eight hours from the moment of my death to choose my successor. You each have special talents. Each of you could take my place and yet, as of the time of this writing, none of you has convinced me, beyond doubt, that you should be next."

"What?" Usman said. "You – you are supposed to be the successor. It's been told this way for years. Since The Awakening years ago. And since the ceremony in the caves!"

Ali read and re-read the orders.

"Be that as it may," Ali finally said, "He did not choose me. The Leader has left it open to all of the tribal heads of al Ra'duzma to decide in forty-eight hours who to pick. All he made specific is where we will meet."

All Ali could see, for the moment, was one thing.

"The place. It's a good one," Ali muttered. "No drones can fly there, and no one can bomb it."

In this place the leaders would have sound cover to meet, select a new leader, and pledge their loyalties – still possibly to Ali, who was widely considered to be the chosen one, but perhaps to someone else. Badi Badi from Yemen, or to any other contender who caught their attention.

Ali's neck twinged like someone had suddenly yanked a cord on one side of his neck. He breathed deeply, rubbing his fingertips into the suddenly strained muscles.

"Something of yours, something of great value, has been stolen," said Usman solemnly.

"I will take it back," said Ali, each word a hard, deliberate promise.

His fury rose and built for what seemed like miles. His thoughts raced.

I gave everything. Everything has been taken from me and I have known nothing but to serve for this call that has not come. The sum of my life. The Leader just tossed it aside in a sentence typed on that crappy keyboard, from his pathetic hole.

To Usman, Ali said, "Leadership is my legacy. Mine. I will have it."

"But how?" asked Usman. "If they do not already know about you there is not much time to convince the tribal leaders."

Ali sat back in his chair, the facts settling where the whirlwind shook them. Before this evening, things had rested in a certain place, for definite reasons. The sudden death of the Leader, and the unexpected vacuum he had left for his succession, had changed facts and upended conclusions.

"I don't understand," Usman continued. "How did they even find him?"

"Someone told the Americans where he was," Ali muttered. "That's why he's dead."

But it wasn't me. Not this time. So who was it?

"Why? What would they get for it? The money?" asked Usman.

Everyone knew about the bounty. The American operatives in the Middle Eastern countries were not subtle about the reward. Lead them to the Leader, walk away with twenty-five million dollars.

"And who knew where he was?" Usman continued.

"Not many. It had to be one of us, I guess. Someone on the inside and close."

"And they'd abandon the mission just for money?"

Usman's uneducated loyalty was so simple, it made Ali half chuckle.

"It's a lot of money," Ali said. "Someone could do a lot with twenty-five million."

And that was when the rest hit him. Ali was a computer engineer; he thought in precise, logical steps. From Usman's simple question, Ali deduced each step that had preceded the evening's assault.

"What would twenty-five million do?" Ali told Usman. "It would fund a major attack - a spectacular one, or a series of them. So, no Usman, I don't think they did it to abandon the mission for money. They sold out the Leader to *pursue* the mission. The traitor wants to take over. He wants to attack."

"But what about you? Everyone thinks you are the successor."

"Not anymore," Ali said. "But you are right. Before they read this instruction, whomever did this probably did think I was the chosen one."

"So why bother? It's well-known that you are to be the next Leader."

Ali shook his head.

"Known, perhaps. But not accepted. If this man would kill the Leader, he'll make short work of the main con-tender. Me. And he must be pretty sure of his second strike to have taken the first."

Usman sucked in air. "He'll try to kill you," he whispered.

"Yes. They will all try to kill me," Ali said. "But I won't let them."

Why? Why strike now? Do they know...about me? Did they find out the truth? If this rival knows my real story, he will tell the other tribal leaders. They will rip me limb from limb.

Several identities ago, while a student at Yale, Ali went by the name "Yassir Metah." Right before graduation, he had left college abruptly, without explanation. Uncle had called. Ali had to leave, without a word to anyone who had become a friend, even a lover, while he wore that cover: College Boy.

As he packed, Ali placed three pairs of socks on his bunk bed. They formed a triangle, made of three black dots.

Camille will know, Ali thought. He had insisted on signs. He had told her that Uncle could never know about her. If he discovered their relationship, Uncle would take him home.

The three black dots in a triangle were to warn Camille that something very bad was about to happen. Life or death.

Then he slipped his backpack over his shoulder and walked out into the cool May night as if to search for a quiet place to study for finals.

A few hours later, Camille Henderson, his girlfriend of four years, came to his dorm room. She saw the black dots.

Yassir Metah was never seen again.

They were just kids then, barely twenty-two years old. There was something about Ali that both had drawn Camille and repelled her, and thus fixated her. He carried darkness behind that toothy smile. Once, in bed, Camille had traced her index finger along a rough scar that broke through the stubble beneath his chin. He had gripped her fingers so hard that one broke, and another dislocated.

She had cried. Ali had not apologized. Ali never apologized. In an odd tone of voice, one an octave deeper than his natural voice, Ali had said,

"Never touch me like that again. And I will not touch you like that again."

They both had known she should have left him. Instead, they shared college, the fear of breaking up always pulling them back together. Then a few days before graduation, Ali left her three pairs of rolled-up black socks on the bed sheets.

There are some small details one never forgets about the people who matter to us.

Ten years after college ended, Camille returned one evening to her apartment in Washington D.C. from her job as an analyst at the Central Intelligence Agency. She could not quite believe someone paid her to speak the language she loved and to study a culture she treasured.

At her door, Camille bent to pick up a scrap of newspaper near her welcome mat. It was an ad for the Central Park Zoo, and the Reptile Exhibit at 4:00pm on July 9.

There it was. A black felt-tip pen had left slight tails on three dots that formed a triangle. The conclusion came fast. Too fast.

"He needs me," Camille whispered.

Camille was not good at intrigue. She was an analyst. Primarily, she considered herself a scholar.

"Something terrible is about to happen," she said. Opening this note was like electrifying part of a city that had been dark for years. Here she was, all lit up.

"Who else would he call? Not his parents," Camille thought. Yassir had confided one night, as a Dura flame log burned short

blue flames slowly in the dormitory fireplace, that his parent had died when he was very young. A gas leak from a cracked transmission, a spark, and at the age of six, her college love had been left to fend for himself on the streets. By some miracle, a wealthy man he now called Uncle had found him, sheltered him, raised him, and educated him.

Camille's train arrived in Grand Central Station the next afternoon. By 3:50 she was handing eleven dollars to the clerk at the Central Park Zoo.

On the sweltering July day, the rainforest exhibit was empty. She walked past the turtles showing their bellies to the plexiglass. The birds made shrill appeals to one another. After twenty minutes, she was drenched.

Yassir had not appeared.

"Beware the madness of spies," Camille muttered, quoting Jean le Carre's warning to covert officers, telling of the occupational hazard of the analyst who craves the action she also fears, who avoids the field but can't stop watching. How she spirals amid shadows she invents.

As she approached the reptile exhibit, the realization hit. All she had seen in the crumpled newspaper was this: she wanted to see her old love. Badly. So she had made up his clandestine call for help.

Camille walked briskly through the exhibit. The path was quite narrow. It led to a dark space. The sign above said "Reptiles."

"Snakes," she spat, looking for the gleaming red EXIT sign. When she spotted it on the other side of the exhibit, she moved toward it. Through the plexiglass, she saw a thick vine dangling. Then it blinked.

Something touched her shoulder.

"Ah!" Camille yelped. She patted her chest frantically, and waved her hands.

"Milly," Yassir said.

Even in the darkness, Camille could see Yassir's broad smile, the white teeth that made his face such a thing of beauty.

"You understood," he said. "You came."

Camille nodded. Ali put his palm against the small of her back. His touch opened a time warp. Camille slipped through it.

"Hi," she said softly.

"I don't have much time," he said, pulling Camille back into a dark corner of the exhibit. His face broke into a wide, white smile. "It's so good to see you."

"Yes," Camille said. Then confusion, old and new, began to blaze. "But it's been ten years! And why? Why this way? What am I doing here?"

Yassir's eyes searched Camille's. "I need you to – I – I know you can do something."

"I'm not sure what you mean," Camille said. She wiped her hot hands on her skirt. The heat made her thighs stick together.

He looked at her hard.

"I know what you do." Ali's voice dove. It cut sharply. He meant to frighten her, and he did. A moment ago she had seen Yassir Metah, the man she had fallen for. Now Ali showed her someone severe and unfamiliar. Someone she had seen only once before.

"That's fine," he said. "I don't expect you to tell me anything. I am here to tell you. I put it in your capable hands now."

"What is it?" Camille reached for his hands.

Ali breathed deeply.

"There is going to be a catastrophe. They are going to use airplanes as bombs on American cities. There's more. One of the planes will have on board a special piece of cargo – a vial with a weaponized form of pneumonic plague, timed for release twenty-four hours after impact. Once inhaled, it will spread quickly between people. They call it the Blood Boiler. Anyone exposed will be dead in a day or two."

Camille stood still.

"When?"

"In a few months," he said.

"How do you know all this?" Camille turned and stared at him.

"Don't," Ali said, as he stood up. "I must go."

"Why are you telling me?" Camille cried. "Why don't you do something to stop it?"

Ali turned back to Camille. "I just did. And I do not, for the life of me, know why."

Then he was gone. A slice of glare blinded Camille as he pushed through the door out into the bright summer day.

Ali knew that Camille and her colleagues used his tip to put an end to the Blood Boiler before it began. They contained the bio-threat, saving millions of lives on the east coast. U.S. military tribunals convicted Uncle Khalid and sent him to Supermax, the worst of all federal prison facilities. It was the end of his freedom, and it was the end of his legacy. The Blood Boiler plot lived on in al Ra'duzma as a joke, and the legacy of KAH as a laughingstock.

In the years that had passed since then, Ali had done everything he could to distance himself from that failure and to mask any connection. So far, no one seemed to have a clue.

Ali spoke with a startling calmness to his houseboy.

"So, Usman. In forty-eight hours I will be crowned or I will be killed. My goal is clear. I will prove my worthiness – again – and I will win allegiance from the tribal leaders."

"What can you do?" Usman asked. "In just two days!"

Ali stood up his full six feet tall. He bent over Usman and put a finger very close to his face.

"I will eliminate the competition. And I will prove that I am the most powerful, and what I have built makes me the deserving *Khaleef*."

"Is your invention ready?" Usman asked, taking a step back.

"Yes," said Ali. He held a generic mobile phone in his hand. "Watch."

He tapped an image of an airplane that sat in a grid among other icons on the screen. "The application can access the ACARS system. Now you can see those green dots? That is every plane in the air right at this moment. My application can collect every piece of data they are transmitting."

"What can you do with that?" Usman asked.

"You'll see soon enough," said Ali. "They all will."

"How do you build something like that?" Usman asked.

Ali smiled. Part of his power was making his methods invisible. His houseboy had no need to know that Ali had a small room in another building stacked with computer servers, linked to the Internet but shielded through a hundred different addresses, and hidden from association with him. That he had piles of mobile devices strewn across a folding table, all of which he had tested and retested.

"Once the sun has set," said Ali.

Usman smiled and dipped his chin.

Privately, Ali added a third promise. He would eliminate the competition. He would prove his merit. And in less than forty-eight hours he also would make sure that no one could reveal the one past mistake he had made, the one that could disrupt his ascent at the last moment. No matter what steps were necessary.

Ali thought of another photograph, one that once sat on Camille's dresser.

It was of him, twenty years earlier. He was wearing jeans and a button-down shirt, sitting on a piano bench. A young woman sat on his lap, her arms around his neck. She had red hair and freckles, and blushed deeply as she smiled for the camera. Behind them in the wood paneled wall someone skilled had etched the letters "Y..A..L..E…"

Camille. You wouldn't tell, would you?

None of his masks ever was real, Ali knew. "College boy" was not real at Yale. "Software engineer" was not real at D6. The only role that had ever rung true was "al Khaleef." The successor to the most feared terrorist organization in the world. Through every role he was given, when every one was ripped away, Ali clung to that. It was all he knew for certain about himself.

You either used power, or you felt it. Ali would get it and he would use it.

Ali knew two more things. One, he would never let them take the leadership away from him. And two, he would prove it was indeed his real, true destiny, that he was built for it, and had every right to claim it. He banished any doubt that ever dared flicker.

At D6, Edwin's cocksureness of himself, and of everyone he encountered, made Ali's doubts flare. It infuriated him. Ali only had been able to tolerate Edwin's presence because Ali was playing a role.

Unfortunately, as it turned out, so was Edwin.

Ali would stamp out his mistake, once and for all, and get on with his future. But he had to do it fast.

He had only forty-seven hours and twelve minutes left until the tribal leaders would meet and choose the successor.

Ali noticed he had left the small leather case on the counter.

"Usman, make tea," he said. "I have to go very soon."

Usman turned to light a match over the gas stove.

"Where are you going?" Usman said.

"I have to do as he says," Ali said. "Meet the leaders in less than forty-eight hours. And before then, I must prove – again – that I'm worth their loyalty. Now. Then. Still. Ever."

Ali turned his back to Usman and pulled the leather case into his palms. He flipped through the sleeves, thin plastic pouches bound within the leather book.

One contained an old toothbrush, its bristles splayed, white powder crusted in the grip.

Ali had paid one thousand dollars to a prison guard from the Columbia Correctional Institute in Portage, Wisconsin, to walk away with an inmate's personal effect. It had belonged to Jeffrey Dahmer, the sociopath who, seventeen times, raped, killed, cut up, and ate boys and men.

The cannibal's toothbrush, in a zip lock bag, was the one piece of luggage Ali had brought on the flight out of Cleveland on a private jet back to Cairo as soon as air space had opened after the Awakening caused the West to shut it down for three days all those years ago.

Now, protected in another plastic pouch, was a piece of the Leader's beard.

Ali closed the leather case and slipped it into a leather satchel he wore like a messenger bag across his shoulder. In the portfolio was the support that Ali needed to clear his path, once and for all. It was just confirmation.

Another interior pocket contained five hundred units each of U.S. dollars, euros and British pounds. His plan was nearly finished. But before meeting with the others at the succession summit, Ali had a great deal to do.

"There is no time. But it is the only way," he said to himself. "First, to England. The place to begin the next phase of my life, and to finally put an end to the last."

Ali had three prepaid mobile phones in the satchel. He sent a text message from one of them. It went to another just like it, which buzzed on the countertop of a small convenience store.

The message read:

Use the stick now. I want to see its mark in the morning.

Then Ali sent another text from a second phone. He knew this would reach a very different device, the latest in stylish personal technology. It buzzed in the inside pocket of an expensive wool suit jacket. It did not matter whether Charles Lincoln, Chairman of Finley's Auction House, saw the text that moment, or after he left the fancy pub and wiped from his lips the streak of beef juice from the roast. Charles was always very good at providing prompt service for his clients, even ones he had not seen in a long while.

The text Ali sent him came from "College Boy," who Charles also once knew as Yassir Metah.

Charles, hi! Yassir here. Will be in UK in am. Must collect my prize you stored so well for me. Where is best? In a rush sadly, as ever! Thx.

For years, Ali had been crouching, peering, hiding. He had planned well. Brilliantly, he thought. But now, the planning was done. Now, it was time to act.

With these two simple texts, Ali had set his plan in motion. Next he would dangle the rabbit's tail, and wait like a wolf in the woods.

CHAPTER NINE

May 22, 4:12 pm
Washington, D.C.

Ascher Silver stood in the back of the small room. A decorated marine, he knew how to fight a battle, but he was just learning how to wage a war. He served as the assistant to the Chairman of the Joint Chiefs of Staff in the U.S. Department of Defense, which meant he assisted the man who had no command under him, but advised the President, the National Security Council, the Homeland Security Council, and the Secretary of Defense.

The Chairman wore a grid of bright medals on the left side of his navy blues. He told Ascher to squeeze into the back of the small room. Ascher stood like an honor guard against the door opposite the wall where the presidential seal hung.

"Open eyes, open ears," the Chairman said. "Either way this goes down."

Ascher could just barely see the screen between the heads that occupied the chairs crowded at the end of a lacquered cherry conference table, ringed with gold. Studying the tops of those heads - the parted grey, cropped black, spiked, straight blonde bob, and several balding pates - he cringed at the human capital collected in this single space.

The Secretary of State, the Vice President, the President, and the Secretary of Defense sat together, side by side, and tense. None had his entourage present.

The Director of the CIA was not there in person. Ascher could see him on another monitor from where he watched in a control room in CIA headquarters in Langley, Virginia. A secure connection patched the Director into the small room at the White House.

This would be a very bad place for a bomb to go off. But this day, these men – and this Secretary of State – held the trigger.

It had taken many years, and many lives and limbs, to narrow the sights on "the Night Walker," a man who stood well over six feet tall. The Night Walker never left the confines of the third floor of the suburban house or stood outside its seven-foot privacy wall, but he would pace on the balcony, many nights, all night.

Laptops were open and cables spidered across the table to secure the top-secret bits that flew through them. But every cabinet member watched the small screen at the other end of the table.

It was a modest place for the leader of the free world to witness the capture of his nation's most notorious enemy. If it went bad, the President and his cabinet members would return to their palatial offices, somber rooms where people expected history to take place. But those rooms also often had recording devices, listening in for posterity, tapes to be released fifty years later. Such devices were not present in this anonymous little conference room. If the operation went bad, someone would just lower the light switch and shut the door.

Ascher craned his neck. He could see most of the small screen showing video filmed from fifteen thousand feet above ground. A camera, attached below the nose of a drone, captured the footage. The feed streamed the video from the drone, through a secure network, into the monitor on the wall of the situation room.

The detail in the images was startling. The technology was much stronger than news reports could reveal to the public. Ascher could see litter, individual pieces of paper, crumpled on the street. He could read the names printed on street signs.

After the helicopters landed, the President, his cabinet members, and Ascher only could see the perimeter team. The Belgian shepherd and his handler, and the translator dressed as a Pakistani police officer, backed off a few disturbed neighbors while two SEAL teams accomplished the missions inside. The SEALs did not wear cameras on their helmets.

The report came by audio only. The transmission rang through a speaker in the small office.

"For God and country - Napoleon, Napoleon, Napoleon," came the voice of the commando who had just pulsed two bullets, an inch apart, into the red laser dot that had settled above the left eye of the Leader of al Ra'duzma.

"Napoleon E.K.I.A.," he concluded. Enemy Killed In Action.

At first, no one spoke. Then Ascher heard the President's voice, serious, without boast. Three words.

"We got him."

Ascher and the assembled leaders would hear later from the SEALS exactly what had happened during the thirty-eight minutes the two teams were inside the Leader's lair, accomplishing the mission and gathering a trove of intelligence.

They watched two helicopters lift off and fly out of view. Then the President and his distinguished advisors congratulated each other.

But far away from Washington, fifteen thousand feet high above the city of Peshawar where the lights were still off and the telephones still jammed, the drone still kept its eye on the smoking lair. It watched the women and children from the Leader's inner circle, bound with flexible cuffs, sitting against an outside wall of the compound, waiting for the Pakistani authorities. It watched strings of spinning lights race through the neighborhoods toward the villa.

Ascher waited respectfully as the top officials in the Executive Branch filed out of the room. The longest manhunt in the history of America had just ended. But he could not take his eyes off the screen. What he saw next was the very first frame of the U.S. military's next manhunt.

Ascher put his hand on the Chairman's shirtsleeve as he passed.

The contact startled the senior official.

"Captain?" said the Chairman.

"Sir, there's a man," Ascher reported. "Going in – back in - to the house. Look."

The grainy screen showed a man moving against the side of the compound. He was inside the twelve-foot wall.

"He looks half the height of the wall," said Ascher.

"Note it," said the Chairman. "Six feet tall, about."

"He has black hair, wearing what looks like a light – not white - a khaki or very dirty – kurta."

Ascher and the Chairman watched as this man entered, disappeared into the house. Ten seconds passed. Twenty. Thirty.

After a minute and a half, the drone footage showed the man reappearing at the doorway. After a brief pause, he burst through the front door, running at full speed. The drone followed him as he stopped at the gate, took several steps backward, then sprinted down the street. The drone kept its eye focused on the house and lost track of the man when he darted into a narrow alley.

"One of the sons?" Ascher asked.

The Chairman studied the screens.

"There were only supposed to be three adult males there. We got them all. Who is this guy? Where did he come from? Where'd he go?" The Chairman barked orders to the Brigadier General operating the computer that received the streaming feed in the room.

"I don't see him, Sir, not yet," said the officer manning the computer. He flicked keys. Four different views from the drone each filled a corner of the wall monitor.

Outside the wall of the compound in Peshawar, a crowd was gathering. Blue lights spun from Pakistani police vehicles as officials arrived at the chaotic scene.

The Chairman looked at Ascher. "If this is a son who escaped, he'll know the whole organization. He could even be the successor. We need to find him now. The nation's top priority is now this man. Find him. You own this."

"Yes sir," said Ascher.

Within fifteen minutes the clip of the last minutes on the video had been copied and analyzed and passed through the government's massive data processing computers.

It found two irreconcilable entries matching the pinpoints that the drone captured when the man lifted his eyes briefly to the sky, noting the precise points where his cheekbones peaked, triangulated to the arch of each brow, and twenty-five other measurements.

One was a Yale college senior photograph from the class of 1990 of a man named Yassir Metah.

One was taken ten years later, in 2000, an employee photograph of a man called Ali Hamini, Software Developer at the company called D6 in Cambridge, MA.

They matched.

CHAPTER TEN

7:30 p.m., May 22
Somewhere in the Caribbean

Edwin Hoff studied the monitors along the wall. He paced along the strip of cement floor in front of them. The poker games were gone. Every screen fed his central program with feeds of data from around the world that could help identify Ali's location.

Edwin was looking for the green light. Since spotting Ali in Peshawar, the bee drones - and Edwin's hack of the U.S. military stream - had not seen him again.

He'll be in disguise by now. But Crosspathz can get through that. You better run, Ali. I'm not the only one coming. They saw exactly what I saw. Someone in the U.S. military wants to find that man who survived the raid and escaped. What's he doing creeping back into the Leader's lair? What does he have to do with the new leadership? I just have to get you first.

The wait was over. Edwin would leave the rig. He would head into a manhunt up against the best of the U.S. Special Forces. He would have to get there first, without anyone seeing him. Not the U.S., who still had all of his biometrics on file from his years in the military elite, including three years as captain of the counterterrorism division of Delta Force.

84

And Edwin had to be sure that the ASP did not catch a glimpse of their operator, the Raptor, presumed rogue until proven dead.

She can't still be alive.

Edwin thought of the ancient leader, the Head of the Association for the Society to Protect. She was a woman without empathy, and with good reason to be so.

But she wouldn't let a little thing like her death get in the way of the RUPD mission. He must be quick and smart. In and out. Intercept Ali before the succession, then disappear. Again. Until it grew another snake head.

Edwin bounced his knee under the desk. "I have to go now. Just one non-trivial problem: where? Give me a clue, Ali. Just one."

Edwin was ready. He was clean-shaven. He dyed his hair chocolate brown and drained the color down the small sink. He cut it clean but left it a bit long, not the most attractive style for his thick thatch, but not a military buzz either. He needed to blend in.

The one place the succession won't happen is in Pakistan. Not now. Then where? Yemen? Saudi Arabia? Turkey, even?

Edwin wore a clear flexible polymer band around his wrist. It was about an inch thick, and had come once in a box from Zed, with instructions to wear it at all times. The device had never made a sound. It had never moved.

But just then, the device on Edwin's wrist began to vibrate. Then it escalated to an urgent buzz.

Edwin pressed his index finger on the screen, which read the whorls of his fingerprint and the depth of each of the ridges on it. He heard a series of beeps, the digital equivalent of iron bolts shifting in sequence behind the door of a vault.

"You're calling me. Why?" Edwin said aloud.

These were the first words Edwin had spoken to another human in many years. But it was no time for small talk. To risk this call, something had gone very wrong.

"Yes," said Zed. "You need a taxi. They tracked my last drop. I'm ...sorry."

"How soon?" Edwin said, his eyes on the clock.

"Two," said Zed.

"Days?"

"Hours. Max. Go now!"

The line went dead.

Edwin opened the door and looked into the hall. The brown Gore-Tex knapsack hung by the stairwell. Edwin snatched it and ran to the bathroom. He reached into his knapsack and pulled out a special contact lens case. He pressed one into his left eye, the other into his right.

He blinked and the lenses settled onto the dome of his cornea. Edwin stared at the mirror. His green eyes, now tinged with a ring of yellow around the iris, flared. The next eyes he saw would belong to someone else. Anyone else. A shiver ran through him until the man in the mirror drew his brows together and stuck out his jaw.

"Focus," Edwin barked. "Be better yesterday."

Then Edwin bolted. The plan he had rehearsed daily had five hundred and twenty-six repetitions in his muscle memory. He did not have to think about how to move, and what to do to avoid capture by the organization that he had once served, before it had betrayed him. He had his own mission now. He would protect the world from terror on his own.

Edwin raced to his bedroom, and pulled the copy of *Howl* from its spot on the bookshelf. He added a ballpoint pen, another gift from Zed, and a small plain notebook, which according to the sticker, had been purchased at a drugstore chain for ninety-nine cents. Then he raced to the kitchen, and grabbed two packets of M&Ms, then a third, and stuffed them into the waterproof inner compartment of the bag. He slung the straps over his shoulders so his hands were free.

Edwin charged to the door of his control center. But just before he left, he turned to look back. He sought one monitor. Edwin called it "Channel D6", his guilty pleasure. Sometimes, when he needed only three of the four hours of sleep he allowed, he would allow himself to watch an hour of "D6," keeping tabs on the goings on of his still-expanding entrepreneurial venture.

His eyes darted to another screen. This one fed information about a particular person, one he found himself keeping frequent tabs on. Edwin was not sure exactly why, and he did not stop to think about it. He had saved her life once, but that hardly distinguished her. Nonetheless, Edwin kept checking in on where she was and what she had gotten into since their last meeting, so many years ago.

A slender woman in her early late thirties was boarding a plane in Cairo International Airport, on her way to Athens. The passenger data feed showed that the flight had been booked only a few hours earlier, and showed her return flight in seventy-two hours.

"What did you do, Camille?" Edwin said. "Must have been something good to earn a quick trip to the islands."

Edwin took a last brief look around his home. Then he turned abruptly and pushed the door open with a hard smack from his out-turned palms.

He charged up the steep iron staircase to the roof of the living quarters where, beneath the towering rigging, he could see across the ocean in every direction. It was sunset and the wind screed through the steel girders. He stared with open eyes but the wind did not bother him. His lenses secreted a viscous material that allowed him to see clearly, fixed on images when he, or they, were in motion, and with acuity to hundreds of yards beyond his normal range.

And that was the least of the abilities Zed had built into them.

"There you are," Edwin said, spotting the stark white wake of a powerboat approaching on the blackening blue water. "And your friend," he said, turning. Another came from the east. "And your backup." Three fast boats were closing in fast on the rig, the net circling in tight.

He had less time than Zed had thought. It would be a matter of minutes, not hours, before the ASP's RUPD team landed on his rig, and broke down every door searching for him.

Edwin looked down to the empty launch float.

Bad day to sink the boat.

He eyed the dinghy from Zed's supply drop, and its ten-horsepower motor.

They could catch that with flippers..

Inside the control room, Crosspathz flashed green. It had made an exact match of the face upturned to a U.S. drone camera in a Pakistani suburb. The video played on the smallest monitor first.

It was Ali. But there was no one in the rig's Control Center to see it.

The feed did not come from a drone or one of his butterfly fleets. It came from a Closed Circuit TV system outside London, England. These cameras were all over the country and provided police with an effective crime deterrent and source of evidence. CCTV cameras were located on street corners, near ATM machines, and outside office buildings.

Ali was standing in front of an office building, next to a sign that held the logos and names of the corporations leasing office space within it. One of these logos bore an all too familiar logo: the letter "D" and the number "6".

He was smiling in full view of the public safety cameras. He appeared to look directly into the camera when he tapped his temple with his index finger - two times. Then he pointed his index finger straight at the camera lens and held it there.

But after all these years of waiting, of watching, Edwin missed Ali's strange reappearance.

Edwin was climbing to the top of the rigging, where he would see the boats approaching. Arm over arm, his Nikes clung to the steel and gave him purchase as if he were scaling a simple ladder. At the top of the rigging Edwin hauled himself up to a small platform. The crow's nest was two feet by two feet, and had walls four feet high.

It contained everything he would need to defend himself.

Edwin checked the four cords that plugged securely into weatherproofed sockets. He unbuckled a waterproof pouch and felt the smooth fabric inside it. He reached over the crow's nest and felt against the wall for one latch, then another. Slowly, quietly, he slipped them open. For the moment, all four walls stayed vertical, surrounding him.

Below, the wind howled, carrying the shouts of the men who had thrown spring lines around the boat launch and were stampeding into Edwin's living quarters. Bullets rang on steel. They shot through the doors to cabin and Edwin's Control Center.

From the crow's nest at the top of the rigging, Edwin focused on the cursor blinking in the holograph of a computer screen that his powerful contacts made appear suspended in his field of view.

Forward slash...B...l...o...w...backslash..

The cursor typed green holographic letters next to the blinking cursor in his field of view:

Then the lenses Zed had built received the electrical impulse his brain made when they formed the image of the symbols that made up the code. The lenses wirelessly sent the signal to the software program running on the computer servers stacked in the former crew quarters on the rig.

The command took effect.

It blew. One by one, the computers in the central room, and the ones stacked in the old crew quarters exploded in clouds of smoke, fire, silicon, copper and metal.

The monitor that held the image of Ali with a finger to his lips, standing in front of D6, sizzled. The pixels fused to black. Software servers in the racks caught fire.

Each screen on the wall of Edwin's network operations control center cracked and smoked. The rig self-destructed.

"Keep going up! He's here somewhere," shouted the assailants.

"There!"

One of the RUPD team spotted movement at the top of the narrow stanchion.

Then Edwin heard a new sound coming through the darkness.

A helicopter was approaching. The rotors beat furiously against the wind. It was coming straight for him. They were coming for him from below, and from above. Straight at his crow's nest perch sixty feet above the oil rig platform, which rose above the waves another twenty feet even in rough weather.

This was why Edwin had planned his defense so well. This was why he practiced it daily.

There was only one thing that could defeat the ASP's sharpshooters and their eighty-thousand-dollar, four-cylinder night vision goggles.

Edwin could just make out movement at the base of the stanchions that held his crow's nest.

He would have only seconds.

The ASP assailants had gathered at the base of the girder that rose to Edwin's crow's nest.

"We tree'd him," boasted one of the attackers.

The four members of the ASP's attack team pointed their barrels up at the crow's nest.

Edwin flicked a switch. One hundred and twenty volts of electricity powered two thousand watts and shot a blazing beam of light down on the gunmen. This carried the full force of a lighthouse lamp, which at close range, blinded them.

He had his chance.

Edwin licked his finger to confirm the direction of the wind. Then he kicked down one wall of the fiberglass crow's nest. It fell outward until it locked like a short diving board, extending several feet away from the direction of the wind. He stepped out onto it. The board had four straps on it, slanted in opposite directions to make two inverted V's, one in front of the other. Edwin stuffed his feet in and tightened the straps. He held the bag of fabric from a straight rod that made a strong, wide handle.

The helicopter was close now, circling the rig. He could see the helmet and goggles of the pilot through the window. From below, shots peppered the rig; he could hear stray bullets ricochet wildly after hitting the steel, the lighthouse glare still trained down on the deck.

On the edge of the platform, hidden behind the blaze of light shining on the guns below, the gale battered Edwin's back sixty feet above the ocean swell. But he had no other choice. He could not go down, and eventually, they would come up. He felt for a pouch of thin lines gathered around a metal ring. When he found the ring, he looped it onto the matching ring attached to two straps that circled his shoulders and came together at his chest over his grey shirt.

Edwin shook the handle on the bag of fabric hard.

Then he jumped. The flat wide board stayed strapped on his feet as he fell fast.

But the wind filled the fabric pouch instantly. It shook out into a large crescent shape. The kite caught the wind like a bucket scooping seawater, and suddenly the bar, which connected to the kite with strong, thin nylon lines, wrenched against Edwin's hands. The pressure yanked against the hook on his harness, fighting his free-fall in uneven jerks. Edwin swung wildly toward the water, his muscles straining to keep control of the rod that held the kite, diving and darting with the whipping wind.

The board strapped to his feet touched the tips of the salty swell, but then another gust filled the kite and carried him off the top of it to another swell. While the lights blazed down, Edwin skipped over the waves away from the rig at a rate that accelerated past thirty knots, then forty, then fifty. He carved the kite's pouch in the air, up, down, hold and around, in the shape of a figure eight as he carved pressure out of the wind, the kite making him leap, pulling him thirty feet into the air. Edwin flipped his body with the board, in a full circle, then double flip, then a triple rotation.

He was off the rig.

But unfortunately, Edwin was also in the middle of the Caribbean ocean, at night. The wind lasted until he had put twenty-five miles behind him, but as it fell, the kite dropped in the water. The board on his feet could float itself, but that was all.

Eventually, the waves flattened.

"'Not a personal flotation device,'" Edwin read, catching a mouthful of seawater. "Thanks for the tip."

Edwin could float in this water for at least twelve hours. Warm water was hospitable, as long as the sharks did not find him. So he swam gently, gathering the folds of the kite sail around the board hoping to keep it afloat until the wind picked up. He rested on his back, watching the stars begin to appear.

But it was not long before he heard the soft regular beat of helicopter rotors approaching.

They're sweeping for me.

Edwin raced through the options. He listened to the sound of the helicopter approach. It was bearing right down on him.

Edwin breathed deeply, then exhaled. He did it again, and again, expanding his rib cage each time, which also expanded his lung capacity. Once his lungs were ready, he could kick his feet up and power down. Even without flippers and weights, he could pull himself down to forty feet below sea level and stay there for eighty seconds. He would dive as soon as he saw the door open and the muzzle of the gun set a precise angle. He would have to dive away from that trajectory.

The helicopter approached slowly. It descended, spreading the waves flat. The pilot opened the door. Edwin whipped his legs in the water like a frog, his strong legs ready to kick him down to a safe depth.

But instead of a gun, a rope ladder dropped from the side of the helicopter. The pilot waved his arms.

"Grab this! Quickly!"

The pilot was grinning broadly.

Edwin began to laugh. He knew that smile so well.

"Zed!" Edwin yelled, a wave catching in his mouth. "You are a titan!"

He spluttered and spat out the warm salt water. His strong strokes cut through the water until he wrapped them through the trailing ladder. The helicopter banked and rose on an angle, as the winch inside it gradually hauled him up.

Edwin looked back over the dark blue expanse of sea. He could not see the assailants. And he could not see the rig.

He turned to Zed and clasped both his hands on his old friend's shoulders. He felt the pointy bones through the flight jacket, and the involuntary shift of the man's muscles responding to an unexpected touch.

It had been a long time since Edwin had seen or touched another person. He began to laugh. The soft sound of delight shook his sturdy shoulders.

Chapter Eleven

9:05 p.m., May 22
Caribbean Sea

The helicopter flattened the waves and rose on the air pressure from the beating rotors. The nose tilted, and the powerful helicopter sped off, putting even more miles between them and the ASP-infested rig.

"Okay, my friend, okay," Zed said. He patted Edwin's hand, which still clutched his shoulder. Zed held out a pair of black headphones. "Put these on before you go deaf."

Edwin put the headphones on. They muffled the whip of the rotors while letting Zed's voice come through clearly. Zed looked at his friend, latching on the wrinkles around his eyes, the extra padding under his cheekbones, which the years had added.

"My god, it's you," Zed finally said, his eyes running up and down the frame of his friend. "Skinny you."

"You should have dropped more peanut butter," Edwin said. "Thanks for coming to get me. How'd you get back?"

Zed shrugged. "I don't think she would have let me take one of her birds. I keep some other friends."

"She? She's not still alive?"

Zed nodded. "She is. She has skin like tracing paper and smells of antiseptic.

Edwin paused a beat. "But she's still looking for me."

Zed nodded.

Edwin stared over the open expanse of ocean. He was looking for land.

"They must have traced my flight plan from the last drop," Zed said. "I'm sorry. I should have been more careful. This one will be very short."

Edwin shook his head sharply. "No. You are outstanding. Thank you."

Zed had taken extreme personal risks each time he had made a supply run in these years when Edwin Hoff was supposed to be dead but needed to eat.

"It was nice to drop by," said Zed. "Even if I never got to…say hello. Though I would have preferred a cup of tea together in my office showing you my latest inventions."

"Speaking of which…" Edwin said.

"All in good time, my friend." Zed smiled. "So impatient. Some things never change. But I do have some good ones."

When Edwin first joined the Association for the Society to Protect, the Head gave him two things: the moniker of "the Raptor," and technical support partner Zed. The ASP expected perfection from the Raptor, so Zed tried to supply him with much more. Over the years, their loyalty had expanded beyond the job, and beyond their respective covers. Zed eventually worked as a scientist at D6.

For what would be his final mission for the ASP, the Raptor went to see Zed for his gear. That day, the door to the small window-less office was open. Partly assembled robots sat on shelves, staring through uncovered eyeballs, showing ghoulish, veiny, red, black, and yellow wires. The duffel bag sat on a pile of magazines.

"What's in your bag of tricks today, Zed?" Edwin asked, as he reached for the straps.

"Ah ah," Zed scolded. He snatched the bag. "This must be introduced properly. Shown respect, like a new friend. Because you will rely on it like an old one. Tea?"

Zed was just under five foot six. His hair was deep black, though he was nearly fifty. Shadows hung perpetually under his brown eyes.

"Seriously? Again?" Edwin scowled. Despite two decades between their ages, Zed was the one solid, sanctioned link in Edwin's life. So he accepted the cup. He sucked at the tea. Spat the hot liquid. He blew at it hard.

Zed sat back in his chair, waiting for his cup to cool.

"It's nice for you to have a break, too. No? Okay, let's see what we've got."

Zed leaned forward and unzipped the bag. He pulled out a small plastic case that looked like it held contact lenses. He unscrewed one cap. Two yellowish discs peered out.

"These protect your eyes on a dive, or a free fall. They have infrared vision. Anything you see scans directly into the hard drive and transmits to me. Now I can see whatever you see."

Zed opened a laptop. "So, vision works when light bounces off an object into your eye. The light goes through the pupil to the lens, which focuses it on the back of the eye. There the retina turns light into electrical charges that tell the brain to produce the exact image you 'see.' These lenses pick up the same impulse. See? I can see, digitize, store, file and search whatever you see."

"That works how?" Edwin asked.

"They're yellow," said Raptor, pressing them to his eyes. The lenses blended with the bright green hue of his eye. An image formed on the screen. It was of Zed's arms, the laptop. Zed's face and eyes. The magazines, door, grey office carpet.

"There's more," Zed said, wiggling his eyebrows. "These lenses are the first known technology to make vision work in reverse. You *think of something, the image forms in your brain, which sends the electronic impulse to your lenses. They pass these signals to the computer, which draws a picture of what you are imagining. Try it."*

Edwin frowned. A random memory filled his mind. The screen showed a man holding out a trophy.

"What did you win?" Zed asked.

Edwin chuckled. "Body-building competition. I got entered."

The computer screen filled with the face of a skinny young boy, maybe fifteen, sitting on stone steps. A black violin case sat at his feet. Four bigger boys, laughing. "Central High Varsity Wrestling" was stitched across their burgundy wool and leather jackets.

"Good friends?" Zed said.

Edwin stared at the monitor. "I trained all summer. I won."

The monitor flashed the face of each of one of those four bullies, pinned, staring up from the mat.

Zed continued. "And she can type. You just visualize the words and symbols."

Edwin clapped Zed's shoulder. "Cool. But the yellow isn't subtle."

"I know." Zed frowned. "We'll improve that. Blink hard to toggle it on and off. And please don't leave it on all the time. I really don't want to see everything going on in that head. Next…"

Zed reached into the bag and pulled out a pair of laced-up Nike sneakers. "Trigger the internal magnet and these will seek the closest steel. You could hang on the edge of a window sill and just worry about the view."

"Not that I'd ever need to," Edwin said.

"Of course not," Zed said.

"You are a titan," Edwin said. Zed smiled and dipped his chin.

As the helicopter flew low over the dark waves, Edwin gripped Zed's shoulder.

"I saw Ali," Edwin said. "He's up."

"I know," Zed said.

"He was at the site of the attack in Pakistan," Edwin said. "Crosspathz made the match from facial recognition the drones picked up."

"Yes," Zed said.

"But now Crosspathz is gone," Edwin said. "I had to blow the network on the rig."

Zed whistled. "You sure?"

"I had to," Edwin said. "That was the protocol."

"So you don't know where we should be flying now," Zed said.

"No," said Edwin. "I don't know where he is. Though my guess is, he's far from Pakistan."

"Yes," said Zed, with a small smile. "He is. But he's closer than you think."

Edwin turned sharply to face his friend.

"Zed. What."

"I built a back-up of Crosspathz, of course," Zed said.

"But that backup was stored on the rig," Edwin said.

Zed smiled. "So I built a back-up of that. Which is right here."

He handed Edwin a flat black glass panel about the size of a paperback book cover, and thinner than a monthly magazine.

"Push the circle," Zed said. "Now, the triangle."

Video played across the glass on the tablet. Edwin saw the last five minutes of the Crosspathz video feed that had come in through the D6 closed circuit camera feed into his control center, while he was climbing the rigging.

Edwin's eyes flared. His mouth opened in a tight circle.

"He's standing outside the UK office of D6? Of my company?"

"It's puzzling, though," Zed mused. "Ali is very careful for ten years not to be spotted anywhere, and then he lets himself be seen twice in twenty-four hours. Once in Peshawar, where he must have known the U.S. would see him. And then he's lurking outside D6 headquarters in England. It doesn't make much sense. Does it?"

The professor pressed his pupil.

"But it does," Edwin answered. "Ali is a logical thinker, if empty in every other way."

"Yes," Zed agreed. "So…"

Edwin crouched forward, as if he could get to their destination first.

"It's so provocative," Edwin said.

"It is," Zed agreed.

"It's on purpose," Edwin added.

"Obvious," Zed said.

"He hopes I'm watching," Edwin said.

"So…"

"So, he wants me to come get him."

"Yes," said Zed. "He's appears to be counting on that. Why now?"

"Because something is happening now that was not happening before," Edwin answered. "Something he has been waiting for."

"Succession," said Zed. "Al Khaleef."

"In the last twenty-four hours, the U.S. just took out the Leader," Edwin said. "The wheels are in motion to pick the successor."

"Ah," said Edwin. "He's using classic deal strategy. If anything can throw a deal off course, it will. So don't sit on your hands and hope it never surfaces. Instead provoke it early and deal with it on your own terms."

"Exactly," Zed said. "You know his fatal flaw. You know what he did, years ago."

"He wants me to reveal myself so he can take me out on his own terms," Edwin said. "His place, his timing."

Then Edwin shook his head. "I'm not the only one who knows. There's a woman. Camille. His old college flame. She was the one he tipped."

Zed looked up at Edwin over the top edge of his aviator sunglasses.

"Where is she?" Zed said.

"Greek Islands," Edwin said.

Zed looked puzzled. "You know this?"

"Yes."

"She's there this minute?"

"Yes."

Zed settled back in the pilot's chair. "You'll be fine. I have built something special for you."

"Good," Edwin said. "I'll need it."

Edwin studied the frozen video screen of Ali tapping his temple. Baiting him. Luring him out of hiding.

"Oh, Ali," Edwin said. "You shoulda brought a bigger boat."

Edwin's every neuron flashed with the adrenalin of battle. But this time, this was no nameless foe. These people had struck, and hurt, America at home. Now they were picking a new leader to carry on the mission and show the others how to do it all over again, only this time, with perfection.

This was a battle long in coming. It was time to put an end to Al Ra'duzma's leadership succession. It was time to put an end to Ali.

"England, then," Edwin said. "It's hair on fire time, Zed. Goose this bird."

Zed smiled. "This one can't get you to England. But I have another bird for you that can. Hold on."

The helicopter banked and began to descend sharply toward a thin strip of white sand picking up the rising moonlight.

Zed settled the helicopter on a paved runway. The blades slowed and eventually stopped. Edwin looked along the expanse of black tarmac, then continued to the end of the runway where the sandbank picked up the moonlight. Beyond it the ocean was dark.

"What?" Edwin said. "I don't see anything."

Zed smiled. "Look closely, my friend."

Edwin scanned the runway, the sky. He began to turn around impatiently.

"Zed!" said Edwin. "What have you brought me?"

"Follow this white line ten paces." Zed pointed down the center of the empty runway.

"Aghhh!" Edwin growled. When Zed was revealing something, he would do it as he pleased. Each time he slowed Edwin down, forcing him to observe, not just act. The exchange of power knit their attachment to one another with sturdy stitches.

"All right," Edwin relented. "Ten paces." He stomped forward, his bowed legs and torso taut.

"Four more," Zed said.

"Oh for..." Edwin complained. He turned to scowl at Zed.

But in that split second, Edwin banged straight into a wall. He leapt back and swore. But when he looked at what he had hit, he saw nothing but space. The runway stretching out toward the sandbanks.

"It was just three, I guess," Zed called. "Sorry."

"What the—" Edwin stood up carefully.

"You are listening now," Zed said. "Okay. So come. I'll show you."

Zed took Edwin's hand and raised it in the air.

"Gently, now," he said. "Push."

Edwin slowly moved his palm forward. Before his elbow fully extended, his palm touched something cold, flat and solid. He ran his hand over a surface that felt like some kind of metal. But all his eye could see was the runway, the sand-bank and the dark waves of the ocean beyond.

"Zed, Zed, Zed," Edwin chuckled. "Cute trick."

His friend Zed, who thought of everything Edwin would ever need, A to Z, and supplied his partner every technical advantage, again had produced something special.

"It's a jet," Zed said. "In a mirrored skin shield. Rather than reflecting the light that lands on it, the mirrors reflect the images facing the other side of it, and vice versa. To someone looking at the jet, they would see the image actually projected through the other side. The skin makes it seem as if one looks right through it."

"Wow," Edwin said. "And anything or anyone inside it is effectively invisible."

"Obviously," Zed said.

"Can I see it without the shield?" Edwin asked. Zed nodded and pressed his fingertips against the scanner.

Now with their bare eyes, Edwin and Zed saw the grey metal of a sleek, small jet squatting on the runway.

Zed smiled. "It's had some modifications."

"I can see that," Edwin said.

"It will go Mach 1. Faster over open ocean where governments don't ban the sonic boom. And she's loaded. Want to see?"

Zed waved his hand over a square grid on the cabin door and it popped open. A small staircase lowered on hydraulic hinges.

Edwin put his hands on the rails and lunged up into the cabin in two strides. He saw two seats side by side. The other seats and comforts he would have expected in a private jet had been removed. The body of the jet had been fitted with rigging that held more equipment in place – a pyramid-shaped capsule about five feet high and four feet wide, and metal slats running along the length of the body of the plane like oars.

"That's your own special little bird," said Zed. "The jet will buy you distance. The controls contain logistics for private airfields in every country in the world where you can land safely. From there the bird will give you about three hundred and fifty miles of range. But she's fast. And also, quite hard to see."

Zed smiled, his lips never parting.

"More modifications?" Edwin asked.

Zed nodded.

"We've made some advances in stealth technology," Zed explained. "Radar-emitted energy catches rounded surfaces – like the nose of a traditional airplane – easily. But it misses flat surfaces until –

"- Until you bank," Edwin interrupted. "When you turn, you're totally exposed to the radar. So we only fly straight."

Zed smiled. "But tactics demand a bit more flexibility. Yes, we make it flat; we add radar-absorbing paint, and we cool the exhaust so there is little heat signature. But here's what's new: plasma stealth."

"Plasma stealth?" Edwin said. "That's just research."

"Yes," Zed patted the edge of the aircraft. "Just research. But at some stage, the test must leave the tube, mustn't it?"

Edwin raised his eyebrows. "How reassuring."

Zed continued. "Ionized gas has a very high degree of reactivity to electromagnetic radar energy. So we use that to our advantage. We wrap the aircraft in a layer of plasma – "

"Like, in a cloud?" Edwin said.

"Exactly!" Zed clapped his hands once, symbols clashing. "You have it. The cloud of plasma is very, very good at catching radar - deflecting or absorbing it. We can manipulate that capacity to reduce the radar cross-section of the aircraft, and make it appear on radar either as nothing at all, or …something quite else."

Edwin had reached the conclusion.

"So you can draw whatever picture you want them to see," he said.

"Like a grand master," said Zed, with a flourish of his right hand.

"Hiding in plain sight," Edwin said. "And in this case? How does my little bird appear on radar?"

"Yours – what else? A kestrel."

Edwin smiled. "The smallest raptor, the one that can hover in mid-air, then attack."

Zed nodded.

"We also use the plasma cloud to control the signature of the craft to the naked eye – by offering the view of what appears on the other side."

"Nifty," Edwin said. "What about the glow? Plasma leaves a glow, right, like a fluorescent light bulb?"

"We've done our best," Zed snapped. "Try to fly during the day."

"Well, that's a relief," said Edwin.

Zed put a tight grip on Edwin's arm.

"You do remember how to fly," he said.

"Hope so," Edwin said.

"Good," Zed said. "Because here is your cover for status: you are an immensely wealthy buyer who flies his own craft. You belong to a club that permits access to private airfields. And, also, you need to actually get there."

"Buyer of what?" Edwin said.

Zed frowned. "Of whatever you want. Art? Jewels? Castles perhaps? What do the supremely wealthy spend their time and money acquiring?"

Edwin thought. His success at D6 had provided him with unexpected billions, but he had never had the chance to spend it. Upon his reported death, his estate bequeathed to one Oliver Kestrel. In the years since Edwin Hoff had supposedly perished, the estate had grown. Fortunately Oliver had proven to be quite thrifty, except for an occasional loss at online poker. Usually to Bunny617.

Zed sized up at Edwin's appearance.

His tan arms stuck out of the bagging edges of a grey t-shirt. He wore faded jean cut offs over his lean, browned legs. The Nikes, without socks. The small brown backpack over his shoulder.

"You have the tan for the cover, at least," sighed Zed. "The very least. Well, you can take the backpack with you. But the clothes... there's a suitcase in the cockpit. A buyer coming to England would be well dressed. Cashmere. Tailored suit. Church's shoes."

"With laces," Edwin said.

Spy tradecraft had a dress code. Operators always wore laced shoes. Loafers could slip off in a sudden dash. Operators preferred overcoats that hung just below the waist leaving the legs free to run. They liked large square pockets that could easily fit a man's gloved hand, wrapped around an automatic revolver in one pocket and a small silencer in the other. Barbour coats were often favorites. Together with a Labrador Retriever on a leash, these coats provided easy cover in the cooler climates. Many a dead drop was made in the park, where it was common to bend over and scoop up something that no one would want to examine too closely.

"Laces? Obviously," said Zed. "You have work to do."

"Anything else in that bag?" Edwin asked hopefully.

Zed smiled again. "Perhaps, my friend. You must go now. You'll be there in less than six hours."

Edwin stood in front of Zed. "Thank you, Zed. I...Thank you."

Zed nodded. "Me too. Me too." He blinked rapidly. "Now, go before I have to create a time warp...No, of course not. That would be preposterous."

Then Edwin turned sharply and climbed into the jet.

Moments later, Edwin stepped into the pilot seat wearing worsted wool charcoal trousers, Church's laced black leather wingtips, and a crisp white poplin shirt with a collar so stiff it stayed in place without buttons. He wore a light blue cashmere v-neck sweater. Gold cufflinks peeked out of the cuffs. His socks were striped, a splash of unexpected and rebellious color.

Gold-rimmed aviator glasses with mirrored lenses shielded his eyes. He wore dark green headphones to protect his headphones from the jet noise. He raised a thumb to Zed, who stood on the runway as the engines warmed.

Zed took a long look at the tarmac. To his naked eye, it appeared empty, stretching to the sandbanks that held off the dark seas.

Edwin pressed the throttle forward. The jet shot down the runway. It lifted up over the beach and bent toward England, racing to the small town where Ali had planted his breadcrumbs.

As Edwin moved through the airspace at blistering speed, he felt unfettered for the first time in years. He lifted the left wing, then waved the right. He tipped the nose up, then made it drop. He carved the air like he was the only swimmer in a flat, clear pond, where his own limbs felt like they extended to the horizon. He could hit nothing. He could break nothing. The black air, all around, buoyed him.

Edwin had trained to live in deep cover for years until called upon to serve a mission suddenly, and without warning. Attachments were forbidden; extraction was permanent. As he thought of the blown computers on his discovered rig, he realized this extraction was no different. It was permanent. There were no attachments. Not even with Bunny617, an avatar for some lonely software engineer somewhere. That was just a blip on a screen, now sizzled. Nothing and no one held him back. Nothing and no one would distract him from completing his mission.

As with every mission, success depended on Edwin's total focus on the goal: Get Ali.

Success would have nothing to do with luck.

Success would have something to do with his training. Edwin had learned to fight with weapons: explosives, guns and knives. He'd trained to fight with anything at hand: fingers, teeth, forks, pens, wire, sharp pencils, and once, exposed broken bone. He had killed men with his bare hands. He had jumped out of perfectly good airplanes, and a doomed one, watching the belly of the crafts pass beyond the laces of his sneakers.

In elite combat training, Edwin had passed the ultimate endurance test - running seventy-five miles fully loaded with an eighty-pound pack, in boots. After he had crossed the line, Edwin counted his squad members. Two were nowhere in sight.

Edwin's feet were bleeding through his socks but he jogged back, in full pack, until he found his men. They were thirteen miles from the finish line and ready to quit. Edwin ran alongside them, goading them on, alternating insults and praise, until every one of his squad finished. He had added the length of an additional marathon to his own run before he counted his complete team at the finish line. Then he collapsed by a tree.

As a captain in the counter-terror squad of Delta Force, Edwin had led his team on more than thirty missions. He could clear the clutter from his mind and theirs, seize their adrenalin, and use it to complete the goal.

Regardless of training, Edwin knew the success of each mission depended primarily on one skill: focus. Complete, utter, unbroken focus on his single goal. Focus.

Edwin maneuvered the jet so it aligned in the green crosshairs at the center of the altimeter. The shortest distance between two points is a straight line.

Get Ali.

CHAPTER TWELVE

Two weeks earlier
2:00 p.m., May 10
Cairo, Egypt

Camille Henderson, in her late thirties, was more fit than she ever had been in her youth. Tennis four times a week and getting out of the office into the field had changed her appearance inside and out. Her hair was a dark ginger and freckles warmed her pale pink cheeks. She knocked on the door of the Dean of the American School in Cairo.

"Sorry to interrupt," Camille began. "I just learned that the woman who...well, she was like a grandmother to me..."

"Oh, I'm so sorry," said the Dean. He noticed that her eyelids were red and puffy.

"Well, not quite yet. It's any day now," said Camille. "She is very old. Over a hundred... it's inevitable... but even still..."

"You'll need to go back to America."

Camille nodded. "Today. Can you arrange for my classes to be –"

"Don't give it a second thought," said the Dean. "Let me know when ... when you will be back."

Camille left his office and walked briskly down the hall-way. She closed the door to her small office and leaned against it, breathing deeply. She blinked away the tears.

Get it together.

Then Camille moved quickly. She unlocked a desk drawer where her dark blue American passport lay next to a line of black ballpoint pens and small dish of pins. She pulled her passport out of her desk drawer; checked it, and put it in a zipped pocket in her leather bag. She checked the bills in her wallet. Then she sat down on her chair and slipped off the flat on her right foot. She gently swept her fingertips over the heavy callous worn into heel. When she found the spot, she slipped one of the sharp pins deep into the callous. She put the shoe back on. With the bag on her shoulder, and a headscarf wrapped around her neck, Camille mounted the stairs.

The helicopter blades beat the air as she stood on the roof of the American University of Cairo.

Half a day later, her eyes bleary from the long flight, Camille pushed the elevator button marked PH in Washington DC's northwest neighborhood, near the zoo.

The elevator brought her up to the Penthouse. When the doors opened, Amanda, the woman who had cared for the billionaire Matilda Mace in the waning years of her life, met Camille with her arms wide.

"Camille!" said Amanda. "She'll be so happy to see you. You are the only person she has been asking for. The children are...well... Mostly they stay in the kitchen fighting over the paintings."

"I'm here in time," Camille breathed. "Thank goodness."

"Oh yes. She's not going anywhere, not without seeing you. She's made that abundantly clear." Amanda put her hand on Camille. "I think she wants to tell you herself...."

"What?"

Amanda made a small smile and wiggled her eyebrows. "What she's leaving to you."

Camille walked down the hall of the elegantly furnished penthouse. She passed the door to the balcony, where they had spent so many hours together discussing men – one man in particular, over and over again, Camille's old love from Yale. She chewed the details over and over as the years passed, perhaps because it just never made sense how he had disappeared one day. Then it did make such terrible sense after all. What she learned about Yassir twisted her life irretrievably, and spun her out to where she now lived, in Egypt, thousands of miles from her country of birth, and wrapped in the restrictions of a foreign land's culture.

Camille reached the double doors. She knocked softly.

There were machines by the bed. But finally, the lights were out. For once, they were silent. The room was half dark, and quiet. Camille could hear only the gossamer breath coming from the small frame reclined in the bed. Her eyes were closed behind bluish paper skin. The bounce of flesh was gone. The skeleton was pressing against the last layer of pumping veins and dimming skin, snaking strands of grey hair.

"Camille," the woman spoke.

"I'm here, Matilda," said Camille, putting her hand gently on the ancient woman's fragile skin.

"And I'm leaving," Matilda smiled.

Camille said nothing.

"But I can't go without giving something important to you," said Matilda.

The words came out slowly, labored breath between them.

"You don't need to give me anything," said Camille, her eyes brimmed and the words caught. "I will treasure our conversations and your friendship, always."

"That, on the wall," said Matilda through the oxygen feed. She raised her bony index finger. "The Picasso."

Matilda looked at the rare painting of a woman, parts akimbo, on the wall opposite Matilda's bed.

"You're giving me your Picasso?"

Matilda smiled. "Yes. That one. And all that comes with her."

Camille balked. The painting was priceless.

"Go on," Matilda goaded. "Look her in the eye."

Camille stood up and walked to the masterpiece. Even up close, an eye was not apparent, certainly not to be found on the figure's face.

"Closer," said Matilda.

Camille adjusted her stance and stood so close that she could see where the horsehair in the master's brush had made narrow troughs in the oil paint.

The eye turned out to be on the elbow. Which was near a set of toes.

Beside the canvas, a scanner read Camille's retina, and accepted her identity.

The wall behind the Picasso slid sideways into a pocket in the wall. It revealed a well-lit closet, painted cream with gold trim, and gold handles on the stacks and stacks of narrow drawers.

"What is this?" Camille asked.

"My jewelry box," said Matilda. "Where I keep my treasures. My memories. Open the drawer with the yellow tag."

Camille saw a yellow tag dangling from a handle. She pulled it gently. A drawer opened. It held a swath of velvet, dark navy, and laden with cut brilliant diamonds, the size of small seeds, beans and peas. There were over a hundred of them.

"My goodness," said Camille.

"That's just one drawer," said Matilda. "Now open the one with the red tag."

Camille felt her fingers slip against the gold knob. This one felt much heavier.

"Tug it," said Matilda.

When the drawer finally slid on its hinges, Camille did not see bright jewels laid out on velvet cloth.

What she found there was something quite else. She swallowed hard, and looked back at the ancient body in the bed.

"That," Matilda strained, "is what comes with her, my dear. And now it is yours."

CHAPTER THIRTEEN

12:10 a.m., May 23
London, England

The cell phone buzzed. It was in the left breast pocket of Charles Lincoln's bespoke suit. Only clients had that number, and only certain clients. Ones who made it well worth Charles's time, over the many years, to respond immediately and no matter what time.

"Yassir! What a pleasure to get your earlier text," said Charles.

Charles Lincoln, Chairman of Finley's Auction House, had fallen asleep in his leather recliner, and still felt fuzzy from splitting two bottles of claret with a young colleague on the eve of their next show. Had he been scheduled to lead this show, he surely would have violated Rule #1 of the Auctioneer's Handbook. Fortunately, that job fell to someone else.

"Yes of course," Charles recovered. "Your treasure is being brought out of secure storage as we speak....why don't you meet me in Upper Chelton...in Oxfordshire...in the morning. Finley's has an auction there. Perhaps you'll find something interesting to add to your collection. It's certainly the fastest way to sign your item over to you ... Wonderful. See you then, old friend. Bye for now..."

CHAPTER FOURTEEN

2:30p.m., May 23
London, England

Between a pub and a cobbler stood a tiny storefront. It was no wider than six feet, enough for a doorway, a single row lined with shelves and a counter. The shelving covered every wall from the floor to the ceiling, stacked with newspapers, magazines, chewing gum, cigarettes, chewing tobacco, brown paper covered magazines, pens, batteries, packs of acetimol and aspirin, stacks of purse-sized Kleenex tissue, coloring books, crayons, magnets shaped like London's red telephone booths and double decker buses, many varieties of chocolate bars and jelly candies, and packets of crisps promoting the flavorful delights of 'prawn cocktail,' 'salt and vinegar,' and 'onion and fig' flavors. There was a vertical refrigerator containing bottled beer, wine, sodas, water, boiled eggs and tomato sandwiches, and a freezer of ice cream novelties and sundries.

In the rear of the shop, one three-foot wide section of the wall hung on hinges. There was no knob, just a hole in the plasterboard. The door opened to a dark hallway that led back to a stairwell down into a dark, damp basement. There, behind a locked door, was a small room. Its walls were black. There was a long table in the middle and a stool on wheels. A task light clamped to the corner of the table directed a cone of yellow light to a circular spot on the table. Near the light was a silver device the size of a thick marker. A wire led from the device to a pump on the floor. A thick cord connected the pump to a socket in the wall.

Ali Hamini sat on the stool, twisting from side to side. The seat needed oil. He pressed the floor pump with his foot. The long steel pen in his hand felt heavy. The pump made it vibrate. Five sharp needles emerged from the tip. He tapped the pump again with his toe. The needles spun. Ali liked the feel of the drill in his hand.

There was a sharp knock on the door.

"Enter," said Ali, as if opening the drape of a circus tent to the first customer in line.

Four men lugged a heavy body through the door. Imad Iqbul, the leader of the North African tribes, was still unconscious when the men made their way through the small shop, down the hallway to the basement room.

They laid him roughly on the table.

"Below the wrist," said Ali in Arabic. One pulled the inert man's arm roughly. His loose sleeve fell down to his elbow. Ali pressed his fingers hard against the inert man's pale stretch of skin.

"Hand me the drill," he said. Then Ali positioned the drill over Imad's arm. "Hold him still."

Ali pressed the foot pedal to the floor, revving it like an engine at the starting gate. This made the five needles agitate vertically, between fifty and three thousand times per minute, each time penetrating the skin and leaving a deposit of black, indelible ink.

"The power of the pen is mightier," quoted Ali. "Yes, yes, yes."

Imad screamed. The men held Imad firmly as he awoke to discover he was prone, bound, and receiving the end of a sharp needle stabbing him with ink.

"Quiet him," said Ali, his voice deep and sharp. "This must be very easy to read."

Ali worked carefully on each letter. There were two words. As he was finishing the last, Imad was sobbing.

Imad screamed out in pain as the awareness settled. It was a tattoo. It was a sin to him. Every member of the North African tribes would see it as a sin, and Imad a sinner. He would lose all of his authority. The North African alliance would fracture.

Ali finished the black tattoo of two words. He leaned over Imad's face.

"You know what it says? *Haram Kafir*," he said. "'Sinful unbeliever.'"

"Ali! Why did you do this to me?" Imad shouted.

"Now you know what I can do to you at a moment's notice, without warning," said Ali. "So every time you see your hand, you know you will never raise it against me. You will support no one but me. I am *al Khaleef*."

"Ali!" screamed Iqbul. "You must remove this sinful abomination. This is...I cannot function...it will not be explainable. My people will not tolerate it."

"I imagine you are correct," said Ali. "And perhaps I will arrange for it to be discreetly removed. After...."

"After what?" said Iqbul, his head twisting from side to side, following Ali as he stripped off the latex gloves and paced around the table in the center of the dark room.

"After you tell your tribes to support me as the successor," said Ali. "After the leadership summit. When you tell them your choice is no longer Badi Badi. It is me. After you all pledge obedience to me, then, yes."

"You don't need just us," Imad gasped, shaking his arm.

"No?" Ali asked. "Who do I need, then? Who else would like a painting like this?"

"You need the Influencer," said Imad. "Rais Abdullah. Fix this now, Ali. I am helping you already. Truly."

Ali was not happy to hear this name again. He was beginning to frame a plan.

First things first.

From the table, Imad looked with dismay at his defiled forearm.

"And you should know... there're others who want it too, not just Badi Badi..." Iqbul said. He fell back on the flat table and closed his eyes, nearly passing out from the pain and the hideous marking on his body.

Ali frowned. He had swung the stick. Now he would get properly dressed to harvest the carrot.

Then he would get to Paris and make his case to the Influencer.

Harvesting the "carrot" would require more time. Though Ali would have preferred to have it in hand when he met the Sheikh for breakfast a few hours later on the other side of London at the Dorchester Hotel.

Ali had a day and a half to get to the summit with all of his supports in place, and all possible detractors eliminated.

As he walked past the bushels of daily newspapers that had just dropped outside the door of the narrow shop, Ali felt his neck twinge. It was not nearly enough time. But he would make it happen.

CHAPTER FIFTEEN

7:00 a.m., May 23
London, England

O n Saville Row, Ali stood on a small, raised square be-tween three full-length, angled mirrors. A much small-er man crouched by his ankles with pins in his mouth and a measuring tape around his neck, straightening the cuffs of Ali's wool trousers.

In the new bespoke navy windowpane wool suit, with gold cufflinks in his light blue Pinks shirt sleeves, Ali looked the perfect banker.

"Mr. Metah," said the tailor. "Could you drop your arm for a moment please. Just so I get the line right. Thank you."

Ali stopped rubbing his neck and let his arm fall against his side. When it did, the folded paper he had been reading floated to the floor.

"You dropped something," said the tailor, reaching for the paper. "Comprehensive Psychiatry? My goodness... a little light reading about the mind's inner workings? I thought you were in software? Goes to show...I guess every-one is into everything these days, with the Internets and googlers and such things."

Ali folded the article, printed on a glossy page torn from the academic journal *Comprehensive Psychiatry*. A section was circled in a sharp black pen.

Some humans carry a variant of the Monoamine Oxidase A (MAOA) gene. Known as the "Warrior Gene," those with this variant are more likely not only to use weapons and join gangs, but also to be among the most violent gang members.

The tailor stood up. "Excellent, sir. That will do you, I think."

"Thank you, John, for accommodating me on such short notice," said Ali.

"Pleasure," said the tailor. "I must say, it's the first time a final fitting has kept as well with so long of a hiatus. You've been keeping quite fit. Not always the case with my clients between the years I must say. Well done you."

Ali looked at his image standing in the fine wool suit that hung crisply on his tall frame. He looked handsome, successful. A face slipped into the perfect picture of leadership. This time. Before it had been in the blue sweatshirt and jeans of College Boy. Then, the wrinkled chambray blue shirt, sleeves rolled up, of Software Engineer at D6. And now, *al Khaleef.*

Ali looked at the measuring tape hanging loosely around the neck of the tailor. It was such a simple, exact technology, to tell something so definite. It must be so reassuring to have a tool that told something so precise about each and every person.

Ali had a sudden urge to take the tape in both fists and twist it around the poor man's neck.

Instead he stared intently at the tailor.

"You think this fits?" Ali's voice fell. It was forced, flat and barely civil. "Do you? Just tell me. Does it really fit?"

"Why, yes," said the tailor, with a note of surprise. "I think it does, very nicely. Would ... would you like to try another style next time? Pinstripes, perhaps, or a houndstooth?"

Ali thought of Edwin. His ratty white t-shirts, his faded, blue jeans, torn from wear, not for style. His stupid sneakers. And his utter cocksureness as he would stomp the halls, splash ink across whiteboards that painted visions of the future world he said D6 would create. How he held scores of people of all ages in rapt attention. Edwin always wanted everyone to know that he knew himself. And he wanted them to know that he saw to the core of the people around him, or even right through them.

Ali could not tolerate being in Edwin's line of sight. He remembered how he had stood up off the carpet during one of Edwin's pointless speeches and walked out of the room in front of the entire company.

Now, years later, the thought of encountering Edwin Hoff made Ali seethe under his stiff white collar.

But it would not be long now.

"Yes, John. Houndstooth next time. I like the sound of that," Ali said.

CHAPTER SIXTEEN

3:05 a.m., May 23
Langley, Virginia

Agent Ascher Silver stood behind the technician at CIA Headquarters.

"Run it again," he said. Ascher had not slept since he saw the man go back into the Leader's lair in Peshawar, Pakistan twelve hours earlier.

The technician pressed replay again.

The video rolled on the screen ahead of him. By now they knew each frame.

"Match the face print," the agent said.

The drone had captured the upturned face of a man exiting the house after the U.S. troops had come in and taken down the hidden leader of al Ra'duzma.

The software program stung the blurry face with over a hundred green dots, connecting them with thin sharp lines between them. These lines made angles that mapped a unique face print.

The CIA's database of face prints ran matches against this image. The database contained face prints from any source that also connected to the Internet, giving each one a general location and identity through this Internet Protocol address. The images came from photos posted on social networks. They came from photos taken on personal cell phones, then backed up on a home computer, and in "the cloud". They came from grainy images taken at toll booths, for driver's licenses, from ATMs, from customs entry points, from the dark eyes recessed in the ceilings above airport security lines, and from the closed circuit television cameras that kept watch on certain neighborhoods in countries like England. The CIA and Interpol shared their massive collections of face prints all over the world.

The computers calculated in zettabytes, the unit of digital information measured by one million, million, billion bytes. This was a lot, considering that a single byte was the amount of data a computer required to encode just one character of text. And one million, million, billion of anything would add up to quite a lot.

"Finding a specific face on this planet consumes just about the same resources of finding evidence of life anywhere in the universe," scoffed the technician. "What do you think this man knows?"

"He's so close to the Leader," said Ascher. "He was right there! He may be a son. He may be the successor. It is paramount that we find him. With this guy in our pocket, we take al Ra'duzma to pieces."

"This is strange," said the technician. "There's no match, not yet. How has he has avoided a photograph, an ATM machine, travel – in the last five, ten years?"

"Keep looking," said Ascher. Under his breath he muttered. "I'm going to get you myself. And I'm going to get the answers out of you. Fuck the rules. You are going to tell me what you know."

When Ascher thought of the dead Leader of al Ra'duzma, his mind locked around a now familiar cadence, one he had heard for years. The first time was the day after he had earned his driver's license. His father's voice was on the answering machine, calling from work. The tape had been copied, and stored and distributed to close family members. Ascher had his own copy on his computer, on his cell phone.

The sound of his father coughing a few times. "God it's getting hot." Willing his voice to stay even, as he strung together random pieces of advice about life. He had ended with "And...and make sure you tell Ascher not to drink and drive."

Ascher never did.

"Well, here's something," said the technician. "I may not know who the Peshawar mystery man is. But I know where he is."

"Where?" Ascher shouted.

"England," said the technician. "The face print matched identically with one belonging to a man who just passed through customs on the first flight to land in the UK. It came in from Peshawar this morning."

Ascher was already running down the hallway, talking into the button on his lapel, listening to the secure bud in his ear.

"We need priority transport to the UK," he said. "The probable successor of al Ra'duzma just crossed their border."

CHAPTER SEVENTEEN

8:05 a.m., May 23
London, England

At the heart of the city, the Dorchester Hotel promised its wealthy patrons an easy stroll through Hyde Park and Kensington gardens, or along the elegant streets of Mayfair to Oxford Street's department stores and specialty shops. At the edge of the same chain of parks and gardens that linked the Royal Family's domiciles at Kensington Palace, Buckingham Palace, and St. James Palace, the Dorchester was a palace for the public, at least those who could pay for it.

A pretty, small garden framed the entrance to the exclusive hotel and separated it from the eight lanes of traffic jostling along Park Lane. From the corner of the garden, Ali Hamini located the three black glass half domes tucked discretely under the eaves of the entrance to the Hotel. One was behind each column outside the entrance, and a third hung above the rotary glass door.

When Ali approached the hotel, the bellman opened his white-gloved hand to guide him toward the reception area. Ali tipped his chin down, and watched his fast feet as he trotted up the slick marble stairs.

The door spun him gently into the foyer of the hotel.

Behind the gilded reception area stretched a space called the Promenade. Column after column of dark salmon marble pillars stretched from floor to ceiling. Velvet curtains draped the edges of private seating areas. Sofas with deep cushions sat paired with low tables, covered in white tablecloths, an easy place to meet for a coffee, to read the paper, or enjoy a more substantial meal.

Ali saw an older man sitting alone. As he lifted his crystal goblet of clear water, Ali saw his gold rings shine from four fingers on his left hand. Like Ali, the Sheikh Malikh Mukhtar wore western clothes: a handmade summer wool suit, but no tie.

The Sheikh cut into his full plate of flat fried eggs, broiled tomatoes, fried bread and a pool of baked beans. Ali noticed there was no bacon or sausage on the Sheikh's plate. A waiter poured a thick black curve of coffee from the spout of a silver coffee pot.

When the Sheikh lifted the porcelain cup, he saw Ali.

"Please sit, Ali," said the Sheikh. "Interesting days."

"Thank you for making time for me," Ali said.

"Ah, no," said the Sheikh. "You are kind to make time for me. At last."

Ali felt the Sheikh's jab, and instantly regretted the trust he had placed in the Leader. He saw now the gaps in his planning, ones his feeling of entitlement had filled. He should have planned even more carefully. He should have found a way to flatter the Sheikh more often, and much before this.

His wounded pride would cost a bit more. But Ali was prepared to pay.

"When we gather tomorrow night," said Ali. "I will show everyone, as promised, how I will put al Ra'duzma at the top of the world powers. I will show you why I deserve your support."

The Sheikh raised an eyebrow.

"I imagine you will not be alone. Badi Badi from Yemen, for one. I hear from him regularly. He's quite a creative young man. Thoughtful. Respectful of his elders."

The Sheikh paused, absentmindedly twisting one of his rings. Each gold band was thick. Two were curved and two were square. The square ones each bore large emerald-cut sapphires. One held a cushion-cut emerald. On the fourth, six rows of seven round diamonds studded the gold rectangle.

"No, I will not be alone in wanting to be al Khaleef," Ali said. "But I am the only one who should become the successor. I am here to ask you for your pledge."

The Sheikh stuck out his lower lip into a small pout.

"What do you have to support your case that you are truly al Khaleef?"

Ali thought of the feeling of the drill buzzing in his hand. Three thousand jabs per minute. But the Sheikh required a lighter touch, and a lure.

"You share my love of art history," Ali began.

The Sheikh nodded.

"While in London, you must have visited the Wallace Museum, not far from here."

"I visit regularly," gushed the Sheikh. "They have a lovely collection of jeweled weaponry."

"Indeed they do," Ali agreed. "One of the best in the world. Do you know the Lopaki Sapphire Dagger?"

The Sheikh placed his hands in his lap, and was now leaning forward, just a slight incline in his shoulders.

"The Lopaki Sapphire dagger. Of course I know it," said the Sheikh. "It was sold at auction years ago for 1.2 million pounds silver."

Ali nodded. "Its handle has four large sapphires built into the gold that are clear and transparent. Truly remarkable.

Another sapphire covers the end of the handle, and when you flip it up—" Ali began.

"—there is a small watch in it," finished the Sheikh. "The sheath is made of eighteen-karat gold, lined with alternating cushion-cut emeralds and yellow diamonds."

"There is a pigeon blood ruby dangling from the tip," Ali added.

They sat for a moment in silence. Then the Sheikh began to nod, and a smile spread across his face.

"You are the one who bought this dagger at auction," he said.

Ali nodded.

"It is beautiful and fierce," said the Sheikh. "A master stroke of the Ottoman Empire."

"That's the one," said Ali.

In the palm of his hand, the Sheikh cupped a loupe, the powerful lens jewelers use to magnify and evaluate the quality and clarity of gemstones. With it he could see any imperfection in a diamond, the exact cut of a facet, the true hue of a ruby.

"Show me," he said.

"I will," said Ali.

"Now," said the Sheikh.

Ali smiled, showing his white, straight, western teeth.

The Sheikh's eyes narrowed. He wrinkled his nose as if he had suddenly sniffed something sour. He clenched the jeweler's lens and put it back in his pocket.

"You don't have it," said the Sheikh, his lips pursed.

"On me? Walking through Hyde Park? No, I do not have it on my person out in public," said Ali. "But you will see it before you are called to vote, that I assure you. And for your support, I will reward you with every shiny, sparkling bit of gratitude I possess."

"Okay," said Sheikh. "If it meets my approval, then you shall have mine. I don't know if that will be sufficient, though, for your goal."

Ali nodded. "There is the matter of Rais Abdullah."

"You can use sticks on some." The Sheikh smiled thinly. "Carrots – or karats - on others. But I do not know how you will persuade the Influencer. Neither of those is likely to work."

"I will show him what I have built. My technology will far outshine any silly shoe bomb," Ali said. "But I need something from you."

"What?" asked the Sheikh.

"I need his address in Paris," said Ali. "And there is not much time."

"Whose?" asked the Sheikh.

"The Influencer's address," said Ali.

"You don't know," said the Sheikh.

"Please," said Ali. "There is not much time."

The Sheikh sat heavily back against the thick cushions and regarded Ali. After a moment he reached into his pocket and pulled out a pen. He slid the cocktail napkin out from under his water glass. He wrote a few words. The blue ink ran where the napkin was wet.

"By the river?" Ali read. A scribbled street address followed the name of the river Seine, which ran through the heart of Paris.

Ali stood up and held out his hand.

"Thank you," said Ali. "You will be well rewarded as my head of finance when I am the Successor."

The Sheikh put his left hand on top of Ali's. Then he lifted his bejeweled fingers in a short wave. As he watched Ali go the Sheikh looked at his other hand. There was a ring on only one of those fingers.

"I love sapphires," he sighed.

CHAPTER EIGHTEEN

8:10 a.m. May 23
Oxfordshire, England

The beautiful village of Upper Chelton settled in the valley between green rolling hills about fifteen minutes from Oxford University. Less than two hours from London, it was a popular destination for weekenders and in the summer, tourists on bicycles.

In the hills, the sheep clumped together, and horses wore blankets as they grazed undeterred by the rain.

The Main Street was lined with buildings made of the honey-colored limestone of the Cotswolds. There were gift shops, clothing shops, tea shops and a coffee shop. There were grocery and fine goods stores and several pubs. At the end of the Main Street several businesses had also taken root, close enough to Oxford to drain its technology brains. One housed the UK offices of the American technology company called D6.

And in the middle of the Main Street, there was an old, glorious inn. The Dashing Hound had provided weary travelers and Royals with rest and respite for five centuries.

In a room on the second floor of the inn, Fiona Tate opened the oak doors of the wardrobe and studied her options. The uniform was always the same. Silk blouses and wool pencil skirts. Tall boots. Sweaters that fell at mid-thigh, and structured blazers. She always brought a selection from her drawer of brightly colored scarves. Even in the spring days, where the breeze could be light and the sun teasingly warm when it bounced off stone walls of the village main street, one had to have an extra layer. And, always, a little flair. Color made the wearer appear more interesting.

Fiona pulled on black matte tights and then zipped the tall black leather boots up the full length of the inside of her calf. Their three inches would establish Fiona at five feet, nine inches tall. At that height, she would command the podium - and with any luck, the people on the other side of it.

She selected a navy shift dress and a bright yellow cardigan that also brought out the blonde highlights in her short-cropped hair, which hung evenly in a bob at the nape of her neck. She looped a finely woven scarf loosely around her neck, so the bright butterflies blended into the folds and tassels dangled. By drawing attention to herself, she could redirect it onto the objects, lot by lot.

Fiona chose pearls for her earlobes and a double strand for her neck. It hung just over her clavicle. She looked like one of the buyers, and she needed to. Fiona needed to use every tool of empathy, conscious or not, to convince the clients of Finley's Auction House to believe her that the prices were what she said they were. This bank of trust took a career to build. She made deposits by cultivating relationships, doing favors, and always, looking to bring to their attention original and valuable objects.

Fiona looked at her watch. The Cartier classic tank, with Roman numerals, gold casing and sapphire in the winding mechanism. Perfection in the timepiece meant precision in the person wearing it.

Charles Lincoln would expect her to be at the Upper Chelton Manor to preview the auction items in less than one hour.

Fiona always looked forward to seeing the real objects in the auction with her own eyes, not just the photographs she had been studying for weeks. These objects had participated in significant moments. Each one was one of a kind.

A narrow road ran up from the town across the ridge of the hillside. Bordered by hedgerows on both sides, it was an ancient pathway first beaten down by the wheels on Roman carts.

A short drive up the hill put Fiona on the grounds of the manor house, which overlooked the valley. From there, the buildings of Upper Chelton looked like cubes of raw sugar, lined side by side and scattered across a green cloth. The estate's sheep slid down the hillsides and spread where the farm manager and his collie permitted them to graze. The cattle, Belted Galloways, gathered in sociable groups of a dozen or so and sampled thistles in the rough.

From the top of the ridge, a long driveway of crushed Cotswold stone wound for a half mile between two rows of tall beech trees, which eventually opened onto the stone courtyard of the Upper Chelton Manor. At the center a stone fountain spouted water up through three-tiered trays stacked on stone carvings of pineapples. Boxwood hedges bordered the fountain on eight even sides.

Fiona followed the butler down the dark hallway, past the massive staircase that turned in the center foyer. They passed a sitting room where six young women and two men sat with their computers on their laps or a covered desk; each buzzing privately into a mobile phone.

Fiona glanced into the room. She saw six pairs of black boots. Six bright colored, jauntily tied scarves. Six sharp skirts. Six pairs of horn-rimmed spectacles. The ones who didn't really need glasses pushed them up on their heads, tucking back their straight blond locks. Fiona looked down past her bright scarf to her own black boots and frowned to see the uniform.

The women were marketing the sale to clients of past auctions, hoping to spin up final interest in the upcoming auction. The phoned-in bids kept tension in the room, as the participants watched the taut faces of the assistants, who in turn listened to the room with one ear and the voice with the other.

At precisely 9:00am GMT, the butler answered the bell. He pulled open the tall oak door and smiled at the handsome man standing there. The guest's black hair was freshly clipped, parted on the side and slightly long in front, as was the fashion. He was about forty and wore an impeccable, dark blue, windowpane wool suit.

"Yassir Metah for Charles Lincoln," said Ali.

"Would you like a copy of the book, sir?" asked the butler.

"Yes, thank you," said Ali.

The butler presented Ali with a glossy copy of a half-inch-thick, glossy paperback volume of photographs. The book. Its cover bore the title:

Upper Chelton Manor: Important European Silver, Armour and Documents

May 3 2011

FINLEY'S Auction House

"The viewing has just opened," said the butler. "Please come this way. There are some very interesting objects, certainly."

"Thank you," said Ali. "I look forward to this."

The butler heard an accent that, like the others, was pure public school.

Ali followed the butler down a dark hallway, passing the door to the room where the Finley's marketing team was working the phones.

A man with silver hair and a bright red face glanced up. The Chairman of Finley's European Department, Charles Lincoln, stood up straight.

"There he is!" said Charles. "As I live and breathe."

Charles turned to follow the new arrival down the hall.

"Fiona," he called over his shoulder, "You must come meet an old friend of the firm."

Charles stopped for a moment to glance in a gilded mirror on the wall near the door. He straightened his bow tie, and pushed his horn-rimmed glasses up the bridge of his nose. He always wore his jacket during the viewing times because one never knew who might stop by. Then he walked briskly down the hall toward the viewing room where he saw that it was indeed his old client, coming out of the woodwork.

"Well! It's lovely to see you, Mr. Metah!" Charles reached his hand out to Ali.

"Hello, Charles," said Ali. "It has been a long time."

"Quite," said Charles.

"I've been traveling, you know. Very busy."

"Certainly, of course," said Charles, glazing the unease of a former client. Sometimes finances changed and made formerly lucrative clients less able to participate. Finley's still required a current bank statement before it would distribute a paddle to anyone, even to a long-time registered client, like Yassir Metah.

"You received my text?" Ali said.

Charles nodded. "Yes, of course I did."

"You have it," said Ali. "The Lopaki Dagger."

"Yes, of course," said Charles slowly. "Just not in hand, not yet."

Ali raised his eyebrows. He did not have time to waste. He needed the Sheikh. He could not proceed without the carrot. Displeased, he breathed in deeply.

"But don't worry," said Charles brightly. "It's coming by taxi as we speak. In the meantime, why don't you look at our show. You might find something of interest, you never know, while you're here. Something perhaps for a special lady, perhaps?"

A gentle joke, a smile, a deposit made in the bank of trust.

Ali smiled stiffly.

"Have you seen the – I can't say 'star of the show' in this case, but it certainly is causing a stir," Charles said.

He guided Ali to a table just to the left of the podium that had been set up in the center of the large hall where later that evening the auction would take place.

Under a locked piece of glass, on black velvet, lay an old, dusty, silver men's hairbrush.

Just then, Fiona Tate entered the viewing room. She walked on tall boots, wearing a smart blue dress, yellow sweater, and bright scarf. The men turned to look at her and she smiled. But when she spoke her voice tucked under itself and she had to cough and start over.

"Mr. Lincoln, hello," she said, a little too loudly.

"Miss Tate. What a pleasure," said Charles. "Come meet my old friend, Mr. Yassir Metah."

"Pleasure," said Fiona, smiling into the dark eyes that shined back at her.

"It is mine," said Ali.

In his western suit, with his western hair, and the unfortunate but necessary encounter with someone who once had known him as such, Ali would be Yassir Metah again, but only for the few hours that it was absolutely necessary. As Ali watched the appealing woman who just had appeared in front of him, however, he realized that living in the skin of Yassir Metah could help Ali Hamini.

"By now, Edwin must be coming," Ali thought. "He'll be all in a froth, exactly as I want him. Now, I have to get him where I need him to be, and when."

"Well, I must take a good last look at these objects in the flesh," said Fiona. "Before the hordes arrive."

Ali's dark eyes followed Fiona as she wandered around the room.

Fiona studied the collection of small pieces of silver. She had her own copy of "the book," which bore glossy pictures of each object up for auction, a description of its authenticated provenance and estimated value. She needed to know these objects and their prices intimately, and memorize the appetite of each potential buyer. For the past weeks, the marketing team had been calling and cajoling clients.

When the auction started, the buyers could be in the chairs, calling in on the phones, or chiming in over the Internet. In a few short hours that room would be filled with tennis match tension as the paddles would raise and bat their bids back and forth, some seen, some unseen.

Yassir walked over and stood next to Fiona. They both looked at the silver hairbrush.

"Can you imagine the hands that touched these objects, and what else they did for humanity, or to it?" Fiona said.

Charles followed his client.

"It is indeed quite an unusual gathering of items," Charles said. "Usually we prize items gilded by the touch of someone who made the world notably better. Like Churchill's footstool. Or Shakespeare's silver spoon. Or the Americans who love those simple, relatively young wooden chairs that their rebels sat on, drinking beer and planning to revolt against the King. But what of the everyday items that belonged to people who wrought evil on the world? I supposed those Revolutionary pieces could count in both categories. Important and revolting!"

Plink, plink, in the bank. Charles counted.

"Mind you, we don't include these items to celebrate their owners. It is instead, perhaps, to reveal something about humanity. These items make us see that the worst of us, are still.....well, Hitler had to brush his hair too. Such as it was."

"Yes, quite," said Yassir. "Like each of us."

"Or, not at all," said Fiona.

Charles frowned. With that retort, Fiona had created friction with a client, even if only for a moment.

Charles put a finger on Yassir's elbow, and said quietly,

"It's been quite safe in our secure storage all these years. I kept thinking you would pick it up, but you never came."

Yassir straightened.

"That was quite a day," Charles said, letting the memory of his career's highest point fill his sight. "It still stands as the highest ... value... ever established for Ottoman Empire weaponry."

Yassir turned his wrist a quarter rotation. Time was moving fast. But he was stuck. He looked sharply at Charles. "When will it be here?"

"It must be in close by now," said Charles. "I'll just check in to be sure where the delivery is just now."

"I need it today," said Yassir. "Tomorrow it does not matter. As much, I mean. I have an early flight."

"I'll do everything in my power, sir," said Charles. "You will have the Lopaki Dagger in your satchel this day."

This was a client who, in the past, had proven well worthy of his investment.

Fiona walked back to the pair of men. "I'm off to the tea shop with the Book to study the fascinating lives these objects have lived, and to put my thoughts together for the auction. We'll see you there, I hope, Mr. Metah?"

She smiled, more girlish than she meant to be.

"Yes, I plan to be," Yassir said. "I'm supposed to be meeting an old friend. I'm wondering if…no…it's too much to ask. Never mind."

"What can we do for you?" Charles asked. "We've known each other a long time, Yassir. If we can help, we certainly will."

"You said you'd be at the tea shop this morning? Just here, down in the town? On the high street?" Yassir asked.

"Yes," said Fiona brightly.

"Would you mind doing me a favor?" Yassir smiled, a broad, white grin.

Fiona caught Charles looking at her intently, his eyebrows tilting. "Of course," said Fiona. "What can I do?"

"Would you buy him a coffee, and make sure you order it with four sugar packets?" said Ali. He leaned in close to Fiona's ear, catching a whiff of the fragrance she wore. Peonies, he thought. And vanilla. "Then, if I may suggest, be on your way. He's a good chum but he's not really a gentleman."

Fiona looked at Charles, who was studying her intently.
"Certainly," she said.
Charles relaxed and patted his client on the back.
Ali smiled, as he set the cheddar on the coiled steel.

PART TWO

CHAPTER NINETEEN

The English countryside arched to meet the descending jet. Edwin saw in the morning light the ancient patterns of rolling green farms where dark green borders separated them into rough rectangles. The hedgerows were so thick no stubborn cow would charge them, and the stone walls kept in everything but the most elastic Labrador thundering over them.

The wheels bounced to absorb the landing, and the jet slowed at the end of a private runway.

Edwin pressed a button on the control panel. The hydraulics shifted behind him. In the rear of the plane, the tail lowered to form a wide opening. The pyramid-shaped capsule slid easily along metal runners to an elevated platform that engaged, locked and lowered the capsule onto horizontal runners.

Next the supports for the long, oar-like bands, which hung along each side of the airplane body, pushed the long panels toward a gear box on top of the capsule. The first one clamped on. The pyramid pulled away on wheels, turned a hundred and eighty degrees, and shifted back toward the jet. The second long panel clamped over the first. Then the third. The capsule rolled back, turned, and a tail component bolted onto the rear of the pyramid. Two smaller blades clamped vertically onto the tail.

In four minutes and thirty-seven seconds, the assembly mechanism produced a six-blade helicopter with a four-blade tail rotor. It held two seats.

Edwin looked at it. "Zed, this pigeon better fly."

Before anyone at the airport laid eyes on the first billionaire of the day to arrive at the private field, Edwin had pulled his tweed blazer over the cashmere v-neck, and buckled the black leather belt to hold the charcoal wool trousers on his hips. He tightened the black laces on his wingtips and stepped into his new form of local transportation.

Within a few miles drive of Oxford University, the D6 UK office filled a floor of an office building at the edge of Upper Chelton's high street. The high street of this beautiful Cotswold village was paved in smooth cobblestones. The buildings and fences were made with the distinctive honey-colored limestone from local quarries. Shops, restaurants, and inns leased space in buildings built of brick and slate, some of which had stood for five hundred years. As people grew taller in each generation, they ducked beneath ancient doorways.

Edwin circled above the office building and the main street. Anyone looking up would see only the sky. Zed's plasma stealth skin wrapped every curve and facet of the helicopter. It absorbed the sound and heat the machine made, and dissipated them through the aircraft.

Just off the main street, Edwin saw a large playground. Sheep dotted a hillside in the distance. Between the playground and the grassy hill were several large paddocks.

Edwin set the helicopter down in the far corner of one where the fences met and where there was no gate. It was at least a half-mile from the street, and the horses would have to exit from the opposite side of the paddock.

"Should be okay here for a little while," Edwin thought. "As long as no one bumps into it, they'll walk right past it."

A mother in the playground might have looked up from her toddlers pressing the limits of physics, their own strength and agility, on the climbing cobweb to notice the two large bays kick up their heels and spook at nothing in particular. And a few moments later, if she looked up again, she would notice the horses had settled down and were posing nonchalantly for another horse person with a flashy camera, too much money and even more time.

The photographer was not tall, or short. She might notice he had dark brown hair. His clothes looked expensive. He wore aviator sunglasses, and had slung a small brown backpack over one shoulder. The spring day was warm and brought the smell of flowers everywhere. The light was a lemon yellow, hinting at the longer days and glistening with the microscopic droplets of water suspended in the air.

Edwin lingered, watching the horses.

If she noticed him, she'd remember what he did right then. But if he did nothing, she wouldn't remember how he came to be standing there.

Eventually, Edwin sauntered along the fence toward the main street.

It was the same with all animals: make no sudden moves.

The heavy wool of his blazer felt stiff and restricting against his neck.

So I'm a buyer. I'll buy a horse maybe. I could buy a hundred thousand of them. He calculated the size of Oliver Kestrel's bank account, and guessed at the going rate for a horse, and added six zeros.

When he reached the road, he looked to his right. Two hundred yards away, up the main street, past the shops and across its traffic, Edwin saw the sign.

"D6," he said, looking at the logo he had once approved, years ago, which now announced the location of the company's new European headquarters and UK office.

They're making it happen...without me...Titans!

The coordinates matched the screen Zed had shown him. *Just hours ago, Ali was standing here, baiting me.*

But no one stood there now.

"So I'm here," taunted Edwin. "And where are you now, Ali?"

The tang of spring grass mingled with light perfumes of flowers. The smell of warm yeast rose in the dewy morning: warm bread, scones, and croissants.

It seemed to Edwin that he had only ever known the smells of sea air, and in it, the taste of metal and dried fish.

Looking down the road to the left, Edwin saw the tea shop, and the sweet steam rising from its chimneys. Its front window bowed into the street.

He could watch from there.

His footsteps quickened as he walked to teashop. Just being near D6 took him back to the deep cover life that had become so much more. The ASP had rules, they had reasons for them, and they enforced them.

But Edwin had loved it.

⚜ ⚜ ⚜

The day D6 went public, Edwin saw calculators in the hands of many of his employees, as they stood packed shoulder to shoulder, waiting for a TV monitor to flicker.

He thought, "Calculating the daily value of stock options will kill D6. Time to crush the calculator and put something in its place that can build a business."

Edwin spotted the man he had hired as CEO across the crowded room. He sprinted toward him and grabbed him around the middle. Edwin hoisted the CEO up over his shoulder. Then he ran with this full-grown adult male over his shoulder to the podium through the crowded room.

Edwin grabbed the microphone. He looked around at the hundred-odd people, most of them men, most of them twenty-something.

"You are all about to become rich!" he shouted. "You will make more money than you possibly dreamed of in this tech bubble. It will go on forever."

"Yeah!" The D6 employees cheered and hooted.

"Now let me tell you why all that was bullshit," Edwin said. "There will be a spectacular crash. All of our customers – these dot-com paper napkin customers - will go bankrupt. Our job is to take their last dollars while we adapt. But we will keep our focus. This company will not just survive. You will not just become very, very rich – you will change the world. D6 software will be in the offices, homes and literally the hands of every person seeking digital information, making every electronic device able to accept and trans-mit data. You will make today's Internet work and you will create tomorrow's. You will do this as the economy fails around you. As your customers die. You will do it by executing one task at a time. Focus on your goal. Next up, world domination!"

Edwin remembered how the room had erupted. How minutes later the stock of D6 was offered for sale to public buyers on the NASDAQ exchange. How an idea for technology and a flawless cover story had

combined to create the reality of a new company called D6, uninten-
tionally turning its founder into a multi-billionaire, and making
everyone in that room, from the office manager to software developers
to sales people, suddenly worth millions of dollars, at least on paper.

Edwin walked to the tea shop across from the UK office of D6 where he could watch for Ali to show his hand. With each step, Edwin remembered the best part of that day when D6 went public. How he had marched out of that conference room and picked up not a calculator, but a marker. How he had used it to cover a whiteboard back and front, with the grand vision for D6. He remembered how his employees packed every square of that carpet, how they leaned forward in the anticipation of what he told them they could make happen.

Except for one person. One man had leaned backward, scoffing at the vision. At D6, Edwin had hired a genius software developer, one who made thirteen million when the company went public. His name was Ali Hamini.

He had put that money to very poor use.

On the high street of Upper Chelton, the bell that hung from the teashop door jingled when Edwin pushed it open. Rich, roasted coffee dripped like honey into white ceramic cups from a triple espresso spout behind the counter.

He sat down at a small table near the window, his back to the stone wall, and looked quickly at the menu.

Cream tea.
Scones and butter and jam.
Clotted cream.

Strawberry tart.
Sausage pie.

Sugar. Melted butter. Salt. Flaky pastry. All right there in the glass cabinet. Edwin swallowed.

Edwin, watching the sign for D6 a hundred yards away from the window, thought of Zed.

Your creativity does not extend to the kitchen. If I ever have to eat another pop tart or canned hot dog.

The bell jingled again. Two men walked in. Edwin kept his chin down but slowly raised his eyes through his glasses.

Suddenly Edwin saw that he had been gone for years, and he saw what those years looked like, pressed all at once onto a familiar frame. He saw the only other person from D6 who had stumbled on to the discovery that for Edwin, starting that rocket ship of a company was just a cover.

Edwin sat very still. He recalled his first class in operative field training.

"Watch how the bodies move. Watch how yours moves," the instructed had advised him. "People recognize each other not so much by faces or hair color, but by the shift of a shoulder, the bounce of a natural step. That's hard to mask consistently."

Hudson Davenport looked about forty, and was a little thicker near the belt. But Edwin noticed the waitress beam at Hudson. Age had only added authority to his appealing style. Edwin quickly took in the ring on Hudson's finger, the heavy bag, and the slight paunch collecting in the middle.

Edwin remembered when he had last seen Hudson in 2001. Then Hudson spent most of his time picking up women, until one day he picked up Edwin's cast-off

Blackberry, and stumbled into a race against time and terror. Then, with D6 nearing ruin, its leader suddenly taken, Hudson had stepped up to save Edwin's company.

Slacker, Edwin thought, looking down sharply. *You made it, as usual, probably by accident. Life just floats you up to the top, over and over again.*

Hudson walked right past Edwin's table. He did not look down. Instead he looked into the case of pastries.

"Agh. Come to me you sweet things," Hudson sang.

"You could chat up a pastry," said his friend.

"These days, Alex, the croissant is my only mistress," Hudson said, twirling the gold band on his finger. He added lasciviously, "And she's plenty."

"Marly's gonna take away your sandwiches again." Alex laughed. "I don't want to be on the other side of that."

Hudson sighed. "Are you listening to the lawn mower commercials yet?" The other man shook his head, still chuckling. Every walk with Hudson was a good time.

Hudson tapped the case and smiled at the waitress. "But ... no. I better not. Not this time. Just a coffee, please, in one of those terribly American to - go cups I'm afraid."

Edwin watched Hudson's brown wingtips, laced tight, scrape the linoleum as he left the tea shop.

Maybe you aren't such a slacker anymore. Are they actually trusting you to run Europe?

Edwin studied the menu again, his head tipped down. Then he snapped at himself.

That time was then; it was always just a game. This time, no distractions, no attachments. Get Ali. Eliminate him. And disappear.

Distraction meant death. It always did in this business - if not for Edwin, then for someone close to him. And anyone close to him was, by definition, a distraction.

But the duty to save the world from the next leader of Al Ra'duzma, from Ali, had summoned Edwin back into the world. And even the slightest taste of human interaction electrified him.

Had someone studied Edwin, this weakness would be apparent.

In the doorway that Hudson had just vacated, Edwin noticed a woman. She had sleek blonde hair cut short in a bob. She was fit, and wore bright, stylish clothes: tall boots, a dark blue dress, and a yellow sweater with a scarf. She slung a large black satchel over her shoulder. He smelled a trail of her perfume— a warm scent lifting off a peony, a hint of vanilla.

Her eyes caught him. They were blue and bright, and pinned right on him.

Edwin flashed a quick smile. Then he scolded himself.

Focus. Do not engage. Focus! Get Ali. He's here... somewhere.

While appearing to study the menu, Edwin assessed his first minutes engaged in the world, with a new cover, after so many years of isolation. It was not impressive.

I'm rusty. Be better now.

Distractions came at him from everywhere: the sweet, yeasty smells from the bakery's kitchen, the appealing shapes in the dessert cabinet, the grace of a woman walking in tall boots; the soft squeak of leather bending.

Edwin focused on his camera, pointed at the floor. The pointy tip of a black boot nudged behind the chair opposite him. The chair legs pulled back.

"Mind if I?" asked the woman with the blue eyes. "They should really put more tables in here. It's just too tight." She had planted herself in the chair before Edwin could respond. "Fiona Tate. Pleasure."

So Edwin waved his hand in acknowledgment. He would bend away like a reed, and gently fade from her experience. The woman kept talking at such a rate that Edwin felt some comfort that with so much pouring out of this woman, she could not possibly take much in.

Edwin reached for the local newspaper folded on the next table and began browsing through it. He sat back in the chair, and tilted away, creating two table spaces.

"Ah," Fiona said brightly, pointing at the article. "Are you here for our auction?"

Edwin shook his head. Despite his intent to disappear in front of this interloper, Edwin began to feel the thrill of sitting next to a pretty woman crawl into his spine. Like it always had, a blush crept into his cheeks.

"No," Edwin muttered.

"Yes," continued Fiona. She tapped the newspaper, her words fueled by the whiff of scandal. "It's all right there in the article. *Important European Silver, Armour and Documents.* Including some quite grisly artifacts. Just imagine the clientele! Hitler's hairbrush will be the top seller, apparently. It's even brought some of our old clients out of the woodwork. We shall see, we shall see."

The words tumbled. She had a fast tongue.

Edwin did not. He sat like a rock.

"Take a look at my book, if you like," Fiona said. She pulled out the glossy copy of *Finley's* and pushed it across the table to Edwin.

"Can I get you something? Tea?" Fiona asks. "I did barge in - least I could do. No. Coffee, right? You are an American, after all."

Edwin looked at her. He had not been near a woman in a decade. His eyes rested on the high delicate curve of her cheekbones, the girlish sprinkle of freckles spreading out from the bridge of her nose. He smelled peonies, lilies, vanilla, mint. Her soap, fading. Her perfume, added on top. Her toothpaste, still fresh.

"Coffee. Okay," Edwin said. "Thanks."

Fiona smiled widely. She held up a finger. "Back in a tick." Then she stood up, took a step backward and tripped on a chair leg. She blushed red. "So sorry...so clumsy!"

Fiona straightened her spine and smoothed her skirt. She turned on her heel and spoke slowly and clearly to the waitress.

"One English Breakfast, please, and one large coffee. With four sugars."

Four sugars.

The words sank like sharp teeth.

"Four sugars?" Edwin said.

"Isn't that just how you like it?" asked Fiona, smiling.

Edwin counted the other people in the teashop.

Her. The shopkeeper. Him.

Edwin looked at the wrists of the older woman working behind the counter. Her grey hair was pinned in a bun at the back of her head. Her apron covered a slim frame.

Distance to woman in boots: one stride.

Edwin swiftly crunched the metrics.

The shop keeper is over sixty. Might have brittle bones. She's behind a counter: three feet tall, glass surface, two feet wide.

Four sugars.

Edwin was on his feet, arms up and out, knees bent. He vaulted the counter and lifted the ample waitress at her midsection. She fell over his shoulder. Edwin carried her gently, but urgently, like a fallen comrade, and scrambled back over the counter.

Then he grabbed Fiona with his other arm and carried her, too, her arms and legs flailing, as he raced out to the cobblestones and to the other side of a large van parked in front of the tea shop.

He flattened the women on the ground with his body.

The three of them lay there for a moment.

Nothing happened. A car honked.

"Oh my giddy aunt!" cried Fiona. Her blue eyes blazed at Edwin. "Get your hands off of me! Look at my clothes! I'm a disaster! And I have to be at the auction! What on earth did you think you were doing?"

Fiona stood up, dusting off her skirt in sharp, angry swipes. Her pantyhose were sprinkled with small stones, and ladders ran, exposing her skin in gaping holes. She glared at Edwin.

Edwin stared at the teashop. The door was just easing shut on its hinges again, a slow, gradual squeak. He watched.

It closed softly.

"Ouch," said the shopkeeper, bending her elbow to see where the pavement had bloodied it. "Blazes!"

Edwin bent by the shopkeeper and took her arm.

"Are you okay?" he said. He could see the wound was shallow, a cement scrape but nothing deep or serious.

"Thank you very much. You've done quite enough already," she said. Blood leaked in rivulets down her arm.

The tea shop exploded. Glass shattered the cars around them. Thick smoke billowed from the store and flames licked the broken window frames. Steel and wood sticks stabbed through the metal and tires on the other side of the van.

Edwin bent over the shopkeeper, his body shielding her from the shrapnel. Then he looked over his shoulder.

The shop was a black, smoking hole. The blast had knocked Fiona to the ground again, but she was already shakily getting to her feet.

Edwin looked at the shopkeeper, who was trembling.

"Wait here for help. The worst is over ."

She blinked.

Edwin reached under the tire of the van where his sunglasses lay. He put them back on. Fiona grasped his sleeve.

"Slowly," Edwin said. "Walk. That's it."

They walked down the High Street of Upper Chelton. Edwin had wrapped Fiona's arm in his and forced them to walk in the meandering gait of people with no particular destination and no one in pursuit. But Fiona's fingers dug into his forearm. He strolled; she walked like her legs were stilts along cobblestones.

As people raced to the shattered windows of the blackened and smoking shop, no one noticed them.

Edwin glanced around the eaves of the shop entrances. Soon he saw it. The black monocular dome: closed circuit TV cameras capturing images of every person walking past or through the shop, silently stripping the cover on which some relied, including Edwin.

This is suboptimal, Edwin thought.

To Fiona he said, "Where's your car?"

CHAPTER TWENTY

9:42 a.m., May 23
Upper Chelton, England

Fiona gripped the wheel of her small hatchback.

"Why did you say that – four sugars?" Edwin demanded.

"I–I – was preparing for Finley's," Fiona started.

"When?"

"Just now," she said. "First thing."

"What's Finley's?"

"It's an auction house. You've heard of it, certainly." Fiona eyed the expensive clothing on the man next to her. "I was looking at some of the items in my next show, to finish preparing. And I met someone. At least, I thought…fingers crossed…you know. He was there, too."

"Doing what?" Edwin cut in. "What did he look like? Did he have an accent?"

"Viewing the objects, obviously. He turned out to be an old client of Mr. Lincoln's. He was medium height. He had dark hair, Middle Eastern looking. And no, no accent," Fiona said. "He was a public school boy, certainly. So I thought, maybe, just maybe something was finally happening…."

She exhaled.

"How old?" Edwin demanded.

"Just about right...maybe forty or so...and no ring," she said. Fiona gave a small, wry laugh. "And of course Charles wanted me to bend over backward."

"How?" Edwin demanded.

"When I told him that I'd be coming to town to study the book, he said that a friend of his would be coming by. Sometime today. A wealthy American school chum, who would be alone. And he asked me if, when his friend arrived, would I buy him a coffee? And he told me to order it specifically - very clearly - with four sugars."

Edwin sat back in his chair.

He nearly did it, Edwin thought. *He pulled me out, he took his shot, and nearly got me with a cup of coffee and four sugars.*

Aloud, Edwin said, "He needed me to know."

"Who is 'he'?" Fiona said. "Know what?"

"Who won," Edwin said.

To Edwin, what was at stake was suddenly very clear.

So. Obvious. Edwin was hunting Ali. And Ali was hunting him, too. And this wouldn't end over a cup of coffee.

Edwin eyed Fiona as she gripped the wheel of her hatchback.

"Where is this auction?" Edwin said.

As they drove, Edwin kept his sunglasses on. He watched the pulse in the side of Fiona's neck: Sixteen beats in ten seconds. Still racing. Then fourteen. Then eleven.

She calms quickly. Despite being nearly blown up. Good.

Aloud, Edwin said, "Drive off the main road. Not far." He wanted to get out of range of the CCTV cameras. In the car, they were protected for the moment. There were questions in need of answers. Then he would let her go.

She was the best way to find Ali. The only way.

They drove along a winding road into the countryside. Along the hills that fell to the edge of the road, where sheep strayed and horses bolted in muddy blue coats buckled below their magnificent necks.

Fiona rattled on. Edwin understood the effects of shock. He was impressed with her effort to recover. The nerves had to run their course, so he listened for more clues that might tumble out with the chatter.

"Why did I wait? Why did I wait? I sound like my grandmother. No granny, no need to buy a new dress yet, yes, of course I'll tell you in plenty of time when there's a reason for it. Other than your own funeral," she muttered under her breath. "So why did I wait for a stranger to walk in? Can't be second in line when a new bloke comes to town - just ask granny. Even if he said that you weren't a gentleman. Even if he told me to buy the coffee and be on my way as soon as I placed the order."

Edwin believed in coincidence: he believed that random facts closely assembled often lay on a single logical link.

He knew some facts. Deductions followed. It was like sitting with Zed, going through the logic step by step. But Edwin had grown used to debating by himself, alternating between blue and green markers on the whiteboard as each voice required.

The Leader of Al Ra'duzma had been killed.

He had to have planned for that moment.

All he had to do, for years living in hiding, was to plan who would succeed him.

Edwin knew a little bit about what one thinks about while hiding for years on end. How something sits, and festers, and then you make the plan, and it becomes clearer and clearer and the mission resolves until it is all you can see against the canvas that never changes.

Get Ali.

So the Leader had to have had a plan. A detailed plan. Dead people quickly lose control of the living, so the plan will order succession to happen quickly.

Ali was in the Leader's house at the very end. So Ali is part of the plan.

Answer found, Edwin paused on one fact that did not fit.

When time was of the essence, Ali baited him to this small town in England. Why? And, in his spare moments, Ali stopped in at an auction house. Why?

When the questions broke down into simple parts, their answers became clear.

Edwin concluded this. Something at that auction was of vital importance to Ali. Something at that auction would help him become the successor. And with regard to Edwin, Ali could be sure of one thing only.

I'll come out to get you.

So Ali had very little time to get what he needed, and he baited Edwin there to kill two birds with one stone.

Fiona had taken a few deep breaths.

"He's not an old friend of yours, obviously," she said.

Edwin caught on the word. It was one of Zed's favorite mannerisms. Everything started with "obviously" when it rarely was, and if so, only to his magnificent brain. But his old friend, his colleague, was far away. Edwin was on his own, with what tools Zed had given him. And suddenly, saddled with a country girl who could not keep quiet.

But for the moment, Edwin needed her.

"No. He's not a friend," Edwin said. "But I need to find him. Quickly."

Edwin recalled the article. Like most things he saw, it opened in his memory like a photograph in front of him. He could read the print.

"The auction. It starts in half an hour," he said.

Fiona stopped at an uphill intersection where four narrow lanes met at the top of a hill, where no car could see another approach. She looked at Edwin.

"It's at the Manor," said Fiona. "They are expecting me."

Then she hit the gas. She lurched into the intersection, stripped gears to slam the car into reverse, backed up, cranked the wheel and sped back over the road they had just covered.

As an elite counter-terror operative, Edwin had been in so many harrowing situations that most were as exciting as tap water to him, but the ride to Upper Chelton Manor would ever stand out. High hedges gave not an inch. The country roads were exactly wide enough to allow two Roman carriages to pass comfortably but intolerant of the size of modern vehicles. Turnouts came at unpredictably wide distances from one another. There was a madwoman at the wheel taking the turns at forty-five miles per hour.

Edwin had a survival skill for every situation.

He buckled his seat belt.

Fiona turned sharply into a gravel driveway through large stone gates. Rocks spun beneath their wheels as she drove past pillars that lined the road, displaying plants/shrubs sculpted into the shape of ten-point bucks, larger than life hares, geometric shapes. Cherry blossoms filled branches with light pink blossoms, and scattered their petals in small carpets beneath them. Bluebells peeked up between white tulips along the edge of the driveway. Pheasants roamed, their long tails balanced behind them. An ostentation of peacocks strutted and flared, having the run of the place but rarely straying from the trough.

The driveway was a half-mile long. No one passed them in the opposite direction as they neared the estate. Fiona pulled around the central fountain into a parking area that already held two dozen cars.

"Amazing home," Fiona marveled at the stone façade of the massive building, with its tall symmetrical windows and wide central steps. "There are twenty rooms in there, at least."

"If he's come for the auction," Edwin said, "then he's still here. You go first, tell me what you see."

Edwin did not want Ali to see him with Fiona. Alone, he had a chance of surprising him. Ali would think Edwin was dead in the honey trap he had laid at the tea shop.

"Perhaps you'd better come with me," Fiona said. "You'll attract notice on your own." Edwin knew she was right, so he followed her.

A man in a three-piece suit stood still at the top of the wide stone steps.

"Good day, Ms. Tate. Welcome. We're so pleased you could join us for this event. This way. And, sir, you too…"

"This is my American friend, Jack Wayne," said Fiona.

"Jack Wayne?" whispered Edwin. "Ridiculous."

Fiona shrugged. "No more ridiculous than the one you gave me."

"I didn't…"

"Exactly," she said. "So from here on, until I learn other-wise, you are Jack Wayne. My new American friend. A colos-sally wealthy client. Obviously."

"Ms. Tate, please," motioned their escort through a door.

Edwin followed her.

"I need a moment to freshen up," she said. The butler directed her to the ladies' room.

Fiona paused at the door. She looked over her shoulder at Edwin.

"Jack, please go in and find a seat. I'll be there in a moment." She headed off to a ladies' room. Once inside she looked closely in the mirror. Dust streaked her eyebrows. Her pantyhose were ripped. She had a long scrape where she landed on the pavement.

Fiona reached into her bag and selected a dark blue pair of pantyhose. She unzipped one boot and pulled it off. Then the other. She rolled a fresh pair of stockings down to the toes, and stuck a foot in. Gently, she rolled them up over her calf and thigh. Then she did the same with the other leg.

She wiped a wet towel over her face.

"The Nikon," she whispered. "The passport. The silver hairbrush."

The images from Finley's Book of items for auction ran through her mind.

Fiona thought about the reserve amount for each and the list of potential buyers the team had marketed to. She thought about how she would fill the bank. She took a deep breath, and left the room, ready to make her first deposit.

Working an auction successfully, Fiona had learned, was like building and drawing on a bank account. Put the right pieces forward at the right prices, you put something in the bank: the crowd goes with you. Take the pressure off at the right time: they thank you. Sprinkle a joke here or there, during one of these pauses: when they laugh, you own them. Then if a piece doesn't sell or doesn't reach its reserve, or god forbid the words fail and you just watch yourself as the surface closes over you, then you will have to make a withdrawal.

Charles had confessed all this to her over a liquid lunch one day when she first came to Finley's.

"My dear, really all you have to remember are the three cardinal rules: No heavy drinking the night before. No heavy drinking the morning of. And –"

"No heavy drinking at lunch?" Fiona had guessed

He laughed, and Fiona did too. "You've got it."

It was, of course, much more. Charles Lincoln had cultivated clients over many years, decades – his whole career. He would do a small favor when he could; then he would be top of mind when someone had a piece, or a friend with a piece, of some value. Eventually large estates would come to him for disposition at the best value – an ambiguous term that appealed both to seller and buyer even though, by definition, both could not achieve it.

"A favor...That's why I agreed to buy Charles's client's friend a coffee. What bloody bad luck," Fiona muttered to her reflection as she dabbed her eyelashes with mascara. Then a chill unsettled her.

Or perhaps Jack Wayne was right. Maybe it wasn't a question of luck at all. The man just used her...and didn't care what happened to her.

This was not behavior Fiona Tate tolerated.

A marketing intern handed Edwin a copy of the Book. She smiled winningly through black thick-rimmed glasses.

"I hope you find something you like here."

The Wealthy Buyer persona was Edwin's "cover for status," the perfectly good reason an operative provides for being who he claims to be. His "cover for action" was his perfectly good reason for being somewhere and doing something. Like potentially purchasing something of great value at this auction of unusual European silver.

Edwin nodded, and took the Book. The fewer people who heard him speak, the better. His American accent was hard to mask, particularly to English ears accustomed to telling county, schooling and class from the lilt in a single phrase. Fiona had been smart to describe him as an American from the beginning.

Fiona and Edwin entered an ornate ballroom with golden painted chairs and red velvet seats lined row after row. The room was wide but shallow. Behind the chairs, floor-to-ceiling wrought iron paned windows provided views of the dense green hedges and delicate yellow roses of the manor's formal courtyard.

A raised podium stood in front of the crowd. Bids made over the Internet would come to the auctioneer through the small grey monitor, about eight inches long and six inches wide, that perched on a stand near the microphone. More bids would come through the telephones. Long tables stretched perpendicular to the rows of seats where well-coiffed twenty-something women in smart, dark-rimmed glasses cocked their heads to the telephone receivers that pressed against their shoulders.

"The phone bank is huge," Edwin heard someone say into a cell phone. "Twelve on one side, eight on the other. Yes, that's the way things are going at this one. Yes, quite."

Edwin shrank back from the hundreds of pairs of eyes suddenly fixed on them. But as he moved along the edge of the room to the back, he relaxed.

Fiona entered, and the conversations dropped.

Everyone looked at her.

She walked to the podium and greeted the crowd. "What a remarkably unusual group of objects we have today. Important items from the mid-Twentieth century, a time civilizations collided. Some are things the worst members of society have used in their common day-to-day life - to remind us, I suppose, of what humanity is capable of and what we must all do to improve and evolve – and control - the human condition. I must make clear that Finley's today will donate eight percent of our profits from the sale to the Midlands Conservation Trust. Some of these objects demonstrate the best of human choices. Some bear witness to the worst.

"Lots twenty-six, eighty-seven, and one twenty-two have been withdrawn. Lots seven through twenty are subject to a reserve. Not subject to a reserve are the remaining lots. So with that preamble, shall we start with the … not unexpected … lot number…one."

The crowd tittered. Plink, plink. Charles beamed.

"She's a natural," he said to another associate. "What better purchase than an hour in the company of a funny woman."

Fiona held forth from the podium.

"First we have Robert Capa's camera, the thirty-five millimeter Zeiss Ikon Contax II. This is the eye that he used to photograph war footage, including the first Americans landing on Omaha Beach. Soldiers who lay dead after a house battle in France. He used it to film creators like Hemingway, recovering from a car accident. His lover Ingrid Bergman and Hitchcock rehearsing a difficult scene. Picasso on the beach with his greatest creation: his son Claude. Creation and destruction. We start this item at fifty thousand pounds."

Edwin listened and watched as the patter began.

"Now sixty. Now seventy to me online. Now eighty. One hundred on the phone. One hundred. Not to you. Not to you, sir. Not to...yes, one hundred and ten thousand pounds."

Fiona paused. She scanned the room. Her eyes fell on a man in a dark suit in the fourth row, near the far side. The man who answered to Yassir. The man who had sent her to a coffee shop when it exploded.

What was he still there for?

But she had to continue. Fiona shifted to the script.

"Do I hear any advance on one hundred and ten thousand for this iconic Ikon?" she said.

The crowd again giggled.

"One hundred and twenty thousand, thank you! One twenty going once, going twice and sold! To paddle one sixteen. Thank you all," Fiona said.

"Lot two." Fiona pointed to the large screen behind her. It filled with the image of a U.S. passport.

"'Honorary Citizen of the United States, Winston S. Churchill," she read. "Useful if you are planning a little trip, perhaps?"

The crowd laughed. "Well, this won't work like a real passport, not even for Sir Winston. But it is the first ever issued by the United States to anyone. Thank you, President Kennedy. Starting the bid at twenty thousand pounds, do I hear thirty? Forty, now fifty, now sixty on the phone. Sixty..."

The words tumbled from Fiona's mouth though her eyes kept darting back to Yassir.

"Now for Lot three," Fiona said.

Edwin slid along the wall to watch from behind the curl of a tall velvet drapery. The number of syllables that fell from Fiona's lips in that first five minutes was more than he had spoken...perhaps ever.

"Where's Ali?" Edwin thought. He scanned the backs of the heads for a familiar crane of the neck, a posture. His facial recognition technology captured hundreds of points on a face; angles of eyebrows, width of the bridge across the nose, angle of cheekbones. From behind, it captured the whorl of natural hair, the arc of a neck increased with age and a sedentary life in front of a computer screen. It accepted color but discounted it since that was the most frequently changed. It studied the roots.

Edwin watched closely. The program hummed, then in the corner of his right eye, suspended in a holograph, it produced three potential matches in a grid laid out in front of him. One was in the fourth row, far to the left. Edwin looked at the hall. A wide door, now closed and guarded, was fifteen strides away. He had to get a better look. Quietly, he eased behind the drapes.

Fiona continued to spin up the crowd. "Now here's something, perhaps the worst of the worst. But its historical value is something that …you will decide. Profits to charity, thank goodness. Lot three is the silver hairbrush that once belonged to Adolf Hitler. One scrape across that fiendish head, every day. You can help the Midlands Conservation Trust beginning at fourteen hundred pounds."

At this, Edwin watched the man in the third row raise his finger. He saw Fiona turn her head toward the gesture, ready to spin it on to the next higher value. But for the first time, her words stopped.

Fiona looked up at the window to where Edwin had been standing. Then she took a sip of water.

"Two thousand pounds. And a half? Anyone?...There in the back... Yes, thank you. Three now. We're at three. On the phones, yes, thank you. Three thousand going once."

"Ten thousand dollars," said the man in the third row.

Edwin recognized the voice, even with the crisp English accent Ali was using. Ali still held the edge of arrogance, the curt dismissive tone that used to light the fuse between them over a whiteboard session at D6.

Edwin's adrenalin surged. His muscles tightened, loosened, and flexed again. He was warming up, though he stood absolutely still.

"My goodness," said Fiona. "Well. The Midlands Conservation Trust will be grateful for this gesture. Do we have any advance on ten thousand. No? Going once, twice, sold to...what is your name, sir?"

"Paddle one thirteen," he said, standing. The man left abruptly to go pay the cashier and leave with his object.

Fiona stepped away from the podium.

"I...I...I'm not well," she said to a young man standing behind her. "Finish for me, please."

Fiona walked briskly out of the hall. Edwin followed her.

"That was him!" she whispered when Edwin caught up to her in the hallway. "That was the man I saw at the viewing this morning. It was the man who told me to buy you coffee with four sugars."

"Where is he?"

"He has to pay, and he has to collect the object from storage," Fiona said. "Come!"

Ali stood calmly by the cashier table. The cashier slowly counted the ten stacks of elastic-bound hundred-pound notes.

"Thank you." He smiled at the man wearing plastic gloves and rolling his purchase in packing paper. "Just a simple bag is fine. I have a plane to catch. They'll take it out when I go through security anyway."

The cashier smiled at Ali. "Let's just double-check, shall we? I hate to mistake when the payment is in cash. It's so final once you walk out that door, isn't it?" She began counting again, carefully selecting each bill and building ten new stacks.

Ali's mouth made a flat line. He waited.

Edwin and Fiona peered around the edge of the door.

"Now what do we do?" Fiona whispered.

Edwin eyed the security cameras pointing from the corners of the hallway toward the cashier. It would be critical to take Ali down somewhere the security cameras would not see him.

"Not here," he said. "Outside."

"Yassir!" Charles Lincoln called triumphantly as he caught up to Ali. "Success, my friend! I have had it delivered! Look."

Charles brought forward a small box. He peeled up the top.

"It is the prize you purchased years ago," said Charles. "The Lopaki Sapphire Dagger. Four sapphires in the handle. Emeralds and yellow diamonds. A watch hidden beneath another at the end of the handle. A ruby on the tip of the sheath. And all the diamonds. It's a treasure trove in one very special item. Lot number two sixty-seven, as I recall."

"Well, I do thank you for arranging delivery of it," Ali said, in Yassir's tone. "And it is quite a good time. I now have a safe place to display it."

"Nice to see you again," Charles said.

"I must go," said Ali. "A plane..."

Charles walked with him to the door. Then he spun on his heel, turning back to the auction where frenzied bidders vied for General Eisenhower's plan for the Normandy Invasion.

Through a large-paned window in a sitting room off the foyer, Edwin and Fiona watched Ali walk down the stairs and stride toward his car. He carried a bulging plastic bag in one hand.

"Run!" Edwin shouted. They broke for the courtyard where Fiona's small hatchback was parked.

Ali's car spun down the drive, spraying yellow pebbles beneath its wheels.

"You. Stay here. I'll get your car back to you," Edwin said.

"I'm coming," said Fiona. She already had her keys out.

"You are not coming," Edwin said. He stopped in front of the car, and stood very close to her, closing his hands around hers.

"You don't want to meet him," Edwin said.

"I've already met him," Fiona said.

"He put you in that tea shop," Edwin said. His green eyes blazed.

"And you got me out."

"Remember that," Edwin said. He let go of her hands. Then, he raised his right hand, dangling the key. Grinning, he pressed unlock, opened the left side door and slipped in.

Fiona opened the door on the right side and sat down.

"Dammit!" said Edwin, hitting the door with his fist.

Fiona was seated behind the wheel. In the small car fitted for English roads, Edwin had beaten her to the passenger side.

"Well done, you," she smiled from behind the wheel. "Keys, please. We're losing him."

The moment would come when Edwin could give her the slip. But right now, he needed her to take him to Ali before he slipped back into the ether and the succession slid on.

Fiona drove fast.

"Did he really try to kill me?" Fiona said. "Or just use me?"

"Don't know. Better for us if it was the latter."

"Why?"

"Because he might still think he got me," Edwin said. "If he had tried to kill you, he would know his plan failed. So now we have the advantage. He doesn't know I'm still coming for him."

Fiona's eyes flashed and focused on the road in front of them.

"Don't lose him," Edwin said, watching Fiona closely.

"I won't," she said. "So who is he to you?"

"Later," Edwin said. "Just stay on him."

He needed to buy just a little more time, then he could get Ali, end it, and somehow reduce the impact of having encountered Fiona. But the less she knew about him the better. So he would try to find out more about her.

"What else did you sell at that place...Finley's?" Edwin asked, gripping the door handle as they rounded a curve close to a hedge.

"Oh gosh," Fiona said. "Everything you can imagine. Some things you can't imagine. Everything from art to Elizabeth Taylor's jewels, to Bonaparte's penis."

"What!?"

"You heard me. Bonaparte's...bone...a part...from the rest of him."

"What did it go for?"

"Ah. I'll have to look that up in the catalog."

A pause.

"I have to ask," Edwin said.

"Massive," said Fiona at the same time. "Like an elephant. Relatively small elephant, but still."

"Really?"

Fiona looked at Edwin. "Of course not. What do you think happens with hundreds of years of desiccation?"

"Nothing good."

"The expression 'shriveled eel' comes up, if you Google it."

"If you what?"

"Google. You know. Search it on the web." Fiona frowned at him again.

"Yeah," Edwin nodded. Isolation on the rig meant he was even less familiar with the way certain words had worked their way into society. He avoided the search engine because more agencies sniffed those searches than anywhere else. He wrote his own spider instead to crawl the public web, and to creep through the cracks in the walls of the private networks.

"Someone kept it?" he continued, mostly to cover his slip.

"Apparently so. And someone bought it. It's been a fairly hot commodity over the decades. Useful conversation starter."

"Huh," said Edwin.

"Yes," sighed Fiona.

In the pause, they came over a curve. Edwin saw the yellow coupe appear for a brief second through a break in the copse, the thick hedgerow lining the roads.

"There! Go. He just turned at that row of trees."

Fiona pressed the accelerator and they shot down the winding gravel road. All they could see were tall trees gracefully lining the sides of the road as it poured over a hill a half mile in the distance. As they wound down a gentle hill, a hamlet appeared that had been invisible from the way above. At the center of the slope they saw a grand house with many gables rising four stories above the ground. Stone walls bordered a green house, and gardens of fruit trees and vegetables. A maze of hedges filled another corner of the grounds carved in geometric patterns, with raised stone beds holding a riot of roses. The lawns were closely clipped leading down and around the mirroring pool. There were stables, a granary with an ancient clock tower overlooking the valley, and there, where a stream carved a path at the bottom, were several small cottages. A low gate built of weathered wood with points across the top swung between stone walls and across a slate path.

"Isn't this private property?" Edwin said. "How can we just drive on in?"

"In England?" She laughed. "Most of it belongs to the Queen, or the nanny state. Anyone can move along a public way. Even in the middle of a gorgeous place like this."

They drove slowly past a man walking in tall green rubber boots and a Barbour coat, a silver whistle around his neck. He stopped to wave them by, his black Labrador sitting leashless by his left foot.

"During the War many of the lands and houses like this were taken for some part of the war effort," said Fiona. "German prisoners were kept on estates like this, free to come and go within a certain circumference. If they broke the rules, they were locked up, I suppose. But really, where are they going to go? Britain is an island, isn't it? I think a lot of them were just as glad to be here, frankly."

"It looks like a working farm, though," Edwin said. A large John Deere green tractor was parked on the side of the road near the small house.

"Yes, and it's a little village. Since machines do so much now, a lot of owners have tenants in the old houses where farm laborers used to live. Like here, probably."

"There's the yellow car." Edwin pointed to a parked car near a small cottage down the hill from the main house. "Stop here."

Fiona pulled the car behind a large tractor. "Now, what do we do?"

Edwin glared at Fiona. "You are done. Stay put. Whatever is in there you want no part of."

Fiona faced Edwin. "That hairbrush is history. It cannot just be lost."

"Stay." Edwin ordered.

Then Edwin got out of the car. He edged to the small stone cottage, and peered through the window. He saw a small kitchen with a round table in the middle.

A silver hairbrush lay flat on the oilskin tablecloth.

Someone rustled behind him. He turned his head. spun on his heel. Fiona stood quietly next to him.

"That's it there," Fiona whispered in Edwin's ear.

He turned on her, eyes fierce..

Obstreperous, Edwin thought.

"That object made evil appear civilized, every day," Fiona whispered. "It forces people to remember what a... human...is capable of doing."

Edwin grabbed her arm. Hard. "You. Don't. Don't get near it."

Fiona glared at Edwin, and shook off his arm in a single jerk. Then she moved to the front door.

"I'll be careful," she mouthed. "It's open."

Fiona pushed the door open and walked into the small cottage.

Edwin recalculated. This was why it was better to be alone. Always. Other people made things worse. They muddied the line. They caused detours and detours led to distraction and distraction led to mission failure. The littlest slips led to catastrophe. He had to get rid of Fiona. But before he did, Edwin knew that she would need his help before she again breathed the air outside the small building.

"Hello?" Fiona called pleasantly as she walked toward the table. No one answered. She kept moving, faster than she spoke.

"Mr. Metah? Yassir? It's Fiona...I went to the tea shop, as you asked. And, well, I just wanted to ask you a few questions...."

She reached the table.

"...About the hairbrush."

"Don't pick -" Edwin said. He kept his back to the wall and edged slowly into the room.

Fiona held the brush in her fist. She was studying every angle of it.

She gasped. "I don't think it's ever been cleaned. Am I looking at flakes of -"

From the door, a man cleared his voice.

They both looked up.

Fiona saw the man Charles Lincoln called "Yassir," a favored client, long lost. The man who appeared at the auction and bought the silver hairbrush that had once belonged to the most despised human being in history.

Edwin saw something else – a living version of the photograph he had stared at on his wall for ten years. The grey bags beneath his eyes were deeper. His cheeks had slumped. But his hair was still jet black. His arrogant, unhurried slouch was the same as he stood in the doorway pointing a gun at them in one hand. His hand held the heavy object very still. In the other hand, he held five blue plastic sticks. C-4. Edwin looked at the small cottage where the walls were made of stone stuck with mortar hundreds of years old.

"Don't move, Edwin," Ali said. He waved the C-4. "I don't really care... as long as you know I sent you."

Edwin calculated. Five sticks would make the old cottage into a pile of rocks in half a second.

"I knew you were still alive," Ali said, his lip lifting in a curl.

Edwin watched Ali's face change. The snarl evaporated. His eyebrows made a tent. Did he see sadness?

On the rig, Edwin had spent hours studying facial expression and the emotions they betrayed. The face told the feelings but never the reasons for them.

"Fiona! I...I told you to get out of the tea shop and be on your way. Now.... it's your own fault. I can't be responsible for what mistakes you made yourself. I told you to... Just - give that to me."

Fiona held out the brush. Ali snatched it, while he glowered at Edwin.

"Both of you, back up," Ali said. "More."

Off the side of the kitchen there was a short flight of cement stairs that stopped at a door only four feet high.

"In. Now!" He banged the gun against the wall.

Edwin watched the gun. And the C-4.

"You first, Edwin. Or I kill her."

Ali held a cellphone in front of them. Edwin could see "7:46:52." The last two digits scrolled rapidly.

"Getting used to this killing business, Ali?" Edwin said. He glanced in his field of view at the clock. He sent a command.

Set timer.

The numbers shifted to 7:44:51.

"You miss a lot," Edwin said.

"Get in!" barked Ali. The whites above his eyes glared. He was chewing his lip. Edwin calculated the range of expressions. Ali showed hate for Edwin. Sadness for Fiona. But above all, there was something else Edwin saw.

It was in the whites above Ali's irises.

Edwin was not sympathetic; he collected the information to identify the weakness in his quarry. But the face told everything: Ali was afraid.

Why is the man with the gun afraid?

Ali shoved them back into the darkened room and bolted the heavy door behind them.

Inside, Edwin and Fiona heard Ali call through the door.

"You have seven minutes, maybe. Don't think you can get out of this one, Edwin. I've beaten you. Again. After all these years wherever you've been hiding, you've lost a step. Or more. You've done exactly as I predicted and as I planned. I must say, I'm a little disappointed in you. Perhaps almost as much as you are in yourself. This is what comes to the arrogant. They fall. They always fall."

Ali rapped his knuckles against the door once.

In their pitch black prison, Edwin and Fiona heard only the sounds of their own breath.

CHAPTER TWENTY-ONE

11:15 a.m., May 23
Upper Chelton, England

In the clammy darkness, Edwin's watch began to glow..
They had less than seven minutes before the timer on the
C-4 ran out and lit the explosive. He kicked the floor. Some
soil moved, but not much.

"I can stand up, but have to duck," Edwin said. "The
roof is five feet from the floor. And I counted seven steps
coming down here, which means there's at least two feet of
dirt above us; maybe more because we drove down a slope
to get here. The cottage is at the bottom of a valley."

"Who are you?" Fiona's shaky words filtered through
the dark to Edwin.

"The floor is dirt. Hard dirt," Edwin continued.
He reached up. "But the ceiling is cement. What is this
place?"

Edwin saw no productive value in sharing his conclusion: they would not be able to dig out in seven minutes.

"It's an old r-root cellar, probably, since it's just off the
cottage kitchen," Fiona whispered. For the first time, she
spoke unevenly. Unsure of her words, subdued.

Edwin's leadership skills flexed deep in his muscle
memory. He led by three principles.

First, lead by example. Second, hold non-performers accountable. And third, suffer together. The next seven minutes required one and three.

Edwin made no room for criticism or assignment of blame. Clear out all distractions. Lead by example. Suffer together and survive.

"How old?" Edwin said.

"Do you think he really has a bomb?" Fiona said.

"He did last time," Edwin said.

"I am an idiot," Fiona said. "Truly. As is was just fine. I had to go seek excitement in the company of strangers. Granny, where have you led me?"

Edwin listened to her speech pattern quicken. She needed to focus.

Talk her down.

"How old is this place?" Edwin repeated.

"N-not that old…. probably, three hundred years, maybe four?" Fiona said, clearing her throat. "I don't like c-close spaces." Her voice raised at the end.

In the dark, deprived of sight, Edwin's other senses switched into high gear. His heart rate, however, stayed low and even. The precise clock in his head ticked off seconds in perfect synchronicity with the glowing numbers on his wristwatch.

Edwin measured the tools he had at hand:

One: The dimensions and structure of this underground cave. Two: An auctioneer who was losing her nerve. Possibly all of them, at once.

Panic eats time. To stop it, teach her to fight. Or put her to work.

Edwin recalled a lesson that he had given, once, on a beach in the Chesapeake Bay, to a redhead named Camille. She was wearing loose khakis recently bought at Wal-Mart, and within an hour, she had learned to conceal a nail in the callous of her foot. The next day, she had used it well.

Edwin checked his countdown. They had six minutes and forty seconds.

In the root cellar, there was no need to fight. So Edwin put Fiona to work.

Fortunately, Edwin had something to work with.

He had an auctioneer, and an auctioneer had to be part computer. So he had at hand a computer filled with historical data about how people used objects, the older the better.

Edwin spoke calmly to Fiona as he felt for the edge. "So it's a root cellar. Is that it? In three hundred years, you think anyone ever used it for anything else?

The walls felt rough.

"These walls are made of cement too," Edwin added.

Fiona's breathing seemed to stretch out a little as she thought. "Ahhhh. I don't know. I can't think!"

Edwin passed his palm along the edge of the wall. He felt a piece of metal. It was a thick ring. He pulled it. Rusty metal squealed. But no part of the wall budged. It was not a doorknob.

"What's this? Come here - feel it," Edwin said.

Engage her sense of touch. Anchor her.

Edwin felt the ring again. It was about four inches in diameter.

The clock showed five minutes and twelve seconds left.

Fiona crouched next to Edwin. He grabbed her wrist and put her hand on the flaking metal ring.

"Feel it?" he said. "Tell me what you think it is."

Edwin dropped to his knees and felt along the bottom edge of the cellar wall. He found the corner and kept edging along on his knees, seeing the lowest part of the wall through his fingertips.

Four minutes, eleven seconds.

"This is...a...ring. Stuck on a wall," Fiona said. "It's big. My whole hand fits through it. Or...wait a minute!"

Edwin heard Fiona's voice strengthen.

Good. She's solving a problem. Not freaking out. Now I can put her to use.

Then Fiona laughed triumphantly.

"Ha! This place isn't just for hanging up roots. It was for keeping the prisoners - during the war! Remember, these estates were conscripted to help out in the War. And the German prisoners lived on some of them with free reign until they broke a rule, or strayed too far. Of course! Where would they find a makeshift jail cell on a farm? The root cellar! It's perfect. So maybe they chained them to a ring in the wall."

"There's only one small ring here," Edwin said. "I've felt every section of the walls. Would they have only kept one prisoner at a time?"

"No," said Fiona. "There were generally teams of workers. Maybe the ring was just a threat. Nobody wanted to be sent to the lock-up in the root cellar. You hear stories about how the prisoners would play with the kids on the farms, teach them German words, and make them toys out of branches. I don't think they were terribly well supervised."

"No," Edwin said. "They weren't. Look at this."

Fiona fumbled through the dark, bent over, tripping once, toward the green glow of Edwin's watch. It was at ankle height, two yards away.

"Look at this," he said. He waved his watch in a circle. The light glowed faintly around crumbling cement. It circled a darker area, about two feet around.

"Is that a ... hole?" Fiona gasped.

"Yes. Now go. You'll fit," Edwin said.

"My gracious," said Fiona. "This must have been dug by malnourished prisoners of war. How on earth are you going to get through it?"

"Squeeze," Edwin said. It was both answer and order. "Go!"

"Where?" Fiona said.

"As far as we can," Edwin said, glancing at the clock in his darkened lenses to confirm what he knew already.

Three minutes, forty-two seconds.

"It looks narrow," said Fiona.

"We have three minutes and twenty-eight seconds before this cave blows," Edwin said. "Go."

"Okay, okay," said Fiona. She dropped to her hands and knees and began to crawl into narrow space. "God, this is…"

"I'm coming right after you," Edwin said. "You keep going if I get stuck. I'll block you."

"Block me? From what?" Fiona said. Edwin could hear her hesitate. Fear rose in her voice.

"Go," Edwin said. "Tell me exactly what you see."

"I don't see anything. It's black."

"Tell me exactly what you feel in your hands. What you smell. What you taste. And move it! Faster!"

Two minutes, eleven seconds.

Edwin wanted Fiona ahead of him for two reasons. If the tunnel narrowed, she could keep going if he got stuck. And if the blast blew, his body would shield hers.

It wouldn't be enough.

Fiona was cruising now, clambering fast on all fours, adrenalin blocking the pain of the grit skinning her knees and sharp rocks slicing into her raw flesh. The walls were so close. They crawled on hands and knees, yard after yard. The tunnel kept going.

"We're going uphill, I think," Fiona said, panting.

Edwin felt the tug of gravity shift his body weight.

One minute.

"Keep moving. Faster. That's it. Good. You are a titan!" said Edwin.

Fiona scrabbled faster ahead of him. Dirt and rocks scraped against Edwin's broad shoulders. He was edging forward on his belly now, pushing the edges with his feet then twisting around onto his side, half-spiraling like a corkscrew.

Edwin's mental clock showed only seconds remained.

"Go!" he urged. "Go go go go go!"

Sixteen seconds. Ten.

Then Fiona cried out. "Ouch!" She stopped moving.

"Go!" Edwin shouted, as the clock in his head ran out.

"I can't! It's blocked!" Fiona cried.

"Put your shirt over your face! Now!" Edwin said.

The numbers on his watch in the pitch black tunnel shone:

Four.
Three.
Two.
One.

They heard a low rumble and the earth shook around them. Dust and dirt flew past them in a gust. Then the air was still. Too still. Edwin coughed under his once blue shirt collar. He could taste dirt. Dust thickened the scant pouch of air around them.

Fiona coughed through her silk scarf.

"What's h-h-happened," Fiona said.

"The blast probably collapsed the root cellar. And the entrance to the tunnel," Edwin said. "So. We go forward."

"Well, we can't," Fiona said, coughing in the dusty thin air. "The tunnel has ended."

"Ended?" Edwin said. "We can move a rock."

He pulled himself up over Fiona's legs and reached over her to feel the obstacle.

"There's a little more space here," Fiona said. "But the tunnel has definitely ended. It looks like they dug no more."

Behind them the root cellar tunnel had crumbled. Tons of dirt and debris had sealed them into this elongated grave.

"This is suboptimal," Edwin said.

Fiona snorted. "Suboptimal? I wholeheartedly agree."

"Move," Edwin said.

His shoulder pressed against Fiona's side as she tried to make enough room for him to see with the dim light of his watch. He could feel her shaking. He sat back for a moment, curled against the wall in the small space. The end of the tunnel was a little larger than the passage had been.

"It's big enough for someone to turn around," Edwin thought. "An option we don't have."

For a moment, Edwin said nothing. They sat with their backs against the wall, their necks curved down, and knees up. He could feel her hot breath coming in short, nervous puffs, against the hairs on his arms that were now coated in dirt. She was hyperventilating.

That was a bad use of good air. He needed to narrow her mind to solve a manageable problem. Go with her strengths. She was a computer of information of how people used things. Old things. Old, forgotten things lost...almost lost.

Edwin held his watch close to her face. For the first time in the tunnel, Edwin could see her eyes, and she could see his. And that was all the faint green glimmer permitted either of them to see. Two faces inside the edge of darkness.

Dirt streaked her cheeks, dusted her forehead. Edwin fixed his eyes on hers.

They were wild, open and blue, and Edwin held on to them.

There was not much air, and each short breath brought the metallic tang of dirt inside his mouth. His jaw closed, and crunched the dirt on his tongue and his teeth.

"Fiona." He coughed. "Think. Why would these prisoners want to build such a long tunnel?"

Fiona held Edwin's intense gaze. She took a small breath, and exhaled. "Escape comes to mind," she said.

"But we didn't crawl over any old skeletons," Edwin said.

"No! Fear!" Fiona shuddered.

"So, why not?" Edwin asked.

It was better to let her discover the hope on her own.

"Maybe they did...escape?" Fiona said. Then her voice fell. "Or, they didn't need to." She twirled her finger, pointing around their small dirt cave. "Maybe the War ended while they were still digging. Maybe they stopped here because they were set free."

"This is..." Edwin twisted to get a better look at the end of the tunnel.

"Suboptimal?" Fiona said.

"I was going to say, it's a nontrivial problem," Edwin said. "You think you know me?"

"A little, perhaps," said Fiona. "By a key phrase or two."

In the green light, they studied each other.

Edwin scraped the wall with his fingertips; he could feel them dig in.

"It's not a rock. Just more dirt. This is as far as the prisoners dug."

"They turned around here, and went back to the root cellar," Fiona said.

"Yes," Edwin agreed.

"But we can't do that," she said.

"No. Ali made sure of that," said Edwin.

For the first time in the tunnel, Edwin could felt how close the dirt walls were.

"We are already buried," Fiona said.

CHAPTER TWENTY-TWO

11:18 a.m., May 23
Upper Chelton

A li ran from the cottage past his yellow car to an old truck. He jumped into the driver's seat. He was breathing hard.

He looked at his watch. He had to be at the summit, in Paris, in thirty-eight hours. Time was passing. All of this strategy would be for nothing if he could not be there to align his wayward supporters and prove to the entire assembly just exactly what it would be worth to them, to the mission of al Ra'duzma, to have him as their leader.

Ali reached into the leather satchel he carried across his body and over his shoulder. He pulled out the phone he used to text the Sheikh.

His thumb flew from key to key.

Am holding Lopaki. CU tomorrow.

Shortly, three dots appeared on the screen. Ali exhaled. The Sheikh was responding.

Good news, came the response.

Ali tapped five keys.

Deal?

No dots appeared. No answer came.

Ali curled his lips back against his teeth.

"Don't be weak," he scolded himself. "You are in charge."

Ali reached into his satchel and felt the reassuring ridges of the bubble wrap that wound many times around the Lopaki Dagger. Tucked into a leather fold, he had the scrap of paper the Sheikh had given him with the address for Rais Abdullah in Paris.

And in the small pouch where one of his three mobile phones rested, Ali held the trigger for the next act of global terrorism that would shake the foundations of the West and remind them that they were at war.

Ali picked up the phone. He turned it on. The screen filled with green dots on a black background. The green dots were moving in arcs. Some were following each other's path. Some moved faster. He pressed a button and saw a sectional view. Instead of moving left to right, he could see the dots in relation to one another, from above and from below. There were thousands of them.

Ali tipped his phone to the right. The dots shifted a hair. All of them. He tipped it to the left. They shifted back to their original lines.

Ali smiled. It was an amazing piece of work. It was hard to let it just sit there, when it was ready to show, and so ready to use. He should be very proud of it. He could feel his heart beat as adrenalin drove through it. He checked his watch.

It was only a matter of seconds before the muffled explosion shook the ground under the truck.

"Good. That's it, then," Ali said.

Now Edwin is buried in a tunnel with that stupid, meddlesome woman. He cannot screw this up for me. She should not have been there. It's her own fault."

He looked back at the phone. The last text message still was his.

Deal?

There had been no answer. Still.

Ali's hands were shaking as he opened the article from *Comprehensive Psychiatry*. In a corner there was a scribbled address.

Oxford Genetics Lab.

"Finish this last piece. Then get...to...Paris!" Ali's order was deep and foreboding, even though he was his own target.

Ali looked back at the dust from the blast that was blowing through the cottage windows. He blinked rapidly.

Time was escaping him. Ali felt control slipping. Doubts seeping.

After a lifetime of assuming false identities, Ali could lose his bearings. He could feel flooded with emotions, too many to control or filter. Usually the walls held and he dutifully felt only what each identity permitted. But not always.

This was why Ali had collected the cannibal's toothbrush, the Leader's hair, and Hitler's hairbrush. To be al Khaleef, Ali needed to have what they did in the very core of his being.

After Ali got out of the truck he slammed the door. Then he walked slowly to the back of the truck, where he picked up a shovel.

Al Khaleef would annihilate this type of sympathy.

Chapter Twenty-Three

11:19 a.m., May 23
Upper Chelton, England

E very instinct Edwin possessed began to kick. His muscles flexed, telling him to thrash and dig and scrape. His pulse picked up.

"Jack?" Fiona said quietly. "Edwin? We're going to…"

Edwin sat back against the earth wall. He stretched his neck.

He counted silently and slowly. *One…two…three.*

His mind fixed on an image of a broken window in an abandoned building. A shadow against an inside wall. He counted off the beat of his heart. He could feel the cold belt of steel against his index finger, the thin rubber against his eyebrow. Waiting. *Four…five…six…* Then one pulse of his index finger. The shadow dropped. *Seven…eight…nine.*

Edwin's pulse was normal again. Sniper training had value whether or not one had a target.

It is crucial that neither of us panic. We need the oxygen. We need energy. We need to think.

He looked at Fiona, her legs touching his in the cramped cavern, just big enough for them both to sit side by side.

We must be a team. Lead by example. Boost morale.

Edwin reached into his brown backpack.

Fiona heard paper crackle and tear.

"Give me your hand," Edwin said.

Fiona put her arm on Edwin's thigh, where dirt was now embedded deeply in the woven wool of his fine trousers. She spread her fingers. In the darkness, Edwin took her wrist, then slid his rough palm down over the back of her hand, to where her fingers joined it.

His thumb pressed lightly into her palm.

Neither one moved for several moments. Their short breaths found a rhythm. Fear bled between them. Suddenly Edwin wanted her. Right there.

"This feels…crazy," Fiona whispered. She did not move her hand. The back of it rested on Edwin's thigh, her palm up, her fingers wide. His thumb had found the surprising center of her nervous system, right in the middle of her palm.

"Yeah," said Edwin.

Just like Lula. Anyone who attached herself to him always ended this way. Always.

Edwin moved his thumb. The paper rustled, and a pile of small smooth discs fell in the center of her palm.

"What's this?" Fiona said.

"Put them in your mouth," Edwin said. He did the same. The sugar coating melted, and then chocolate smoothed over his tongue. Grains of dirt crunched between his teeth.

"Smarties," Fiona said.

"M&Ms," Edwin said.

Soon the sugar hit their bloodstream, providing an instant chemical lift to their morale.

"Ha. We have proof," she said. "At least of that. A receipt of provenance to go with the rare article. You are American, after all."

"Yes," Edwin said. "I am."

"But you don't know what Googling means," Fiona countered. "Have you been stranded on a desert island for the last decade?"

Edwin said nothing.

"We're at the end of the line, it appears," Fiona said. "So, perhaps words should be said. Life regrets?"

"You first," Edwin said.

"That," Fiona began, then started coughing. This was happening frequently now as the air thinned and the dust thickened. "That my beloved auction items have lived more daring lives than me. Until this afternoon, that is. And see how well that turned out. I've spent too much of my...all too brief, as it turns out... time...bored, actually. What a pity. You?"

Edwin paused. He was calculating the volume of the space they occupied, the amount of limited oxygen that was there to begin with, and how much they consumed per minute. Talking was a good way to keep Fiona from falling asleep in the depleted oxygen, a state she would not wake from as it decreased.

"If you are bored," Edwin said. "You should ask more questions."

After a moment, Fiona said, "Like what?"

"Ha," said Edwin. "Do better."

"Okay, then, how about this. Do you have any regrets, Jack Wayne?"

"Attachments," Edwin said. Using only one word spared their air.

"Having the wrong ones," coughed Fiona. "Or not having enough?"

"Yes," Edwin said. His eyes were beginning to swim. He and Fiona both were becoming hypoxic. "My turn. What's the hardest thing you ever had to do?"

Fiona didn't answer at first. Fiona was remembering the sound the door to the field hockey coach's office
always made when the latch fell behind her. The shameful
thrill of being chosen, still, even after so many new classes
came in. How powerful she had felt that day she raised
the field hockey stick and brought it down so fast on his
reaching fingers. How he had screamed and writhed,
how the bones sounded when they cracked under the
second blow. Two weeks later, when he walked by her in
the hallway, with his hand still in a cast, she watched him
look beyond her, and sling his arm around one of her
teammates.

Fiona was the chosen one no more. Wasn't that what she
had wanted?

Then Fiona answered Edwin. "I learned how to stop
stuttering."

"Did you ever!" Edwin laughed. "You stuttered?"

"Badly. All through school."

"How did you stop?"

"Eventually I had to."

"Must have been hard."

"Excruciating. Kids are very unkind. But I...I finally
wanted to be heard."

"What did you say?" Edwin asked.

"Enough," Fiona said.

In the darkness, the minutes passed. Their breaths fell
short and shallow.

"So, Edwin Jack Wayne, whoever you are," Fiona said.
"I'd like to know something before I slip away here. Who is
the man I'm spending the rest of my life with?"

Edwin was quiet.

"Your secret is safe with me," Fiona whispered. "Let's
just say I'll take it to my grave."

Edwin was amazed at Fiona's sense of humor, even in their bleak circumstances.

"Hudson would have liked you," he said. "A lot."

"Who's he?"

"A guy I used to work with. He loved the ladies and they returned the favor times ten. I think he's married now though. Sorry. He's a slacker, anyway."

"Ah well," Fiona coughed. "So then. Who put us here? Why is he after you?"

Edwin let a long beat fall before he spoke. It set up the drama. He needed to shock her - to spike her adrenalin - and focus her on survival.

"Ali is a terrorist," he said. "The chosen one. He is the successor to lead Al Ra'duzma."

"What?" Fiona's body suddenly tightened, shifting the soil. "That man? Who I talked to? Who blew up the teashop and the cottage? Who bought the brush? Who I thought was attra....oh my god, I have no sense whatsoever." She stopped to cough violently.

Edwin continued. "I have been looking for him for years. But he wants to kill me first."

"Why?"

"Because I know who he is. I know what he's done. And he cannot be Leader with that vulnerability."

"What did he do?"

"That's another story," said Edwin. "But believe me. He has been training for his entire life to take over a global network of terror cells. It's called al Ra'duzma, and he has been a long-term project of the prior Leader. He's westernized. By now he knows us too well. He even feels loyalty to some."

"Any...attachments?" she asked.

"Yes. He formed a serious attachment while at college in America and it made him very weak."

"Was she a religious fanatic, too?" asked Fiona.

"Religious?" Edwin scoffed. "This has nothing to do with religion for Ali and his gang. It's about power - and money – and respect. What most criminals really want – he's no different. They're no different. What is different is the scale. Ali wants recognition from the world. Ali wants power over everyone. Starting with me."

Fiona looked shocked. Edwin saw this as progress and continued.

"He betrayed his own people, at their most critical moment. Because of him, a plan to spread pneumonic plague over the East Coast failed. Because of him, his bene-factor, who saved him from an orphan's short and bleak life on the streets of Saudi Arabia, is spending the rest of his life in a U.S. federal prison."

Fiona swore under her breath.

Good, thought Edwin. *Now at least she's stopped writing her own obituary.*

He continued talking. "But here's the thing. None of them knows what he did. I do. And so does she."

"She?" Fiona said.

"The attachment. From college," Edwin said.

"Poor woman," Fiona breathed. "Does she know that he's coming for her, too?"

Edwin thought for a moment. Fiona was right.

"No," he said. "Camille is on her way to Greece for a little rest and relaxation. She has no idea that Ali is ...activated."

Edwin flipped on to his knees and began scratching at the clay.

"Maybe we're not too far from the surface," said Fiona hopefully.

They clawed at the close roof, and at the walls. Small pieces of dirt scraped down on them.

"Look," Fiona said. "This will help, a little. Here's a spoon." She tapped it on the wall. Edwin heard metal scrape dirt. "Gosh, they dug this whole thing with a spoon? Give me that light."

Edwin shone his watch on the object. Fiona spat and rubbed the bottom of the blackened spoon. The crusted dirt fell away, and some metal began to shine.

"This is a silver spoon, and its engraved," she said. "'CWD'. Hmm. Pre-wars. Worth something."

"Nice. They served prisoners meals with silver spoons?"

"They didn't have plastic forks in those days. Still, I would have expected tin. Silver is a bit unusual."

Fiona began feeling around the dark edges of the small space. She felt a ridge, an arc of metal. She scraped at it, and pulled out an object the size of a large rock, but much lighter.

"Ha. Look at this. Here's some tin. It's a bowl, buried in the wall."

"We didn't find any digging tools this whole way, and now at the end, there's a spoon and a bowl," Edwin said.

Edwin leaned his head back against the tunnel's end and coughed. His watch glinted off something. Quartz crystals in the earth, maybe.

Still sitting, he reached up and touched the roof of the tunnel. He tried to pick the bright stone out of the dirt, but it would not budge. He grazed the flat plane with the tips of his fingertips up and down. Dirt slipped away. The bright spot became a circle. A perfect circle in the middle of a flat plane. In one direction, Edwin felt smooth lines. He ran them sideways, and felt rough edges.

"This is a piece of wood," he said. "With a nail head in it. Get on your knees and press your shoulder against it. We'll do it together. Now!"

Fiona focused on the task in front of her.

"One, two, three!"

The old piece of wood would not budge.

"Okay, pull it instead." Edwin said. They gripped the edges. "Now!" It gave on the first try. The wood crumpled onto of them.

Dim light filtered to the spot where they sat but no air came in. A thin layer of waxy material still sealed the opening above them. Edwin scratched it.

"Feels like plastic," Edwin said.

Fiona looked up. "It's got a shape on it. She pushed gently and a section separated. Light and air rushed into the tunnel. They could see the thick brown dust hanging in the air, making them cough.

"Wait a minute," Edwin whispered. "Let your eyes adjust to the light. We don't want to go into that blind."

But, Fiona, squinting, had already stood up and was poking her head up.

"Ha!" Fiona cried.

Edwin pulled her back into the tunnel, covering her mouth. "Stop. You can be heard. We don't have a lot of options for cover. Tell me what you saw."

Fiona's eyes danced. She was giddy. "That covering is old linoleum. I saw shelves. I saw cans on the shelves. I saw long rolls of cling film and tin foil."

Edwin looked puzzled. An image of the oil rig's storeroom, after a supply drop, came to his mind.

"We're in a pantry," Fiona explained. "In the big house, I think! The prisoners…they didn't build this tunnel to escape! They dug it to sneak a meal! Probably from the kids who lived on the estate and saw the soldiers as playmates. That's why there's a bowl and spoon here. Not to dig – to dine! That's why it's silver, not tin. A child would not have known the difference. He just would want to help a hungry friend and would have shared what was his own."

"Wait," Edwin said, holding her shoulders. "We're about to walk out through someone's pantry into their home. We need to get out and back to your car without being seen by anyone who may be the slightest bit suspicious of the second unexplained explosion in the neighborhood."

He stared at Fiona in the light. He could see the whites of her eyes, the stirring blue, in a face coated with mud. He wiped his thumb gently against her cheekbone.

"And you are covered with dirt."

"Usually, pantries are off of kitchens," Fiona said. "And kitchens in houses like these would have a service entrance. Also known as a discrete exit."

"Good. Wait here." Edwin pulled a ballpoint pen out of his pocket and from its tip popped a thin blade. He sliced slowly through the flap of linoleum. Then he slowly edged up.

He saw this.

Shelves upon shelves upon shelves. Cans of Heinz baked beans and bottles of unopened ketchup and Heinz creamy salad dressing. Jars of mint jelly and raspberry jam and Cumberland berry sauce. Wide tin cans of brightly wrapped Nestle chocolates. Stacks of red and orange jelly jars. Rolls of biscuits, some with chocolate covering. Soups, soups and soups. Jars of granola and cereal boxes lined one next to the other. Pasta curls in clear containers, and glass jars of thick and chunky tomato sauce. Cadbury's Flake chocolate bars, Cadbury's Caramello. Cookies and biscuits blended with confection. Boxes of cider and cranberry juices.

And, as Fiona had said, rolls of aluminum foil, and transparent, plastic cling film.

Edwin reached into his backpack and extracted a roll of duct tape.

A few moments later, Fiona crept across the quiet kitchen, her dirty feet swaddled in clingy plastic wrap and duct tape. No one was there. The deep blue AGA stove warmed the room gently. A large oval table filled the center of the large room. Sparkling brass kitchen implements and horse brasses decorated the walls. Windows over a large split sink showed a view through massive trees of the farm giving way to a duck pond, and growing barley fields rolled gently into one another. Breezes smoothed their light green tops, gusting from one patch to another.

Fiona lifted the latch on the heavy oak door and it swung on well-oiled hinges. She stood in the servants' hall, two feet from the door that led outside, past the garbage cans, and the road that would wind through the farm buildings back to the public way.

"Edwin, come. Hurry!"

Edwin did not appear.

Just then the latch on the door to next room began to rattle.

Fiona shrank back, softly closing the door. Standing in the servants' hall, her feet wrapped in cling film, but otherwise covered with dirt from head to toe, Fiona peered through the edge of the curtain that covered the glass pane of the door.

Into the kitchen walked the man they had passed on the road, his tired, wet dog loping beside him.

"Poor boy," said the man to his dog, taking his cap off and smoothing his thatch of thick white hair. "Warm yourself up. Bed."

The dog padded straight to the brown mat that lay in front of the AGA, the wide, deep cast iron stove that always held a different temperature in each of its four ovens, and added a constant comfort of warmth to the kitchen. The dog circled and lay down in a curl, with a heavy sigh.

The man lifted the shiny lid of the hottest burner and slid a tin teakettle on its steel plate. Soon it began to steam.

Fiona barely breathed when the dog picked up his nose. He stood up, and walked toward the pantry door.

"Oh no," she whispered.

The dog wagged his tail.

"You know what's in there, don't you, old boy," said the man. "You want a bickie?" said the man. "Well, I don't know about that."

He selected a tea bag from a china canister. When the teapot rattled, he picked it up and poured hot water over the teabag. He dropped in a teaspoon of sugar, and stirred with a bright silver teaspoon.

Fiona could just read the engraving. Three letters: C. W. D. She gasped.

The dog whined at the pantry door, scratching it with a paw.

"Off," ordered the man. "Here."

He spoke in short clear commands. The dog turned abruptly and gazed at his master.

The man sat down in a chair by the oblong oak table that filled the center of the kitchen and held a tea biscuit near his chest.

"Hup," he said. "Poor hungry thing. What else am I to do?"

A woman's voice called from the other side of the door.

"Darling, could you give me a hand?"

The eighty-pound Labrador, with greying eyebrows and beard, put his forepaws on his master's lap. He waited.

"Don't you tell on me, you naughty devil," said the man to his old friend, who eyed the biscuit, and promised his soul. "Go on then, greedy boy. Now, bed."

The dog mouthed the biscuit and took it to his lair on the warm brown mat.

Then the man drank his tea. When it was empty, he pushed his palms on the table and stood carefully. He walked stiffly to the steps leading from the kitchen, his dog a half step behind him.

The kitchen was empty. Steam hissed from the teapot.

The door to the pantry cracked open a quarter of an inch.

Edwin peered out. Fiona saw that his cheeks were bulging. Chocolate smeared his upper lip and honey colored crumbs stuck to his lips.

"Let's go!" Fiona whispered. Edwin ran through the kitchen with his feet swaddled in cling film and duct tape. Fiona held the door open. He clutched a roll of biscuits his hand. Cadbury's Caramello bars stuck out of his dirty jeans pocket.

"What on earth?" she said.

"Eat when you can," Edwin said, chewing. He swallowed. "Let's get on grass."

They snuck behind a low wall of Cotswold stone, built from flat slates carefully stacked. A livestock gate barred the old Roman road, two ancient gullies carved by old wooden wheels and now horse and footpaths, where anyone had right to walk on a beautiful spring evening. White sheep, some with black faces, grazed in clumps. Farther off the rapeseed fields bloomed swatches of brilliant yellow, and stray red poppies stitched the edges of the road, where wind fell and left their seeds.

The grass swallowed their footprints. Fiona broke into a run, but Edwin put his hand on her arm.

"Slowly," he said, forcing them both to walk casually down the hill toward the cottage. "Everything chases a running rabbit."

Fiona's car was still where they left it, shielded by the tractor.

The empty cottage appeared unaffected by the explosion that had blown through the root cellar.

Fiona and Edwin got into the car, and drove away from the cottage along the narrow road alongside the fields fenced in by flat, delicately stacked stones.

The car's reflection filled the wide side-view mirror attached to the tractor's door.

From beside the tractor, Ali watched through the large side mirror until the car turned at the edge of the estate.

He dropped the heavy shovel to the ground.

"Stupid woman! Why did you get in the way?" Ali said.

Ali looked at the silver hairbrush in the sealed clear plastic bag.

I spent half my time getting the carrot in hand, and as a bonus this silver hairbrush relic. Edwin, for the moment, just for the moment, I will allow you to wait.

Ali held a piece of paper. It was a map. There were two hastily drawn blue marks. Once circled the Oxford train station. The other was around a laboratory, called Oxford Genetics Labs.

He could be there in twenty minutes. He had no time to spare.

Ali had to know.

CHAPTER TWENTY-FOUR

1:00 p.m. May 23
Upper Chelton, England

Fiona drove down the long driveway of the estate until she caught a glimpse of herself in the rearview mirror. She looked at Edwin. They were covered in dirt.

"Right. We look like chimney sweeps," Fiona said. "And I'm hungry. There's an inn in Upper Chelton where I have a room. I'm afraid your lovely clothes are done for."

Edwin looked in the mirror. She was right. He was streaked with dirt and mud. It was in his eyes, around his nose, shaking out of his hair. Edwin needed to stay forgettable. The sight of a pair who looked like they had just crawled out of their graves would stick in the mind. Raise questions.

Edwin looked at Fiona, sunlight catching her hair, streaks of mud making it browner than blonde.

With me, she's toast. I need to go.

But first, Edwin needed a lot of hot water, and soap. Fiona could make that happen.

Ten minutes later they were back in the main town. They could see fire trucks and police maintaining a yellow-taped perimeter of the teashop.

Edwin caught a glimpse of a man wearing a dark blue jacket and Ray-Bans. He was chewing rapidly on a piece of gum. Dead giveaway.

"The Americans are here. FBI, CIA probably," Edwin said.

"Why would they be here, in little Upper Chelton?" asked Fiona. "Wouldn't they be a bit tied up with Peshawar today?"

Edwin studied the man looking through the wreckage at the teashop. The panel on his blue jacket read "Captain A. Silver."

Edwin said, "They saw Ali go back into the house. They picked him up from the CCTV feed here."

"How is that possible?" asked Fiona.

"Data," said Edwin. "Big Data."

Edwin knew exactly how exposed he was out in the world amidst the security cameras and tracking devices. Crosspathz was his own invention but he had respect for what covert agencies could build with code. His mission was getting harder. The longer it took to get Ali, the more risk one of these cameras would upload his face print and apply one hundred points of green light to each of his unchangeable features. He could not risk much longer the chance they would match his face print and discover they had caught an entirely different animal.

Edwin looked at Fiona and said, "I need you."

Fiona blanched. "Ah. I'm flattered. Oh. Er, in what sense, exactly?"

"To get us cleaned up," Edwin said. "Without anyone noticing. Then I need you to get as far away from me as you can."

The inn was a quarter mile down the high street of Upper Chelton. Its three-story façade was made of honey colored limestone, with sharp-peaked gables and sturdy bay windows. Small wrought iron squares held warped panes of glass. In front of the entrance, a tall iron post raised a coat of arms bearing the words "The Dashing Hound" in black iron. Gift and clothing shops continued the main street façade in the same yellow brick, with wrought iron windows, on either side of the inn.

Fiona turned the car sharply into a narrow driveway, parking next to a dumpster in a tight lot behind the inn. Steps led to a small door. Next to it Edwin saw the flat slats of an industrial vent. The kitchen.

"Stay here," she said. Fiona climbed the steps and slipped through the door.

Edwin twisted around, instinctively looking for two exit routes. He did not like this place. He could not see around the dumpster. He could not see the exit. They were parked in a stone courtyard. The only way out appeared to be through the entrance - an easily blockable one-way driveway that emptied on to the High Street. Two miles from the headquarters of D6.

Suddenly something crashed on the roof of the car, right above Edwin's head. Edwin crouched. He held his pen like a dagger. He would make short work of whatever it was.

Nothing happened.

Edwin's eyes darted around the car. The windshield. The driver's window. The passenger window. The rear window. Back to the windshield.

Still, nothing.

Then Edwin saw, dipping over the top of the windshield, two small black triangles. Next came a small round face and two yellow eyes with a pink nose.

"Oh for - ," Edwin said, when a tabby cat slid down the windshield. "I need hot water. And soap. And food. Then I can figure out where Ali went with that hairbrush, and why."

Fiona, her face clean, and hair scooped up in a cap, appeared through the service exit holding a large key. Edwin followed her up a dimly lit back stairway to the room on the third level.

Blue and yellow flowers covered the walls. A four-poster bed filled the center of the room. A white duvet was puffed across it. Six pillows lay against the headboard. A wool blanket, cornflower blue, was folded across the foot of the bed.

"You first," she said, pushing opening the door to an elegant marble bathroom.

Edwin closed the door. The bathroom had a wide alabaster sink. Against the wall stood three horizontal rails, heating the thick white cotton towels that folded over them. There was no shower in the room. Instead, hot water tumbled from a shiny chrome spout into deep, white tub.

Edwin huffed. He had not had a bath since he was six.

It was a far cry from the oil rig's shower. That was an upright shower with loud tin walls and a metal spout that dripped a thin stream of lukewarm water down over him and down through the grate in the cement floor.

Edwin put a large white towel on the floor next to the tub and stepped in the middle of it. He unlaced his Church's brogues and pulled them off. He moved the shoes to one end and peeled off his filthy cashmere sweater and caked wool trousers, shredded at the knees and elbows, rolling them tightly and placing them next to the shoes. He stepped into the tub water, which quickly turned brown. Then he rolled up the towel around his filthy clothes. There was a little dirt on the floor, but his tracks were gone.

Edwin lay back in the deep porcelain tub and sunk below the surface. The heat went through him. He sat up and reached for the soap: a purple cake molded in a flower and smelling of lavender.

"This is obstreperous," Edwin said, using a favorite word, often incorrectly, for anything that annoyed him. He scrubbed his skin and his hair. He sank beneath the surface again to rinse it.

Under water Edwin did not hear when the bathroom door opened, or moments later, when it shut.

Edwin surfaced, and he lay still in the hot water, breathing the moist clouds of steam. He stood up, the water sluicing off his chest and legs.

Edwin reached for a hot towel, and wrapped it around his waist. He scrubbed his hair roughly with another towel, and then looped it around his neck.

That was when he saw that his clothes were gone.

And my shoes! Zed's shoes!.

He wrapped the towel around his waist and slowly, opened the door to the room.

Fiona sat on the bed. She held the tightened strings of a large plastic bag.

"Your clothes are irretrievably filthy," she said. "These should be about right. For a wealthy client of Finley's."

"Where are my clothes?" Edwin asked.

"Binned it," Fiona said. "All of it. Now it's my turn. Ooh. You smell lovely. Like a spring bouquet. Quite an improvement."

Edwin scowled. Fiona moved past him, pressing her thumb against his clean wrist.

A smudge of fingerprint stayed on his arm.

Fiona closed the door to the bathroom. While she ran a clean bath, Edwin dressed.

He moved as fast as he could, pulling on the tan kha-kis, white t-shirt and blue chambray shirt that Fiona had brought him. He pulled on the loafers.

"No laces." Edwin frowned.

Edwin peered out the window of the room. It opened over the courtyard where they had parked, one floor below. He pushed it open, and jumped up onto an iron railing to the ledge of the dumpster.

The cashmere sweater and wool trousers he could let go. But not the shoes. Not these.

The brogues were not on the pile of garbage. But they were in the steel bin.

They were clinging, suspended, to the side of the dump-ster where their magnets had found metal. Edwin reached in and grabbed the pair of dirty shoes, and stuffed them into the plastic bag Fiona had brought the clothes in.

Edwin looked at the car. He could take it and go. Now was the time to make a clean break from Fiona and find Ali.

"Ali. Where are you?" Edwin muttered. "Why do you need that hairbrush? Most importantly, where are you going next with it?"

But as he put his hand on the car door, the kitchen vent released the smell of roasting meat, steaming vegetables. Edwin was famished. He had not eaten anything except the biscuits in over twenty-four hours.

Edwin had not eaten roasted meat in over ten years. There were some things one avoided when living on an oil rig - lighting a match was one of them. Everything he ate was microwaved or toasted or out of an MRE packet.

"Eat when you can," Edwin said.

When Edwin opened the door to the room, Fiona was clean, and dressed in tight black leggings, a graphic long sleeve t-shirt and a buttonless sweater that opened in the front, dangled to her mid-thigh. She wore short black boots with a low heel.

Edwin could not take his eyes off her.

"Who drew on you?" he said, pointing to her shirt.

Fiona glanced down at her get-up.

"Me, I suppose, thank you," Fiona gave an approving nod to the mirror. "Style. It's important. It makes people think you have something to say, something that's worth listening to. Something….unique."

"I like to have laces on my shoes," Edwin said. "That way they stay on. No matter what."

Fiona looked at Edwin, bewildered.

"Thanks for that," she said. "Now, let's eat. I'm starving."

The pub at the inn was half full. Edwin chose a booth in the back corner. Edwin sat with his back against the wall, facing out, so he could keep a peripheral eye on every other diner and anyone who approached. To elongate his view, he picked up the napkin holder and placed it at the edge of the table, near the aisle, tilted on an angle. The face worked like a side mirror. In its reflection he could see that the waiter was already coming to take their order, his white shirt and black pants stark against the oak paneled walls and heavy wool drapes. He lit the small candle in the middle of the white tablecloth.

"He'll have bangers and mash," Fiona said. "I will as well, thank you. And we'll have two of your strongest cappuccinos. With extra sugar on the side, please."

Fiona smirked at Edwin. "Spare your voice."

Edwin was quite sure Fiona did not know who he was, but she was making it all too clear that she knew who he was not.

"It's been a remarkable day," Fiona said. "Someone tried to blow me up...twice. Got buried. Escaped with a chocolate thief."

Then the humor fell from her face.

"Now I'd like to know who you really are, and why this happened."

Sometimes, Edwin thought, the best place to hide was in a very bright light. Around a spotlight, one could slip away in any direction.

"Obviously, I'm not a wealthy...buyer," Edwin said. In this glare, he painted his second cover. "I'm an operative for the U.S. government. I'm supposed to track him down and bring him in for questioning ... and then back to the U.S. for justice."

Fiona's eyes narrowed. Edwin's answer just led to more questions.

"Hmm," she said. "That's the first time someone has actually told me they were a spy. Bit unusual."

Edwin did not want Fiona to question his newly explained cover for status. So he shined the light on Ali. Real light. Then he would make the most of his unwanted companion's talents.

Three core principles of his combat training came to mind:

1) *Your goal is to kill.*
2) *Everything you can reach is a weapon.*
3) *Nothing is off limits.*

Edwin had at hand an inquisitive specialist in old and rare objects. If pointed in the right direction, she could help. Already she had found the hairbrush, and Ali.

"Ali wants to succeed the Leader of al Ra'duzma and run the whole global terrorist organization. This must have something to do with that. He would not waste time right now running around the English countryside unless it was going to help his bid."

Fiona stared at Edwin.

The waiter arrived with two plates. He put one down in front of Edwin. It held piles of mashed potato, a lump of butter melting on each. Two browned, thick sausages, covered with brown gravy and sautéed onions rested on the side.

Edwin loaded his fork and stuffed it into his mouth. Chewing, he said, "So the real question is this: why does a terrorist – this terrorist - want Hitler's hairbrush?"

Edwin swallowed, cut another slice of sausage, smeared it with mashed potato and soaked the forkful in gravy. He filled his mouth and groaned. "God that's good." He swallowed half of the cappuccino, then, his lip smeared with froth, dug back into the sausages.

"It was disgusting," Fiona said, recoiling at the memory of the cold lines etched on the handle. "It was caked with dust and god knows what. It looked like it had never been cleaned. I cannot even imagine. He wanted it badly enough to drop ten thousand pounds on it." Fiona dipped her head, and drew her brows together.

Confusion, Edwin read in lines of her face.

"What?" he said.

"It's just that…Charles said this same client once paid well over a million pounds – that's close to two million dollars – for the Lopaki Dagger from the Ottoman Empire. He asked Charles to keep it in storage, and it's been there for years. Out of the blue, he texted Charles late last night and demanded to pick it up today. That's why he was at the auction today."

"What's so special about the Dagger?" Edwin asked.

"The jewels," Fiona said. "They are spectacular."

"What's on it?"

"It's actually called the Lopaki Sapphire Dagger because it has four large sapphires in the handle, at least. A ruby. A yellow diamond. Lots and lots of smaller diamonds. All set in eighteen-karat gold."

"Sharp blade. But soft gold. Lousy weapon," Edwin said. "But it would be easy to chip the jewels out."

"Each is very valuable. The piece is an artifact of the Ottoman Empire, but each on their own would fetch a pretty penny," said Fiona.

"So we have a wealthy terrorist gathering up jewels on the immediate verge of his succession," said Edwin. "The Dagger is a bribe. And maybe also a weapon."

"And, he fancies the macabre," Fiona said.

"What's macabre?" Edwin said.

"Dead people's stuff," said Fiona, slicing through the sausage. "How ghoulish."

Edwin replayed in his mind the video he had seen of the Leader's lair. Ali had returned right after the Seal Team had left with the body.

"What do the Leader of a global terror organization and Hitler have in common?"

"They are devil spawn," said Fiona.

"Exactly," said Edwin. "He's not after the hairbrush. He's after the hair. Or the skin follicles. Now he has Hitler's DNA, and the Leader's."

"He has what? The Leader of what?"

"Al Ra'duzma."

"My heavens," said Fiona.

"He must have wanted to get his DNA on something," Edwin said. "That explains why he went back in. It was his absolute last chance."

"What's he going to do with it?" Fiona scoffed. "Build the ultimate Frankenstein?"

"That's not possible," Edwin said. But he had been away for a long time. "Is it?"

"Who knows what they can do with genetics now," Fiona said.

"Someone does," Edwin said. "We need an expert."

"Where do you think he is now?" Fiona asked. "Do you think he's looking for us? Or do you think he's looking for her?"

"For who?" Edwin asked.

"For that woman. His attachment. The other person who knows what he did?"

Edwin smeared his index finger against his empty plate and licked the last salty streak of gravy. Camille.

"Quickly," Edwin said. "We have to go."

Fiona paid the check.

Edwin appeared to be staring at the window, but he was studying the feed through his lenses. Crosspathz fed him views from his butterfly drones, and from the central computer on the oil rig, but the system had lost Ali. Edwin fed the last data he knew: the time and place in latitude and longitude of the cottage where they had escaped through the tunnel.

A large squadron of Edwin's bees was monitoring England. Edwin had more eyes than CCTV. And fortunately, he could also see through any other big data collection system. He would eventually pick up Ali, now that he was on the street. It was only a matter of time.

"He may have jewels, but he's running out of time," Edwin said. "Which means he's wrapping up any loose ends now. We need to find out what he's really up to."

Twenty minutes later, Fiona and Edwin drove into the parking lot of Oxford Technology Partners. She parked the small car next to a building. The sign outside read "Oxford Genetics Labs."

CHAPTER TWENTY-FIVE

3:00 p.m. May 23
Oxford England

Edwin and Fiona walked down the hallway of the office
building. When they reached Office 324, she knocked.
Edwin kept his hat low, his face down. He tried to fade behind her. He wanted the scientist they were about to meet to
remember that Fiona was with someone, but later, when he
would try, he would only recall "hat, average height, brown
hair maybe. Glasses? Not sure." Minds would fill and empty
with so many details of the world swirling past them, that
often the best disguise was simply the one that made the
least impression.

"Dr. ... Bart?" Fiona said, reading the stitching on
his white lab coat. "We're hoping you can help us. We're
researching a story..."

"Screenplay," Edwin said.

"Yes, for a film," Fiona said. "Imagine a guy who's traips-
ing through the countryside gathering up ghoulish items.
Collecting DNA from really bad people ..."

"From killers," Edwin said. "Serial killers."

"Ooh," said Dr. Bart. "And he's going to clone a bad guy
by act two, is he? Or a whole farm of bad guys, perhaps?"

"Could he?" Fiona said. "What could he do with it, really?"

"Clone? A person?" The scientist laughed. "Well, I think right now the best your villain can do is isolate the bad genes, to see what's there. Doing anything with them - like cloning - is much more complex."

"What's a bad gene?" Fiona asked.

Dr. Bart tried to be more helpful. "How about gene therapy? There's been some debate in the community about something called "the Warrior Gene.""

"Warrior gene?" asked Fiona.

"It's a variant on the MAO-A gene. Some humans carry it, and the initial research shows that carriers may be more likely to join gangs, use weapons and even turn out to be some of the most violent gang members," said the scientist. "Perhaps your villain wants to use that, sort of like Gatorade for his troops. Juice up the ones he has already to be more prone to killing and violence. Here's an article on the research."

He handed Fiona a glossy magazine. Just then someone knocked at his door.

"Excuse me for a moment." Dr. Bart said. He stood up, leaving Fiona and Edwin alone in his office.

"Eesh," said Edwin. "I hope they have Jack the Ripper's grave site under lock and key."

"They don't," said Fiona. "They never figured out who he actually was. Some fanatics think "he" might even have been a "she." But just imagine if dead did not mean gone forever. Gravesites would be under lock and key."

"Hairbrushes too," said Edwin. His mind raced. "Ali may be tapped to be the successor, but he still has to prove he's worth it to the other tribal leaders. Maybe this gene therapy sauce is part of his bid. Whatever he's doing here, though, he must be getting help from someone. He's got a base some-where. And local support. We need to find his support fast."

"I...I'm not sure I can help with that," said Fiona. "I'm better with found objects than lost people."

"True," Edwin said. "We don't need an auctioneer. We need a spy."

And not just any spy, Edwin thought. He needed the spy who, the bees told him, had recently boarded a ferry to an island off the Greek mainland. The spy who accidentally uncovered what Ali had once done to betray the organiza-tion he now set out to lead. The spy who liked to sit behind her desk, far away from the action in the field, until one day the CIA named her a conspirator to commit domestic terror and treason against the United States, naming her Public Enemy Number 1. That was when, years ago, Edwin had saved her for the first time.

Many years earlier, Edwin had watched Camille, his new recruit, as they sped across the Chesapeake Bay outside Washington, D.C. in a high power motorboat Edwin had bought in cash off a dock. It had been only a few hours since Edwin had rescued Camille from an interrogation room in the CIA, and so far they had evaded capture by the FBI, the CIA's Office of Special Services, and the D.C. Metropolitan police. They had only their own running lights as com-pany across the dark expanse of water. But Edwin knew that would not last, not on this touchy evening, hours after the worst terrorist attack on American soil, when airplanes were grounded, every odd sighting subject to search, and every person in America was on high alert. Not when every American security force had just been given a picture of

Camille, and a shoot-to-kill order, for this alleged terrorist consort.

Camille sat in the corner of the cockpit of the powerful motorboat. She gripped a cleat that was bolted on to the deck. Her face had lost its ruddy complexion. She had gone very white.

Edwin saw a small cove, its white strip of beach stark against the dusk. They did not have time for this. But the lesson had to happen.

Edwin slowed the boat and took it in to very shallow water where he idled the engine, than ran up to the bow and tossed the anchor. He returned to the cockpit and pushed the throttle in reverse gear. The boat backed down on the anchor.

"I know one thing, Camille," Edwin said, glaring at her. "Before this is over, you are going to get caught. You are going to get tied up. Maybe by the good guys. Maybe by the bad guys. Both think they have pretty good reasons to do it. It will happen."

"What?" Camille wailed. "What's going to happen to me?"

Edwin heard her fear surface. That was good. Any survival skills he taught her now would bind to that raw fear, and they would come out along with the fear when she felt it again.

"So treat it as fact," Edwin said. "And prepare. To the beach!"

Edwin dropped his jeans and pulled on swim trunks over his boat shoes. In a swing of his arms, Camille was around his shoulders like a yoke. He jumped into the water. She shrieked. But she did not get wet. The water only reached Edwin's waist. He trudged through it for fifteen yards until he deposited Camille on her feet in the sand.

For the next thirty minutes, Edwin taught Camille three skills of hand-to-hand combat. How to plant one's feet for optimal balance. How to compromise an opponent's weight and force to use it against them. And one more.

Camille was covered in sand. Edwin wrinkled his lips. He pushed his tongue to the side of his cheek and rolled it forward. A small nail stuck through his teeth.

"You keep these on you. Always. Very useful tools. Keep one in the tips of your shoelaces. One in your cheek, but don't swallow it. Let me see your palms."

Edwin flipped over her hand. He smoothed his thumb across it.

"No. Too soft. If you had callouses like mine you could keep one right thee in the hard skin."

"How about my heel?" said Camille. "Walking around in flats all summer turned all those blisters into rocks. My pedicure lady tries to go after them with a razor."

"Excellent!" cried Edwin, squatting back on his heels. "That's even better than a hand. They check your palms and they take off your shoes. But they don't expect the backs of your heels to be packing."

Edwin watched Camille kick off her shoe and produce the advertised callus.

"Whoa, nelly!" he said.

"Gross, I know," she said.

"No," Edwin said. "Fabulous."

"So, like this?" Camille said. She took the small nail and slipped it slowly into the hard skin on the back of her heel. Not even a wince. Camille beamed.

"Your shoes must really suck," Edwin said. But he was pleased. The terrified rag he had carried to the beach, paralyzed by the many scenarios she could conjure for being caught and restrained, now sat upright on Edwin's shoulders as he waded back to the boat. She had had a creative survival idea. The fight instinct just might have a chance.

They pulled out of the harbor alone in the dark. But neither state would last for long.

Years later, the day after the United States had killed the Leader of al Ra'duzma, Edwin's bees told him that Camille Henderson was exploring a different beach, this one on a Greek island. He had to find her before Ali did.

In the Oxford Genetics Lab, Edwin took Fiona by both shoulders.

"Stay with Dr. Bart," Edwin said fiercely. "Find out everything you can about this MAOA gene variant, what could be in that hairbrush, and what Ali would have to do to make the gene variant useful. I'll be back. In a few hours."

"Where will we meet?" Fiona asked. "You will...you'll come back, right?"

Edwin glared at her. There was still a streak of mud behind her ear.

"Focus," he said sharply. "You have one goal. Find out what this Ali can do with this hairbrush and what he can do with any warrior gene. Why would he stop now to do this? It does not make sense yet. You will make sense of it."

"But where are –" Fiona began.

"Stop," Edwin said. His grip hurt, and it surprised her. "You will think of nothing else. Not where I am. Not when I'll be back. Solve your task only. Here's why: anything else you do in the next hours is a distraction. Distraction will defeat you. If you lose focus, innocent people will die.

"You will solve only this: What can Ali do with this gene? What is he trying to do? Why is it so important to him? Fiona, focus. You will be a hero."

Fiona blanched. Then she turned sharply and went back into the office of the DNA expert to wait for him to return and find out what Ali could possibly be doing with Hitler's hairbrush and a terrorist's relic. And she would think of nothing else.

Fiona felt a surge of adrenalin. Her mind was clear. It was like waiting behind the curtain for the bell that was about to announce the start of the most important auction of her life.

From the hallway, Edwin watched the door swing on its hinge.

Just before the door closed, Edwin opened his palm. A small bee scooted in to the room behind Fiona. It settled in the shadows, absorbing images of its surroundings through each panel of its multifaceted eyes. Edwin pushed through the door to the stairwell and climbed three flights to the top of the roof. He twisted the dial of his watch. In six minutes, he felt a breeze. He could see and hear nothing. But when the breeze stopped, he walked forward two paces into the view of the buildings he had been watching until he felt the special metal surface of his helicopter that landed to meet him.

In the echoing stairwell, the door closed. A man was leaning against the wall behind it. His hair was black, and hung low over his eyes. In his hand he clutched a small zipped leather satchel. Without moving, he watched Edwin lunge up the stairs, and take the turn. He checked his watch.

"It's close to the witching hour," said Ali. "One day since the succession clock began. One day until I must be at the summit. What I have planned even trumps what I will eventually do to you, Edwin. Although the third time's always the charm."

Once he heard the door to the roof close, Ali walked to the hallway door. He pulled it open. In less than a minute Ali had his hand on the doorknob of the same office where Dr. Bart was explaining to Fiona Tate how gene therapy worked.

Ali hung at the door for a moment, overhearing this exchange.

"So, with the right gene then, someone could theoretically inject a group of young men and juice them up," said Dr. Bart.

"You mean, make them even more violent?" said Fiona.

"All of them. Yes," he said.

"Or even, with an army of them?" Fiona asked, her voice rising. She felt a chill thinking of videos of furious young men in the desert, rifles overhead, fabric around their faces, with a genetic encouragement to be the most violent shot into them, like breeding particularly angry bulls.

"Yes, it could be used…therapeutically, if you will, to reduce the likelihood of any soldier feeling human empathy."

"Reduce?" Fiona asked. "Or even erase it altogether?"

"Possibly," said the doctor. "It's theory, of course. If I could prove that, I'd surely get my knighthood. 'Sir Henry Bart.' I like the sound of that."

At that moment, the door to the office swung open. Fiona and Dr. Bart turned to the familiar wheeze of the well-oiled hinge.

Ali stood in the doorway.

Fiona felt her heart begin to race. But then her fingers closed reflexively in a tight fist, as if gripping the handle of a heavy wooden hockey stick.

"Focus," recited Fiona under her breath. "Ask more questions."

This helped clear her mind and prepare for battle. What did he want to do with this? Who better to tell her?

Ali was furious. There she was again. "You shut up," he said. "I have some questions for this man. Then I will deal with you."

An hour later, Ali grabbed Fiona by the shoulders and opened the door of Lab 243. Fluorescent nightlights hummed in the empty pale hallways of the Oxford Genetics Labs. He pushed Fiona forward.

"I told you to get away from that café!" Ali shouted, his fingers digging into Fiona's arm. He hustled her down the hall to the elevator.

"You also told me to buy your friend a coffee with four sugars," Fiona said. "You might have included a suffix... something like... 'before the tea shop blows to high heaven.' Something like that would have been nice."

Ali listened for a shake in her voice. He heard none.

"I told you to get away from the café. That's what I told you to do after you bought the coffee. It was a simple instruction. I thought the Finley's team was always so good at following simple instructions," Ali said.

They were outside now, walking swiftly down the street.

Fiona put her free hand in her jacket pocket, and folded it around something small. A few strides later she discretely removed her hand, and let the object fall to the sidewalk. She put her hand back in her pocket for several more steps, then repeated the motion.

"If you had listened, you would be fine. Instead you ... now you have to come with me. There is no alternative. None," said Ali.

"Where are we going?" Fiona said.

Ali did not respond as he strode quickly down the street, his fingers gripping her elbow until they reached Oxford Station.

Fiona saw Ali check his watch, check it again.

"Are we late for something?" she asked.

"Nearly," Ali said. "Just, come, please. We have some trains to catch."

Ali bought first class seats on the next trains to St. Pancras Station. There they would switch to the Eurostar and travel beneath the English Channel to Paris. He and Fiona sat side by side as the high-speed rail journey began. She glanced at his knees. They were caked in dry brown dirt.

Fiona was scared, but she did not show it with a tremor in her words. That, she would never do again.

Instead Fiona asked questions.

"How did your trousers get so filthy?" she said.

Ali did not reply. Fiona studied the dirt. He had tried to brush it off but it was embedded into the fibers of the dark trousers. He had been kneeling in the dirt. She glanced at his fingernails. They had sharp, freshly trimmed edges.

The dirt was the same rich brown she and Edwin had washed down the drain at the inn hours earlier.

"Were you ... trying to dig us out?" she asked.

"No," Ali muttered. "It's two hours to Paris. Twenty minutes under the seabed. Only twenty minutes."

"Paris," thought Fiona. "Not how I'd hoped to see the Eiffel Tower next."

Then she thought of Edwin. How would he ever find her?

CHAPTER TWENTY-SIX

5:15 p.m., May 23
Paris, France

"*Le Burger Tres Grand*," ordered Rolf Valet. "*Oui, avec des frites.*" The fast food restaurant on the Champs de Lye was crowded. Rolf was in his mid-fifties, and heavy for a Frenchman. His daily trips to the fast food chain made him look more like an American than his compatriots, who satisfied themselves with a croissant, real butter, and rich espresso.

Rolf held his tray, looking for a place to put it down. His watch said 9:03 pm; the plastic seats in bright orange, yellow and red – colors that someone learned stimulated the appetite and which now branded most fast food settings - were all full. But the hard seats discouraged lingering.

He made his way to the condiment table, eyeing the tables. He pushed a lever to fill ketchup pots. He snagged a handful of salt packets, popped the tops and shook them over his fries. He folded a few into his mouth.

Then Rolf saw a seat open when a man stood up, rather quickly.

He carried his tray over. He was so intent on grabbing the seat that he did not notice the man he took it from was in some distress. He sat down, unwrapped his burger, and took a large bite. He closed his eyes and chewed. The chewy meat and salty juice tasted good. The bun was springy and sweet. It was exactly what he expected. Exactly what he got every day. He took another bite and another. He grabbed a handful of the *pommes frites*, dipped the fries into a thick squeeze of sweet, savory ketchup. He folded them into his mouth.

Rolf was on his third fistful of fries when he took his eyes off his food and noticed something was very wrong. The man who had vacated the seat was still in the shop. But he was leaning heavily on the rubbish can, his lips frothing.

Rolf took another bite, slowly.

Then the man by the garbage fell. Someone cried out. The man heard shrieks, and soft cries, and moans.

Rolf stopped eating. He looked around, and watched as one by one, five other people fell to the floor. They writhed in pain; their mouths bubbling white. Then they each lay still.

"*Mon Dieu!*" he cried.

That was when his stomach lurched. He felt like something inside his gut was cutting its way out.

The coroner received the first phone call, then the second, then the third. Later, the news would report that within minutes of one another, hundreds of patrons at twelve different fast food restaurants around Europe had collapsed, frothed at the mouth, and died shortly thereafter.

Coroners later found that in each one, salt packets plucked from the condiment tray had been laced with cyanide.

CHAPTER TWENTY-SEVEN

3:30 p.m., May 23
Upper Chelton, England

Crime scene spotlights bore down on the rubble of the teashop.

Ascher Silver kicked a pile of dusty plaster and separated rocks with his boot. Picked up a piece of twisted black metal in his Gore-Tex gloves. He examined it closely.

"It's an espresso spout," he said to the man next to him, as they pored through the rubble of the teashop in a small village in the Cotswolds. The store had exploded for no reason, about two miles from the spot where a face print-matching program had identified the individual who had gone back into the house in Peshawar moments after the Seal Teams left with the corpse of the former Leader of al Ra'duzma.

Ascher frowned.

"This is a long way from Peshawar, and very soon after the take down. Assuming the program is right – which it probably is not - what would have made this individual bolt for England right when the succession sequence must have begun?"

"The technology is pretty good," said his partner.

"It's not perfect," said Ascher. "It never is perfect."

Nonetheless, there he was, picking through smoking parts, chips of pottery, broken glass, and bent stainless steel.

Suddenly phones began ringing and beepers went off.

Ascher grabbed his phone.

"Silver," he said. "What's up?"

"There's been another attack," said the voice. It was the analyst for the Agency's Europe desk. "A big one, in Paris, Belgium, Munich. Cyanide-laced salt capsules dropped at burger joints. Go secure."

Ascher plugged a long string of numbers into his phone. It whined back at him like he had dialed an old fax machine. Then it engaged again. The line was secure.

"Someone named Usman of Pakistan is claiming responsibility," said the analyst. "The press is calling it the 'Burger Bomb.'"

"Is this our guy?"

"No," said the analyst. "I'm sending you the picture. Totally different guy. But HUMINT says he's now a main contender for the succession."

"How did you get this picture?"

"Al Jazeera had it a minute after the calls started coming in from the restaurants. It's like a marketing strategy sequence:. surprise, impact, owner, image."

"So is our guy working for this Usman?"

"Don't know. Maybe they are rivals."

Silver whistled. "How many contenders are there?"

There was a long pause.

"We don't really know, sir. This attack, now, seems to indicate that a ...competition may be under way."

Ascher swore under his breath. "It's going to be open season. They're all going to try to earn it."

"What, the top job?"

"The face of fear," said Ascher.

"Look on the bright side, sir," said the analyst. "They'll probably try to kill each other off, too."

"Well, there's that," he said, exasperated.

"Yes. Works for the mafia."

"Stay on this," Ascher said. "I don't like this westward movement, so quickly. England. France. What the hell are they doing here? Who are we looking for?"

"Yes, sir," said the analyst.

"I'm going to France," said Ascher.

On the second of his three pre-paid mobile phones, Ali watched media reports as the train raced. The picture Al Jazeera released of the self-proclaimed Burger Bomber made him shake.

There in front of the world, proving his claim to succeed the Leader, and admitting to the mass murder of scores of westerners in multiple European countries, was none other than Usman.

Usman. The messenger. Ali's house boy in Peshawar.

Traitorous swine. He's been watching my every move. He knows my plan and he has used everything I knew to outflank me. Bold and sinful little traitor.

Ali breathed in very deeply. This helped him draw the energy from his fury and concentrate it like a primed weapon.

Usman was only ahead for the moment. He did not know about Rais Abdullah, because Ali did not know about the Influencer until the last moment. Usman did not know where he was. And Ali had his address.

Still, the boldness of Usman's attack worried Ali. He must believe he had plenty of support to make such a move.

Ali paced, rapidly assessing the strength of his position against his competitors.

Did his shaming tattoo work enough punishment on Imad to guarantee his fear of worse reprisals should he displease Ali? Did the Sheikh truly believe he will have the carrot for him? Or were they all hedging their bets until the very last moment?

The answer became clear.

It does not matter. I simply must get the Influencer in my pocket, irrevocably and before anyone does more damage to me.

Ali's mind clicked through the steps of his new plan. He would be prepared. He would deal with Usman. But one thought still rankled.

What does Badi Badi have yet in store?

Without knowing, Ali prepared his counter attack. He did not need to know exactly what Badi Badi would do to sully him, because he knew this:

Badi Badi just needed to inflame the insecurities of the decision makers, and pin the cause on Ali.

The same strategy could work for Ali.

Part Three

CHAPTER TWENTY-EIGHT

9:30 p.m., May 23
Skyros, Greece

The narrow path wound up the steep slope to the top of the island, between the close, white-washed stone houses. Goats pulling carts were the only vehicles allowed. Older women, dressed in black, sat in the doors of their homes for hours, and watched.

Camille Henderson picked her way carefully over the cobblestones until she reached a small café. It had three small tables tucked between the wall of the café and the path. Her calves strained from the incline, and the long walk up from the beach where the hotels and clubs collected most of the tourists. When she arrived at the tiny restaurant, she inhaled deeply and let out a long breath. The lights twinkled in strings draped along the canopy. Between pairs of faces tipped toward one another, candles glowed in yellow tins on the white tablecloths. It was prime dinner hour.

"Just for one," Camille said to the host, a lanky young man.

He smiled, and directed her to a small table under the awning. The lamp lit a bright line on his thick black hair.

"Not for long, I am sure," he winked. "A pretty woman soon finds company on Skyros. You'll see."

Charmer, thought Camille.

He placed the menu down on a small table. It had two seats.

Camille chose the one with her back to the restaurant wall. Since her field training, she could not select a seat without reciting the rules of tradecraft. Always protect your blind side. Always find two exits before sitting down.

Camille put her large satchel down on the paved patio next to her chair. She wore a long black drape of a dress that touched the top of her woven sandals. Lamplight bounced off the whitewashed houses that lined the cobblestone path. She noticed a young, dark haired couple next to her, leaning forward on their elbows. Periodically one or the other would tap the ash off the end of a burnt cigarette.

Camille inhaled deeply. The acrid smell of smoke reminded her of Matilda, and her stern counseling sessions on the balcony, years ago.

"Get over him!" Matilda had ordered.

Matilda. She was such an interesting friend, all these years. It was time to answer the question she had asked, the one that made Camille seek out this island, and a moment to think.

"The Picasso...and all that comes with it," sighed Camille. "I could not have thought more highly of anyone, Matilda, and it still turns out that I underestimated you."

When Camille first met Matilda, Camille was a young, single woman living in D.C. She had thought she was just lucky to live in the same apartment building with a woman, in the tenth decade of her life, who was so engaged with the status of the world's most vulnerable, and its most powerful.

"Ha!" Camille had scoffed. "And I thought I was looking in on you."

Just then, Camille noticed an old woman watching her across the path from the cafe. She was dressed in black, the uniform she had worn every day since her husband had died, and what she would wear every day, until she joined him.

Camille thought the woman looked at her. The woman's expression slid into on a long, disapproving frown. Suddenly, she tipped her chin up. Something above the dark roof of the café had caught her attention. Then, a few minutes later, she returned to her needlepoint.

The watching widows on this island knew all, especially she who lived across from the local cafe.

Between ordering her meal and receiving it, space fell where Camille had, for the first time in a long while, not a thing to do. She had no one to talk to. The Agency had given her three days free on a Greek island, supposedly to rest. Ironically, this order became cover for action for her actual purpose: to think about the offer Matilda had made, and decide whether to take it.

What would she do with that Picasso, and all that came with it? The gift would change her life. It was an unfathomable fortune which brought with it immense responsibility.

Camille felt suddenly unmoored without the magnet of necessity ordering her choices. Her thoughts began to race, so she practiced breathing deeply, in then out. Eventually she became fully present in her new, empty schedule.

The waiter arrived with a plate full of a doughy, round, grilled pita, layered with slices of spiced meat that had been shaved off the stacked layers of meat that rotated upright on a spit. The souvlaki was covered with fresh chopped tomatoes and red onions. A nest of thin, crispy fried potatoes filled the plate. There was a side bowl of tangy, cool tzatziki sauce.

Camille went first for the sauce, a salty blend of yogurt, garlic and cucumber. She scooped a dollop of the white sauce onto the souvlaki. She glanced around. Then she folded the thick pita and took a large, unladylike bite. Pieces of slick tomato and yogurt sauce slid out over her pinky fingers.

Across the cobblestones, the old widow watched. Camille ignored her. She raised the preposterously stuffed souvlaki to her lips for another bite. It was so good.

Still chewing, Camille put the food down on her plate, and bent to look for the napkin that had slipped off her lap.

But when she looked up, her plate was empty. The food was gone.

A man now sat in the chair across the table. His mouth was completely stuffed. His bright green eyes danced. Camille noticed they had a slight yellowish tinge at the edges of the irises.

His skin was tight against his cheekbones. His hair was dark brown and longer across the brow. He wore khakis, and a buttoned-down blue shirt.

"Edwin?" Camille whispered. She had not seen him in many years, not since he had left her in a Cambridge multi-family house, with the terrorist Khalid al Hamzami, "Uncle" to Ali, bound in duct tape. As she focused on his face, Camille's thoughts ran.

Did he know that she had used the tricks he had taught her on that beach, that she had used the thin-gauge nail to escape a murderer's assault and send a terror mastermind to prison for the rest of his life?

Edwin could not know that to this day, on this Greek island, she still wore a sharp thin nail in the callous her work shoes built. Just as he had taught her to do on a beach on the Chesapeake Bay years before.

Edwin could not know that, because of him, Camille had left her analyst job, left the safety of a CIA desk job, to join the field operatives. That now, she worked with the unseen colleagues who ate lunch on the other side of the divider in Langley's cafeteria.

Edwin could not possibly know that Camille now sat on the brink of another profound decision. So why was he here?

Camille gaped at Edwin. Here was a man she'd spent only a few hours with - from the time he sprung her from the wrong side of an interrogation room in the CIA, swept her down a heating duct into a mulch pit and out of the CIA's protective fencing in a trash truck, through Union Station and Wal-Mart and a fast cruise up the eastern seaboard to Boston. Here was the man who saved her life, and in less than forty-eight hours, changed it forever.

And now, here he was years later, appearing out of nowhere to eat her dinner.

The waiter floated by. He lifted the empty plate in front of his patron's new guest.

"Shall I bring you another order?" he asked.

Edwin flashed two fingers. The waiter nodded and disappeared. He returned with two full plates, and a small copper pitcher of Retsina, a local white wine with the flavor of pine sap.

"On me," said the waiter. "You see, I told you Skyros would not leave a beautiful woman alone for long."

"Water," Edwin said. "For us both."

When the waiter left, Camille leaned over the table.

"Edwin!" Camille said. "What are you... how did you? Am I in - ?"

She looked around frantically. Despite her field training, color rose fast on her chest and cheeks. "The last time you appeared without warning, I was answering questions while strapped to a board, heels higher than my head, listening to a tap start to run water through a hose."

"No," Edwin said. "You're not in trouble. But you will be. And I am now. I need your help."

Camille patted her chest rapidly. "Okay, well, phew, that's a relief, sort of," she said. "What kind of help?"

Edwin watched her. There was an unusual quality to being in her presence. This woman knew something about him. That he once lived, before the oil rig, before he ceased to exist. He did have a history. She bore witness to it. Suddenly, sitting across from Camille, Edwin felt like he had just put his frozen fingers over a heater. His veins were cracking as the heat rushed through them.

Briefly, silence fell between them. The vacuum made Camille talk.

"I'm in the field now. I'm an operative."

"I know," Edwin said.

"You do?" she asked. "How?"

"I've kept tabs on you," Edwin said.

"I don't even want to ask," Camille said. "How?"

"Bugs. And software. Software bugs," Edwin said. "So they sent you on three days R&R. Must have done something good."

"Why are you here...now?" Camille said.

Edwin waved her off.

"Your old friend. Yassir – Ali – whatever - is stirring things up," Edwin said. "I've been watching him. Also."

Camille picked up a salt packet and ripped the top off it.

Edwin's fingers clamped down on her wrist. He twisted it, and put his other hand under hers. He poured the salt packet into it. Then he chucked it over his left shoulder.

"Salt's not good for you," he said.

"Why?"

"You're really off-line out here?" Edwin said. He pushed her satchel toward her with his foot. "Turn it on."

Camille reached into her bag and retrieved a mobile phone. She punched a long series of digits into it. The long code provided her access to a secure stream of reports.

She gasped.

"Ohh...They hit twelve restaurants in Paris, in Brussels, and Munich, beginning at 8:03 p.m. GMT with cyanide-laced salt packets? One hundred and thirty-two dead."

"That's not going to be the end of it," Edwin said.

"How do you know? They usually strike simultaneously, not in succession. Twelve at the same time – that should make someone's point."

"Yes. Someone's," Edwin said. "But not someone else's."

"I don't follow you."

"The Leader of Al Ra'duzma is dead," Edwin said.

"Yes. That I do know," Camille said. "Quite well."

It was private boast, but Edwin caught it. He would follow that up but first he needed Camille's complete attention.

"So now there will be succession," Edwin said. "They will fight for it. Whoever wants the mantle will have to earn it. They'll have to become terror to lead it, like the previous Leader did –"

"That scraggly beard, that frozen gaze fixed on his fiery future," Camille said.

"Yes. We can all see his face - every one of us on this planet who lives near a television or computer screen," said Edwin. "And your old friend is into this one, too, up to his neck. Again."

Camille shook her head. "No...not...Yassir?"

"His name is Ali Hamini," Edwin said. "As you know. And yes. He was there the night they killed the Leader."

"Where?"

"In the Leader's house. In Peshawar. I saw him," Edwin said, his green eyes fierce.

"How did you-" Camille frowned.

"The same software we used to find him in Cambridge," said Edwin. "But a few versions improved. Like forty."

"He was in the Leader's house?" Camille said. "Living there?"

"Unclear," said Edwin. "But he knew the layout well enough to go back in – and he needed to go back in badly enough – in the seconds after the Seals flew off and before the Pakistani security service came in."

"Why? What was in there? Treasure? Proof of guilt?"

"Maybe the Leader's will," said Edwin. "He only had one thing to pass on."

"The crown," said Camille.

"Yes," said Edwin. "And since then, Ali has taken some steps."

"Oh, Yassir," said Camille, shaking her head, remembering a friend from another pocket of time.

"No. No. His name is Ali. Whoever he was with you at Yale was…"

"An act," Camille said sadly. "I know…it was just a performance."

"Yes. It was just part of his uncle's plan then," Edwin said. "He was a pawn that chose – chose – to turn knight, and is now making a play for king. And the plan now - whatever it is - is already in motion. Get this - within hours of the take down, Ali was in England. And there's more."

"What could be more?" asked Camille.

"He's baiting me," Edwin said. "He stood outside – somewhere – where he knew he'd be seen by the cameras that feed a network that is non-trivial to hack, but not impossible. He stood in a certain place where he could very well guess that facial recognition software could catch him. And that I would see him. And he bet that I'd come get him."

"That's a lot of leaps," said Camille.

"Not so many," said Edwin. "He was standing outside the UK office of D6. That was my company. My cover, I mean."

"Where he used to work for you?" Camille asked. "So what did you do?"

"I bit. I went there. He tried to kill me today," Edwin said. "Twice."

"What? Ach. I guess I still have trouble with my Yassir being your Ali," Camille said. She still resented the collision between her fantasy of how things had been and the disturbing, repeated confirmation of how they actually were.

"Get over it. Quickly. Yassir was just his cover. Just a cover. Covers aren't real," Edwin insisted.

"Felt real," Camille said.

"It's not," Edwin snapped. "Not really. Underneath it all, it's just cover. How can a cover ever be more?"

"Really? D6 is still trading on the NASDAQ last I checked." Edwin shifted in his chair.

"Look. Two people know what Ali did to mess up the last attacks. Me. And you. The wheel of succession is now in motion. Since it started rolling, he has deliberately lured me to a place where he set a trap and tried to kill me. He missed. He tried again. You have to be prepared."

Camille looked confused. "Why?"

"Because he's coming for you, too," Edwin said. "You know what he did. You can expose him and defeat his plan to become the successor. You have to see him coming. And you must help me get to him first."

Camille's eyes opened wide as she listened. Her cheeks went pale under her freckles.

"We don't have much time," Edwin said. "There's a twist. Ali thinks he's the chosen one. But someone else wants the job and they are going to prove they deserve it."

"Starting with the mass poisonings."

"At least."

"Did he do that?" Camille said softly. "Yas…Ali?"

Edwin shook his head sharply. "I don't think so. Someone named Usman of Pakistan has claimed it. And that's exactly what has me worried. Because now Ali – and anyone else who wants it – has to outdo the Burger Bomb. He knows it. And he's up to something."

"What?"

"He must be making his own case. And he's in England. Maybe on his way somewhere else. Somewhere nearby. Europe actually makes sense for the succession. It's the hardest place for Americans to watch them with drones."

"So one might think," said Camille. "We have to find Ali."

Edwin noticed that she no longer referred to this man by the name she had originally known. Yassir was the love of her life. Not Ali.

He was getting somewhere. So he struck.

"I know where the succession is going to be," Edwin said. "They're all going to be there. All of the tribal leaders."

"Where?"

"In Europe. Ali is in England. Or was. A few hours ago, I was in the same room with him."

"But he got away."

"Actually, I did. But he's doing something strange. He's spending valuable time collecting strange objects."

"Like what?" Camille asked.

"Hitler's hairbrush."

"What?" Camille said. "How?"

"Auction," Edwin said. "And…"

"And what?"

"I think he has something from the Leader. Like, hair, maybe."

"Why on earth – "

"I think he's collecting DNA from the worst of the worst. The Leader. Hitler. Who knows what others."

"Why?" Camille asked.

"That I don't know. Yet. But he wanted to get me out of the way at the same time."

Camille's brows drew together. She thought for a moment.

"The way to find the operators is to find their helpers," Camille said. "When the cells operate in Europe, they have help with housing, documents, food, clothes, jobs. They have hosts who blend them in until they strike. That's their strength. We use it against them. Judo."

Edwin nodded. "Ah. So that's why you are here. Because we need to find Ali's European base before the succession takes place," Camille said. Then she added with resignation, "And before he does something else to prove that he deserves to lead the worst of the worst."

Edwin nodded. "Sorry about your vacation. Sounds like you deserved it."

Camille studied Edwin. "I had some thinking to do," she said. "But I know what the right answer is. At least, one of them."

"You were involved yesterday," Edwin said. "With the takedown of the Leader."

Camille dipped her chin. "It was a team effort."

"You found his compound," Edwin said. "You know how to do this stuff well."

Camille smiled. "No. But I did find something else."

"Good," said Edwin. "Now find Ali's European base. Rat-ass fast."

Camille flopped her hands on her thighs. "How am I supposed to do that? I'm on a Greek island. Even if I catch a ferry in the morning, I won't get to Cairo for another day, best case."

"I'll get you there before dawn," Edwin said. "Come."

Edwin's chair legs scraped the cement floor.

Across from the cafe, the old watcher shifted her thick thighs on the stone stoop. She leaned back, squinting in the darkness. But when she cupped her fingers together like a visor, she thought she saw the silhouettes of a man and a woman, her dress flapping at her ankles, trotting across the roof, above the lights of the cafe. They appeared to stop walking.

The man turned sharply. The widow had the distinct impression, from the way his shoulders squared and his head cocked, that he was looking at her through the darkness. She watched him touch his wrist.

Then all she saw was blazing light. It blinded her completely. She turned away, blinking. When the spots cleared in her vision, the rooftop was empty. The man and woman were gone. All she could see was a faint glow against the clouds in the distant horizon, and the thin hum of electricity in the wires that now snaked up the goat path to bring light, sound, TV and Internet to most of the homes.

Camille tucked into the small passenger seat behind the pilot, her legs stretching beneath his seat. "So I see you've kept up with technology in the last ten years. Where did you get this bird?"

Edwin handed her ear protectors that also contained a microphone and a speaker so they could communicate in-flight.

"Airmail," he said.

Cruising at three hundred and forty miles per hour in Zed's stealth helicopter, it took less than two hours for Edwin to fly Camille to the roof top of the American University in Cairo.

"You only have two hours to get the identity of the Helper. We need the name and street address. Three, tops," Edwin said. "You are behind."

"And you?" asked Camille. "Where will I find you?"

Edwin looked through the lenses at the screen that rendered in his field of view. What he saw there told him exactly where he was now most needed. In England, as soon as possible.

"I'll let you know when I do," Edwin said. "I have your number."

"How?" Camille asked.

"Irrelevant," Edwin said. "You find the Helper."

"This is impossible," Camille said.

"Make it happen," Edwin said. His green eyes, tinted yellow around the edges of the iris, blazed at her. "You will be the hero, Camille. Also something you are very good at."

Camille stepped down on the rooftop of the building and crouched beneath the blades of the helicopter.

She had no time. But fortunately, this time, she knew exactly where to begin. And this time, she had every resource at her fingertips.

"Ah, Uncle Khalid," Camille mused. "It's about time I looked in on you."

There was no guilt in her voice, and no affection whatsoever.

What Edwin had seen in his lens view was this.

Bee #27 was off line. That was the drone he had deployed to watch Fiona Tate and the geneticist, Dr. Bart. But it was not watching them anymore.

As soon as Camille's feet hit the ground in Cairo, Edwin visualized a command:

"Review record," he thought. Then, he thought the stroke that issued the command. "Backslash."

The program responded. It replayed the last twenty seconds of digital recording that Bee #27 had filmed. It showed this:

Fiona and the scientist, their hands and feet duct taped to metal chairs. Tape over their mouths. A face sneered contemptuously, filling the lens.

"Ali," Edwin said through his lips, which pressed together in a flat line of fury.

Then the film showed Ali's thick fingers, dirt-stained nails, snatching the drone from its perch, and ripping off its small wings. Then the view scrambled. The last thing the recording showed was of the dust balls that settled where the wall met the linoleum floor of the laboratory.

Then the video image bounced, fuzzed, and went black.

Edwin powered up the rotors and lifted the helicopter off the roof of the American University of Cairo. As he gained altitude, he tipped the nose toward the Northwest.

Camille had reached the top of the roof access staircase enclosure. She turned back and saw just a ripple in the air, heat rising, and the hazy neon glow of a dust cloud dissipating in the starlight.

CHAPTER TWENTY-NINE

1:00 a.m., May 24
Oxford, England

The jet flew swiftly and low over Europe and the English Channel to a still, private airfield. A short while later, a small helicopter lifted off, and ten minutes later settled on the roof of the Oxford Genetics Lab.

Edwin raced across the roof, opened the door, and thundered down the stairs to the third floor. He gently pressed his fingers against the door to the hallway and scanned the span of linoleum, lit a whitish green by the fluorescent bulbs.

The hallway was empty. The door to Lab 324 was shut.

Edwin walked briskly down the hall. He put his hand on the knob, and opened it slowly. He stepped back, flat against the wall, as the door swung wide. He peered through the doorway.

The chairs along the lab benches were all empty and still. The computer at Dr. Bart's desk was on. Calculations whirred; a program was running.

At first, Edwin saw no one.

Then he heard shoes scrape at the floor, like someone trying to stand up. The sound was coming from behind the door he had just opened.

He turned back and shut the door.

Dr. Bart crouched on the floor. Surgical string - the tough nylon used to bind torn flesh - was wrapped around and around his wrists and his feet. It cut deeply into his skin. Some blood streaked down his fingers and ankles.

A strap of duct tape covered his mouth. His eyes bulged with fear.

"This will hurt," Edwin said. "Sorry." He ripped the tape off the man's face.

"Ach!" cried the scientist. Edwin took a ballpoint pen from his pocket, and pressed a button. In a single swipe the narrow blade slit through the suture string, freeing the doctor's hands. Another freed his feet.

"What happened? Where's Fiona?" Edwin demanded. He kneeled by the doctor, examining him closely. Aside from a rectangular red abrasion stretching from cheek to cheek, Dr. Bart appeared unharmed.

This Edwin noted. Dr. Bart had seen Ali's face full on. Yet he left him alive. Detained, but not harmed.

Ali misses his targets... a lot, Edwin thought. *At least so far. But he'll get better. And once he crosses that line, killing won't be a problem for him anymore.*

Dr. Bart spoke quietly, his voice shaky.

"A man came in right after you left. He must have been here...he must have been watching us."

"You and Fiona?"

"No. The three of us. He came in right after you left. Immediately after."

"What happened? Tell me exactly." Edwin said.

"This man came in. He had dark hair, dark eyes," began Dr. Bart.

"Did he speak?"

The doctor nodded. "He had a public school accent. Not an American, like you."

Edwin was suddenly aware of his own exposure. And that he, too, would face the same decision Ali had.

Dr. Bart knew what Edwin looked like. He heard his voice. He would report it to the police. He would call them, eventually.

Edwin knew that operators often hid in plain sight. But sometimes one needed the opposite. Sometimes operators hid behind a veil of the absurd. Especially where anyone who ever retold such an outlandish tale would seem stark-raving mad.

"I'm with the CIA," Edwin told Dr. Bart. "We've been looking for that man. He's linked to a group that believes in colonizing life beyond this planet. And we think he's right."

Dr. Bart gasped. "That's why he's collecting all those samples?"

"The hairbrush," Edwin nodded.

"Not just the hairbrush," the doctor said. "He had a portfolio of them. There were four unique genetic samples."

"What were they?" Edwin said.

The scientist shuddered. "I didn't like being around them at all, not even microscopic slices of them."

"What did he have?" Edwin demanded.

"He had scalp cells from Hitler's hairbrush. He had a long, straggly piece of white beard hair."

Edwin nodded.

That's why Ali went back in. He must have been lurking, waiting for years, months. And then the chance to get it was almost gone forever.

Edwin asked, "What were the other two items he wanted you to look at?"

The scientist made a face. "He had a toothbrush. He said it belonged to Jeffrey Dahmer. You know, the cannibal who did unspeakable things to seventeen boys and men before he cooked and ate them."

There was a long pause. Dr. Bart looked ill.

"Do you know what I'm likely to find in genetic material clinging to a cannibal's toothbrush?" he said.

"His gum cells?" Edwin said.

The geneticists nodded. "And...his... meat."

"Eesh," Edwin said, his stomach lurching. "What was the fourth sample? Who did it belong to?"

The doctor shook his head. "I don't know yet. The fourth sample contained fingernail clippings. He had all of them in plastic sleeves of this leather pouch. Like... mementos."

The scientist got to his feet and looked at the clock. Then he raced to the computer. "We don't have much time."

"What did he ask you to do?"

"He demanded I compare the genetic patterns. He had the article recently published on the Warrior Gene...that one I was telling you about...and he wanted to see if any of them had the Warrior Gene that I was telling you about. And, if any matched, in any way. Then he told me to post the results on this website before 5:00am GMT or else.... then he took her."

"And he left you bound and gagged? How were you supposed to do what he wanted?"

Dr. Bart shrugged. "It's almost like he had two minds. One didn't want the answer at all."

Edwin was studying the screen. "Did he tell you what would happen if you don't post the results?"

The scientist looked up. Edwin saw sweat beading on his forehead.

"He said he'd drop Fiona's head from the tallest tower by 5:15pm."

Edwin tasted bile in his mouth.

No. Fiona is not... Not this time. Find her. You are behind. Dig!

Edwin sucked air sharply into his lungs, and exhaled, each three times. His mind focused.

"5:15pm. The Tallest Tower," Edwin said. "The summit must be soon after, and near enough, to the Tallest Tower that Ali could be in both places almost at once."

That would be exactly forty-five hours after the leader was killed. The Leader could have set the timing for the succession ceremony as his last act. Forty-five hours would be a strange number, but not forty-eight. Forty-eight would give the tribal leaders enough time to travel from anywhere in the world. And forty-five would still leave enough time – a few hours – to travel to the ceremony. But where? Where would they all gather?

Edwin clicked through the logic, obvious step by obvious step.

Somewhere central. Somewhere safe. Somewhere many roads lead to and from. Someplace where Middle Eastern faces seem familiar.

Edwin saw the full opportunity take shape before him. He could take out the entire next generation in a single strike. He just needed to find out where they would gather. And be there waiting.

Edwin had less than twenty-four hours to discover the meeting location somewhere in Europe, he thought, and to get there.

Before then, he had to find Fiona. He thought of how she fought for the relic she believed held a better purpose for the future than it had in the past. How she kept her sense of humor even while buried in a lightless tunnel. His palm on hers, feeling her pulse.

"The tallest tower must be Big Ben," said Dr. Bart. "The Tower of London actually isn't that high. It's an old prison fort. Now they just keep the crown jewels there."

Edwin looked at the website and the authentication code. The numbers locked like a pdf in his memory - a photograph he could store, file, retrieve and use when he needed. This capability required no technology - Edwin was born with it - though Zed had developed technology to extend Edwin's extraordinary talent.

"You do what the man said," Edwin told Dr. Bart. "Do not leave this chair. Do not speak to anyone. Find out what he's looking for in these samples and post it by 5:00am. Whatever you find, post it by 5:00am."

"But what about the police?" asked Dr. Bart.

"Plenty of time for that later. If you call them now, they'll ask you a million questions. They'll take you down to the station. You'll tell them about the CIA agent investigating extra-terrestrial terrorism. They'll have you psychologically evaluated. They'll look into every corner of your background."

"Ah...oh, I see," the scientist pulled back. "Right." Everyone had his secrets. Edwin did not need to know their particulars to leverage their power.

"You won't get back here for days," said Edwin. "Fiona will die. You will have ordered her execution."

Dr. Bart gaped. "I...Right. I think I'd best work on this then."

"Good," Edwin said. "You will save Fiona's life. And probably life beyond this planet, too."

The scientist gave Edwin a curious look, then pulled his chair back and typed his password into the computer.

Edwin ran out of the lab. He bolted up the stairs to the roof, where the helicopter waited. Once inside it, Edwin pounded his fist on the seat.

"Where are you, Fiona? This is why! This is why! This is why I said get as far away from me as you can."

The ASP code flashed in his memory as clearly as a photograph.

Sec 1.2.10 No Attachments.
The Operator shall not form or maintain any significant personal relationship(s) during the Term of this Agreement other than with the assigned technical support. Any such attachment will lead to immediate termination.

The rule did not specify to which party termination would apply. But Edwin knew. Lula had paid for his lesson.

For Edwin, the cover of "Start-Up Founder" had been beyond fun. It was compelling. In that cloak he rose to the top of the technology world in the boom. He became a kind of celebrity, until the call to extract came, as it always did. From every other mission, he had extracted so easily. It had not been hard to disappear from the fire-fighter team in Atlanta, or from the temp worker office pool in Austin. The ski-bum winter in Colorado had been fun, and good practice for his winter SERE skills (Survival, Evasion, Resistance and Escape). But each time, when the call had come, Edwin was ready to go.

But leaving D6 had been hard. Edwin was supposed to be a grad student studying obscure mathematics, but he had become a technology wizard with global celebrity status. He had become wealthy, distractingly wealthy. And he'd had an attachment.

Generally, things did not just happen to Edwin Hoff. He made them happen. As a boy who loved math and orchestra, but not the teasing this attracted, he sought weights, muscles, and guns. In the military, he learned to master everything that a man's brains and strength could control, including the men who could master both.

In this assignment, however, he had encountered something new. At D6, as its founder, leader, and visionary, Edwin tasted the thrill of personal recognition, public and private. He became the popular kid. Women liked him. He had mastered "cool." He had friends. And he liked all of it.

This was a problem.

When extraction came, Edwin should have left. He should have been gone for good. He should have taken care of business and gone to meet the Head of the ASP as per his orders.

But he did not.

This cover was so much easier than his real job, so much more fun. It let him be productive and creative. And for the first time, he had grown close to someone.

To a lot of people, actually.

Zed, his support in cover and in the ASP. Sterling Davenport, his investor. Jameson Callaghan, the CEO he had hired. Nancy, his administrative assistant. Over a thousand other people he employed, who counted on him for a paycheck, to pay their rent and feed their kids. He thought of the good-natured playboy Hudson Davenport and his silly grin that helped him close deals and floated him up and over trouble. And Lula. He thought of how her brown hair rested on her shoulders in the mornings, just before she tied it up in a bun under her cap at the café. She was simple and easy and innocent, everything he was not. They weren't just attached. They fit.

When Edwin Hoff should have been on his motorcycle speeding toward a meeting location in Washington D.C., he had this thought instead, idling at the Cambridge exit on the Massachusetts Pike:

Did Edwin Hoff matter to them?

He checked his watch. There was no time, not even for a brief detour.

So he had to be quick.

Lula lived in a small studio apartment in East Cambridge, near an area of promised redevelopment. He cut the engine when he was a hundred yards away.

"Be quick," Edwin told himself. "You're a blip to her. Get your damn focus back."

When he peered above the bay window into Lula's apartment, he lost it completely. Lula was slumped at her computer, typing slowly. Doing email. Behind her was a small television set. It was playing the news, the same news every channel was playing that day, showing photograph after photograph of smiling faces that were now becoming familiar touch-points to a shocked, grieving country.

Edwin saw a familiar face flash by. It was his own headshot from D6. He was beaming.

When Lula saw Edwin's photograph flash by on the news again, and again, she broke down. Her hands covered her face. Edwin heard hear her cries through the window, which was open a few inches. She shook with sobs. She wept.

Edwin's hands were on the window sill when he noticed the door to Lula's apartment. It was habit for Edwin to map all entrances and exits in every room. He noticed changes.

A new slice of light came from the hallway.

Someone else was in the apartment. Edwin silently stepped back into the shadows, still watching. If Lula had a friend over, she did not act like it. In her private grief, her legs gave way and she lay face-down on her bed.

Edwin did not like how upset she was. He did not like how she cried in her pillow. This would give someone opportunity and purchase.

Lula sobbed.

It happened very quickly. From behind her partially closed door, a figure in black clothes edged into the room.

She did not see him.

Silently he pulled the edges of her pillow up around her ears and twisted it hard.. Lula lay limp.

Edwin raged. His gloves were stripping the paint from the windowsill. He was about to blow through the window when the attacker turned toward it. He bent down.

Edwin ducked under the sill.

He heard the window slide up half way. Then he rose slowly.

Inside, the attacker had turned back to Lula's body. He yanked her jeans down to mid-thigh. Then he left.

What Edwin saw made him stagger back into the shadows. It changed everything. He knew Lula's killer.

Edwin had trained him. He was an ASP operator.

For several minutes, Edwin stayed still, calculating.

There was no next cover for him. He was not supposed to survive the mission the Head had just sent him on. They already were cleaning up what was left of Edwin Hoff.

The RUPD hunt has already begun.

Then Edwin swung through the window. With a gloved hand, he held Lula's limp body. Beneath a thick film, his yellow eyes blinked back to focus.

The Head of the ASP had betrayed Edwin. But he had learned something about himself during this cover, as Start-Up Founder.

He was an entrepreneur at heart. He could start, and finish, anything he chose to do.

That was the moment that Edwin Hoff embarked on the biggest start-up experience of his life, against the most hostile and well-funded competitors. He would take down the global terror network on his own.

Fortunately, he had plenty of financial resources to achieve it. As long as no one found him.

On the rooftop of the Oxford Genetics Lab, Edwin pressed the button that made the rotors of his helicopter begin to spin.

He was furious.

Not a day back in the world, and he already had imperiled another innocent woman.

Just a cup of damn coffee in a teashop and now Fiona was fighting for her life.

Edwin knew what the outcome would have to be. His years of training built behaviors into his muscles and his brain that defended against the distraction of human empathy.

"The mission is all. It has to be. My purpose on earth is to wipe out terrorists, not an auctioneer who stumbled into the fray."

Especially not one who wore leather boots and graphic t-shirts and smelled of peonies and vanilla. One who showed no fear, barely, even at the end of a long, narrow tunnel several feet below the roots of the grass.

"If this were just a match of courage, Ali, she would cream you," Edwin said.

And Edwin knew this. Fiona was the best link to finding Ali. Until Camille showed up with the Helper's address.

"I'm coming for you, Fiona," he said. "And I'm coming for him."

Edwin tapped into a larger monitor in the helicopter that grasped the feeds and pulled the data into Crosspathz. England was an excellent place to be found. It was not such a good place to get lost. Ali had picked a good place to lure Edwin, but not to escape him.

The country was covered in Closed Circuit TV cameras, which captured and stored footage of people passing by street corners, banks, and office buildings. It deterred crime and provides law enforcement with live video of those who took the ill-advised risk without deep prior thought.

But the visibility cut both ways. For Edwin, each camera also would feed the ASP's monitors.

Even if the Head was dead, she would not kill the order to find him. They were still coming for him.

These CCTV feeds also were an intelligence goldmine for the CIA. One analyst studying footage and face prints pressed the digits on her phone as fast as she could. She reached Ascher Silver's secure line. He was in England, kicking through the rubble of a tea shop.

"Ascher!" she said. "A face print for the Successor matched someone who just went into a building in England. Oxford Genetics Lab."

"Address!" he barked. He looked at his partner. "Change of plans."

CHAPTER THIRTY

1:15 a.m., May 24
Oxford, England

Inside the helicopter squatting on the roof of the Oxford Technology Lab, Edwin watched the CCTV system through the monitor in his lens. He could see the streets below. He studied the live feed for anything out of the ordinary. A pattern. A disrupted pattern.

Then something odd caught his eye. When he looked out the window, his lenses could fix on an object on the ground, moving or still, and magnify it.

The object was square, cream colored, about the size of a deck of cards. When he zoomed in, Edwin saw that it had five thin extensions splayed out on one side.

"That looks a little bit like a hand," Edwin said. "It looks a lot like a hand."

Then he saw another one, about fifty feet down the street. It was exactly the same size as the first one.

But the trail ended there. Edwin switched CCTV camera views to the one that covered the next span. He did not see any more of these objects.

Conscious of becoming a subject of the video cameras, rather than a consumer of their feeds, Edwin slipped out of the helicopter. He clamped a line to a hook on the belly of the bird, and ran for the edge of the building. The streets were abandoned. Clipped in to the harness, Edwin rappelled face-first down the side of the building.

He reached the ground in less than two full seconds. He adjusted his gait, and sauntered, hat low, to the place where he had seen the hand.

Curiously, there were no birds. No scavengers in search of carrion. It had been hours since Ali had taken Fiona; the natural environment would have detected the dying flesh by now.

But when Edwin approached the white hand, he smiled. It was not rotting flesh. It was a rubber glove.

"From the box in the laboratory," Edwin said. "She's leaving me bread crumbs!"

Edwin reached into his backpack and flung a bee into the air.

"Find the crumbs, bee," Edwin said, watching the drone feed in the field of view his contacts displayed. Soon, the small drone found the next glove, and the next, casually dropped along the main road. They led right to the entrance to the Oxford Train Station.

"Fiona! You titan!" he cheered.

Edwin trotted back toward the laboratory building. He was crossing the driveway when four dark SUVs screeched to a halt outside the building. Edwin shrank back behind a hedge and watched.

A team of special ops soldiers, fully armed with night vision goggles on their helmets, emerged from the large vehicles. They surrounded the building.

They crashed through the front door. Edwin could hear them pound up the stairs. He already knew their target destinations from his own training.

They were sealing the perimeter - all points of access and egress - and the roof,. where their goggles would let them see his helicopter, plain as day.

Edwin spotted the drainpipe. He looked down at his brogues. They were beautiful stitched leather, laced up tight. And they had come from Zed.

Edwin sprinted for the drainpipe and leaped at the steel. The magnets in his shoes held close to the pipe, giving him leverage as if his feet were on steps. Edwin shimmied up the pipe. It was four floors to the roof. He could hear the soldiers pounding up the stairs.

"Go! Go! Go!" Edwin urged himself.

It could all end here if they caught him. Ali would kill Fiona. He would take over al Ra'duzma. Then the new leader would disappear to carry out his plans and make his name. Camille would be his next target. And Edwin would be answering questions from the wrong side of an interrogation table while Ali and his gangs caused more trouble.

Fiona will not pay for this. Get Ali. Before he takes over. Before he gets Camille. Before he can do whatever he has up his sleeve.

Edwin reached the roof. He stayed low, looked around. He could see nothing but a rappelling line snaking from a spot in the middle of the roof toward the edge.

He heard the door to the rooftop rattle. They would be through it in twelve seconds, max.

Edwin sprinted to the rappel line, coiling it fast. He waved his hand in the air and the helicopter's door responded. It slid quietly open. Edwin climbed into the cockpit and flicked on the rotors.

"Up, bird!" he said.

The roof door burst open.

"Windy up here, mate," said one commando.

"Wind tunnels," said the other. "From the other buildings. Birds love it. Look."

He pointed at a small falcon that appeared to be hovering just above their heads in the center of the roof. From within the stealthy helicopter cloaked in shape shifting plasma, Edwin watched the commandos below.

Seeing nothing, they left roof.

Edwin smiled as he flew higher, and banked.

"Okay...plastic glove... So Fiona, where did you go next? You have to come up somewhere," Edwin said. He ran facial recognition software against every camera showing people emerging from every station in the London Underground. No match.

"Where do these trains go? Schedule!" Edwin barked.

A line-by-line schedule for the Oxford Train Station scrolled in front of him.

The next three went to St. Pancras Station..

Why there, Ali?

Edwin circled the helicopter, watching the buses pull into Oxford Railway Station.

You have to come up, Edwin raked one hand through his hair. He scanned the map of the London Underground.

Unless ... you don't.

What Edwin saw on the map told him where they had gone and where they would emerge.

The meeting is not in London. The tallest tower - it's not Big Ben at all, Edwin thought. *That train is going to St. Pancras. But you're not going to London. You're going under the English Channel, to Gare du Nord. You're going to Paris.*

Edwin paused.

"Where there is a tall tower," he said. "The Eiffel Tower. That's where they're all going.. The succession meeting is in France."

France has a large population of Muslims, so the tribal leaders would blend in easily. Because France was on the continent, they could travel by land, with relative ease and comfortably concealed, and reach the destination within forty-eight hours' drive from Greece, Italy, or Turkey, porous borders nearest to their countries of origin. And the U.S. cannot fly drones over the land of their closest allies. Not easily, anyway.

Edwin toggled on his lens and thought out the content that would appear as a simple text message on the secure phone of Camille Henderson.

MEET ME IN PARIS. LUXEMBOURG GARDENS. WITH HELPER ADDRESS. UR BHIND.

Paris. But why take Fiona? Why is he risking the complication?

Edwin banked the helicopter and powered east, following the track toward London. The inevitable conclusion came quickly.

Because Fiona isn't just a complication. She is a prop. He's going to use her to prove he should be the successor. He's got something dramatic planned. And he needs Fiona to outdo the Burger Bomber.

This was suboptimal. But it could not be the whole plan. It was not original. A new leader needed a new kind of bang.

Edwin thought about the news footage he had seen over the years during the war on terror. It was all too familiar to see live decapitations.. The act required very little investment and, at least initially, scared lots of people. Which was exactly what the next leader of Al Ra'duzma needed to do. Unconsciously, the tip of Edwin's index finger grazed the three-inch braid of healed flesh along his neck.

The West is too soft. Too sympathetic to the individual. They are so exposed. And Ali knows it.

Edwin flew over the Oxford Railway Station where Fiona had dropped her last glove. A hundred feet up, he pressed a button. Two bee drones dispatched from a small door in the belly of the helicopter. They engaged, and quietly drifted into the tunnel system, programmed to find and film the path underground to the Channel, and whoever could be riding in a train going through it.

An hour later, while the drones flew undetected through the Channel, Edwin and his stealth-wrapped helicopter flew over it.

Chapter Thirty-One

11:30 p.m., May 23
Cairo Egypt

Behind the empty football playing fields of the American University in Cairo, Camille turned back to watch Edwin fly off, but he was already out of sight.

She had to find the answer and bring it to Edwin in a few hours. On the other side of the Mediterranean. On the other side of Europe.

"I need to speak to Zubani," Camille said to her boss, Vernon Keely. "Now. Don't ask me why."

After what Camille Henderson had done for the United States of America, and for the rest of the world, for that matter, Vernon Keely would give her whatever she needed to get her job done. Successful field work relied as much on their operators' instinct as skill; Henderson had both. From now on, he would only grease her path. And perhaps even learn something.

"I need the figs," she said, opening her palm. "And the honey bear."

Moments later Camille sat across from a small young man in an orange jumpsuit. Whaleed Zubani's hands were cuffed in front of him, chained to his waist. Drool seeped from the corner of his mouth until he sucked it back.

The three plump figs were delicately arranged in a white paper basket. Camille popped the top of a clear plastic bottle, molded in the shape of a bear, and tipped it upside down. Thick amber oozed out, layering haphazard lines over the ripe fruit, piling into pools around each piece.

"I came to see how you are doing, Whaleed. I love figs," Camille said in Arabic, with a small smile, confessing to her captive. She could see saliva reforming in the corners of his mouth so she picked up one of the juicy figs and bit into it. "Just perfect! Do you get these in here?"

Whaleed shook his head.

Camille knew exactly what he ate. In the last three weeks, and for the next several years it would be a mix of bread, broth, water, rice, and sometimes chicken. The food in these places was minimal. Outside of constitutional protection, war criminals were kept barely nourished, never satisfied. Then a plate of fresh fruit became powerful leverage.

"No? Oh, that's too bad. They're really good." She paused. "Would you like one?"

He looked away. Camille pushed the tray toward him.

"Take them, Whaleed. Go on. Please. I brought them for you."

Whaleed's mouth made a stiff flat line. "I'm only in here because of you."

Camille shook her head. "No. You're here because of you. You did a very, very good thing. Today the world's a better place than yesterday. Much better than the day before yesterday."

Whaleed looked at the fruit. Then at Camille. He reached tentatively for a fig. Camille sat back. He could not move his shackled hands far enough to reach the plate.

"May I?" she asked. She spoke in fluent Arabic.

Whaleed nodded.

Camille picked up a fruit and dipped it in the thick honey that had pooled at the edge of the basket. She put it in Whaleed's mouth. He chewed, a sound of pleasure in his breath. When he finished, he looked up at Camille.

"Another?" she asked.

He nodded. She fed him fruit by her hand, like he was a baby. When the plate was empty, she called for more. She fed him until he shook his head from side to side.

"Thank you," said Whaleed.

His brown eyes held hers. He chewed slowly what remained in his mouth, and sucked the sticky seeds from his teeth.

"I need your help," Camille said.

"Again," he said. "I've done everything I can."

"You have done everything you can. You have," Camille said. "This request is much easier than what you already have done to help your fellow man."

Whaleed looked down at the empty cardboard basket. "What?" he muttered.

"I need to know who the helpers are in Europe. In England and France, particularly."

"I don't know," he said.

Camille frowned. She put her fingers on the plate and slid it away from Whaleed.

"Except there is a story of one who has been there for many, many years,"

Whaleed said quickly.

"Who sent him?" Camille pushed the plate two inches back toward him.

"Her," said Whaleed. "It's a woman. She has been there for decades."

"Who is her husband?"

"He was a doctor. But he died. She lives alone. She was sent after he died."

"By whom?"

Whaleed looked at her. "He was a good friend of her husband. The one who built the whole operation. Until the Great Awakening."

Camille asked, "What happened then?"

Whaleed shrugged. "The infidels caught him. Their news stories said he had a trial and he went to prison. He had planned a beautiful attack but he never returned."

Camille sat back. "Are you talking about KAH?"

KAH. Khalid al Hamini. The man she first knew only as "Uncle," the man her first love treated as his parent, his guide, and his mentor. Ten years later she learned exactly what course KAH had sent his charge along. The fact that an innocent freckle faced coed had fallen for the dark brown eyes of his nephew was of no importance to him at all. She was a twig in his way, to be crushed under his wheels or snapped in half and tossed aside.

Despite all that planning, thought Camille, *things didn't quite work out the way he had planned. And that's why I am sitting where I am, and Uncle is enjoying a much different view.*

Camille thought of Edwin.

"Yes," Camille said. "KAH would know who the Helper is. He sent her to Paris in the first place."

Whaleed snatched the last fig. "You could ask him, but he's disappeared off the face of the earth."

"Fortunately," Camille said, "Sometimes a person who disappears off the face of the earth is lurking just beneath it."

Camille left the interrogation room with an empty ceramic plate. She closed the door. Vernon was pacing in the hallway.

"Figs?" he asked.

"Psych 101," Camille said. "You are much more likely to persuade someone after you feed them. I learned it in college. That, and that people have an innate fear of snakes and sharks."

"Snakes I could have brought you. A shark might have been tough challenge," said Vernon.

Camille shrugged. "You catch more flies with honey, anyway."

Camille closed the heavy door of her office at the American University of Cairo and picked up a phone. She dialed a series of numbers. When the solid tone rang, she entered the code.

Thousands of miles away, the phone rang. In Boston it was mid-afternoon.

A woman answered. "FBI Boston. Agent Marly here," said Christine Marly, a Field Agent in the counter-terror division.

Christine Marly had risen from recovered lawyer to beat cop to FBI field agent in Boston. She and Camille had entered the field roles at the same time. Because of their connections to a planned attack years earlier, they had formed a bond of trust that helped them and helped the country communicate covert information between the CIA and the FBI.

"It's Camille Henderson."

"Hey...I hear congratulations are in order for you," said Marly.

"Teamwork," said Camille.

"And one less bad guy in the world," Marly said.

"Maybe more," said Camille. "I need a quick favor. I need to talk to a prisoner. And I want to see him."

"Okay. When? This week?"

"Now," said Camille.

"Now? Like today?"

"No. Like in two minutes. Immediately," said Camille.

"Who is he? Where is?"

"He's in Supermax," said Camille. "I need to speak with KAH. Make sure he's wearing the contacts."

"Oh, he wears them every day. We get a lot of intel from that technology. It doesn't hold up in court because it's self-incriminating, but it gets us good stuff we can use after they are in the can for something else," said Marly.

Years earlier, Camille had proposed a theoretical new technology to the best technical minds the CIA employed. The challenge was this: could they reverse the physics and chemistry of vision to capture images the brain thinks about, or remembers?

This was not her original idea. But Camille never would tell them where she had seen it before, or who had invented it.

The guard's metal baton rattled the cell's steel door and zinged through the prisoner's metal fillings.

Two men to each side, they shackled his feet and his hands behind him. They walked him down the hallway until they reached the metal door that opened and closed around them. They moved into another holding area. Eventually they reached a small, empty room with a single plastic chair facing a large monitor.

The mastermind of a failed plan to release a bioweapon in the atmosphere above New York City shuffled in chains that bound his ankles and his hands. He wore a bright orange jumpsuit, the same color – the same uniform - that he had worn for ten years, and would wear for the rest of his living days in the highest security federal prison in the United States, buried beneath a mountain. The guards brought him into a grey room and pushed him down into a single chair.

KAH could not see the small camera embedded in the facing wall, or the small microphones in the ceiling tile above him that would capture his image and voice and transmit both to a secure monitor on a desk in a small office tucked away in the English Department of the American University of Cairo.

Camille Henderson's "cover for status" was to be an English professor at the University of Cairo. Vernon Keely, her boss at the Agency, was also the dean of the department. She could travel the world ostensibly for research or for academic conferences, or to help out non-profits. This was "cover for action," which would explain why she was where she was, doing what she was doing.

There sat Camille Henderson, waiting for the feed to connect her to the one person who had, ten years ago, attempted to infect and destroy millions of American lives. In fact, he had succeeded in exploding only one. Hers.

"To whom am I speaking?" KAH asked in English. "You see me, but you have no courage to show me your face."

"Put me on," said Camille.

"What?" Marly asked into the microphone. "Really?"

"Who's he going to tell? He gets thirty minutes of sunlight a week. Do it. I need to mine him."

The twenty-four-inch panel on the wall of KAH's interrogation room flickered.

Then he saw a face he knew well. Someone who had interfered with his plans many years before. Someone he blamed for the catastrophic failure that put him into perpetual confinement and worse, a legacy of shame.

And Camille looked into the eyes she had last seen burst wide with surprise when, years earlier, she had duct taped his wrists to his ankles in an old apartment in Cambridge, Massachusetts. A short time later, she had called the FBI dispatcher. Within two minutes sirens whipped blue and red bands of light outside a two-family home in East Cambridge. The team wore bulletproof vests, and tested their triggers. The team at the front door with the battering ram found it unnecessary. The door was unlocked. When they crept upstairs, and down the hall, they found their Most Wanted, Camille Henderson, presiding over a bound and seething mastermind who, if properly persuaded, could provide exact details of the failed plan to spread weaponized pneumonic plague in the atmosphere over the east coast of the United States.

These several years later, through the video monitor to the interrogation room in Supermax, deep beneath a Nevada mountain, Camille watched KAH recognize her.

"You," he said. He spat on the floor.

"Hello, Uncle – may I still call you Uncle?" Camille said. "We were so close to becoming family."

"No." KAH moved his lower jaw, then pursed his lips and spat. A thick white glob flew at the screen.

"I do hope you are enjoying your stay with us," said Camille. "Let us know if we can make you more comfortable. A new pillow, perhaps?"

"What do you want?" He coughed.

"I wanted to congratulate you, actually."

"For what?"

"Your mission appears to be coming true," said Camille.

"Oh? We don't get much news."

"There have been a few developments since. Recently, in fact. Your leader was killed yesterday."

KAH's eyes widened.

Camille was counting on that. She knew to keep talking, so KAH continued to sit there silently and fume, all the while exposing his thoughts to the software in the lenses, which read the electronic impulses his mind produced of the images he visualized.

So she leaned into the microphone on her laptop, which transmitted her voice to the interrogation cell.

"Yes," she said. "And congratulations are due to you, too. Your long game is finally at an end. You have won. We hear that Ali is next in line. He's to become the next leader of Al Ra'duzma."

A broad smile spread across KAH's face.

"Yes, it could still all work out the way you planned it," said Camille. "Except for one thing."

"What's that?"

"Well, Yassir – sorry, Ali – has to be at the succession ceremony by the end of the day. But he doesn't know where it is. He needs shelter. And he's in Europe somewhere."

This was the moment. Camille had led KAH's brain precisely where she wanted it to go. She could follow the map on the computer of the impulses and images his brain created as he followed her thoughts. Step by step, like a prosecutor on cross-examination, she extracted each small, innocuous truth: not from his speech, but from his thoughts, and in the electronic imagery they printed on his brain. They made electronic signatures, which the contact lenses captured. Strung together, these images told an important story. While KAH thought he wore them to see just a few feet further, and to focus on objects just a little more clearly.

When Camille created the urgency, the need and the problem, KAH's brain leapt to the solution. He did not speak. His expression did not change. But as he sat there, Camille watched his thoughts take shape on the screen of the computer that sat on top of her desk in the English Department in the University of Cairo.

"There is a helper," Camille read. "She is in Paris. Her first name is Raisa. Raisa de la Seine. She looks like she's in her late twenties...."

But then, Camille saw more. KAH's brain was racing through images. It paused on one of brightly colored stones, separated into orderly piles on a clean white bed sheet. Then KAH settled on an image that startled her. What KAH projected in his mind, Camille had seen before, with her own eyes.

KAH was remembering a photograph in a wooden frame. The picture showed a much younger KAH with his arm around the skinny shoulders of a coltish six year old, all arms and legs.

It was a photograph Camille had seen nearly every day for a period of four years. It had been propped on top of the folding desk in the small cramped dorm room of her boyfriend.

Camille recognized the photo of a young Yassir, taken when he was about six years old.

So there is a connection this de la Seine woman, and Yas- Ali. KAH must know she's the helper..

Aloud Camille prodded KAH. "So, who can help your Ali?"

"I will never help you," seethed KAH.

"No, I thought you'd feel that way. Still, worth a try. Until next time. Don't worry. I'll know where to find you."

Within the hour, Camille buckled her seatbelt on an oil sheik's private jet.

"Tutoring English has its perks," she muttered as the Embraer lifted off toward Paris.

Camille had to find a young woman named Madame de la Seine, who opened her home and provided food, Metro maps, and, Camille hoped, a place of refuge for newly arrived young men from Saudi Arabia, Egypt, Syria and Afghanistan, just trying to figure out how to make very short lives in Paris.

Chapter Thirty-Two

2:00 a.m. May 24
London, England

Ali clutched Fiona's arm and directed her on to the Eurostar train boarding at St. Pancras station. He would not let her get away, not now.

As the train entered the tunnel, Ali watched the bright strip of lights flash by. It reassured him. It gave him the illusion that this was just a trip on a regular subway train. He could push away the thought of the tons of seawater above them that could trickle in through a small crack, building up pressure, until….

Ali shook his head. He felt the long, thick object in his satchel. The dagger was secure, and with it, the support of the man who ran all of al Ra'duzma's finances. Ali felt sure that the Sheikh, with one final look through his loupe lens, would back him for successor. And if Imad wanted the tattoo removed, and with it the permanent stain of sin that would compromise his own authority – not to mention fear risking Ali's future wrathful surprises - he would pledge the North African tribes to support Ali as well.

By this time tomorrow Ali would be al Khaleef. The Successor. King. But as the train greased the tracks, Ali could not enjoy the anticipation.

There were too many open questions. As they cruised under the ocean, he considered the odds, the complications, and how to anticipate and plan for them.

Could Usman succeed somehow without the Sheikh's money and Imad's North Africans? Potentially. Particularly if Usman had gotten to the Influencer, somehow. Usman had surprised Ali. Ali did not like to be surprised. He began to plan for how exactly he would deal with the traitor.

He needed the Influencer on his side. First order of business was to find Rais Abdullah and win him over.

Something still rankled Ali.

"The Leader spent so much time talking about Badi Badi from Yemen...how he was so impressive and so creative and so this or that," said Ali. "What did he know that I don't?"

High above London, Edwin turned the helicopter south toward the Channel. Suddenly, Edwin heard a series of beeps from the monitor. He glanced at it. A screen image froze, highlighting the faces within in green. The tiny bee camera had located Ali and Fiona sitting side by side in a train.

The other drone showed a second train barreling into the tunnel behind them.

"Go, bird," Edwin said, gunning the throttle. The train that went under the English Channel connecting England to France – London to Paris in two hours – soothed with the free flow of commerce the hundreds of years of war that the impenetrable ocean border had fostered.

That train went one hundred and eighty-six miles per hour. Edwin's bird could double that on a clear night.

Inside the tunnel, Fiona and Ali felt the train brake suddenly. It came to a complete stop.

"What's going on?" Fiona said.

"I don't know," said Ali. "I don't know." He looked around frantically. "This is not good. This is not good."

"Is this an attack?" Fiona whispered.

Ali looked at her. The train had stopped dead, deep under the sea bed. The lights inside the train shone brightly.

He swallowed, aware of Fiona's calm demeanor. She was so unlike the one he could see in his mind's eye, a much younger girl, on the verge of womanhood, with eyes just as blue, skin impossibly perfectly pale, waving a blue and white banner at an American football game in November.

Ali felt a burst of fury. He did not like being trapped. Not anywhere. Definitely not buried under the sea. The spasms began zinging along his neck.

"It'll be fine," he whispered. He slid low in his seat, and raised his knees. He wrapped his arms around them tightly.

When his trouser leg lifted, Fiona saw the large knife in a sheath strapped to Ali's calf.

"Are you...are you getting in a crash position?" Fiona said.

He shook his head. "My neck hurts."

Fiona stopped looking at him, but she heard his rapid, uneven breath. Something had overcome her captor. He appeared to be having a panic attack.

"You're claustrophobic," she said.

Ali shook his head. His fingers covered the knife. "Be quiet."

Fiona watched the perspiration bead on his brow.

She tried to sound reassuring when she spoke to the madman beside her. If he stayed calm, two things could happen. He would not use the blade on her in a moment of panic. And, she could still find out what he was up to.

It could matter to quite possibly a large number of people. Like all of Paris?

This focus kept her panic at bay. She clung to it. Fiona thought of the Finley's catalog. Now she too was earning the right to be amongst the objects in its pages.

"We'll be out in a minute," she said.

Ali nodded.

A few moments later, they felt the pistons engage. The engines coaxed the train forward. As it gathered speed, Ali put his feet on the ground. He took his hand away from his calf, and pulled down his trouser cuffs. He sat up straighter, and checked his watch.

"I just need to get to the Influencer as soon as possible," he said. He felt the crinkled piece of paper with the address near the Parisian river.

Ali needed something else. He needed to log in to a website by 5:00 a.m. That would clear the path for everything. That was his ace.

"So what do you need me for?" Fiona said.

Ali looked at Fiona. He reached up to her hair, and smoothed it. Fiona recoiled, but Ali continued tracing his finger through her hair, to her ear, to the edge of her jaw and along her throat until it came to a rest in the center of her clavicle.

"Every presentation needs a spectacular kickoff, don't you think?" Ali said. "To make sure people are listening to what comes next. I do. I'm sure I do."

Then he looked out the window. The white lights streamed by in an unbroken line.

In Calais, France, Edwin hovered in the helicopter over the Channel exit. A wall of cement dammed a valley of electrical wires and poles. Three tunnels bore through the wall: two for transport and one for service.

The small monitor in his lenses suspended a picture of a graph in front of his eyes. The bees were tracking the train that Ali and Fiona rode in. They told him its speed, and the precise distance it had to travel to reach the edge of the tunnel.

Edwin set a countdown. He would follow the train until they got off in Paris and put an end to Ali there.

"Which world war is this, then?" Edwin wondered as he waited for Ali's train to emerge from the tunnel. "Five? Six? Ali and his tribe are making it the world's next war. And in a few hours I'm going to put an end to it. And to all of them."

Edwin calculated the time in his head.

"The train should be here by now. What's going on, bees?"

Their green dots stayed fixed in the monitor; they had stopped. But they were still filming. The drones told him Ali was in the fifth row of the second carriage. Edwin pulled in close; he wanted to see his nemesis with his own eyes, in that split second before the train gathered land speed and blurred past him. He had to take care though, as the wind shear coming off the train's friction could spin the air to ground pressure beneath his blades, a pressure which they required to hover safely and undetected.

He could feel the air disruption as the train approached. It was edging out of the tunnel, gathering speed. It was moving much slower than it would have been had it not stopped mid-tunnel. Edwin waited. He made the helicopter descend until it hovered twelve feet above the ground, parallel with the train's windows. He flew alongside, following the bees. They had found an attractive source and were gathering at a particular window as the train came through the tunnel.

Edwin saw Ali. But Ali saw only the shape of a small hawk, a kestrel, hovering alongside the moving train. Then Edwin revoked the plasma shield.

For a split second, Ali shrank back. Instead of a bird, he saw the shape of a small helicopter flying by his window. He saw the pilot.

"Edwin," he gasped.

"Edwin!" Fiona shouted.

But their cries were lost in a thunderous explosion. Clouds of black smoke burst out of the tunnel behind them. Orange flames licked the mouth of the tunnel, pressurized air, on fire, racing to release in the atmosphere. The power of a train exploding in the tight confines of a tunnel shot out metal projectiles like a massive shell exploding down the barrel of a rifle.

The fragments and pressure blast caught Edwin's helicopter and tossed it like a cheap lawn chair in a tornado. Up it went into the air, spinning stem over stern, over and over, until the winds released the battered craft and it crashed in pieces on the ground.

CHAPTER THIRTY-THREE

2:52 a.m., May 24, 2014
Calais, France

The metal blades of Edwin's helicopter sprawled on the field, twisted and bent. The glass had shattered.

Over a hundred feet away, behind a clump of grass, Edwin tucked in the folds of his jacket. The ejection mechanism triggered when the gyroscope signaled that the spin was irrecoverable, and propelled Edwin into the air at a safe enough distance from the rotating blades. The folds of his jacket had released, ballooning like two parachutes between his arms and torso. The billowing pockets held a firm edge at the far end, enabling Edwin, once he had caught the air, to glide in a direction away from the crash, descending at a rate of three feet across to one down. This was Zed's fourth version of the flying squirrel suit, and a high-tech cousin of the wing suit favored by some extreme athletes.

The train carrying Ali and Fiona had continued on out of sight. Edwin listened but did not hear its brakes squeal. Instead he heard the distant sirens howling. Judging from the sound of their approach he had four, maybe five minutes before the authorities would arrive.

Instead of stopping, Edwin realized the train carrying Fiona and Ali was picking up speed, putting distance between itself and the explosion behind. Trains have little options for maneuvering but to go forward. Edwin guessed they would clear the vicinity of the explosion, then schedule a planned stop for a full inspection well before they reached Paris.

The second explosion that people heard happened outside the tunnel. It was much smaller than the first. Investigators would think it was part of a fuel tank that exploded at the same time. With the train parts scattered over the countryside, it would be hard to sort out the fragments of steel that had originally framed the blades and body of a small and unusual helicopter.

Edwin took inventory. Though he had not slept in over twenty-four hours, his adrenalin was pumping. He stretched each arm and leg. Nothing hurt. He stretched his neck. Fine. Fiona's train was long gone into the distance.

"Arghh!" Edwin growled. "There has just been a major terrorist attack at the mouth of the Channel Tunnel. I'm on foot. In the middle of the night. Too damn close to it."

And too damn far from her.

Edwin checked his clothes. His khakis and blue chambray shirt fit the part; he was grateful for the unexpected change to a more casual look. He had his brown Gore-Tex backpack still strapped to his shoulders. He slid it off and opened it. Then he extracted the precise tools for his next cover for status.

Edwin held a ballpoint pen. And a well-thumbed copy of Alan Ginsburg's *Howl.*

"Now I need a tree," Edwin said. "A big one, close by."

In the darkness he trotted across the uneven grass. Lights began sweeping the landscape as the officials gathered around the destruction. Helicopters flew overhead.

Edwin dashed under the dense, drooping boughs of a chestnut tree. He sat down heavily against its trunk. He put his pack over his lap. And he closed his eyes.

Edwin had learned to sleep anywhere, at any time, under any level of duress. These two hours of rest for his body and mind could make the difference in the battles that would come with daylight. His reflexes would be sharper. His decisions would be better.

The last thing I want to do is to walk aimlessly at an odd time of night through a small village while all of the public safety officials of France, England and Interpol arrive. But a writer out of cash and on the road with Alan Ginsburg ... where else is he going to sleep?

It was 3:12 am, by the green digits in the corner of his view. Two hours would be plenty. He leaned back against the trunk of the tree and set his internal alarm clock.

"One hundred and twenty minutes," Edwin said.

Then he closed his eyes, and slept.

CHAPTER THIRTY-FOUR

4:30 a.m., May 24
St. Denis, France

The train stopped at a commuter rail station in a suburb outside Paris. Ali jumped off the back platform and pulled Fiona along with him.

"Don't even try it," he said.

They walked through the farmer's market that was just setting up in the dawn light. Wooden crates held stacks of spring lettuces, pods of asparagus and piles of artichokes, fennel and leeks. Bright flowers soaked in deep, wet pots. Cubes of fresh-churned light yellow butter sat under wax paper, immune to flies. Glass bottles stood in rows, full of milk, thick layers of cream below their tight tin caps.

Restaurant buyers would be there soon, stocking their kitchens with fresh produce well before the patrons would request their breakfast omelettes.

Coming through the other side of the market, they saw a taxi.

With his satchel over his right arm, Ali opened the back door and pushed Fiona into the car.

He barked an address to the driver. It was for a street address in the center of Paris, along the River Seine.

Thirty minutes later, Ali sat in an old baroque chair, covered with faded grey velvet, face to face with the Influencer. When they had arrived, Ali had shoved Fiona into a hallway closet and locked it. She would not disturb the pitch of his life.

"What is your claim, then? What can out-do cyanide-laced salt packets? Exploding tunnels? Or is this one in the closet your only plan? A decapitation for all to see? Buh. That is so catty copy," Rais Abdullah said, unimpressed. "Why should I give you this chance, now?"

"She is just a side show," said Ali. "An inconvenience turned to opportunity."

"Now, that's a good skill," said Abdullah. "Show me what you have and why should I put my support behind you. Something you seek at such a late date."

Ali pulled out his phone.

"An app? Buh," came the blast of French contempt.

Then Ali turned on the device. He showed the Influencer how he could capture the green dots, and with a turn of his hand, how the gyroscope in the device could send a message that made each of them move too. And so much more.

By the time Ali had fully demonstrated the potential of his hand-held demon, an entirely different expression had settled over the Influencer's face.

"It is impressive," said Abdullah. "I will think about it. I will make my decision known to the others before the meeting tonight. Now go."

On the way to the bedroom, Ali saw something through the open door to another bedroom that caught his eye. It was a tattered old suitcase, covered in carpet.

It had been his once. He had taken it to college. And when he no longer needed that cloak, he tossed it out. His houseboy had picked it out of the trash.

Ali turned back to the Influencer.

"Usman is here?" Ali asked.

"Not at the moment," said Abdullah. "Go put your things down. Have a rest. This will all be resolved this evening, as the Leader has told us it should be. Exactly forty-eight hours after his demise."

CHAPTER THIRTY-FIVE

5:10 a.m. May 24
Calais, France

E dwin opened his eyes one hundred and eighteen minutes after he closed them. The sun had already woken
the farmers.

"I hope Dr. Bart posted those results," Edwin said. "He
keeps Fiona safe or he's toast."

Now Edwin had to get to Luxembourg Gardens in the
heart of Paris. He blinked his eyes and muttered a command.

"Where am I?"

The floating image in his lenses produced a bird's eye
roadmap; then a version in relief, then a photographic
street view showing where the road nearest to his field met
with two others.

"Three roads meeting. There's a cafe. Or a garage.
Maybe both," Edwin said. He did not want to hitch a ride to
Paris in a milk truck. Slow. Too risky. They'd close all roads
and inspect everything, everyone.

Hitchhiking near a terrorist attack. Suboptimal. Bad plan.

Then Edwin thought of another option. It involved
some degree of exposure. It involved a former colleague.
A former— attachment, of sorts. But it just might work.

Slacker. You better still be doing your rounds in Europe.

Edwin blinked his eyes, and his lenses adjusted. In his field of view, a blue monitor appeared, with a blinking arrow. He began to think about code, semantics that would speak with other computer languages that would let him in through the hatch he had created, over a decade earlier, to let him in and out of every secure system in the company he had created: D6.

This time, he only needed the employee directory.

"D-a-v-e-n-p-o-r-t" he thought, and each letter appeared on the screen in front of him. "Hudson" Edwin whispered. The microphone embedded in his skin behind his left ear lobe captured this input. In a millisecond, a phone number appeared. The cursor flashed, then wrote, "Shall I dial for you now?"

Edwin nodded his head. The gyroscope captured the motion of his head up and down.

The transistor implanted behind his right ear lobe created a very small sound that at such close range, only Edwin could hear it ring. He breathed slightly easier when the tone adjusted and he heard the ring reach to a different continent from the one he had dialed, located in Cambridge, Massachusetts.

"Allo!" answered a cheerful voice, with a fake French accent. "Davenport 'ere."

Edwin said nothing.

"Cato? Is that you? I told you not tonight. Really. I mean it. Aha - zer you ah!" Hudson Davenport was a poor, but enthusiastic, mimic of Peter Sellers.

Edwin heard Hudson cough, then drop the Pink Panther routine.

Hudson said in a plain voice, "Can I help you? Hello?"

Edwin looked at the grasses waving in the field. The early morning sun spread gold across the lush green blades.

Edwin unscrambled his voice for a single word.

"Slacker," he said.

Then he thought the command that made his voice audible, comprehensible, but unrecognizable. The screen processed it.

Hudson was wordless.

Then, very tentatively, he said, "Edw-?..Is this? Are you-?"

"Shut up. Just tell me where you are," said Edwin, his voice mechanically altered and disguised.

"Amiens, France," said Hudson slowly. "Seeing customers north of Paris. We head to the city later today."

Edwin spoke quickly.

"Are you alone?"

"No way!" Hudson exclaimed, hoping to confuse the young man who sat opposite him at the steel woven cafe table. The man was a recent hire to manage sales in France with whom Hudson was about to begin a long day of visiting customers.

"Get alone. Do you have a car?"

"I could," Hudson said. He eyed his colleague, who was sipping cappuccino.

"How far are you from Calais?"

"Agh...I don't know," Hudson said.

"Know," Edwin said.

Edwin heard him typing on the phone.

"Google maps says it's like an hour and a half drive," Hudson said finally. He had walked out of the restaurant in the hotel where bleary business people were getting ready for the day. "What are you doing there?"

"I'm not there. But I'm close. Can you get to this town – G-u-i-n-e-s?"

"Yeah, okay, when?"

"Five minutes ago," said Edwin. "Get there as fast you possibly can, slacker. With wheels. And alone."

"Where, exactly?"

"Look for a small café. Pink cement walls. Lots of flowers in baskets. Clay pot roof tiles. Called 'Brasserie' something."

"Thanks for narrowing it down," said Hudson.

Edwin disconnected the call.

He trotted down the hillside and behind tree cover that edged the roadside. The branches of the trees were remarkable, their leaves seeming to shoot upward so an artist would have to use upward brush strokes to capture them. As the dirt shifted beneath his feet, Edwin saw more spinning blue lights of the French police descending toward the latest terrorist attack on their soil. The morning shift.

He blinked, and the images that his bees had sent him of a pink café in the nearby town transformed to a map which showed him the farm fields to keep to and the roads to avoid as he jogged four kilometers to the small town of Guines, France.

Ten minutes later, just as the first morning news came on the air, the planner of the Channel Tunnel Attack revealed himself.

CHAPTER THIRTY-SIX

1:00 a.m., May 24
Washington, D.C.

The technician at the Association for the Society to Protect waited nervously as he watched the last minutes tick past.

The phone rang. He picked it up and heard the long steady tone. He looked at the crumpled piece of paper he had retrieved from a flyer advertising whale watches by the ocean. He punched in the code.

"Go," said a deep voice. "The Head is listening."

The technician tried to keep the tremor out of his voice.

"The uh, we successfully placed the bug in one of the drones Zed built. It went live yesterday. We picked up a read from it. In France. The RUPD operatives are on their way there now."

"France," said the Head. "Find him. As soon as possible. Do not lose him again."

CHAPTER THIRTY-SEVEN

5:30 a.m., May 24
Charles de Gaulle Airport, France

As the twelve seat Embraer jet began its descent, Camille watched the video on the small monitor that rose from the center table between the pair of plush leather seats.

Through her noise-canceling headphones, Camille heard the testimonial video.

"It took you ten years to find our great Leader. It took me one day to strike back. My name is Badi Badi. Yesterday we struck your fat Western bellies that have gorged on the flesh of the world, leaving the rest of us without. Today I struck your fastest train. Now you will think of me before you put anything in your mouth. Now you will think of me before you make a move. You know I can get to you, any one of you, as and when I choose. Yesterday you won a skirmish. Today I moved the battle forward. Fear what tomorrow holds for you."

"So you want the job too," Camille said to the screen. She was surprised to feel so relieved. The face did not belong to Ali. Not for the moment. But according to Edwin, in a matter of time, it could soon. And if she saw Ali's face it would mean something even worse had happened.

We're watching a shoot-out between the world's worst terrorists, giving it all they have to earn the top position. And we're their targets. This is definitely a non-trivial problem.

Camille studied every element in the field of view the camera provided. The pale grey paint chipping on the wall. The top of an old suitcase just inching into the frame. A thick pipe in the corner. Camille compared the width of the pipe to the speaker's face

Sewage. There's a toilet above. Maybe a full bath. Old paint. Maybe lead.

She studied the angle of the light on the subject.

He's standing near the corner because he wants natural light for filming. This is an apartment building. One wall of windows. The other side is a hallway.

The video ended.

"Impressive salvo," said Camille. "Will it be enough to win the pledge of loyalties from the faction leaders?" She felt chilled and fearful. But not for what Badi Badi would do next.

Oh, Ali. What will you have to do to top him? Or this Usman?

The Interpol report fed up to Camille's secure tablet as she heard the landing gear engage.

There were two women named Madame Raisa de la Seine with addresses in Paris. One was in a shabby neighborhood near Montmartre. The other was on Rue du St. Germaine in the 16th Arrondissement, a mile from the Eiffel Tower.

Camille looked at the time stamp in the corner of her screen. She passed her thumb over it. A countdown alarm appeared. There was no time to check out the addresses first. Above all she had to be in the Luxembourg Gardens to meet Edwin.

CHAPTER THIRTY-EIGHT

5:30 a.m., May 24
Calais, France

At the edge of the farmer's field, Edwin saw a rusted metal bicycle with a large wire basket hanging over the back wheel.

"Cover for action," he thought. This was tradecraft - the plausible reason he could give for doing what he was doing, where he was doing it. His "cover for status" - the plausible reason he could give for being who he said he was - Edwin needed another prop. He felt in his brown backpack for the rectangular shape that was about a quarter of an inch thick. It was still there.

Edwin pushed the bike over the clumps of grass and dirt until he reached the second road that led to and from the village. Hudson Davenport would be there soon.

"Now, wander!" Edwin ordered himself.

He wanted to stand on the pedals and churn the wheels as fast as he could go. Instead, he pedaled lazily, weaving along the roadside as he scanned the countryside. He was traveling along empty farm fields, marked by tall trees at the borders. The early dawn glazed the light green sprouts. The morning smelled of spring grass and wet dirt. Somewhere the smell of yeast rose in hot plumes through chimneys.

Bakers were pinching wet dough into croissants, baguettes, tartes tatin, then sliding them on metal trays into hot ovens for the earliest risers. Edwin passed small rectangular white signs that told him the next towns were near.

He could hear more emergency vehicles wailing. A gendarme slowed as it passed him. Edwin raised a hand in acknowledgment.

The vehicle pulled to the curb on an angle that blocked Edwin's path. The officer opened the door and stood behind it. He stuck out his palm.

"Arretez!" the policeman commanded.

Edwin stopped pedaling.

He put one foot on the ground. The other stayed on the pedal. He looked down at his rusty front wheel. He would have to escape on his brains.

"I'm a tourist. Too-reest," he said.

"Americain? Anglais?" said the policeman. "What are you doing here? Alone? Where are your baggages?"

"I am un poet," said Edwin. "I don't need much. Just this. Okay?" He asked permission to slowly reach into his small backpack.

The officer raised his chin.

"Okay," he said.

Edwin pulled out a small book. It was a long, challenging poem.

The policeman took the paperback.

"'*owl*, by Alan Ginsburg?" read the policeman.

The corners of the volume were curled, and the laminate was peeling off the cover.

Edwin had spent many hours reading it on the rig, in the sunshine. Anchored to a girder with his Nikes.

He still had no idea what the book meant.

But without anyone to talk to, the words created by another person, in his own language - however unfamiliar the message - was a strong link to the life he had left. And it was the one part of Lula Crosse that he could hold in his hands.

She was saving him again, though he had cost her everything. The irony made Edwin angry. But he pushed it down. Focus.

"I bike, I see, I think, I go to the cafe and write," Edwin told the gendarme, with an unfamiliar sing-song cadence.

"You are Hemingway, eh? Another? Bon. Go, then." Satisfied, he waved Edwin forward, toward the town. "You can find a nice cafe in the village. Better find an 'otel, too, for tonight."

More officials raced by, sirens blaring. No one stopped Edwin again. They raced past him to the north, screeching tires toward the wreckage that Edwin was putting further behind him with every crank of the pedals.

When he was alone on the road, Edwin tightened his grip on his handlebars. He stood on the pedals and pushed hard, ungainly but faster, toward the village.

"Find me, slacker!" Edwin said, scanning each passing car for the silly grin of Hudson Davenport.

But sometimes, even when time is of the essence, there is nothing to do but wait.

Edwin put his borrowed bicycle in a rack with two others near the post office. He surveyed the town. The sun was coming up, promising a warm spring day. Three roads came together in the short span that was its main street. There was a boulangerie where Edwin saw fresh baguettes sticking pointed ends out of baskets on display. In a butcher shop, cured meats hung from the window display. A florist stacked baskets of spring blooms on staircased benches and hung overflowing baskets of blooms from the windows. Another small shop proffered baskets of produce, colorful and vibrant, light green stalks of leeks, artichokes with clenched leaves, plump peapods, frizzy heads of lettuce.

Edwin walked to the produce market. He saw baskets of plump red strawberries.

"Vas-y!" Go ahead, called the grocer, encouraging Edwin to try the berries. "Ils sont magnifiques, non?"

Edwin popped a berry in his mouth. He had not tasted a fresh strawberry in a long, long time. He chewed, then swallowed the sweet fruit and its juices.

Edwin nodded, and tipped his hat. Absolutely magnificent.

"Good," he said.

He picked up a box of berries and reached inside his pack. Different pockets contained different monetary units. The Euro had greatly simplified commerce - and espionage. Covert operatives needed fewer denominations to tuck into their pouches.

His box of strawberries in hand, Edwin popped one into his mouth. Then he scanned the roads. Nothing.

"Shlacker," Edwin muttered as the juice leaked from his lips. He swallowed. "You better be on your way here."

"Ah, there it is," Edwin said. On the corner, he saw small round tables with woven iron chairs. The glass windows were painted with his favorite word. "Cafe."

Edwin chose a seat with his back to the restaurant and where he could see, up and down the road.

Though minutes ticked off in his brain, he could relax his guard in one respect. Ali was on that train. The train was somewhere else. For the moment, there would be no counter-attack. This was no stroll in the countryside, either. Fiona was still with him.

The waiter approached.

"Eat when you can," Edwin thought, reciting a critical lesson from his Survival, Evasion, Resistance and Escape training.

"I'll have two chocolate croissants and a large cappuccino," Edwin said. The waiter nodded and disappeared.

Shortly he returned with a basket containing a folded white napkin. He placed it next to Edwin's plate. Then he settled a bowl-sized mug in front of Edwin. Cream frothed in small bubbles. Someone had dripped the espresso in the shape of a heart. Cocoa powder was sprinkled across the surface.

Edwin opened the napkin and sweet steam rose in the morning air. He lifted one of the croissants. Flakes of golden pastry drifted as he put it in his mouth. He bit, tasting the thick strip of soft dark chocolate that ran through the croissant and balanced the savory buttery bread. In two bites, the pastry was gone and he was licking flakes off his fingers.

Edwin gulped the cappuccino, watching the road over the lip of the mug. He noticed the waiter watching him. His mouth full, Edwin pulled a pad of paper from his back pocket and double-clicked a ball point pen.

This time, an ink tip appeared.

"A poet?" Edwin thought. He began to rethink his choice of cover for action. But he had to stay consistent in this town, close to the explosion, and where a policeman and two shop keepers had had a good look at him.

The waiter eyed his blank page, pursed his lips.

Edwin wrote three words. "Strawberries are red."

Edwin was dabbing his finger to the plate to capture the last flakes when he heard something coming down the road, wheezing like a sewing machine. He looked up to see a very small car, optimistically branded "Deux Chevaux."

"More like One Goat," Edwin muttered. The car pulled to the side of the road, and the stringy engine sounds ceased. Edwin watched as the driver got out.

The years had not changed Hudson Davenport very much. He still was fit. He stood and stretched in the street with that same easy smile. His chocolate brown hair was still thick. Edwin took in grey flecks in Hudson's hair and the longer laugh lines around his eyes. He wondered what Hudson had done, and with whom, while those lines slowly deepened.

Edwin dropped money on the table for his meal and stood up slowly. He took the strawberry basket with him. Every fiber was pushing him faster; he breathed deeply, he slowed his movements. He had to remain forgettable.

"Get in," Edwin said to Hudson as he slipped into the side seat. "We'll talk on the way. First give me your phone. And your laptop."

"Laptop? No one travels with a laptop now. So heavy!"

Edwin spluttered. "Give me everything electronic now, slacker."

He took out the battery of Hudson's phone. He pulled out his ballpoint pen and with a click, produced a very thin, sharp, blade. He poked it into the edge of the iPad. Then he reached up to the hands-free phone microphone in the car, and strapped a piece of duct tape over it.

"Drive. Fast. Toward Paris. I need to be in the Luxembourg Gardens yesterday."

Hudson got in, turned the key and the sewing machine wound itself up. They drove out of the village, on to the main road.

"Faster," Edwin barked. "Fast as you can."

"Um ... so," Hudson said. "Hello."

Edwin looked back at him. "Strawberry?" He shook the basket at Hudson. One berry skittled around the box.

"So ...," said Hudson again. There was a long pause. The sewing machine strained up a hill.

"So ...," said Edwin.

Hudson took this as encouragement. It was how he saw most signs. "So the last time I saw you someone shot you off your motorcycle."

"No, the last time you saw me I was drinking a cup of coffee on Charles St. in Boston."

"Right, but then...around the corner. I heard a shot. The crowd said you got shot and some street bum carried you off... " Hudson said, remembering the confusing end to Edwin Hoff that Hudson witnessed over a decade before.

"Drive," Edwin said. "I need to get to Paris as soon as humanly possible. I'm behind."

From the corner of the café, a man with shaggy blonde hair and thick wire frame glasses paid his check and rose. He wore a black leather jacket. He walked out of the café and swung his leg over a motorcycle.

Then Lars Grundek, ASP operator, followed the small car out of the village toward Paris.

CHAPTER THIRTY-NINE

12:00 p.m., May 24
Paris, France

In Luxembourg Gardens in the heart of the city of lights, an American tourist was easy to spot. At any time of day, she walked fast in her jogging shoes, fist around her purse, straight through the park to reach her destination unmolested, and only a few minutes late. A Parisian found a bench and sat on it.

Edwin could not bear to sit. He had been forced to sit for years. Instead, he paced around the boat pond.

Between the pond and the benches near the wooded area stood a crepe stand. It had a short line when Edwin joined it. He tried to appear patient, watching with the others as the chef poured thin yellow batter onto a convex griddle, lifting it with a long thin spatula, flipping it and folding it over sliced bananas and Nutella. He folded the moon into a half, then that into a triangle with a rounded edge. He shook clouds of powdered sugar over the top.

The next customer ordered a savory item. The chef layered slices of ham on top of shaved asiago cheese, which melted as the next crepe cooked.

Edwin looked around. He could not see Camille anywhere. He gritted his teeth. The timing was just too tight.

She would have had to find the answer almost immediately. But Camille had always proven so resourceful.

"Pour vous?" asked the crepe-man, when Edwin reached the front of the line.

"Chocolate-banane - deux," said a woman behind Edwin.

He turned to see Camille, and smiled. They collected their crepes and moved to a bench near the boat pond. She sat. Edwin stood. They ate.

"What did you learn?" Edwin said.

"I got a name," Camille said. "Interpol produced two addresses in Paris."

"Where?" Edwin said. His voice was terse.

"One near Montmartre and one in the 16th Arrondissement," Camille said, describing two neighborhoods of Paris.

"The 16th? Isn't that one of the wealthiest?"

"Yes."

"What's a twenty-five year old doing living there?"

"I don't know. The other area is grittier," said Camille.

"Let's go there first," Edwin said. "I'll get a car. Or a bike."

Edwin stalked the locked, parked cars on the edge of the road, until he found one. He had his hand on the handle, when he noticed the red flashing alarm light inside. Time was wasting. He moved to the next.

"Yoo hoo," called Camille.

Edwin looked up. Camille stood next to a taxi, holding the door open.

In ten minutes, the taxi delivered them at the address of an old cement building.

"Look," said Camille, pointing at the panel on the door. It was in Arabic. "There's a mosque next door."

Edwin watched as Camille knocked on the door. A young woman opened the door. After a few words, Camille trotted down the steps.

"She's running a daycare," Camille told Edwin when she returned.

"Is it a front?"

"She's watching six toddlers. That's enough terrorists under one roof," Camille said.

"The mosque - is it a front?"

Camille ran a check on her iPhone. "There's no known suspicious activity at this location. Not with Paris, not with us, not with Interpol."

"So it's...," Edwin paused.

"...a mosque," Camille said. "There's religion and then there's criminals. Our job is to separate the two."

"My job is to get Ali," Edwin said.

"You mean stop the succession," Camille said, looking at him.

"Get Ali," Edwin glared at her. "I told you years ago he was into it up to his eyeballs. He financed the attempted bio attack – and when we stopped him the first time he doubled his money and tried again."

"He owed his uncle," Camille muttered.

"No," Edwin said. "He's been programmed. He has a mission. Everything he has done has been a front to get to this very moment in his life when he can take over Al Ra'duzma and use all his knowledge of western culture – learned at Yale, learned from you – "

"– and from you," Camille parried. "You hired him at your company."

"That was different," Edwin spluttered. "He was supposed to be a grad student at MIT. He was a genius. We weren't scanning for terrorists."

"Not even you?" Camille said. "I'm surprised. What happened to your...focus? D6 was just cover, and covers aren't real, right?"

Edwin curled his lips into his teeth. He said nothing. Camille had aimed well, and she stung him. D6 had sent him into orbit with the unexpectedly public life of a tech billionaire. This had greatly displeased the ASP, his true employer. Edwin could deny the impact his cover life had had on him. But when he was alone on the rig, when he tuned in the special monitor to watch what was happening in the D6 closed circuit TV network, he knew this. D6 always had thrilled him to his toes. And it still did.

"He seemed like a smart guy," Edwin said finally. "An arrogant jerk, but smart. Almost as smart as me."

"Yes," said Camille. "Sometimes it's hard to tell the difference."

"Look," Edwin said. "Whatever came before, it's clear now. He was in the Leader's house when they got him. He went back in after the Americans left and before the Pakistani ISI arrived. And he's taken a hostage."

"He's the chosen one. Al Khaleef. So he thinks," said Camille. "Then there is this Badi Badi. And Usman, the so-called Burger Bomber."

"And they want the job too," said Edwin. "And they each have to do two things to get it."

"Scare the crap out of everyone," Camille said.

"Yes. Burger bombs and train blasts - done," Edwin said. He would use everything at hand to motivate Camille to find Ali. Even if he suspected that Camille's goal was far more sympathetic than his. "And there's more."

"What?" she asked.

"They are going to kill Ali," Edwin said. "Because they each have to remove the competition."

Camille paused. "We have to get to him first."

"Exactly," said Edwin.

The taxi sped through the streets of Paris to the second address Interpol had produced. It belonged to a grand apartment building not far from the Eiffel Tower.

"This is a very expensive place for a helper," Camille said. "This kind of place gets noticed."

"But this kind of place gets a lot of deliveries," said Edwin. "Cover for action. Messages can come and go in flowers, packages, errand runs. People are always coming and going."

"Okay," Camille said. "So what do we do?"

"Send her flowers," Edwin said.

Edwin hung by the doorway while Camille walked catty-corner across the street, past the boucherie's meats, the gro-cerie's produce, and the boulangerie, where local families picked up their bread on a daily basis. Camille bought a large bouquet from the grocerie.

Then she walked back to the door and rang the buzzer.

"*Nous avons des fleurs pour vous, madame*," she said.

"*Merci, venez.. Troisieme etage*," said an older woman's voice.

"She's not in her twenties," Camille said to Edwin as she entered the elevator and pulled the wire grate shut.

"Maybe she has a maid," Edwin said. "I'll stay out here. Be quick. Drop the flowers and report. Meet me across the street in the cafe."

Behind the diamond steel shapes in the elevator door grate, Edwin watched Camille's feet rise up and through the ceiling. Then he crossed the street and went into a café.

A motorcycle idled near the butcher shop. Its rider wore a black leather jacket and helmet. He spoke into a small headset.

"Lars, I have him in view. Thirty feet away. Am I clear to kill?"

"No," said Lars Grundek. "You are not. But do not lose him. Bring him to me. And then the Head will put an end to this hunt personally."

Edwin studied the cafe's seating options. He counted the areas of egress. It was on the corner of two busy streets. He looked down each; there were off-shoots and angles. Plenty of options should he need one. He picked a small table where his back was in the corner, where he could see all approaching. As he walked to his chosen seat, he adjusted the napkin container on the table in front of him, like an extended rearview mirror to catch anyone approaching. The glass wall of the cafe would reflect any other inconsistent motion.

Edwin pulled out the tattered copy of *Howl* and his pencil. He looked around. There were several people sitting by themselves in this cafe, each with a pen or a poem in hand, each becoming the next Hemingway. He wondered how many of them had used those hands they wrapped around pens, shaping delicate phrases, to kill.

Edwin's eyes scanned the pages but he focused only on his peripheral vision.

Something did not feel right. Edwin scanned the tables. Something was out of place. The pattern was broken somewhere. The tables were laid with rolled napkins around cutlery. Each had an ashtray and napkin container.

The napkin container. That was it. At one table, Edwin saw that the reflective aluminum face had been shifted on a ten degree angle from the other place settings. He followed the reflection of the turned facade until he met the cold face of a man he knew. He had last seen him years before, through a window, crushing the windpipe of Lula Crosse.

Their eyes locked.

"He made me," said the ASP operator into the microphone. "I have no choice. I must take him out now."

Edwin stood up abruptly. "Everything chases a running rabbit," he muttered.

Edwin tipped over a chair, and leaped over the brass railing of the cafe. He bolted down a street, then right down another alongside the tall grey facades of the regal apartment buildings in the 16th Arrondissement of Paris.

The man in the black jacket crashed over the tables and chairs. At other café tables, more hopeful poets looked up, horrified. Then, finally having had an experience, they scribbled down how they felt about it. The operator leaped over the railing seconds behind Edwin. He barely saw Edwin turn at the corner by the flower shop.

Edwin rounded the corner at full speed. He knocked a hanging flower pot from its post, and held it for two strides. Then the bright red and yellow blooms and green stalks fell with their dirt in a clump on the ground behind him.

Seconds later, the ASP operator ran over the broken plant. He could not see Edwin. He looked down the empty road lined with the grey stone facades of elegant pre-war buildings. Then the operator saw another, narrower street bend off at an angle. He ran down it. A woman walked by him with a worried expression. He slowed to a walk, studying the entryways to the buildings. He did not see any other roads. Perhaps there was an alley further along, between the elegant archways capped in green iron awnings.

The woman turned and scowled at the operator. He tucked into the closest door as if to examine the names at the ringer.

The green iron awning above him was strong, and bolted into the steel girders behind the cement facade. It was strong enough to hold a grown man's weight, for a short period of time. The time it took to wrap around two fists the ends of a green wire used to hang a flowerpot.

While the man posed in front of the names beside the door, the woman turned the corner and was gone.

That was when Edwin dropped on the ASP operator like a wild cat from a tree. The thick flower wire cut through his windpipe as the angle of Edwin's falling weight broke his spine.

"Lula," Edwin said, a sad apology in the sharp word. Then he walked slowly down the street, leaving the assassin crumpled on the ground.

Be better yesterday. Edwin scolded himself. *There will be more. They know where I am now. They know I am alive now. There will be many more soon. That old bird does not give up. She does not give up.*

So until Camille resurfaced from the apartment that possibly housed the Helper, Edwin would keep moving. He would know every road around this Helper's spot. He would watch everyone come and go. And after he got Ali, and stopped the succession, he would not be seen again. But he had to find him. Fast. Before things went very badly for another innocent woman. He wondered how Fiona Tate was faring in the extended company of one who aspired to be the world's next ace in the terrorist deck of cards.

CHAPTER FORTY

5:00 p.m., May 24
Paris, France

The elevator opened on the third floor. Camille knew instantly that she had been fooled. She had no idea where to turn next. All she knew was they were out of time and options. Bile rose in her throat.

"No, no, no. This is wrong," Camille said..

She's an old woman! KAH told us the Helper is in her twenties. This is way off.

To Camille's eye, the woman who met her at the elevator was in her mid-sixties. She was draped in a black cloak, with a black head scarf.

Behind her Camille saw a long greyish blue hallway, paint peeling off ornate balustrades and mantles around wide doorways. A chair was covered in grey velvet that still showed some of its original garnet near the deep seams. A small glass lamp sat on a side table. It was filled with beach stones that shone beneath the bulb's warm dome. Green malachite. Purple amethyst. Blue lapis and striped agates.

Nothing has changed here in fifty years. Including the rent.

Camille studied the woman's face. She took in the round of her jaw, the formless thick shape of her bending frame.

She had dark eyes that hung heavy bags. A black scarf covered her hair.

But then something caught Camille's eye. She could not explain why it held her attention, but it was just enough to make her stay, and ask some questions.

"Madame de la Seine?" Camille read, looking at the card on the flowers.

"*Oui, c'est moi,*" the woman said. She reached into a purse to pay.

"*Non,*" said Camille. "*C'est un cadeaux.* From the store." It's a gift.

The woman shrugged and turned to put the flowers on the side table. As she turned, and bent her head, Camille saw something that explained everything.

"My lord," thought Camille. "It can't be."

"*C'est tout?*" the woman said. Is that all?

"No, that is not all," Camille said. She abandoned French for Arabic. She spoke in the dialect she knew best, that of the hometown of her first Arabic tutor.

Madame de la Seine stiffened, very slightly.

Camille took a deep breath, and said, "I am here to give you your family back."

The woman turned to Camille. She spoke in English.

"I don't know who you are," she said. "But you have confused the translation. You mean 'take me back to my family.' But the boys are my family. All the boys who come and go. And I can look at them. And hope for them."

Camille saw in Madame de la Seine a wistfulness, a look of deep sadness.

"And I help them adjust. Give them a fresh start in a new world."

"To be martyrs?" Camille countered. "They could be so much more."

"Martyrs...buh. Why? Because of their beards, our devotion to Muslim tradition?" Madame de la Seine pursed her lips in contempt. "No, no. I feed them. I give them warm food, so they can study ... learn a trade ... and earn a salary so they can start a family...what every mother wishes for her boys."

She said this too firmly, Camille thought.

"Maybe," Camille said. "But that's not why Khalid al Hamzami set you up here decades ago."

Madame de la Seine blinked rapidly. She said nothing.

"What did you wish for your boy?" Camille said softly. "Before..."

The woman raised her eyes. They were black with anger. "I don't have a son," she said.

Camille spoke very softly. "You did, Raisa."

Madame de la Seine shook her fist. "How do you know my ...my...you must leave now."

"Your friend, the scientist, Khalid al Hamzami, told me your name. And he told me how he came to your door. He told you that an American bomb fell on your husband's car. That he and the boy were both killed."

Her eyes looked black. Through a flat thin mouth, she hissed. "How do you know this?"

"The Americans call your husband's old friend 'KAH.' He's a very bad man. He'll live the rest of his days beneath a mountain in Nevada where he sees the sun for fifteen minutes a day because he once helped execute the biggest attack on American soil, and because I helped stop him. He told me all about you. Everything I needed to know."

Madame de la Seine sat down on the cracked white vinyl of a kitchen chair that wobbled on bent aluminum legs. She rested her elbows on the table. Her head hung low as she spoke.

"I had nothing. I had no reason to live. The bombs took my life, too. Eventually, Khalid took pity on me. He breathed his own air into my lungs. He brought me to Paris, he told me to help the boys. I found I could...I could hope for them. He kept sending them to me, just for a few months, then new ones would come. I wouldn't let any of them stay more than a few months."

"And did you ever see any of them again?" Camille asked softly.

Madame de la Seine shook her head as her tears began. Full drops welled at the bridge of her nose, and streaked down her face.

"Is anyone here now?" Camille asked.

She nodded. "There are three. One just arrived a few hours ago. One came yesterday. Another comes and goes."

"The newest one...where is he now?"

"I showed him to his room. He bathed. He asked for something to eat."

"What did he ask for?"

"Figs," said the woman. "He asked for figs with honey."

Camille felt her spine tingle. Yassir's favorite snack.

"He's here?" she said. Her mouth was suddenly dry. "In the other room?"

Madame de la Seine shook her head.

"No. He's not here. He turned on the computer, saw something, and left very quickly."

"What was he wearing?"

"He was fancy. Very western ... blue suit, a tie. They needed a thorough wash but they were quite expensive-looking."

"Can I see the room?"

The woman walked her down a long hallway, past a room containing a small toilet and sink, and another with a full bath. The back room was a small rectangle. The long wall was lined with books. There was a futon mattress unrolled on a wooden frame, made up in fresh linen. Against the wall leaned an old suitcase, its carpeted exterior in tatters.

Camille balked. She knew that suitcase. Yassir had brought it, clean and new, to college. It was gone the night before graduation when she had gone to his room and had seen only three rolled up socks in a triangle on his bed.

She turned slowly to the glow coming from the screen of an old computer on the desk. It was on a website that made no sense to Camille.

www.OxfordDNAlabs.co.uk? What was that for?

Walking back to the hallway, Camille noticed another small bedroom. It was painted grey. It was empty. There was a thick pipe running from ceiling to floor in the corner. A window let in a lot of natural light.

She had seen that before too. It was the background to the tape Badi Badi had released in which he took responsibility for the Channel bombing.

Camille spun. "Who else did you say is here?"

"No one, now," said the woman. "There's been another young man for several weeks. Another came yesterday, as I said. But they all seem to be out now."

"He stays in this room?"

"Yes. I have several bedrooms. It's rent-controlled. I've been here over thirty years. It's a lot of space for Paris, and at 1970s rates."

"Where is he now?"

The woman puckered her lower lip and shrugged.

"Buh," she said, making the noise that in French can mean, I do not agree, I do not know, I do not care. "The new one left a few moments before you got here. He said it was time to show the girl the sights of Paris."

"The girl?" asked Camille. "Wasn't he alone?"

"No, he had an English girl with him. But of course she cannot stay here. If they marry, I will help them find another place."

Camille's mind raced. She must find Edwin now. She would bet a plate of figs that room down the hall was where Badi Badi filmed his testimonial video to make his bid to succeed the Leader.

If Yassir returns here tonight, he won't leave.

"Madame de la Seine," said Camille. "I need to show you something."

She held out her mobile phone. Wherever she went in the world, she carried photographs with her. Some were recent, of her travels to the great pyramids, and to Gibraltar, and the Kennedy Center by the Potomac River in Washington D.C. One was of a magnificent Picasso that hung on the wall of a private home. One was a photograph she had scanned in. It was taken in college, outside the dining hall. She was sitting on the lap of her college boyfriend, Yassir Metah.

Madame de la Seine looked at the picture, and back at Camille. Then she sat down heavily in a chair and bent over the armrest, facing the wall.

Camille soon left Madame de la Seine's apartment. She took the elevator to the street level and pushed open the heavy door. She did not see Edwin, so she moved slowly along the sidewalk toward the shops.

Suddenly Edwin appeared at her side.

Camille jumped, patting her chest rapidly.

"Cool as a cucumber, as ever," Edwin noted.

"Where did you come from?" Camille's cheeks blushed.

"Just hanging around," Edwin said.

"How did you get that mud on your face?" Camille said.

"Stopped to smell the roses," he said, wiping it off.

"Watch out for the thorns," Camille said. "You're bleeding."

She held his hand upward. A fresh red line cut straight across Edwin's palms.

"So? What did you find out?" Edwin said.

"A lot," Camille said. "Ali was just there. With a woman."

"Good," Edwin said.

"Good? He has a hostage and that's good?"

"She's still alive. That's good," Edwin said.

"He was looking something up on the web. This," Camille showed Edwin her palm. She had scribbled the website down.

"Don't worry about the computer," Edwin said. He stared at the website address and soon a screen flashed in the upper right corner of his field of vision.

"What's his password?" Edwin said. He looked at Camille, and thought "C-A-M-I-L-L-E." Stars filled the box, his eyes moved over the button and flared. The eye movement sent a signal to the program, in effect, hitting "return."

Red letters responded "Incorrect password."

"Come on, think," said Edwin. "What would no one else know, but he would never forget? Almost no one else."

Camille thought for a moment.

"Timothy Dwight was the name of our residential college at Yale. Where we lived for four years."

Edwin tried it. Red letters responded.

"No. Think."

Camille paused. She remembered a happier time, a smiling Yassir on a spring day, sitting shirtless in the window of their freshman year dorm, as light as the warm breeze. It must have been a very secret moment of pleasure for him, and of rebellion, she thought, given what else was on the agenda.

"Try, 'Entryway E'," said Camille. The randomly assigned entrance to the hall of their freshman rooms. Names assigned, lives begun, friendships made and held forever. Bonds forged, and over time, welded, strained, broken, mended, mourned, celebrated.

Edwin tried it. "Camille – you are a titan."

Edwin had accessed the secret site where the DNA researcher had posted the results of the analyses of Ali's bizarre packet of sloughed flesh from some of the nastiest pieces of protein ever produced.

"He's testing for the warrior gene. Four samples. The results show that three have it and one does not."

"What were they? What were the samples?" Camille asked.

"Hitler's hairbrush – skin cells, hair follicles. The Leader's hair. Jeffrey Dahmer's toothbrush. Mass murderers and a cannibal."

"And the fourth?"

"Unknown," he said.

"What was it?" Camille asked. "The last sample?"

"Fingernail clippings, the report says," said Edwin.

"I know who the fourth is," said Camille.

Edwin nodded. "Me too."

But in that moment, everything had changed. Edwin realized he now had a new weapon at hand.

He was already working it into the next phase of his mission.

"I don't want to kill Ali," Edwin said to Camille. "I don't want to capture him."

"What do you mean?" Camille gasped.

Edwin's face was stern.

"I want to flip him," he said. "Ali has no soul. We will give him a seed of one. And he will fight to keep it. He will fight for us because we gave it back to him. He will fight against those who took it from him."

Camille frowned. "But he's gone now. Raisa said something about sight-seeing."

"At this hour? It's getting dark - what can they see?"

"In Paris, the city of lights?" Camille said.

Edwin followed the glow of lights in the darkness that had descended around the 16th arrondissement. The nearest tourist site was lit like a candle that shone the brilliance to all around.

The tallest tower. One made of puddled iron, when the invention of steel was too new to trust to the structure designed to be the gateway to the Paris World's Fair of 1889. A tower so tall it was preserved not just because it attracted tourists, but also because it was very useful for transmitting electronic communications.

Edwin broke for the door. "He's at the Eiffel Tower. Unless we stop him he's going to decapitate Fiona just hours before the succession summit begins."

"You think?" Camille said. "But how does that compare to blowing up the Channel, or a mass simultaneous poisoning?"

"It doesn't," Edwin said. "Fiona's severed head is just Ali's warm up act. He has something massive planned, and it will happen at the meeting so no one can top him."

Camille breathed, "Oh god."

"Get Ali," Edwin gritted as they raced to the elevator. "We're behind."

Chapter Forty-One

5:30 p.m., May 24
Paris, France

Raisa de la Seine, the Helper, sat for a long time in the stuffed armchair, absorbing all the American woman had just told her. What she had shown her. How Ali Hamini looked at college, when he had just grown into a man. Now he was middle aged, and wanted to be al Khaleef. The Influencer, Rais Abdullah, who lived near the Seine, calculated what this information meant, and what she would do with it.

She could hear the bath running. Eventually, she rose and walked slowly down the hall. She reached into a linen closet and selected a clean, folded towel from the back of the closet. She lay it over her left arm. Then she knocked on the bathroom door.

"Usman?" she called. "Do you need a fresh towel? I have one for you."

"Thank you," he called back.

She opened the door. It was good that he was already in the bath. The water muffled the gunshot and the blood drained down through the pipes without leaving a stain. Wire cutters made short pieces of the bones, all of which fit, chunk by chunk, like the remnants of roast lamb into her new macerator in the sink.

PART FOUR

CHAPTER FORTY-TWO

7:30 p.m. May 24
Paris, France

Tourists milled around the massive base of the Eiffel Tower. The lights sprayed the iron latticework in gold. Edwin and Camille reached the snaking line of tourists who had set aside two hours to marvel at the tower while waiting for a chance to ride the angled elevator up through one of the massive feet to the first or second viewing level. Some planned bravely to take the small lift to the very top, dangling hundreds of feet in the air amid the iron girders and millions of rivets that held the trusses together.

"Closed? *Ferme? En greve! Buh!*" People in the line frowned, disgusted. Someone threw paper on the ground. The line began to disperse.

"What's going on?" Edwin asked Camille.

"They've closed the tower," Camille said. "*En greve* means 'on strike.' Parisians do it all the time to try to get better wages."

They ran to the front of the line. A wire was stretched across the entrance gate to the tower. A piece of paper taped in the middle posted this in black ink:

En Greve. La Tour Eiffel est ferme.

There did not seem to be any workers there to support it, or to guide anyone.

"No," Edwin said. "Something's wrong here. The cables are running. That elevator is still running."

He looked through the lattices.

"I see them," he said. "Ali is taking her up. Stay here."

Edwin leaped the line and sprinted to the door that said "ESCALIER....STAIR." His footsteps rang on the metal planks as he raced up the staircase.

He could see two heads through the window in the elevator as it rose languidly through the iron lattices.

On a normal night, viewers inside would catch glimpses through the golden lattices of a spectacular scene of Paris, the city of lights, as the evening closed in. The Arc de Triomph and Haussman's broad boulevards stretched out like spokes. The bateaux mouches – fly boats – floated down the Seine to both provide and participate in the special vistas of Paris. To the west, in the dark woods, the Bois de Boulogne, strangers knew exactly how to find each other.

But this was not a normal night.

Inside the elevator, Fiona faced Ali, not the windows. He was tapping his fingers rapidly against the screen of his mobile phone.

"What are you looking for? Why are we here?" Fiona demanded. She was not cowering. She was not shaken. Humans, like any animal, have two instincts when attacked. Flight or fight. Fiona unleashed the latter.

"The scientist's results, dammit. They were supposed to be there well before now. I can't wait any more. We're running out of time."

His English was perfect. But his public school accent was slipping. He was beginning to sound, Fiona thought, a lot like her friend Jack Wayne. American, northern east coast.

Ali looked at Fiona. "Stay still. I'm going to need to film you." Ali pointed the phone's camera at Fiona and pressed a button.

The elevator stopped.

"We have to switch here," Ali said. "Get out." They marched up a flight of stairs to the car that would continue up to the second viewing level.

Edwin was out of breath. He paused, just for one moment, and saw them switch to the next car. He saw her face.

"Fiona!" he whispered. Her brows were drawn together tightly. Her beautiful blue eyes were pinned on Ali. Her mouth was a flat line.

Edwin smiled. She was furious! Good. Fighters had more time. She might just make it.

This, and years of pent up isolation, sent adrenalin through Edwin's fatiguing legs. Before the elevator began its ascent through nineteen more stories, Edwin was two strides ahead and up the next set of stairs.

CHAPTER FORTY-THREE

7:30 p.m., May 24
Paris, France

Camille watched Edwin power up the Eiffel Tower steps. It was the first time in many years that Camille had known with any certainty where Edwin would be for the next hour.

She dialed carefully. When a man answered, she said two words.

"Eiffel Tower."

These two words meant the operation was a go.

CHAPTER FORTY-FOUR

8:00 p.m., May 24
Paris, France

"Let me go," Fiona demanded. "You don't need me for your big plans."

"There's no other way," Ali said. "There are no stairs. Just the elevator to the top. You're coming with me."

"Why?" she asked.

They rose through the open iron lattice of the Eiffel Tower.

Edwin's heart was thumping in his chest. His legs burned with lactic acid.

He calculated the distance to the top. There was no way he could make it in time.

Ali and Fiona boarded the smallest elevator. It would lift them to the top of the Eiffel Tower in minutes.

The doors closed. The gears engaged. The giant cables rolled forward again.

Edwin sprinted from the stairs to the empty space where the elevator had been. His legs were exhausted. But his arms were not. Those years he spent swinging from the steel trusses of his oil rig made Edwin feel right at home in the elevator shaft of the Eiffel Tower. So did his brogues, manufactured by Church's and customized by Zed, Cotswold dirt in their treads.

The lift rose another hundred meters in the air above Paris. When it reached the top, Ali and Fiona stepped out onto a metal grate. They were alone over the landscape of the city, the railing caging them in and bending backwards overhead, protection for those bent on self-destruction.

"Stand here," said Ali. He pushed Fiona against the metal. Out of his pocket, Ali pulled wire cutters. He clipped through four wires then pushed them out with both hands. When the metal bent outward, it made a space wide enough for a soccer ball to fit through.

"That will do," he said. Then he duct-taped the phone and the telescope, so it hung steadily. He pressed the video recording button.

Ali put the cutters on the floor and reached down to his leg. From a leather strap under his trouser leg, he gripped the handle of a jagged blade. It was eight inches long, and serrated - a hunter's knife that could cut through skin, sinew and bone.

The frame of the video showed Ali standing behind Fiona. She could feel his halting breath against her neck. He adjusted his grip on the handle. Fiona felt the cool blade touch her neck.

Something crashed against metal. The floor plate rocked and rattled.

Ali turned sharply. Fiona ducked out of his grasp. He lunged for her and caught her arm. He yanked her back and clutched her to his chest.

Edwin was two yards away, crouched like a rugby player; his base sturdy and solid on strong, thick-muscled thighs. His torso was a thick taut rectangle. His arms flexed and square. His hands were open, fingers curved like talons.

Ali swore in Arabic.

"Let her go, Ali," Edwin said.

Edwin broke for the phone. He shut off the video and pulled out the battery.

Ali twisted the blade, which made his hand turn slightly. His fingers, curled on the handle of the knife, faced Edwin.

It was then that Edwin noticed white, uneven lines at the ends of Ali's fingertips. His fingernails were recently clipped.

"Let her go, Ali," Edwin said. "You've never actually killed anyone. Not yet. Somehow, you still have a chance."

"Excellent," said Ali, shaking off the sweat that dripped into his eyes. "You are here too. As I had hoped."

"Why did you fish for me?" Edwin said. "Standing by the CCTV cameras at D6? You knew the data would be picked up, show you to anyone looking for you."

"Yes," said Ali. "Exactly. And I knew you would be looking too."

Edwin frowned.

Ali laughed at his fresh score. "You're in my way," said Ali simply. "For what I must do next. There can be no one who doubts me. No detractors."

"Because I know what you did last," Edwin said. "You tipped Camille. You threw your uncle's plot and now he's the goat. His legacy is failure."

"Yes. You know," Ali said. "And that's a problem."

"So does Camille," Edwin tested.

Fiona's fingers dug into Ali's arm.

Edwin could see him wince at the pinch.

"You going to take out Camille, too? You had that chance once. You didn't do it then. You won't do it now."

Ali wiped his forehead with his shoulder. Edwin saw him hesitate. So he changed his pace and angle of attack.

"You're not who you think you are," Edwin said.

"Shut up!" shouted Ali.

"You're not," said Edwin calmly. "I saw the results from the lab. The four samples. You had the Leader's beard hair - that's what you went back into the house for after the Seals took him down. You had Hitler's hairbrush and flaky scalp remnants. You had Jeffrey Dahmer's toothbrush – particularly gross, Ali. A cannibal's toothbrush - you've been carrying it around all this time? Really, really gross, Ali."

"I had to know," he said. "I had to compare them."

"Yes," Edwin said. "You did. So you would know if you have what it takes to be the worst, to lead the worst."

For a moment Ali glared at Edwin.

"I did not see the results," he said, shouting over the whipping wind.

"I did," Edwin said. "Let her go, I'll tell you."

Ali tightened his grip.

"Now," Edwin ordered. "Let her go. She is irrelevant to your goal. Stop complicating your own strategy. Not worthy of you, Ali."

Ali looked like he was about to erupt. Finally he shoved Fiona away.

"Get out of here!" he hissed.

Edwin reached for her. When his hand touched her wrist he could feel her pulse – faster than normal but, surprisingly, not frantic. He dipped his head to her ear.

"Go. Elevator. Fast," said Edwin. "Find a redhead pacing at the base of this thing, and sweating a lot. That's Camille. She'll help you. Stay with her."

"I'll stay with you," Fiona said.

Edwin waved his hand sharply, pointing toward the elevator.

"Go now!" he said.

Fiona turned and ran to the elevator. The doors opened and she hurried in, beating a button on the instrument panel. The doors closed around her.

Ali and Edwin faced one another high above Paris as darkness consumed the city of lights.

"The results!" Ali demanded.

"Three had the Warrior Gene," Edwin said. "One did not."

"Which ones?" Ali demanded.

"Don't flatter yourself," Edwin said. "The nail clippings came from an average guy. Just a guy."

Ali blinked rapidly. He took several deep breaths, and turned to look out over the city.

Edwin watched Ali. Now was the time to flip him.

"I told you," Edwin said. "It's all up to you. Every choice. What you do now. What you do next. You can't identify some map in your DNA and blame it for what you do."

Ali's face stayed blank.

"Before you make a mistake that puts you with your uncle under a mountain for the rest of your life," Edwin said, "there's something more you need to know."

Here Edwin paused. Ali looked at him.

"You need to know how you got here in the first place," Edwin said. "When others chose for you."

Ali spat on the ground. "Uncle saved me from every day of dirt in my mouth and nothing in my stomach. I owe him this."

"You don't," Edwin said. "He stole everything from you before he ever gave you a thing. Talk to Camille. She's down there. She has the real proof for you to know something true about who you are. Drop the knife and go talk to her."

Ali raked one hand through his hair, then the other. He shifted his weight nervously from one leg to the other, holding the knife tightly.

"No one will ever choose for me again," Ali said.

Edwin heard the thump of a helicopter blade beating the air. He knew the sound stealth aircraft made on their approach. By the time you heard it, it was much closer than you thought.

"Back!" Edwin shouted, tackling Ali around his midsection. They rolled behind a metal girder as a helicopter rose up beside them, its blades whipping ten yards from the Tower. Bullets strafed the floor. A troop of black hooded commandos swung on dark ropes through the girders of the Tower.

"Follow me!" Edwin barked to Ali.

The years on the oil rig proved an excellent training ground for what Edwin had to do next. He found a path through the lattices of the tower in the darkness, and swung himself down rung over rung, clinging to the frames, and sliding where possible down the giant iron triangular girders. He showed Ali the way.

Ali caught his foot on a step. He fell through the air, landing on a girder ten feet below.

Edwin heard him cry out. He swore. He turned to see the commandos descending above them.

Edwin climbed back up to where Ali hung and grabbed Ali. He reached into his backpack and pulled out a small package of dental floss. He wrapped it around Ali's shoulders and under his arms several times. He wound duct tape over his palms.

"Jump," Edwin ordered.

Ali looked shocked. Edwin kicked his feet out from under him, and he fell. But Edwin caught the slack and braced against the girders. He lowered Ali to a platform. Then he tied the dental floss lines in three quick hitches around a beam and slid down it rapidly, his palms protected by the smooth side of the tough tape, until he reached the same platform.

The commandos were above them, fast roping through the rigging.

"Ground," Edwin said. "Now."

When they landed at the foot of the tower, Edwin and Ali raced to find cover.

"Here!" Edwin barked. The two men jumped into the lights of the spinning merry-go-round, hung on for half a rotation, then sprinted behind a clump of dark trees in the Champs de Mars, the leafy park surrounding the Eiffel Tower.

Fiona stood behind the tree, next to Camille.

And there was a third person with them. She was in her early sixties. She wore a headscarf, and peeking just below her left ear, was a dark mole.

Madame Raisa de la Seine. Or with a slightly different pronunciation, Rais Abdullah, who lived by the central river in Paris, the Seine.

"Come," she said to Edwin and Ali, whose chests were heaving and necks were slick from exertion. They could see the helicopters above, and the troops on the ground making a perimeter.

Madame de la Seine was a droopy woman. She carried a loose sack over her shoulder, which swung like another appendage next to ample flesh. From the sack she pulled a large map of Paris, which she unfolded and hung between her hands. Looking every bit of a modern family, the matron with two couples, the group passed through the police presence that had suddenly descended on the Eiffel Tower plaza to track down the Person of Interest the U.S. military had spotted going back into the Leader's lair moments after he was killed.

And, milling about the closed entrance to the Tower, were three shaggy haired, unnoticeable tourists. Men in their thirties, of average height and weight, though beneath their casual clothes, very fit.

A beam of light flashed through the woods.

Edwin looked up. "I need to go now," he said.

"Take this," said Camille, pushing a prepaid mobile phone in his hand. "I'll call you when we learn the location of the summit."

Fiona grabbed Edwin's hand, to his surprise. She leaned her head against his neck and they strolled like lovers through the Champs de Mars towards the river Seine.

This was an entirely unfamiliar posture for Edwin. His feet found a new pace.

"Where is he?" whispered one of the ASP operators.

"Thought I had him in the woods. Was sure I did, but now he's gone," said the other.

"Be patient," the Head's voice streamed through their earpieces. "He's here, very close by. Within two hundred yards. Find him."

"Spread out," said the operators. They moved outward toward their teammates who had set up the perimeter around the Eiffel Tower and its grounds, where a bridge led across the river.

As Fiona and Edwin crossed the busy street toward the river, Edwin sensed two objects shift position. They both moved two yards closer. Like floats on a net, closing in.

"Come!" Edwin grabbed her hand. "Now - run!"

They raced along the edge of the River Seine. Footsteps broke into a run behind them.

"They found me. Dammit! That video from the tower. They must have tapped it, and matched my face," Edwin said.

"Isn't that one of them also – up there?" Fiona had spotted a man in a baseball cap and running shoes attempting to look casual. He was leaning against a railing. One of the large, wide tourist boats slipped along the black water below them. Edwin saw narrow cement steps edging down the inside of the bank.

"Go!" he barked. Edwin and Fiona jumped down to the platform and into the black water.

CHAPTER FORTY-FIVE

8:45 p.m. May 24
Paris, France

Ali and Camille stopped behind Madame de la Seine as she put her hand on the steel knob of a heavily plated gate interrupting the length of cement wall, twelve feet tall. It had been left unlocked. She pushed it open and hurried them inside. They stood in a lush garden, where hulking objects rose in the shadows at unexpected intervals. The sculptures of Rodin were everywhere, thinking, and posing.

Madame de la Seine had many friends scattered throughout Paris who could open doors for her, mostly because they were the ones hired to guard them. This one worked security at the Rodin Sculpture Gallery.

Now, for the first time, they could breathe.

Camille turned to Ali and addressed him by the name of the man she knew. She reached for her old friend from college.

"Yassir," Camille said finally.

Ali turned to her. His voice was warm, familiar, and sad. Apologetic, she thought. "Milly."

"You need to stop this madness," Camille said. "Whatever you are doing. It's not too late."

"It is too late, Camille," Ali/Yassir said. "It's always been too late for me. That's my life. This is my plan. This has been the plan ever since … Uncle saved me."

"But that's just it," Camille said. "You weren't abandoned."

Ali frowned. "My parents died. The Americans killed them. I was a dirty starving child on the street and Uncle dusted me off and fed me and set me on the path. This path is the only path."

"Look where that path took him," Camille said. "He's living like the criminal he is now and has ever been."

"Stop talking about him like that," Ali threatened.

"You don't see it," Camille said. "Come."

She put her hand on Madame de la Seine's forearm and brought her face to face with Ali.

He looked at her, then over her at Camille, shaking his head with frustration.

"What?! Move, woman!" he shouted, his nerves taking his manners.

This time it was the older woman who spoke. "You were not abandoned," said Madame de la Seine. "You were taken. From me."

"What?" Ali said sharply. He took a hard look at the older woman. Camille turned her slightly. Now Ali could see what Camille had spied in the apartment earlier that afternoon. It was why she showed Raisa de la Seine the picture she carried with her everywhere of her college love.

There was a mole below Raisa's left ear, just outside the trim of her headscarf. Just the same as showed clearly in the photograph of young Ali at college, his head slightly turned, with Camille.

Camille spoke quickly. "The planners needed a young smart boy to form and shape in Western ways. A boy who, even at a young age, showed a knack for organization and planning. They had to give him a reason to hate the West forever, and feel unrelenting loyalty to the planners no matter what they asked of him. This would be the boy to ascend to the head of the organization one day. In fact, the Leader was a placeholder, only waiting for you to ascend. The planners chose you first."

"My parents died in the car crash," Ali said.

"No," Camille shook her head. "When your father refused to go along with their plan, they killed him. They told your mother that you had died, too. Then they sent her away and gave her a salary and a home and a job."

"And you," said the woman, "thinking you were lost to the world, believed you must forever pay a debt to the one who lied, and said he found you."

Ali looked from Camille to the Madame de la Seine, and back.

"She is your mother," Camille said. "He is your son."

Ali was stunned. His voice left him. The structure of his life spun and flipped as he stood amongst the statues in the sculpture garden. As the objects straightened into a new order, he realized the planners had indeed chosen well.

He was someone who could destroy from within.

"I have to be at the summit of tribal leaders in ninety minutes," Ali said finally. "If they choose Usman or Badi Badi, they will seek me out and kill me. I must be there. I must show them why I am worthy."

Madame Raisa de la Seine, the Influencer, smiled at this man, her son, who consumed her vision. So much had been taken from her, she felt entitled to any reparations she chose.

"You will have no issue with Usman," she assured him.

Camille handed Ali a small thumb drive.

"Take this," she said. "This should help."

CHAPTER FORTY-SIX

8:45 p.m., May 24
Paris, France

Fiona felt the cold black water of the River Seine close around her. The metallic noises of Paris near midnight, of lights and voices bouncing off metal and cement, and small engines pushed to their street limits, all disappeared. She heard the dull thunk of diesel engines churning the water.

She came up slowly, gulped a mouthful of air, and settled below the surface. The current shifted her body so it followed parallel to the river. It was getting drawn closer to the sound of the engines. Closer, faster, and more powerful.

The water pulled at her. The current was so strong.

She realized this too late.

The bateau mouche was dragging her under. She began to kick hard but now the power of the current drawn into the boat's engines slipped under her, pulling her down. She kicked and clawed and came up, shouting.

"H-h-h-hel-l" and down again. Then she felt a thick belt suddenly surround her midsection.

Edwin.

He kicked his powerful legs hard, one arm around her waist.

They reached the surface. With his other arm he gripped a low panel on the side of the boat. He had his fingers around a metal cleat and lay on his back. The water split around his shoulders. His other arm grabbed Fiona around her waist and held her on his belly like an otter holds an oyster.

"Grab my neck," he ordered sharply. "Tight." She locked her arms around his neck as the water flowed over his head and past hers. When she was secure, he took his arm from her waist and held it above his head. With two arms locked on the boat, and Fiona flat against his torso, Edwin kicked up his feet toward a steel line that connected the stern of the boat to a decorative flag post. He needed to lift them up and out of the heavy drag of the wake.

They missed.

He tried again. With a massive thrust of his lower torso, he popped Fiona into the air and his legs locked around the wire.

They were free of the pull of the rushing water below. Edwin's arms were tiring.

"Get on the boat," he said, his feet now higher than his head and outstretched arms. Fiona felt like she was going headfirst down a slide.

She slid over his shoulders and his head, and clambered over his outstretched arms. When she was secure on the after deck of the boat, Edwin twisted like a gymnast, arm over arm, until he was face down. He let go his arms, flying away from the stern of the boat but the using that force to flip all the way around the wire where his legs were still securely locked. Then he shimmied down the line to the afterdeck.

He smiled at Fiona. "Hi," he said. "Bored yet?"

She smiled back. "This has been a very interesting day."

Edwin nodded. "The good: we're a half mile ahead of them," he said. "The bad: they know exactly where this boat goes."

"And it doesn't go fast," added Fiona.

She looked around at the monuments lining the banks. The Louvre was on their left; Musee d'Orsay behind them to their right. Notre Dame loomed.

"I have an idea," she said.

CHAPTER FORTY-SEVEN

9:00 p.m., May 24
Paris, France

The bateau pulled up to a quai on the other side of the river, to unload and pick up tourists. Fiona led Edwin by the hand as they ran through the streets of Paris.

They came to an old courtyard built of red brick. The low brownstones had the feel of once having been the only center of an ancient town, eventually turned to modern condos.

"Le Marais," said Fiona. "Number ninety-seven. He's a client of Finley's."

They ran to an apartment building. Fiona ran her fingers across a panel of bricks, then pried one loose. A brass key glistened.

"We're in!" she said.

Then Fiona closed the door behind them.

They stood in a dark foyer, breathing hard from their sprint.

"He travels a lot," she said. "He said I could stay whenever I'm in town."

"Boyfriend?" Edwin asked.

"No," said Fiona. "He's not very...."

"Interesting?" Edwin asked.

Fiona and Edwin looked at each other. The dark, close space, the heavy wool coats hanging from the walls surrounding them, brought back the moment at the end of the tunnel, when all each could see was the other's eyes in the light green glow of Edwin's watch.

"No attachments," she whispered.

Edwin knew that after this night, Fiona would not be able to find him. He could find her – he could find anyone, anywhere – but he would not. He would never put anyone else at risk ever again. Never.

Eventually, it was time to go. The summit would be in an hour. Edwin got to his knees on the carpet. In the dark hall, he kissed Fiona's shoulder.

"I have to go," he told her, flashing a quick smile. "I'm… sorry."

Fiona nodded, and watched him slip out of the servant's entrance to the back alley behind the apartment.

Fiona found the bathroom and turned the taps. Hot water filled the deep porcelain tub. As it filled, she studied her hands. Deep under her nails, she still saw dirt from a Cotswold farm. It was the kind of dirt that desperate digging put behind the nails of those not born to burrow beneath the surface.

"If you are bored," she said aloud, "you should ask more questions."

She blew bubbles that had gathered around her bent knees.

"Who is Edwin Hoff, really?"

Fiona got out of the tub and wrapped a towel around her chest. She twisted another around her hair like a terrycloth turban.

In her client's study, she found a tablet.

She selected the familiar icon with the big "G". Then she typed the search terms:

Edwin Hoff D6.

A long series of articles and photographs appeared. She read each one through to the end.

"Oh golly," she said.

Fiona dressed quickly. She wiped down the bathroom, and put the key back behind its rock. She walked out into the Parisian evening feeling alive, content, happy, and switched on like never before.

Fiona felt questions pouring through her. Most importantly, this one:

"Where will I see you again, Edwin Hoff?"

She did not ask when, or if. Those questions did not occur to her.

PART FIVE

Chapter Forty-Eight

9:00 p.m. May 24
Paris, France

A helicopter circled above Paris. Ascher Silver rode inside. He peered into the night sky as they passed along the Seine. He spoke into the microphone against his jaw.

"What's going on there?"

"That's the Musee de l'Orangerie."

"What's that line of cars?"

"A party?"

"They look like they're just arriving, not leaving."

Ascher checked his watch. "Land on the roof. Now."

In the old rent-controlled apartment, Ali dressed carefully in the white kurta the Helper had laid out for him.

"Abdullah, de la... the Helper... the Influencer," he thought. Ali finally knew something that would not change. He knew why he had been orphaned. He knew why he had been chosen and molded and pushed from one profile into another. He knew why his life had taken him to the streets in the first place, destroyed in order to be saved and indebted forever. They needed to make a westerner and they had chosen him. *Al Khaleef.* The Successor.

For the first time in his life, Ali understood the facts. They ran through him on high voltage circuits.

He looked at himself in the cracked mirror, black hair hanging straight, creases in his face drawn by worry more often than humor. Behind him decades of old greyish blue paint peeled off the walls in patches. In the inside pocket of his kurta, he carefully inserted the thumb drive that Camille had given him. If Ali needed to use it, he would.

Ali was already well prepared. He had the carrot for the Sheikh in his satchel, gleaming in gold, sapphire, yellow diamonds, rubies. He had drilled the indelible stick into the arm of the North African tribal leaders. Usman, the traitor, had gone utterly silent. Someone had influenced him to withdraw, apparently.

There is still Badi Badi.

But above all, there was the solution that Ali had been building for years.

This was the meeting he had anticipated for most of his conscious life. It had hung out there as ballast against whatever he thought, wherever he went, always he knew - even if no one around him did - that one day he would come to take the leadership role of this loose association of furious people. He approached the meeting with the gravity and determination he always had imagined; but with an entirely different goal in mind.

What he had learned in the last hours had changed everything.

Ali rode in the back of a hired Mercedes, which pulled up behind a line of other BMWs and Aston Martins and Maserati's in the valet line outside the Musee de l'Orangerie.

One valet approached the Mercedes, and muttered to his colleague as he went by, "Another fundraiser."

"*Ce soir? Après tout? Buh!*" The other exclaimed in surprise and disgust. Tonight? After everything? Unbelievable.

Ali watched as a single man emerged from each automobile and made his way to the intimate museum that housed the oval galleries and Monet's Les Nympheas, the murals that stretched around the gentle curves and bathed the viewers in the peaceful impression of immersion in water lilies.

The Leader had laid out the specifics of the succession meeting and had distributed them to each division leader who had pledged him loyalty, and to three others – Ali, Badi Badi, and Usman. He had chosen Paris, and the cover for action of wealth, to hold this meeting. In Paris, American drones could not fly. And in a museum so cloaked with masterpieces seen by some as the most creative of humanity's works, no civilized nation would order a bomb dropped from above or a shot fired from within. Under the cover of a free democracy and among priceless creations of free minds, this group would gather to select the person to whom they would pledge a life of loyalty to destroy the West.

After the twenty-seven men arrived, they locked the doors from within. Cans distributed around the room emitted white noise, which would muffle any speech in the room and add a second subtle layer of protection to anyone who might be listening. The Arabic dialect would add another natural defense. The security cameras would collect views just like any other fundraiser, those of men mingling around the artwork, waiting for the candidates to make their cases.

Ali, through his mobile phone, rolled out the code that easily accessed the security system and made video of the first twelve minutes repeat in a never-ending loop. Now what actually transpired would do so off the grid. It should buy him enough time for the last exchange, and the real presentation.

The Sheikh came to greet Ali. As they embraced, Ali slipped the golden sheath into the deep pocket of the Sheikh's kurta. Other men surrounded him with the obsequious greetings directed towards one who would soon rise.

Ali saw the Sheikh slip off toward a panel of water lilies, where he brought out his monocular lens, and examined the package in close detail.

At 10:15 p.m. in Paris, exactly forty-eight hours had passed since the death of the leader of al Ra'duzma. Ali rose. He steeled himself to speak.

But as he stood up, another man jumped to his feet. He was shorter than Ali, with small black eyes and round wire glasses.

Badi Badi sang like a preacher. "In the past two days, our mission has suffered its greatest loss," he said. "But we have also hit the West as hard - even harder - than ever before. My colleague shot the poison in their fat bellies. And I made the underground train tunnel explode. My colleague Usman has delegated his support to me...so I now ask for your pledge of loyalty."

There was murmuring. From across the room, the Sheikh nodded at Ali.

Deal.

"But this man, Ali, is surely the chosen one," said Sheikh Malikh Mukhtar. "It is what the Leader planned for all these years."

"Is it?" said Badi Badi. "Or has he - have we all – been fooled by this imposter?"

"Imposter? What are you talking about?" said Iqbul. Ali noticed how his sleeves hung low, the edge falling to his knuckles. They covered his defiled arm completely.

Badi Badi pointed a thin index finger at Ali.

"This is the man who sold out our leader to take the reward of twenty-five million American dollars."

Silence fell over the men, who now turned to Ali.

"And it's worse than that," said Badi Badi. "He's not one of us. He's one of them! He has been for years. When he was in the West, they turned him! He was to assimilate in the West, quietly, until called upon. Instead, Ali told the Americans about the plot to release pneumonic plague over New York and Boston as part of the attack on America – what his own uncle – our great KAH - had planned. They stopped it - and now the man who once saved him lives out his days in an American prison."

"How do you know this?" Iqbul demanded.

"His own uncle told me. Imagine his rage at the betrayal. Stupid Americans give their criminals lawyers. The lawyer found me and gave me KAH's message. It all makes sense. Where was Ali? Boston. Where was the vial purchased? Boston? Where was it to board the plane? Boston. Where did the seller get caught? Boston. Where did KAH get caught?"

Ali tried to speak but no words came. His silence made room for a flash verdict. Four men grabbed Ali and pinned him to the floor.

"Boston!" cried Badi Badi.

"It is time for new leadership," urged Badi Badi. He stood over Ali, and drew a short dagger from his kurta. He put it on Ali's neck. "In the last forty-eight hours, the world has come to know my face as the one to make them shiver. What has Ali done? What has he ever done but destroy our plans? He is an investment misplaced and one long ago lost."

"Wait!" cried Ali, his cheek pressed against the cold marble floor. He reached his arm out. In his tight fist Ali held a two inch long, half inch wide stick of plastic. It was a jump drive - an insertable, moveable device that someone could use to copy a computer file from one machine, then tuck into the inside pocket of his kurta, and pull it out someplace else to install in a new drive.

"He's lying to you to cover his tracks. Look. I have proof. He is your leak! This is the man who gave up our Leader forty-eight hours ago."

"Let him up," called the Sheikh. "Hear him."

Ali shook off the dust, and straightened his robes. He moved calmly, aware that the group was watching him closely. Each gesture, each display would be measured by the pack to sense where he fell in the leadership hierarchy. He would move with purpose and without fear; with confidence and without apology. It was with these small movements, as much as his grand vision, that he would win their pledges of loyalty and ascend to the Successor, *al Khaleef.*

Ali pulled a small laptop from his satchel, and plugged in the drive. He pushed the drive into the small rectangular slot on the side of the computer. He clicked on the single file it held. A grainy video played.

In the film, captured by a small hidden camera, a man sat at a cafe table. The video clearly captured his face.

It was Badi Badi. He was glancing around in every direction. Shortly, a woman joined him. She had very pale skin, and red freckles. A lock of ginger hair escaped her head scarf. She wore a long skirt, a flowing *shalwar kamese* and slung a bag from her shoulder. It was loose material that looked like it had expanded to carry the daily grocery haul.

Simply from the tilt of the woman's head, Ali knew who it was.

Camille, on assignment in the field.

The gathered group heard Badi Badi's recorded voice. He spoke in short sentences, each a dart that revealed, then retreated. "Follow the messenger," he said.

"How do we find him?" asked the woman.

"I want to see the money first," he said.

In the video, Camille pushed the satchel toward Badi Badi and let him peer in.

"Twenty-five million U.S., in hundreds," said Camille. "This is five hundred thousand. The down payment. You get the down payment for the messenger. You get the rest of it as soon as we get him. And you'll need a strong goat. It will be too heavy for you to carry."

Badi Badi nodded. He pulled a folded piece of paper from his pocket.

"Find this license plate. It is the messenger's car. He uses it to run commands from the Leader out, and to take information back to him. Follow it to his home. You'll see the home is much grander than a mere messenger could afford."

"How does he pay for it?" Camille said, opening the paper. She saw only a string of numbers and letters.

"He has a wealthy roommate," said Badi Badi. "A very wealthy one."

Then he stood up abruptly, slinging the satchel over his arm. "Follow the messenger."

The camera continued to film Badi Badi as he sauntered off into the crowded street, his right shoulder heavy with the bounty the Americans had offered to anyone who served up the head of al Ra'duzma .

In the museum, the tribal leaders turned on Badi Badi.

"You? You betrayed him. Us! And for a bribe!"

Badi Badi held a sharp dagger in front of him as he backed toward the wall.

"He was done! He was impotent in that house. The mission was suffering. He is martyred like he asked so many of us to be, and now I...we...we have twenty-five million to fund our mission."

"You lie! Sinner! Infidel!" came cries from the mob.

Badi Badi bolted for the exit door and slipped through it.

"Leave him," ordered Ali.

Amid the chaos and confusion, Ali offered a way forward. Ali absorbed uncertainty. He found that this power felt full and natural.

"He is irrelevant to us. We are here to complete the succession as our Leader provided," Ali turned slightly, addressing each person in the gallery. When his eyes settled on someone, he held his gaze for just a moment longer than expected. "Now, before I ask for your pledge of loyalty, I will show you how I will destroy the West, with your support."

The ceiling lights dimmed. Small spotlights shone soft pure light on each of the masterpieces. A white screen descended from a slit in the ceiling. Ali held a phone in his hand and pushed a button. The image he saw in his palm was mirrored, and expanded, on the large display.

"The West puts an irresponsible value on the single soul – the individual person. This is why the Awakening, years ago, was so remarkably effective. They knew each name of each passenger. They showed us, over and over again, their smiling photographs. We struck where they felt it most deeply.

"Protecting every single soul also guides the strategy of their defenses. Since the Awakening years ago, it's much harder to commandeer passenger aircraft. They are not so soft. Also typical, the West fights the last war, not the next one.

"Let me show you how we will wage this war, and win," Ali said.

"There is an event held every year in the Italian Alps known simply as 'Cortina'. Leaders of every stripe – congressmen, senators, the vice president, and heads of all of the major U.S. corporations and universities – are desperate to get an invitation to Cortina. Ostensibly it is to participate in the panel discussions about how to improve the state of the world and guide its future, in the way westerners see it. But mostly they go so others deemed just as important can see them. They bring home the badge of honor of having been invited, and they wave it in front of those who were not, those less special, less intelligent, so much less worthy.

"They also extend the invitation to future leaders. So the current and future brain trust of the Western political, academic, artistic and corporate worlds are all there for the same week, every winter.

"The same sins that have always weakened the West blinds their leaders: hubris, pride, ego. They don't think closely enough about the position of Cortina. It is high in the Dolomite Mountains. There is one road in to the valley. The mountains lock in the hotels. They would have very little room to maneuver, should they need to.

"Now that I have shown you my target, I will show my forces."

Ali raised his phone. The screen showed a black background with thousands of green dots moving slowly along different arcs.

"This is the ACARS system. The Aircraft Communication Addressing and Reporting system. It is how America and Europe air control track every plane in the sky. It takes in information about each plane, its flight plan and its current positioning and altitude. They do this so they can keep track of planes and if necessary, send information back to the computers on the planes to alert them to unexpected obstacles in the environment: weather, mountains, other planes.

"I have planted some code in the ACARS system so that it accepts me as a trusted member of the system. I get refreshed information every thirty seconds, right here.

"And this is the good part. When I choose, the ACARs system will accept information from me too. I can tell the planes to avoid immediately a lightning strike, another phantom plane in its path, to change course, to descend, to find a landing point of my choosing. Whether or not there is an airport there. Even in a small valley in the Dolomite Mountains."

Ali paused to let them absorb the potential.

"But surely the pilots can override any computer information that doesn't seem right to them," said Iqbul. He hastened to add, "It's very clever, nonetheless."

"Yes, of course they can. If a pilot notices, they can override the automatic response to my Trojan horse ACARS message," said Ali. "And I would be dumbfounded if any passenger plane pilot accepted my message."

"So what is this worth, then?" asked another tribal leader.

"Thank you for asking," Ali said. "It's this. Here is where the West makes itself so vulnerable. Do you know how boring it is to fly the same routes over and over again? If a pilot has no single souls to watch out for, don't you think one might be tempted to switch off for an hour or two, letting autopilot and the trusted alarms signal anything wrong? So who would fly big planes, full of fuel, but no precious souls?"

He looked around the room. Their faces tipped up to him and to his invention. Ali felt his blood surge. This, he knew. He was *al Khaleef.*

"Look at this screen. At any one time, there are a thousand cargo planes in the air at once, over the U.S. and over Europe. Watch the screen."

There was a simple form on the screen. It read:

Destination:
Latitude:
Longitude:
Altitude:

Ali filled it in while they watched.

Destination: **Cortina Italy**
Latitude: **46.537 degrees**
Longitude: **12.139 degrees**
Altitude: **0 feet. Ground level.**

"Ready?" Ali asked. "This is just a demonstration, but watch the screen."

Ali tapped the screen of the phone with his index finger. The command was sent and infiltrated the air control system.

Some of the green dots on the black map began to shift course. Some altered their directions entirely. For fifteen seconds, a thousand green lights drew toward the top cuff of the boot from every part of the globe.

"They respond to my command. This means I have my own air force," Ali said. "When the leaders of the Western world next assemble in one confined space, I will order the entire fleet to crash en masse on top of them."

There was a silence. Then Iqbul, leader of the North African tribes, clapped his hands together, holding them low, in front of his waist.

"*Al Khaleef!*" he said.

The Sheikh joined him. Soon the room was thundering with applause.

Ali beamed with pride. *Al Khaleef.* The goal he had always sought. As he stood there, Ali located the first elements of what was real in him and unchanging.

The power he had always yearned for, felt real.

Fury felt real. But he did not hate the West. He really did not care about it. Ali felt fury for those who stole his life, his family and his soul.

Vengeance felt real. He would use power, al Khaleef, to punish those who stole his life and dismantled him.

Camille felt real.

But that was all he had, for now. Ali imagined it was something like a soul, loosely stitched.

One by one, each man who led a tribal faction of al Ra'duzma bent before Ali and kissed the back of his hand. In this ritual of *bay-a*, they pledged their lifelong obedience, and within each promise they passed along the loyalty of all those who had offered the same to them.

CHAPTER FORTY-NINE

10:15 p.m., May 24
Paris, France

Badi Badi found himself alone in the dark stairwell. His footsteps echoed as he shuffled, trying to decide on a direction. Up? Down? How would he get out before they found him? His breath heaved.

Badi Badi heard a sound and jumped. Then, there was nothing.

His eyes were adjusting to the dim light cast by the red neon "SORTIE" signs. Exit. He decided to go down the stairs. It would lead somewhere - maybe to a tunnel - which would let him come up somewhere else.

It would turn out to be a bad decision.

As he reached the landing, the last thing he would see was a pair of fierce green eyes of a man in a crouch, arms and fingers out. The only sound in the corridor was the cracking of a man's third, fifth and seventh vertebrae.

After disposing of Badi Badi with his bare hands, Edwin stood by the door of the central exhibit hall. Surrounded by painted watercolor murals, masterpieces all, the leaders of the tribal factions of al Ra'duzma each kneeled before Ali and each kissed his hand.

Edwin magnified each face. His lenses locked on the dimensions of the bone structure, measured the depth of fatty tissue, and the distance between the eyes. Each face was stored in the database, marked in a file as Top Leader. There were twenty-seven of them. Plus Ali.

Edwin studied and stored the faces in this single gathering of men with the ambition to be the world's worst terrorists. He looked at the walls behind them covered in pastel paintings of water lilies. Walls and walls of masterpieces by Monet and other impressionists.

The decision was easy. There would never be a better opportunity to cut off Medusa's snakes.

Kill them now.

But Edwin had no C-4. Duct tape and M&Ms would not do this job.

He stepped over the crumpled corpse of Badi Badi and slid quietly down the bannister so no footsteps would echo in the hallway. He went down to the basement to the utility room, where the oil heater burned. It was a large tank. Once the flames began it would trigger the oxygen suck.

Natural light came in through a mottled glass window at the top of the wall, an in-ground window well. Edwin calculated he would have just enough time to crack the glass and squeeze through it.

There would be casualties.

Ali got here all on his own..

Edwin pulled out his pen, and clicked it twice. A sharp, short blade emerged. He positioned it along the seam of the oil tank. But just as he was about to jab it into the steel and release drops of oil onto the delicately burning flame beneath it, pebbles pelted the window, wave after wave.

He knew that. It came from a propeller of a tactical fighting helicopter.

The SEALS are on the roof.

Edwin pocketed his knife and bolted from the boiler room. He could not hear the soldiers but knew their tactics. They would be setting up a perimeter. Pairs would be stationed outside each door. They would be on the roof, looking down.

So Edwin went up.

But when he peered along the roof edge, Edwin saw an empty helicopter. It bore the insignia of the U.S. Air Force.

A hood covered his head. He was on the ground, his wrists duct taped to his ankles in less than five seconds.

It was a move he knew well. He should have been waiting for it.

The U.S. forces were after Ali.

But the ASP was after Edwin.

"Edwin Hoff," said Lars Grundek, grinning at him through his wire frame glasses. "After all these years. We got you."

"So," Edwin said. "You going to do this here? With the Air Force in the neighborhood?"

"Lucky you," said the man. "After all this time, the Head wants to finish you personally."

Moments later, Edwin sat in handcuffs in the back of a black car. He used the minutes to rest his muscles for what came next.

After all these years, she never lost focus. Not once. And as soon as she had a chance she found me.

It took a lot for Edwin to admire someone. Even more to fear them. There was no other person he held in such awe as the Head of the ASP.

CHAPTER FIFTY

11:00 p.m., May 24
Paris, France

L ars Grundek drove Edwin, handcuffed, to a brownstone in the Fifth Arrondissement in Paris. He brought him into the building, and forced him up two flights of stairs until they stood on an ornate Oriental carpet running through the wide hallway outside a closed door. He knocked, and another operator opened the door.

Lars pushed Edwin inside, his shoulders flexed but useless against the binds. He brought him over to a wing chair, upholstered in light blue silk.

"Sit down. Have a snack."

With a slice of a very narrow blade, he freed Edwin's hands. He clicked his thumb and the blade retracted into a sheath that looked like an entirely normal ballpoint pen.

"Orders," muttered Lars.

Then he left Edwin standing next to the wing chair.

Edwin sat in a wing chair facing a table covered by a white linen tablecloth.

There was a silver tea tray covered with a white doily. Butter made grease stains around small squares of dark chocolate cake, éclairs bursting cream from both ends, and yellow round biscuits crowned with crystalized sugar.

Chocolate mousse stood still in small clear cups. There were strawberries coated with white chocolate. At the center of the table gleamed a large silver pot of coffee next to two white porcelain cups in saucers, a pitcher of cream, and a bowl of white sugar cubes.

Edwin reached for a cube of sugar, then sharply withdrew his hand. "It can't be her, still," Edwin told himself. "She'd be over a hundred."

No one came.

He stood up and paced the room. He examined the walls. One had a very tall window flanked by gold drapes. The door he had come through led to the hallway. A second door led perhaps to a bedroom or a private study.

Edwin studied the paneling for hidden breaks. Was there a third door, a secret door? Were they watching him through the mirror that hung in a gilded frame opposite the fireplace? There was a small settee and a light yellow silk couch, its opposing grains creating the appearance of stripes.

He sat back down in the blue wing chair.

At that precise moment, the chair Edwin occupied began to turn beneath him. It rotated one hundred and eighty degrees.

He looked up into the face of a woman. Her eyes were clear blue, nearly the color of his chair. Her hair had a ginger hue and hung to her shoulders. He could see freckles on her cheeks.

"Camille?" said Edwin. "Where's the Head?"

Camille smiled. "Coffee?" she said.

"This is not possible," said Edwin.

"It is," said Camille. "I am the Head of the ASP."

CHAPTER FIFTY-ONE

11:15 p.m., May 24
Paris, France

In the elegant sitting room, Edwin stared at Camille. He sat with his elbows square on each wing of the blue silk chair. His feet were flat on the carpet, just slightly behind the chair legs, and his thighs were tight. At any moment, he could spring.

"How?" he said.

Camille smiled. "Matilda Mace bequeathed her control to me upon her death. Your RUPD mission was still top of mind even at her end. I did not know exactly what I would do about it. And then, you came directly to me."

"And what will you do about it?" Edwin said.

"That depends on you," Camille said. "I did not want this job, not at first. When I first met Matilda, I thought she was a lonely old billionaire closing it out and wanted someone to talk to from time to time while she looked at her paintings. She happened to live upstairs from me in my apartment in Washington D.C."

Camille paused, and smiled at Edwin. "Of course, as you know, there are few real coincidences in our line of work. Anyway, her assistant called me out from where I was stationed in Egypt. I came to have a last goodbye. She was lying in her bed, looking at a Picasso on the wall."

Camille's gaze was distant, and she laughed. "'Look her in the eye!' Matilda had said. Have you ever tried to look a Picasso in the eye? They are not in a normal location. When I finally found it, there must have been a retina lens behind the paint because it recognized me. The wall behind painting swung open. You'd never believe what was in there."

"What?" Edwin asked.

"Inside there was a room with lots of cabinet and drawers, each with different labels on it. I opened one...there were hundreds of uncut diamonds lying there on black velvet. Then she told me to pull a tall cabinet door that had a red tag. That held something ...well, something unimaginable."

"Try me," Edwin said.

"Behind the door with the red tag, there was another room. It was stacked with monitors, files and documents. Then we had the most amazing conversation. Do you know why Matilda built the Association for the Society to Protect?"

"I have some idea," Edwin said. "Tell me what she told you."

So Camille related exactly what Matilda had told her that afternoon she summoned Camille to her bedside from across the world.

Camille began.

"'This I bequeath to you,' Matilda told me. 'In 1939, they had me in a hospital bed. They were doing biological experiments on humans like we were lab rats. Well, this rat got away. I hid in a cart under seven dead, oozing bodies they wheeled out like garbage. I ran from the dump to the forest and made my way to Switzerland. A farming family took me in for months. Eventually they wrapped me in wool blankets and put me on a dairy truck to the south of France. I got on a boat to America and met a young man who had just inherited sixty thousand dollars. We married and lived in New York. He invested it in things like Coca-Cola, and razor blades, and shipping containers. And I cultivated our art collection. It allowed me to go anywhere, meet anyone, while I secretly built an organization called the Association for the Society to Protect. The ASP. Its sole mission is to prevent the spread of biological and chemical weapons. We are friends of all nations but obey none. I hire only the best fighters there are from every nation.'

"So I asked her, 'What do they do for you?' She looked surprised at my question. 'For me? They don't do anything for me – it's for the world. They do what is necessary to stop the release of bio threats. Whatever their cover for status, they only really have one mission. I call upon them when I need them.'

"'Do they ever leave?' I asked her.

"'Never. Exposing the ASP would be catastrophic for humanity. Really, it is not too much to ask.'

"'What if they try to leave?' I asked her.

"Matilda's violet eyes darkened. 'Then there is a mission made for them.'

"'To do what?'

"'To declare them RUPD. Rogue Until Proven Dead. The team pursues the rogue until they get evidence of his death.'

"'What if he …apologizes?' I asked her.

"'No,' said Matilda. 'There is no room for apologies, no room for second chances. Order in the ASP requires the leader to hold non-performers accountable. It is the bond the other operators require of their leader. If one – even a special one – is allowed leeway, all order breaks down.'

"'But why choose me?' I was sputtering. Not my proudest moment. 'I'm just an English teacher in Cairo. I can't manage this organization!'

"That made Matilda smile. Of course, she knew what I really did for a living. For some reason she said this instead:

"'Of course you are, dear. Why you? Because I trust you. Because you have a potential not yet reached by your current...occupation. And because you have no...attachment.' Which was embarrassing. But too true. She let me off the hook by adding, 'And because of one more thing.'"

"I asked what that was. She said, 'The ASP has already saved your life, once.'

Here Camille stopped the story. She looked up sharply at Edwin. She remembered the first time she had seen his face, years before. She was at work at the CIA, lying on a board. She had been strapped to it for nearly two days.

When the CIA's Office of Special Services suspected an employee of spying for the enemy, they interrogated the suspect in a particular room in the Agency. It had a very bright white light, which never dimmed, and buzzed like insects were drawn to it, for hours on hours on hours.

They brought a hose. Camille remembered how the tap water thundered into the bucket. They tipped up her feet. She could hear the water sloshing as they brought the bucket near her head.

Then a man had appeared from nowhere. He immobilized her attackers, and pushed her to freedom through an air duct into a mulch pile.

"It was only then that I finally understood where you had come from," Camille said. "That day, I was on the phone with Matilda arranging a time for tea. I told her what room I had been called to but I did not tell her what it was for. She was the only person who knew that room... Thank you, by the way."

Edwin blinked. "You're welcome."

"Shall I go on?" Camille asked.

"Yes," Edwin said. Lars Grundek had not appeared in the room, though Edwin knew he must be close by, watching, with other associates.

"So, by this point, Matilda was lying back against the pillow, her eyes shut. She was breathing very deeply."

"'You sent Edwin.' I said to her. 'Edwin is...one of yours?' Matilda opened her eyes. 'Is? No.'

"'He's not yours?' I asked her.

"But Matilda was fading. Each sentence seemed to take oxygen from every vein and require a full replenishment for the next. But she spoke eventually."

Edwin coughed. "What did she say?"

Camille sighed. "She said, 'Edwin was my best.' So I asked where you were. I asked if you had died. She said, 'He may have. He is still declared RUPD.'"

"I knew she wouldn't stop," Edwin said.

"So I asked her, 'you have a team looking for him now?' And she said 'No. I don't. Now you have a team looking for Edwin.'

"Then she told me to go into the room and photograph everything. She said she would send everything to me in Cairo. That I would have all of her teams reporting to me. That I was her successor. She sent me off to Greece for a few days to think about it."

Camille and Edwin sat opposite each other in the blue wing chairs. She looked at him.

"So there I was in Greece, thinking it over, wondering where on earth you were, and you came right to me."

Edwin frowned.

Camille continued. "And thank goodness you did. It's quite dangerous to try to go rogue from this organization."

"Yes," Edwin said. "It was dangerous to have friends, too. Deadly, even."

"That remains so," said Camille. "But it does depend on who your friends are. And you, Edwin, are my friend."

"What does that mean?" he said.

Camille fixed her blue eyes on his. "I want you to come back to the ASP. Come work for me."

"Or?" Edwin said.

"There is no 'or'," said Camille. "It's simple. You do the work you do best. You help me rid the world of bio threats wherever they are, without regard to border or flag."

"Or ... attachment," said Edwin.

Camille looked grim. "I know about Lula. I'm sorry. And I know about the rule. But it's there for a reason, Edwin. There is still the same risk that attachment leads to distraction, which nearly cost you your mission. That cannot happen."

"I know," said Edwin. "Never."

Camille paused. She shrugged. "At least, not much."

They looked at each other. Edwin realized that he was looking at perhaps the one person in the world who bore witness to the pieces of him. All of him. Even under the rules of the ASP.

Camille put her hand in her pocket.

The motion made Edwin balk. He watched as she carefully withdrew it.

In her hand, Camille held a deck of cards.

"So, Oliver Kestrel," she said. "I'll play you for it. Five Card Draw? Texas Hold 'Em?"

"Cards?" Edwin asked.

"Yes," said Camille. "If you win, you forgive my debt. If I win, you come work for me."

"Your debt?" Edwin said. 'What debt?"

"132,055 big ones." She smiled.

Camille shuffled the deck of cards and split it. The stack in each palm arched and fell together. Camille tapped the edges on the table to align them.

Edwin was dumbfounded. "You are Bunny617."

Camille grinned. She dealt two hands.

"With me, Edwin," Camille said.

It was not a question.

They played for several hours. At the end of the match, Camille flipped over a hand of four aces. And with that, she won. But Camille would never know whether Edwin had fought that hand, or given it to her. It did not really matter. Because Edwin was back.

EPILOGUE

E dwin had very little time. He pulled his motorcycle to the quai by the river's edge near the great cathedral. Golden lights made massive dark beasts of the intricate gargoyles on Notre Dame. In the distance, the white capstone of Montmartre rose like a half moon. The museums were closed, clutching and protecting their masterpieces.

Across the river stood the old red brick quarter of Le Marais. There was a key behind a brick that opened the door to an empty apartment. As the engine idled, Edwin thought of Fiona, and the crazy electric intimacy they had discovered there.

It was sugar. It was sheer joy. Out of her presence, he could remember it, but not feel it. That would not ever be enough, Edwin knew. But it would have to be. Contact with him was not safe for Fiona, and it never would be.

Edwin had work to do.

He felt the throb of the city at night. Cafes hummed. He thought of the coffee and wine, filets of fish drizzled in light tangy sauce, fresh strawberries dripping with chocolate.

And people. There were people everywhere.

Edwin left his motorcycle and walked until he stood directly across from the Notre Dame Cathedral. He saw the chalk mark on the streetlight. It was at hip height, where the hand fell naturally, a white horizontal line dashed across the black paint. He tucked his chin into his leather jacket, and turned left down the boulevard to the entrance of the first jazz café he saw.

The sign to the Blue Jazz Café hung flat against the stone façade. Edwin looked down. There he saw the white spot on the ground. He recognized the dusty pattern made from another piece of chalk, crushed by a shoe. Another operator had loosened a hole in his pocket, slipped the chalk through his trouser leg to the sidewalk and stepped on the nib.

This was the site of the dead drop.

Edwin went inside. The jazz café had a long oak bar. It was a busy night and the man on the sax was blowing hard. Edwin chose the third seat from the end.

The bartender noticed the man in the leather jacket eventually. "A glass of wine, monsieur?" he asked.

Edwin nodded. "White Bordeaux, please."

The bartender smiled. "But of course. What else, a California Chardonnay?"

The man who spoke had provided Edwin with the proper phrases – his "bona fides" as they were called in trade craft. So Edwin answered, as per his instructions. "That stuff is cough syrup," he said.

The bartender poured a glass and placed it on a coaster. He put both in front of Edwin, and turned back to the cash register behind him.

When the bartender returned to face his customers, the glass of white Bordeaux was still there, untouched. But the man in the leather jacket was gone. So was the coaster.

As Edwin walked hastily down the street towards Notre Dame, he looked at the coaster in the palm of his hand. His lenses magnified the very small print on what appeared, to a normal eye, to be a small price sticker. The print displayed his new orders for a personal meeting.

Edwin flicked the coaster into the river. The cardboard circle floated until it grew soggy and sank. Edwin swung his leg over the Ducati, one recently purchased from the account of Mr. Oliver Kestrel, ostensibly for the loner's joy ride around Europe. He gunned the throttle and tore into the night. But this time, not too far.

His orders had said this:

ASP Operator:	The Raptor.
Mission:	Personal Meeting with asset to build plan to identify & destroy al Ra'duzma.
Date and Time:	May 26, Noon.
Location:	Zurich, Switzerland.
Site:	Banhoffestrasse. Lindt Chocolatier.
Special Considerations:	Plan must be in place by May 28. Handle on this asset is weak.
Contact:	Al Khaleef.

Camille had ordered Edwin to meet with Ali within the next forty-eight hours. They would capitalize on the moment of weakness when Ali was turned against his people and grateful to Edwin and to Camille. They would use this handle - tradecraft terminology for the leverage one side used to successfully recruit an agent from the enemy - to work together to take down their common foe.

Somewhere in that city, and spreading outward from it, men and some women planned destruction of the Western world. Edwin would take them down, now that he had a man on the inside. A brilliant man, quite like himself, but with many more shades of black.

But Edwin would have to move fast. Vengeance could burn an uncertain flame.

The End

ACKNOWLEDGMENTS

I would like to thank the readers of <u>The First Secret of Edwin Hoff,</u> who, after meeting *Edwin*, asked to see him again. This book is here, now, for you.

Many thanks to my agent, Josh Getzler, and Danielle Burby and Tanusri Prasanna at Hannigan Salky and Getzler for your enthusiasm for *Edwin Hoff* and your guidance to bring out the best stories in these books.

To Kate Brauning, for her insightful and detailed edits which elevated <u>Rising Aces.</u>

To Jerry Dorris, for his gorgeous graphics and talent for getting readers to judge a series by its covers.

To my friends - authors, readers, 9Yo's and kind souls - you light up my life and you are all heroes in my book (if not in this actual book.)

To my mother, Phoebe B. Boyer, who is a lawyer, natural advocate and the best book publicist out there. To my father, Dr. James Boyer, for encouraging me to explore other countries and always to create more options. Many of the scenes in the books come out of your life lessons. Thank you both for your never ending supply of love and support for *Edwin* and for our family.

To my parents-in-law, Juliet and Christopher Bourne, who helped me get right so many aspects of this book, from cover to cover, including word choices that work better in

English English, French spelling, tricky typos and specific details that make the story more authentic. Thank you for spreading the word about the *Edwin Hoff* thrillers so enthusiastically in England and beyond. Above all, thank you both for your never ending supply of love and support for *Edwin* and for our family.

To my big sister, Phoebe C. Boyer, who always has my back no matter what. Me, yours too. Always.

To my sister-in-law, Vanessa Alexander, and my brothers-in-law, Todd Snyder and Bruce Alexander, and my nieces Phoebe I. and Georgia, and my nephew Jacob - thank you for your constant love and support. (For the careful reader, yes, there's a thing with Phoebe's in my family).

To all of my aunts and uncles and cousins, thank you for encouraging me throughout my life. For *Edwin* I also owe specific thanks to Jonathan and Annie Whaley for helping me understand, if not totally accept, the physics of flight for *Edwin's* travels. And to my aunt Lois Hager, whose book club read <u>The First Secret of Edwin Hoff</u> and so graciously welcomed me to visit. Her sharp eye and copy editor's skill have made Rising Aces a much cleaner read. To my aunt, M. Christine Boyer, who took me to Greece after high school for a wonderful adventure in which souvlaki in a hillside café played an unforgettable reassuring roll...and which reappears in a pivotal scene in <u>Rising Aces</u>. And to my uncle, John Bennet, who always has the first copy of any work his nieces and nephews produce, and makes sure the rest of our large family has the chance to clap for it too.

To Sophie and Jessica, my greatest works of art. You inspire me everyday with *your* creativity and the things you say and the ways you grow. I love you.

And for Julian...who made this possible, and everything else. Time to ship, and write more! I love you.

THE FIRST SECRET OF
EDWIN HOFF

Also by A.B. Bourne
c. 2011 Watch Hill Books

The First Secret of Edwin Hoff is a thriller about an elite commando living the unexpectedly public life of a billionaire tech entrepreneur. But when Edwin is called to stop a bio-attack planned to release from a 9/11 plane, he does what a Seal Team 6 fighter would do for his next act, and more. Under deep cover, he protects the world from terror while turning the folks he meets into heroes.

Edwin Hoff is a fictional character inspired by a real person: Danny Lewin was a Counter Terror Captain in Israel's equivalent of Seal Team 6. He trained to rescue hostages and kill terrorists with his bare hands. Later he went to MIT for his masters in math and founded Akamai Technologies, becoming a billionaire overnight. The author worked for him there for two years until, on September 11, Danny went to visit customers in California. He boarded AA Flight 11. Amid the horrifying tragedy, Danny left behind this puzzle:

On September 10, he packed up his office. No one knows why.